Caro Fraser was educated at Glasgow High School and Buchan School, Isle of Man. After attending Watford School of Art she spent three years as an advertising copywriter before entering London University, King's College, where she studied law. She was called to the Bar of Middle Temple in 1979, and worked as a shipping lawyer before turning to writing. Caro Fraser has been writing full-time for the last seven years. She is married to a solicitor and has four children.

BY THE SAME AUTHOR

The Pupil
The Trustees
An Inheritance
An Immoral Code
Beyond Forgiveness

Judicial Whispers

CARO FRASER

PHŒNIX

A PHOENIX PAPERBACK

First published in Great Britain by Orion in 1995
This paperback edition published in 1995 by Phoenix,
a division of Orion Books Ltd,
Orion House, 5 Upper St Martin's Lane,
London WC2H 9EA

Fifth impression 2000

A CIP catalogue record for this book is
available from the British Library.

Printed and bound in Great Britain by
Clays Ltd, St Ives plc

For Jim

Chapter one

Anthony Cross woke suddenly in the grey half-light of morning and knew that he had been dreaming of Leo. He closed his eyes again quickly, trying to summon back the feeling of safe happiness, of intimacy recaptured, but already his mind was breaking the surface of his dream like a stone left by the tide. He lay nursing his sense of loss for a moment or two, then turned his head upon the pillow to look at the girl sleeping next to him, at her blonde, anonymous head, her hand upon his shoulder. He moved the hand gently away and rose, pulling on his robe, and went through to the bathroom.

There he stared briefly at himself in the mirror, at his own handsome features, slack with sleep, and wondered why he had these dreams. He passed a hand through his dark hair, yawned, and began to run his shaving water. The dreams occurred every few months, like strange, tender echoes. Although each dream left in him a small, hollow pain which he could not fathom, he welcomed them. They took him back in time as though to some forgotten country.

Anthony began to lather his face, remembering the closeness of the hours he and Leo had once spent together, working, talking, sometimes just dawdling time away. He dipped his razor into the water and watched the scum of lather and tiny black bristles float away from the blade. He wondered if Leo ever dreamt of him – and then pushed the thought away as absurd. What might have happened if the affair had not ended before it had even begun? Anthony often wondered this, often wondered what depths there might have been to their unexplored relationship. But now they worked together, side by side, barristers in the same chambers, and there was no hint that such intimacy had ever existed. They met only in the company of others now, and every encounter was hedged

1

with a casual remoteness.

Perhaps, thought Anthony, as he rubbed his face with the towel, the dreams were a kind of compensation. Compensation for loss, the loss of Leo's company, smiles, attention, conversation. Perhaps the pain of losing such a close friendship had not died away in his heart after all; perhaps it was merely buried, so that the recollection of that which he had lost floated to the surface of his subconscious as he slept. Perhaps.

He went through to the kitchen where his flatmate, Adam, was already dressed and gulping down coffee.

'Hi,' he said. 'Want some? I'm off in a sec.'

'Yes, thanks,' said Anthony, and put a slice of bread in the toaster.

'I taped the cricket for you,' said Adam, then added, 'since you and Lizzie seemed to have gone to bed early.' He grinned at Anthony and handed him his coffee.

'Oh, thanks. Yes,' replied Anthony abstractedly, thinking with guilt and boredom of the girl still sleeping in his bed.

Adam studied his face, able to gather what was in Anthony's mind. Another one for the chop, he thought. Adam, with his sandy hair and pale, thin face, thought that if he was tall and good-looking like Anthony, and apparently able to have any girl he wanted, he'd manage to look a bit happier about it. He turned and rinsed his mug out under the tap. 'You in tonight?'

'I think so.' Anthony took his toast from the toaster, and rummaged in the fridge for the butter. 'Then again, I don't know. I never know.'

'Okay. See you later then.'

'Bye,' said Anthony.

He drank his coffee and ate his toast, then went back into his bedroom to dress. He moved about quietly, closing drawers and cupboards gently so as not to wake the girl. He was tying his tie when she woke; she simply opened her eyes and lay gazing at him sleepily. He looked wonderful, she thought, in the dim light, the raised collar of his white shirt framing his lean face, his dark eyes expressionless. He glanced at her, turned down his collar, and bent to fasten his shoelaces. His demeanour had a telling remoteness about it, each movement

2

was made with a brisk finality. But she was not sufficiently awake to read any of the signals.

As he came to the side of the bed to pick up his watch, she stretched out lazy arms to him. 'Do you have to go just yet?' she murmured, and kissed him gently.

'Lizzie,' said Anthony, a note that was almost one of pain in his voice, 'I'm going to be late.'

She merely smiled and drew him towards her again, but there was a stiffness about him, an impatient reserve, that made her drop her arms. She lay back and looked at him as he straightened up and took his jacket from its coathanger. Something in the atmosphere made her feel suddenly like an intruder.

'Will I see you tonight?' she asked. She knew the answer but still she had to ask.

Anthony hesitated in the doorway. What should he say? 'Lizzie –' he began, then stopped. Say something final, he thought. Tell her. No, then there might be tears and awfulness, and he'd be late. He glanced at his watch. 'Lizzie, look – I'm really busy for the next week or so. I don't know. I'll ring you, okay?'

She said nothing, merely lay there, feeling the space between them widen into infinity. Anthony added, 'There's some coffee left in the pot. Help yourself to breakfast.' And he went.

He clattered downstairs and out into the early September sunshine, hating himself. What did you do when the whole thing had become stale and lifeless, when there was no point in going on? Nothing, except let it peter out. Anything was better than tears and scenes. But every relationship seemed to end in this way. Perhaps it all came too easily. Perhaps it was just as well; he didn't want to become serious about anyone again, not after Julia.

In the train he took some papers from his briefcase and tried to concentrate on them, but the dream of Leo hung about him like a scent that clung to the air, imparting itself to everything, distracting him. He could not recall any detail of it, except that Leo had been there and things had been happy. The happiness of dreams, he mused, elusive and wonderful. The best kind of happiness. Am I happy now? wondered Anthony. He supposed he must be. He should be. At twenty-four, he had a new and flourishing barrister's practice in one of the best sets of commercial chambers in the Temple, he shared a decent flat in South Ken with his friend, Adam (which was a bit of an improvement on life in a tiny semi in East Dulwich with his mother and his brother), and he had a good social life, money to spend, girlfriends . . . I must be happy, he thought, and stared sightlessly at the window opposite, wondering why, in that case, he ever stopped to think about it.

The dream was still so present in his mind as he strode swiftly from the tube station through Temple Place that it came as a real shock when he bumped into Leo Davies hurrying up from the Embankment.

'Good God!' said Leo, steadying himself from the slight collision. 'Hello.'

'Hello,' stammered Anthony. 'Sorry. I'm in a bit of a hurry. Got a con at nine and a summons at half ten.'

'My bloody car broke down halfway along the Embankment,' said Leo and sighed, passing a hand over his hair. 'I had to leave it there. Must ring the AA from chambers.' Although he was only forty-four, his hair was silver, lending his gaunt good looks a maturity they would not otherwise possess, for his smile was brilliant, boyish, and his blue eyes candid and restless. He was of Anthony's height, but more squarely built, and was expensively dressed, almost to the point of dandyism.

They fell into step together as they made their way to chambers. There was an uneasy silence between them. They were not accustomed to being alone in one another's company, these days.

Anthony muttered something inconsequential about a recent House of Lords judgment and Leo uttered some words in reply. He glanced at Anthony, feeling in his heart the faint pleasure he always felt when looking at the young man. Then he made some remark about his car and Anthony laughed. Leo loved to see him laugh. It's absurd, he thought, that we hardly ever speak to one another these days. Ridiculous. That business was all finished a long time ago. None of it mattered

4

any more.

'Look,' said Leo, stopping at the foot of the steps to 5 Caper Court, 'what about a game of squash this evening? Ring up the club and see if they have a court free. Yes?'

Anthony was startled. Leo had not invited Anthony to spend time with him since the day he had got his tenancy.

'Yes,' he replied hesitantly. 'All right.' They went upstairs together. Anthony's room was on the first landing, Leo's on the second. Anthony paused at his door. 'I'll see you later, then.' And he smiled at Leo, his happiness so evident that the older man was touched, first with pleasure, then with a slight misgiving.

'Six thirty,' said Leo. 'Try to get a court around then.' And he passed on up the stairs to his room.

At six fifteen Leo was sitting at his desk contemplating the document which lay in front of him. The desk itself was of pale ash, its surface devoid of any other object save the document. All the furniture was of the same pale wood, quite unlike the old, dark, comfortable furniture favoured by most other barristers. No cosy Dickensian shades hung around Leo's room. All was austere, clinical. There was no friendly muddle of papers and briefs lining the shelves and windowsills; everything was neatly tidied away behind the doors of expensive, functionalist cupboards. Even the pictures that hung upon the wall were anodyne modern abstracts, and not the usual charcoal sketches of the law courts, framed water-colours of ships or landscapes, that hung in the rooms of other members of chambers. It all seemed of a piece with the man himself – one of them, yet set apart from them in unusual ways.

Leo was one of the most exceptional advocates in the Temple, with a mercurial personality and a ready wit, and was popular in chambers. Life always seemed to lighten up when Leo was around. He was charming, amusing, and although he moved within the well-defined codes of the Bar with deference and circumspection, there was a certain unconventionality about him; he was an elusive man, and few knew anything of his life outside work.

As he sat studying the document, all his customary energy and restless habit of movement seemed concentrated and contained. The evening light that fell through the window glinted on his hair, and the angular shadows beneath his brow and cheekbones lent his face a brooding, hawklike quality.

The document was headed 'Lord Chancellor's Department. Application for Appointment as Queen's Counsel'. Beneath the word 'Title' were five little boxes, marked 'Mr', 'Mrs', 'Miss', 'Ms' and, slightly larger than the rest, 'Other'. Leo sighed and passed his hand over his head. 'Other'. That about sums me up, he thought.

He rubbed his hands over his eyes. At forty-four, he supposed it was about time that he did this. It was part of the plan, the next step up the golden ladder. There was almost an inevitability about taking silk which bored him. He would achieve this just as he had achieved everything else – his successful practice, his cars, his clubs, his houses in Mayfair and Oxfordshire, his polished circle of social acquaintance. All a long way from the Welsh mining village of his childhood, where he had struggled to free himself from his beginnings and to create a new identity. This would be part of that identity, part of the image which he had cultivated as assiduously as his own charm and urbanity. Leo Davies, QC. Another stitch in that tapestry of his life, the one behind which he could conceal himself from the rest of the world.

He sat flipping through the pages of the form, wondering how long it would take for his income to climb above the half million mark, once he had taken silk, when there was a knock at his door and Anthony came in.

'Hello,' said Leo, glancing up.

'Hi. Squash courts are all booked up, I'm afraid. They've got some competition ladder or something. I don't know.'

'Pity,' said Leo. 'I could have done with a game. I'm right out of condition.' His voice still held an attractive Welsh cadence. He leaned back and flexed his arms above his head, studying Anthony. The young man's face was leaner now, and without any of the softness which had caused Leo to fall in love with him some eighteen months before. Nearly two years. It seemed like a lifetime ago. Well, thought Leo, that had all ended as soon as it had begun. They were friends now, colleagues, no need to let the slightest shadow of it hang between them. They never alluded now to anything in the past, and Leo had hidden away any lingering traces of his former love as easily and effectively as he hid so much from himself and others.

'What's this?' asked Anthony, coming over to the desk and squinting down at the paper. Leo was about to pull the document away and fold it up, but stopped. Why shouldn't Anthony know?

'Application to take silk,' he replied, and leaned back again. 'Have a look, if you like,' he added, and Anthony picked the paper up and flipped through it curiously.

'Listen to this,' said Anthony, smiling; he read aloud: '"Have you ever had an action brought against you in respect of another matter involving you personally, or under your supervision, for professional negligence? Have you ever been subject to the disciplinary process of the Bar without the matter having been dismissed? Have you ever been adjudged bankrupt, made a composition with your creditors, or been sued to judgment for any debt?"' He looked up at Leo and laughed.

'Well, quite,' replied Leo, dryly. 'Instead of "yes" and "no" boxes, they should put one marked "no" and the other marked "forget your application, in that case".' He took the document from Anthony, folded it up and put it into his breast pocket. 'Well, if we can't have a game of squash, a vigorous drink seems like the next best thing.'

They made their way downstairs and out into Caper Court, where a light drizzle had begun to fall; the flush of golden light at the end of the September day was beginning to be eclipsed by banks of grey cloud. They ran through the cloisters and over King's Bench Walk, out into the back alleys of Fleet Street. Leo paused in the doorway of the pub before going in and tapped his breast pocket lightly.

'I'd rather you didn't mention this to anyone. The silk thing, I mean.'

Anthony gazed at him and raised a hand to brush away the surface drops of rain from his dark hair. He nodded. 'Of

7

course. But why did you let *me* know?'

Leo looked back at him candidly. All that ground was too well trodden. Anyway, he didn't really know himself. Something to do with the slender thread of once-shared intimacy which he liked to feel still bound him to this young man, however loosely. He wanted Anthony to know things, wanted to share whatever hopes and disappointments there might be. But he could not acknowledge this.

'Probably,' he replied, 'because you happened to come into my room when I was reading the bloody thing. I was never a good dissembler.' No, never. At that moment someone brushed between them and went into the pub. 'Come on,' said Leo, and Anthony followed him in.

He was pleased to be alone with Leo once more. Tonight's invitation to a game of squash had seemed to him like a return to old times; perhaps the defences were coming down, and he could enjoy Leo's solitary company as he had once done. It struck him as strange and propitious that he should have dreamt of Leo that very morning. For these reasons, he was conscious of a vague disappointment when he saw Stephen Bishop, a fellow member of chambers, sitting alone at a table with a pint of beer and the *Financial Times*. He looked pleased to see Leo and Anthony, and folded up his paper.

'What will you have?' he asked them.

'Large Scotch, please, Stephen, since I happen to know you can afford it,' replied Leo, settling himself into a chair. 'William told me this afternoon about your disgustingly fat fee for that Harvey case.'

Stephen smiled and took his glasses off to polish them with a large handkerchief. 'Yes, well, you know, some of us are just born to greatness. But I have to admit it's nice to get the odd moneyspinner.' Stephen was a portly, cheerful man with an easy manner and a mild nature. His practice was steady but unremarkable, and he never let it interfere with the harmony of his life at home with his wife and four children. He was liked and respected at the Commerical Bar, but he never brought to his cases the energy and dedication that Leo did. Safe, but unexciting, was the verdict on Stephen. He put his glasses back on and turned to Anthony. 'What about you, Anthony?'

'Just a small Scotch, please,' said Anthony. 'I still have some papers to look at tonight.'

Stephen fetched the drinks and sat back down.

'So,' he said, 'how's the day been?' He glanced at Leo. 'Still plugging away at that supply contract dispute?'

Leo yawned and rubbed his jaw with his hand. 'Yes, unfortunately. But surprise, surprise, Stott has to go off and sit on some judicial enquiry for the next four days, so it's been adjourned till next week. Since I don't have anything else in particular to occupy me, I think I'll absent myself from chambers for a few days.'

Anthony felt a little pang. It was absurd, he knew, but he liked to know that Leo was around, liked to hear him whistling on the stairs, to catch an occasional glimpse of him at tea or in the clerks' room. When Leo was away, life for Anthony, even though he was remarkably busy himself, became a little bit emptier. Leo just had that kind of personality, that was all.

'What will you do?' he asked Leo, and took a sip of his Scotch.

'Oh, go down to the country, I think, drink in the last of the summer in peace.' He thought briefly of his house in Oxfordshire, and of its present occupants. 'Relative peace,' he added thoughtfully. Without looking up he could feel Anthony's eyes on him, knew that he was wondering who would be there with him. Was he jealous? Well, thought Leo roughly, knocking back the remains of his drink in one, it didn't matter to either of them if he was. That was all water under the bridge. And why was he even thinking like this? It had been a mistake to ask him for that game of squash this evening. It just made life more complicated.

'I wish I had somewhere worth retreating to,' observed Anthony. 'I mean, somewhere like your place,' he added awkwardly. 'If ever I get anything adjourned, there's always another piece of work to plod on with.'

'Oh, what it is to be young and thrusting and ever so popular with solicitors,' laughed Leo. 'I remember being like that – don't you, Stephen? Never turning work down, working all the hours God gave, buttering up your clerk, trying to cultivate a worldly image.'

Anthony smiled, and Leo was charmed to see him colour faintly.

'Yes,' observed Stephen dryly, 'I understand that we're *particularly* popular with lady solicitors.'

'Oh, balls,' said Anthony. 'Anyway, no doubt it's all very well when you're middle-aged and established and don't have to keep chasing fee notes.'

'Less of the middle-aged,' said Leo. 'I feel quite coltish as I sit there in number five court, listening to Marcus Field enlightening us all on the official policy of the Government of Qatar towards brokerage commissions. Thank God I'm off the hook till next Monday.'

Stephen drained his glass and shook his head. 'I'm glad I'm not Anthony's age any more. Too much cut-and-thrust . . . You have to be so energetic, so determined. Exhausting, just to think of it.'

'Not thinking of retiring, are you, Stephen?' asked Leo jokingly, crushing out the butt of his cigar.

Stephen smiled. 'The fees at Marlborough won't permit it, I'm afraid. Got to keep slogging away. Anyway, see you chaps tomorrow. I'd better be making a move.' He rose and picked up his newspaper. 'Goodnight.'

When Stephen had gone, Leo sat in silence with Anthony for a few seconds, then picked up his empty glass. 'Another?' he asked Anthony.

Anthony hesitated. He felt tired. He had an interlocutory application in the morning and he hadn't even looked at the papers yet. But he wanted to stay. He glanced up and smiled. 'Yes. Okay, another, thanks.'

Leo brought the drinks and sat back down. Anthony looked on idly as Leo lit another little cigar, watching the lean, fine hands he had always found so fascinating. He enjoyed watching Leo, enjoyed his restless, elegant movements, the way he turned his head, the way the side of his mouth jerked when he made a joke. His mind strayed back to Leo's remark as they had entered the pub earlier and he asked, 'Isn't Stephen senior to you in chambers?'

'Yes. He joined two years before I did. Sixty-two.' Leo blew out a little smoke and looked at Anthony. 'Why?'

Anthony looked uncomfortable and turned his whisky glass between finger and thumb. 'Isn't it . . . I mean, wouldn't you expect him to take silk first, or something?'

Or something. Still with that charmingly juvenile sloppiness of speech when embarrassed, thought Leo. He looked levelly at Anthony. 'In the normal course of events, yes.' He paused and leaned back. 'But one can't wait around for ever for Stephen to dither his way through life. He should have applied two years ago, if he was going to go for it.' Leo stroked the glowing edge of his cigar against the rim of the ashtray. 'Maybe he did. Maybe he was turned down. All I know is, one has to be loyal to oneself, not to the other members of chambers.'

'But don't you owe the rest something? I mean, we are all one set of chambers.'

'There is something you have to learn, Anthony,' replied Leo, and his voice was hard, the blue of his gaze quite cold. 'And that is, that you must put yourself first. Every time. Look.' He leaned forward. 'I've run every case for the past two years without a leader. And won most of them. The time is right for me. I'd be a fool to pass it up this year. I don't care what Stephen does or doesn't do.'

Anthony thought for a moment. 'But what effect will it have on Stephen's career if you're successful? Could he still take silk?'

Leo looked carelessly away. 'Probably not.' He drew on his cigar. 'Almost certainly not. If it were to happen, one could take it that the Lord Chancellor's Office had assumed that he wasn't going to apply – or that they were sending out a signal that he wouldn't get it if he did apply. Either way, the writing would be on the wall.' He did not look at Anthony as he spoke. 'Besides,' he added, 'even if he did apply next year, there wouldn't be enough work to justify another silk in chambers. There would be Sir Basil, Cameron, Roderick, Michael – and myself.'

You're so confident, thought Anthony. But of course you are. Why shouldn't you be?

He nodded and said, 'So that would be it – for Stephen, I mean?'

'Well, I suppose so,' replied Leo. 'Otherwise we'd be top-heavy. We might be, in any event. Unless Sir Basil retires.'

'That's not likely, is it?' asked Anthony in surprise. Sir Basil Bunting, the head of chambers, was, admittedly, in his sixties, but he seemed to be riding with magnificent serenity on top of a lucrative and immensely successful practice.

Leo smoked in silence for a few moments. This was something he had thought about. Poor old Stephen was one thing – well, he had had his chance and not taken it. Why should Leo care? Considerations of Stephen were easily dismissed. One was loyal to oneself. Sir Basil was a different kettle of fish. Leo knew that Sir Basil's practice wasn't quite as flourishing as Sir Basil liked to make it appear. Clients nowadays liked younger men – they liked people on their own wavelength. Solicitors were the same, too, and God knows they seemed to be getting younger by the minute. If Leo took silk, he was confident of mopping up a good deal of work from the juniors in chambers. Sir Basil could be squeezed out. And that, thought Leo, might be no bad thing.

Just when Anthony was beginning to think that Leo hadn't heard what he had said, Leo turned to him and flashed a wicked, attractive smile. 'You never know what pressure might be brought to bear on Sir Basil,' he murmured. 'We might just have to hope that the Lord Chancellor wants another High Court judge.'

Anthony drew in his breath and stared at Leo. Will I ever become as ruthless? he wondered. Leo glanced briefly back at him and wondered the same thing. He had detected a slight toughening in Anthony over the past year or so. That touchingly tender aspect of his character seemed to be rubbing away, as the work poured steadily in and the money in-creased. Or was that just a physical illusion, something to do with the fact that Anthony's face was older, less boyish, that he wore decent suits and shirts now, that he was more confident – even a little arrogant – as his practice grew more successful?

'Don't worry,' he said, and drained his glass. 'It's not as bad as it sounds. And don't feel too sorry for Stephen – he's doing very nicely. Anyway, you never know – maybe he's applying for silk this year, too.'

And we know which of you is more likely to get it, if that's the case, thought Anthony. One way or the other, Stephen was the loser, and Leo, it seemed, couldn't care less.

'Want a lift anywhere?' asked Leo as they left the pub. 'The AA seem to have remedied its little defect.'

'No, thanks,' replied Anthony. 'I'm going back to chambers. My papers are still there.'

Leo nodded, and the two men said goodnight and went their separate ways.

In the kitchen of Leo's Oxfordshire house, a young, blonde-haired woman was carefully laying sheets of pasta on the bottom of an oblong dish.

'It's not a problem for me,' she remarked over her shoulder to the boy who stood looking out of the window, arms folded, at the dusk falling on the rainy garden. 'I go back to Oxford in a month's time. It's just been another episode in my life.' She paused briefly to gaze at her handiwork before moving back to the stove to stir a white sauce. 'I like to think of my life as a series of episodes. Nothing final. Nothing static.'

The boy turned to look at her. Like her, he was blond, but taller, and his face wore a sullen, dissatisfied expression. The girl's face was airily serene as she moved about her tasks.

'Don't give me that. You love him.'

'Oh, of course I do!' She turned in smiling astonishment. 'He's divine, an utterly divine man. I love him to death. He's the most wonderful fuck, and he doesn't care in the least for me – that's why he's so attractive.' She turned back to her work, still smiling. Then she added, 'He doesn't care for either of us. We're just a – summer dalliance, you might say.'

The boy turned to look back out of the window. 'At least you've got something to go to. What have I got when it's over?'

'Oh, get a job, James.'

'That's a laugh.' He picked up a knife from the draining board and fiddled with it, running his thumb along the blade. 'Anyway, I don't want a job. I want to stay here.' His voice took on a plaintive, childish tone. 'God, Sarah, I really don't want to have to go.'

'You're just insecure,' remarked Sarah. 'Pass me that grated cheese, would you?'

'So what do I do? Go back to being a photographer's assistant? Let him drop me just where he picked me up? No thanks. He owes us something, doesn't he?'

Sarah flicked her hair back from her shoulders and licked at the finger she had just dipped in the sauce. 'Not a thing. Not me, at any rate. After all, he's paying us for being here – for being his . . . ' She paused and laughed, then sighed. 'His companions. He's fun. He's amusing. This was just a holiday job – I told you. My parents think I'm working as a cook for someone.'

'Well, you are.' James's voice was sulky, bored.

'That's all they know.' She began layering mince and pasta together. 'Put it down to experience, James.'

He said nothing, and she turned to look at him. Seeing the forlorn expression on his face, she came across and put her arms gently on his shoulders. 'Come on, cheer up. We've had a good time, had a laugh, haven't we? Anyway, it's not over yet.' She gave the tip of his nose a soft, pecking kiss.

'That's not the way you kiss me when we're in bed with him,' said James, staring into her eyes.

She smiled back. 'No – but that's work, isn't it?' She watched his troubled face and her smile faded. 'Oh, James, what is it you want? Why can't you just make the most of it, and be happy?'

'Because it's different for you, Sarah! Your family have got money. You've got something to fall back on. What have I got? You'll just swan off back to Oxford and forget about all this – '

'Well, I wouldn't say that.'

He ignored the interruption. ' – while I'm just sort of – thrust aside!'

'Well, face it.' She took her arms from his shoulders and went back to the dish of lasagne. 'He doesn't need you. You can see the kind of man he is. We're just a little diversion in his life. Nothing special. He doesn't want anyone to come too close. There's nothing you can do about that. Anyway, let's change the subject. What do you want to do tonight? Pub?'

'That's just about all there is to do, isn't there?' said James

14

angrily. 'He leaves us stuck here in this hole from one weekend to the next, expecting us to stick to his stupid rules, and be all bright and cheerful and eager to please when he turns up on a Friday night! I'm fed up with it. He's not the only piece of excitement around here, whatever he thinks.' James rammed his hands into his jeans pockets. 'I met this bloke when we were in Ryecot. I'm going to ask him back.' His voice was dogged.

'Don't be a berk, James. You know what Leo said.' Sarah began to pour the cheese sauce carefully over the last layer.

'What's the point of having a place like this for the whole week if we can't share it with a friend or two? I need a bit of company.'

'Thanks. What about me?'

'Well, like you said, that's just work, isn't it?' He looked at his watch. 'I'm going to ring that bloke now.'

'Fun for me,' murmured Sarah. 'I'd better see what's on telly tonight.'

'If you're very good,' said James as he left the kitchen, 'we might let you watch.'

'Ha, ha' said Sarah to herself, as she stared admiringly at her lasagne.

She was watching the late-night film when she heard Leo's car pull up in the driveway, the beam of its headlights brushing the curtained windows with a faint arc of light. She thought of James upstairs in bed with his friend. Leo's bed. She knew she had at least thirty seconds in which to call up to them, warn them, and that James might just, possibly, be able to get him out through an upstairs window in time. She couldn't be bothered. She heard the car door slam, then his feet on the gravel, and snuggled a little lower in her armchair. She was fed up with James, anyway. Always whining round the place. And with him out of the way, who could say how things might develop? Maybe she could make her position that little bit stronger. A man like that. Life would become divinely simple. She'd never wanted to settle down, but if it could be someone like Leo . . . Some hope, she told herself, and smiled wryly at the television screen as Leo opened the front door.

'Hello,' he said, as he came into the room.

'Hello,' she replied, and smiled winningly, briefly, at him round the side of the armchair. Then she stared at the television again. Her heart was thudding a little at the thought of Leo finding James. 'A midweek surprise,' she murmured. 'Just as well I made some lasagne this afternoon. I was going to put it in the freezer for Saturday.'

'Good.' Leo rubbed his face and gazed blankly for a few seconds at the television screen. 'I need a drink. No – I think I'll go upstairs and change first.'

'That's a good idea,' said Sarah. 'I'll fix you a drink while you're up there. You'll need it,' she added under her breath.

It was difficult to concentrate on the film with doors banging and voices shouting and feet thumping on the stairs, but at last they died away. She heard the front door close. Leo came into the room.

'I've poured us both a drink,' she said. 'Yours is over there.'

Leo picked it up. 'James is packing,' he said. He crossed the room and switched off the television, then turned with a sigh to Sarah. 'I'm afraid,' he added, 'that you're next.'

She smiled the impudent, tantalising smile that he had always liked. 'Oh, well. All good things come to an end.' She raised her glass. 'Cheers, anyway.' She took a sip. 'Can I at least stay tonight?'

Leo pushed back a stray lock of grey hair, then tugged his tie loose. He sighed, the anger gradually dying away. That bloody boy. He had known it was a mistake to let it all go on this long. It should have ended ages ago.

Sarah put down her glass and rose, moving forward to embrace him, pressing her body gently against his. 'After all,' she said softly, 'two's company. And three *was* a bit of a crowd . . . ' She kissed him, parting his lips gently with her tongue. As he put his arms round her waist she felt some drops from his glass of whisky fall on the back of her skirt. His hand was shaking. She knew that his anger at the discovery upstairs had left a little legacy of excitement. Weird old Leo.

'All right,' he replied. 'Just for tonight.' He had always preferred her to James, anyway. She was far more inventive. He would be sorry to see her go, in a way. 'You go first thing in the morning,' he added, more firmly.

'First thing,' she agreed. Probably, just as well, really. She had enough saved for a couple of weeks in Cyprus with Alicia. And there was always tonight. 'First thing,' she repeated with a smile, before he closed his eyes to kiss her properly.

Chapter two

The grounding of the MV *Valeo Trader* off Almirante on Monday, the 8th of September, was of significance to several people, but Felicity Waller, as she rummaged through her knicker drawer in her Brixton flat, was not one of those immediately affected by the event. Her ultimate involvement would be of the most peripheral nature, largely confined to the misfiling of relevant documents and the photocopying of a series of nautical charts in the wrong order and at the wrong size setting. But as the vessel, with its cargo of lemons, mineolas and bananas, lay with its hull resting on a sandbank in the Pondsock shallows some .32 miles west of its putative position (based on the chief officer's navigational chart), bathed in the gentle glow of a Pacific sunrise, Felicity was troubled by nothing greater than the task of finding a pair of run-free tights for work.

The possibility of the tights being clean, too, did not enter into it; she merely wanted a pair without rips or holes. She wished to make an especially good impression that day.

'Bleeding bloody hell,' murmured Felicity, as she pulled from the drawer the only remaining undamaged pair, lime-green Sock Shop originals. She glanced across at the crimson Lycra skirt and black sweater which she had salvaged from the weekend laundry bag (which she hadn't managed to take to the launderette) and thought that at least she would look colourful. That might cheer her new boss up a bit. As she scrambled into yesterday's knickers and hooked herself into a greying M&S bra, 36D cup, she told herself she would not go to the pub tonight. She'd stayed too long last night, she admitted to herself, ruefully surveying in the mirror her round, pretty face, smudged and drawn with lack of sleep and the remnants of mascara. Why couldn't she stick to all the good resolutions she made?

Today was the day she had intended to turn over a new leaf. They were giving her a second chance at work (which was decent of them, even if they were a load of old wankers), by letting her work for this new partner who was starting at the firm. Some young woman. She'd meant to go to the launderette last night, have a bath and wash her hair, get to bed early, get up first thing, have a decent breakfast for a change. It was to have been the dawn of a new Felicity, punctual, clean, orderly, a credit to this Miss Dean person she would be working for. If only Vince hadn't brought that dope round . . .

So much for my good intentions, she thought, and gave the bag full of dirty washing a kick as she went through to the kitchen to plug in the kettle and find a fag. She scratched with her fingernail at a little blotchy orange stain on the hem of her black jumper as she waited for the kettle to boil. What could that be from? she mused, trying to remember what she'd eaten over the weekend that had been orange.

She made two cups of tea and padded along the corridor of the tiny flat to her brother's room.

'Gordon Bennett!' she muttered, putting the mug of tea down on the floor next to the bed, and moving across to open the curtains and one of the windows. 'Smells disgusting in here!' She poked at the lumpen human shape beneath the bedclothes. 'I'm off in a minute. Don't spend all day hanging round here watching videos with Vince. Get down the Job Centre.'

The heap under the bedclothes groaned and shifted. Felicity sighed and left the room. She hesitated in the hallway, then went into the living room. On the wicker sofa lay another heap of humanity, its ragged brown head protruding from beneath an unzipped sleeping bag. Felicity stood looking down at it, and then said, 'Good morning, Vince.'

Vince pulled the sleeping bag down from his face and smiled at her. Even first thing in the morning, when he was hungover and unshaven and his hair was matted and sticking up, that smile melted her heart.

'Mornin'!' He suddenly reached out a hand and tried to pull her down towards him, but she gave him an indignant kick

19

and pulled away.

'Get off!' she exclaimed. 'D'you want a cup of tea?'

'I want you, is what I want,' replied Vince, crinkling his eyes and folding his arms underneath his head as he surveyed her.

'Now, now,' replied Felicity. 'What about Carol? What would she say if she heard you talking like this?'

'Carol's blown me out,' said Vince, still smiling. 'So.'

' Oh, yeah? You need a good blowing out, you do. I'll get you a cup.'

She went back into the kitchen, took a swift draught of her tea, and thought about this. How wonderful if Carol had given him the push. Then again . . . she needed someone like Vince like a hole in the head. That's the way it goes, she thought as she waited for the kettle to boil again. You fancy someone for months, you begin to get the idea he fancies *you* a bit, and then it all happens at the wrong moment. It was important for her to clean up her act for the next couple of months, make a good start with this new boss. If she lost this job (and she very nearly had, what with that business on Sandra's birthday when she'd had one too many Malibu-and-Cokes at lunchtime and fallen asleep at her word processor), then they would be right in it. Rent not being paid, bills not met. Oh, no, tempting though he was, Vince was one of those things that would have to be put on the back burner.

With this resolve, and adopting her new persona as competent and sensible secretary to one of the thrusting new partners of Nichols & Co, solicitors, she took Vince his tea with a cool, polite smile.

As she struggled out of his arms and pulled down her sweater five minutes later, she made one last effort at salvaging her dignity.

'Don't think,' she said, standing up and patting her curly hair down, 'that you're going to get the chance to do *that* again in a hurry.'

'Tell me about it,' said Vince with a smile. 'Did you know you've got amazing legs?' He lay back and yawned.

Felicity glanced at her watch. 'God, I'm gonna be late! Help! Listen, don't you go leading my brother astray. He's going to be looking for a job today, right?'

'Yeah, yeah.' Vince reached up and pulled Felicity back down on to the sleeping bag.

While Felicity was busy making herself late for work, Rachel Dean, who was to be the fortunate recipient of Felicity's secretarial services henceforth, was herself getting ready for her first day at Nichols & Co. She sat in the quiet of her pretty little kitchen in her Fulham flat, eating muesli and drinking Earl Grey tea, while the discreet voice of Radio 3 issued forth the news, followed by Haydn's Symphony No. 29. She glanced at her watch, rose, and rinsed out her bowl and cup and saucer. She was a slender, fine-boned girl, quite tall, with a graceful hesitancy of movement. She was wearing a new suit for work that day, fine grey wool with a faint pinstripe, a cream-coloured silk blouse, and her black, sleek hair was drawn smoothly back from her face.

She went into her bedroom – the bedroom which she herself had decorated in rose and white when she had bought the flat a year ago, working away at this and all the other rooms painstakingly at weekends, until each was perfect and to her liking – and shook out her bedding. Then she folded her silk nightdress and slid it beneath her pillow. She picked up her briefcase from beside the desk, on which stood a small computer and word processor, and went through into the living room. She surveyed its immaculate silence for a moment, then left the flat and went down to her car.

Little pangs of nervousness kept leaping up in her stomach as she drove to work. She felt just as she had on the first day at her new secondary school when she was twelve, fifteen years ago. But what was there to be nervous about? She had ability, she knew. That was why they had given her this partnership. It was only a salaried partnership, but time would change that. If she worked hard enough, got a big enough client base, they were bound to give her a share of the equity in a couple of years' time. Nichols & Co had no female equity partners – she was determined to be the first. She lifted her chin slightly as she thought of this, and turned the car smoothly into Commercial Road. The motivation was pride rather than ambition. And besides, what else was there in her life apart from work?

She parked her car – a smart little blue Fiat with a spotless interior, no litter of maps, paperbacks, cassettes and sweet wrappers – in the back streets of Shoreditch, and reached the offices of Nichols & Co in Bishopsgate at nine o'clock precisely. She gave her name to the receptionist, who smiled sweetly and said, 'Oh, yes. You're starting today, aren't you? I'm a bit of a friend of Felicity, your secretary. She's ever so nice.' Rachel smiled a small, chilly smile, still trying to quell the unreasonable little starts of nervousness inside. Well, thought Nora, this one's a bit of an ice queen. And she stabbed a red-enamelled nail at one of the buttons on the switchboard.

'Hello, Denise?' said Nora, with practised nasal resonance. 'Is Mr Rothwell in yet? Only I've got Miss Dean here. She's starting today. Yes, that's right.' The vowels stretched like elastic. 'Right. Thanks ever so.' Nora flipped a switch and smiled up at Rachel. 'If you'd like to go up to Mr Rothwell's office – fourth floor – Denise will meet you at the lift. Mr Lamb will be joining Mr Rothwell and he'll show you your office.'

Rachel thanked her and went over to wait for the lift. Nora ran an expert eye over Rachel's trimly clad figure. Good legs, nice face. Definitely more of a looker than the other three women solicitors in the firm. Only a matter of time before the office wolves got to her. And, thought Nora, as she patted her stiffly lacquered chestnut hair, there were more than a few of them about, as Nora herself could testify.

'Good luck, dear,' murmured Nora as the lift doors closed on Rachel. Then she turned back to the flashing light on the switchboard, cancelled it with a smart flick of her crimson fingernail, and sang into the mouthpiece, 'Good morning, Nichols and Co. Can I help you?'

While Rachel made polite small talk with Mr Rothwell, Felicity stood wedged between a glum body of office workers all the way from Clapham North to Moorgate. She'd hoped she might get a seat so that she could do her make-up, but now even the possibility of a quick sprint to the Ladies at work to do it there seemed to be receding.

'Come on, come on!' she muttered under her breath as the train ground to a halt between Borough and London Bridge.

Minutes passed like ages. The rest of the passengers sighed, shifted their weight, rattled their newspapers. No one looked at anyone else. Eventually the train lurched forward, and at nine ten Felicity was struggling breathlessly up the stationary, out-of-order escalator at Moorgate.

She scuttled through the revolving doors of the offices of Nichols & Co at nine twenty. 'Morning, Nora!' she called out, and Nora fluttered a manicured hand back at her and replied, 'Morning, Fliss! I'd go up the back stairs if I was you, love, because Mr Lamb's going round like a bloody Dalek, checkin' on everyone.'

'Ta.' Felicity dodged up the stairs just as the lift doors opened, and took them two at a time to the third floor. She hovered by the fire door, waited until the coast seemed clear, and then sped across to her desk. Four pairs of eyes, those of Felicity's fellow secretaries, watched her as she stuffed her coat and bag hurriedly under her desk just as the figure of Mr Lamb, the office manager, appeared from the lift. He came over to her desk, smiling unpleasantly and tapping his thigh with a sheaf of papers. He was a squat, balding man in his mid-fifties, obnoxiously officious, and with a personal relish for humiliating the more attractive young female members of staff.

'Good morning, Felicity,' he said. His voice had a nasal Essex twang which Felicity particularly disliked. He stood tapping his thigh for a few more seconds. Here it comes, she thought, and tried to quell the heaving of her chest after her sprint upstairs.

'Morning, Mr Lamb,' she murmured.

'Not a very auspicious start to the week, really – would you say?'

'Sorry, Mr Lamb?' Felicity looked up at him with wide brown eyes, her voice soft and surprised.

'I happened to be coming out of the lift as you were making your way up the back stairs. Twenty minutes late. Bit of a record even by your standards, wouldn't you say?'

'The train got stuck at London Bridge,' replied Felicity, and began to open her desk drawer as though preparing to start work.

'Yes, your train *always* seems to get stuck at London Bridge, doesn't it? I really don't understand how nobody *else's* train ever gets stuck.' Mr Lamb seemed to be enjoying his own heavily sarcastic humour.

'Yes, well, sorry, Mr Lamb.' Felicity stuck her chin in the air and looked straight at him.

'Apart from being late,' continued Mr Lamb as he surveyed her, 'I think it would be an idea if you managed to make yourself rather more presentable for the office.' Felicity's ample bosom heaved slightly with indignation, and she thought she caught Mr Lamb's eye flicker to it. 'Since this position as Miss Dean's secretary is by way of being something of a second chance for you, I'm surprised that you haven't tried to smarten yourself up a bit.' There was a pause, in which Felicity sat glaring at her keyboard. 'As I say, not the best start to your week. Fortunately for you, Miss Dean is with Mr Rothwell at the moment, so you've got time to hang your coat up and make yourself look a bit tidier. Comb your hair, I'd suggest.' He turned on his heel and strode off up the open-plan office.

'Yes, Mr Lamb, no, Mr Lamb, sod off, Mr Lamb,' murmured Felicity, and pulled her coat from beneath her desk and went to hang it in the cupboard.

Felicity was aware, as she walked back to her desk, of the watchful eyes of the other typists focused on her. She was not popular with them. They were all middle-aged, moralistic, and spent much time discussing knitting patterns, diets, and their grown-up children. Felicity was very much an outsider. They were not overtly unfriendly to her, treating her with a sort of caustic tolerance, but her very obvious sensual attractions had an almost animal effect upon them, so that their voices would fall and their glances slide away when she arrived. Her blowsy cheerfulness and rude banter made them uneasy. They did not approve of her clothes and had suspicions about her lifestyle. They took satisfaction in the fact that Mr Lamb did not approve of Felicity either, but they knew that his disapproval masked an aggressive fascination with the swing of her hips and the curve of her breasts.

The Menopausals, Felicity called them.

Only one of them, Doris, ever went out of her way to be friendly to Felicity, but it was a friendliness that Felicity mistrusted. Doris was a plump, soft woman in her fifties, the oldest of the secretaries, with a sweet voice and a permanently sympathetic expression, which was somewhat marred by the bright watchfulness of her small eyes. They were eyes that would fasten confidingly on those of her listener, and all Doris's communications seemed to have a confidential, secretive quality. She would show little acts of kindness to Felicity, bringing her the occasional coffee, consulting her on the choice of wool for a matinee jacket for one of her beloved grandchildren, showing her photographs of herself and her husband on holiday in Spain. But in spite of these little displays of affection, Felicity mistrusted Doris. She suspected her of tale-bearing, of gossiping, of spreading rumours about what Felicity did out of office hours. Give her Louise any day. A bit sharp-tongued, but at least she was straight up and down with it.

As Felicity sat back down at her desk, Doris smiled across at her. 'Ooh, Felicity,' she said in a voice like Dralon, 'have you seen this new lady partner yet, the one you're working for?'

'No,' said Felicity, 'I haven't.'

'Oh, no, you wouldn't have, would you? You were just a tiny bit late again, wasn't you? Well, she's ever so lovely, Felicity. Really elegant – beautiful suit she has on.' Doris's voice was humbly rapturous.

Felicity took all this in with interest. 'Does she seem nice, then?'

'Well, I wouldn't know, Felicity. I haven't spoken to her yet. But she's got one of those looks – you know – '

'Stuck-up,' interjected Louise, in a tart voice, not looking up from her word processor.

'Ooh, no!' said Doris gently. 'No. She did look very proper. But I wouldn't call her stuck-up. No.'

'You'll have to watch yourself round her,' remarked Louise to Felicity. 'That's all I'd say.'

God, thought Felicity, this didn't sound too promising. When Doris had gone back to her word processor, she got up and went into Miss Dean's empty room. She surveyed the

25

desk, pulled open a couple of drawers. It was her job to keep Miss Dean supplied with all her bits and bobs, stationery, paperclips, stuff like that. She'd better get some. It wouldn't take two minutes.

She trotted down to the post room, where the stationery was kept, selected some pens, paperclips, Post-it notes and a hole puncher, then stood exchanging banter with the office boy and gossip with the post girls. She glanced at her watch. She'd been down here nearly fifteen minutes, she'd better get back. But she couldn't resist putting her head round the door of the telex room and saying hello to the boys, and since Terry had a copy of the *Sun* and the *Sunday Sport*, she had to have a quick look at her horoscope and read the problem page in the *Sunday Sport*. Disgusting, it was. Made you wonder if they didn't make it all up.

By the time she had giggled her way out of the telex room and stopped at reception to tell Nora, who was a Scorpio, the gist of her horoscope, it was past ten. Mr Lamb was waiting in Miss Dean's room with Miss Dean.

'Miss Dean and I have been waiting for you, Felicity,' said Mr Lamb in cold and meaningful tones, 'for ten minutes.'

'Oh, have you, Mr Lamb?' replied Felicity. 'Ever so sorry. I've just been getting Miss Dean some things.' And she tumbled her cache of pens and paperclips on to the desk and held out her hand in greeting to her new boss. 'Hello. I'm Felicity.'

Rachel Dean looked at Felicity as she shook her hand, and saw a pretty, untidy-looking creature with garish clothes which did nothing to conceal an extraordinary figure. She smiled warmly at Felicity because one couldn't help smiling at her, but her first impression was that this scatty-looking creature did not give the appearance of being a model of efficiency. Rachel had had secretaries in the past; some had been a positive asset, some a liability. Felicity, she suspected, fell into the latter category.

Felicity, looking at Rachel, marvelled at what she saw. I wish I was that slim, she thought, and had cheekbones like that and smooth black hair all swept back. Dead sophisticated. I want to be like that. I want to wear a suit like that and have a knockout smile that looks like vanilla ice cream. Some hope, she thought. She smiled bravely at Rachel and watched her walk round behind her desk, wondering how much her shoes had cost.

'Thank you for getting me these,' said Rachel. 'It's dreadful to start off with not even a paperclip to your name. I wouldn't even know where to get that sort of thing.'

'Oh, I'll take you round in a bit, if you like, introduce you to the chaps, show you where everything is,' said Felicity brightly.

'Miss Dean has met most of her colleagues already, Felicity,' said Mr Lamb, 'and I think you've wasted enough time this morning chatting your way round the building.' He turned to Rachel and gave her his best smile. 'I'll leave you to get on, Miss Dean.' And he strutted out.

'They're not all like him,' said Felicity. 'He's a prize one, he is. Would you like a coffee, Miss Dean?'

'Please call me Rachel. Yes, I would – black with one sugar, please.'

'It wouldn't go down too well with Mr Lamb if he heard me calling you Rachel,' said Felicity doubtfully. 'He's a real one for form. He'll never call you anything but Miss Dean.'

'God, I hope not,' said Rachel. 'Still, office managers are a breed apart, aren't they?'

'I don't like to think of them breeding, much!' said Felicity with a giggle, and Rachel laughed, too.

While Felicity fetched the coffee, Rachel sat down at her pristine desk and began to sort out the jumble of stationery which Felicity had dropped on it, quite glad to have something to do. She'd have to start ringing round soon, reminding people where she was, chasing up contacts. The first day in a new firm was bound to be a bit blank, she supposed. Still, here it was, a new beginning.

Felicity came back with the coffee.

'Here we go,' she said, her tongue between her teeth as she set Rachel's plastic cup down in front of her. 'Cheers!' she added, saluting Rachel with her own cup.

'Cheers,' said Rachel.

'So,' said Felicity, 'what d'you want me to do, then?'

27

'Well, I don't exactly know, Felicity. I haven't really got much to do myself. I have some phone calls to make, and with luck I should get a couple of files from my old firm this afternoon. They'll need to be photocopied and the originals sent back. I have some letters to get out – do you want me to dictate a couple to give you something to be getting on with?'

'If you like,' said Felicity. 'I don't really mind.'

'Well, I have to send out a standard letter to a list of different people, telling them where I am and so on. Not very exciting, but I suppose you like to keep busy, don't you?'

Felicity's eyes widened. 'Well – yes, generally,' she murmured. God, this one seemed a bit keen. Working for Mr O'Connell had been a doddle, since he was out at the pub half the time, but Miss Dean seemed quite a different proposition. Oh, well, she'd just have to stick to her resolution. She would become amazingly efficient; Rachel would tell everyone what a marvellous secretary she had, and how lucky she was. She'd show that bunch of geriatrics. 'Anyway,' she added, thinking of what Rachel had said, 'why can't you just ring your old firm up and tell them to get your stuff round here, pronto?'

'Well, there's a certain protocol about these things – I mean, a way of doing it,' she added, seeing Felicity's blank expression. 'I'm effectively leaving one firm and taking quite a bit of business with me. Not that there are any hard feelings about it, but they're not likely to fall over themselves to pass things on. I suppose I'm quite lucky that I haven't got clients ringing me up right now, asking me to do things on a case when I haven't got the file in front of me.'

'Right,' murmured Felicity. And the phone rang.

'Speak of the devil,' said Rachel, and picked it up. Felicity fluttered her fingers and trotted out, deciding to pop down to accounts and have a little natter with Moira. Mr Lamb could hardly have a go at her for not getting on with things when there was nothing to be got on with.

Michael Nikolaos was a small, shabby Greek shipowner, with a small, shabby office in Piraeus. Since he had been telephoned by the master of the *Valeo Trader* with news of her grounding, he had been sweating and cursing and trying to get hold of Rachel Dean. He loved Rachel, he trusted her, and she had steered him through a number of problems over the years. He often thought he must be beset by more difficulties than any other shipowner in Greece. He was probably right.

It had taken him a while to track her down to her new office, and by the time he had poured forth his troubles he was agitated and miserable. He should never have bought reefer vessels. He had enough problems with bulk carriers without adding to them with refrigerated cargoes.

'Well, all right, all right,' Rachel was saying soothingly. 'We'll arrange for a surveyor to inspect the hull as soon as we can and see what the prospects for refloating her are. Who are the agents at Almirante?'

'I think it is – yes, it is Stern. Stern.' Mr Nikolaos tapped his forehead impatiently with fat fingers and wiped away some beads of sweat. Piraeus sweltered in the September sun. His desk was a mess of papers, and on the corner of it his second phone had begun to flash.

'Very well, I'll get on to them now. And we can get someone down to talk to the master and the pilot.'

Mr Nikolaos groaned. 'There was no pilot on board. The master say he sail without a pilot.'

'The vessel sailed out of Almirante without a pilot?' Rachel sighed and made a note. Where did Mr Nikolaos get his masters from?

'Yes! I don't know why – but, yes! This is dreadful business for me, Miss Dean. If the vessel is damaged they will have to jettison cargo. Then I am sued for short delivery – this is too many troubles for me! And we don't know what is damage to ship . . .' His voice trailed away on a bleat of panic and despair.

'Calm down, Mr Nikolaos,' said Rachel as kindly as she could. Poor old Mr Nikolaos, one disaster after another. Still, at least it was a new case on the first morning of her new job. God bless him. 'We don't even know if there *is* any damage. So let's just wait and see what the surveyor says. All right? Now, you get those documents over to me as quickly as you can. I'll be in touch this afternoon.'

As Mr Nikolaos put one phone down and picked up the

other with trepidation in his heart, Rachel sat back in her chair and looked up to see the figure of Roger Williams, one of her partners, standing in the doorway. He was a square-faced, plump man with warm eyes that held the eyes of others just a shade too long, and a habit of making himself as proximate to women as possible when speaking to them.

'I've come to tell you I'm taking you to lunch,' he said with a smile.

'Thank you,' said Rachel, and smiled brightly back. Roger and four others had been present at her final interview, and she knew that she should be grateful for the fact that he had probably been one of those most in favour of her joining Nichols & Co, but she wished that everything he said didn't sound so much like an insinuation.

'Just you and me and Fred Fenton. You've met Fred, haven't you?'

'Oh, yes. Yes. I was introduced to him this morning.' That was a relief – someone her own age. Fifty-year-old males could get a bit oppressive; they always seemed to think that a young woman was some sort of challenge they had to rise to. It could make social occasions tiresome.

'Right you are,' said Roger. 'See you downstairs at twelve thirty.' He paused, leaning against the doorframe, sliding one hand into his trouser pocket. 'Settling in all right, are you? Got a decent secretary?'

At that moment Felicity came tripping back, bringing Rachel some tapes for her machine. Roger glanced at her and laughed. He looked back at Rachel. 'Well, ask a stupid question,' he said, and raised his eyebrows. He turned to Felicity. 'Hello, Felicity.' His expression as he gazed down at her, watching her fiddle with Rachel's dictaphone, was one of supreme self-assurance, the powerful male animal in a male-dominated office exerting authority over the inferior female minion.

''lo, Mr Williams,' murmured Felicity coolly.

'Boyfriend been keeping you up late again?' Roger continued to regard her. 'You'll have to tell him to give it a rest now that you've got some real work to do, for a change.' And he smiled back at Rachel, glanced at Felicity again, and sauntered off.

'Isn't he lovely?' remarked Felicity cheerfully. 'He's a pig, he is.'

'Felicity! He'll hear you!' said Rachel. Her phone rang again and she picked it up.

'So what if he does?' murmured Felicity to herself. She'd never told anyone about the time he tried to grab her tits in the lift – it would just have been more trouble than it was worth and the end of her job, more likely than not. But she'd be ready for him next time. Just let him try. Her meditations were interrupted by the sound of Rachel's voice.

'Okay, there's something for you to do now,' said Rachel. 'A messenger has just dropped off two of my files from my old firm at reception. So if you go and fetch them and bring them to me, you can make a start on photocopying them.'

'Okey-doke,' said Felicity, and headed for the lift. She could have a look at that astrological computer print-out that Nora had had done at the weekend while she was down there. Wouldn't take more than five minutes. And if Rachel was going out to lunch with porky Williams, maybe she and Moira could nip out to the pub for a few drinks and a bit of a giggle.

Chapter three

Three weeks to the day that Felicity had vowed to mend her ways and become a paragon of secretarial virtue, she was shaken awake by her brother at ten past nine. It took a lot of shaking to rouse her. At last she rolled over, pushing a tangle of hair from her eyes and squinting up at him. Vince, who was lying next to her, muttered something and pulled the duvet around himself.

'Christ! What time is it?' she said, her eyes beginning to focus.

'It's ten past nine, Fliss. You've slept right through your alarm.'

Felicity groaned and reached out a hand to the clock radio blaring tinnily on the floor by her bed. She shut it off. 'God. Oh, God. Sandy, I feel dreadful. Oh, God.'

At last she managed to pull herself out of bed and make her way to the bathroom, where she stood swaying uncertainly by the washbasin. Slowly she turned on the cold tap and splashed water over her face. She stood there, her face dripping, leaning on the basin for a moment, then reached out for a towel.

In the kitchen Sandy was making her some tea.

'What am I going to say, Sandy? I'm going to be dead late.' She slumped down in a chair. 'I've never felt this bad before.'

'Yeah, well, you're doing too much stuff, I reckon.'

'That's great, coming from you.'

'Yeah, well, why don't you say you had to go to the doctor's, or something?'

'I've said that twice before to her. I reckon I'm going to cop it this time. And she's *so* nice to me, Sandy, she always sticks up for me . . .' She took the tea that her brother handed to her. Her hands were shaking slightly and her face was pale and hollow-eyed. She had only had four hours' sleep.

After a pause, she put down her tea and stared at her hands. 'Sandy, I don't think I can make it without something. I'll be like a zombie, otherwise.'

Without a word Sandy left the room. When he came back he handed her some pills.

'Coupla chalkies. Here you go.'

She took them and swallowed them with some tea.

'Listen, Fliss, you've got to slow down a bit. I mean, Vince is my mate and all that, but – '

'But we need my job, right?' She glared at him. 'Because I'm the only one in this stinking flat who can be bothered to get off their bum and go to work every day. Right? Well, don't you think I'm getting a bit sick and tired of propping you up? I'm entitled to my fun, too, you know. Why is it *me* that's got to get up each day and have all the hassle and aggro, while you sit around doing nothing and having a good time?'

Sandy leaned back against the sink. His spindly arms stuck out from the overlarge T-shirt in which he slept.

'I don't have that much fun, actually. It's effing boring half the time. I sometimes think I'd rather have a job.'

Felicity stood up and pulled her jacket from the hook behind the kitchen door. 'Then why don't you bleeding go and look for one?' she demanded, and left the flat, banging the door as hard as she could.

The amphetamines were beginning to take effect by the time she got to the office. She managed to slip into the Ladies and apply enough make-up to disguise the ravages of last night's session, and she even managed a bright, defensive smile as she slipped into her chair under the watchful gaze of the Menopausals. She had begun to sort through the papers next to her word processor when she heard Rachel's voice.

'Felicity, may I see you for a moment, please?'

Oh, God, here we go, thought Felicity. She went into Rachel's room.

'Close the door, please, Felicity.' Felicity closed the door.

'I'm really sorry I'm late. I had this dentist's appointment I forgot to tell you about. I would have rung in, but – '

'Save it, Felicity.' Rachel gave her a stern look. 'The dentist's appointment is not the point. The point is that I had to send out two copies of the surveyor's report on the *Valeo Trader* urgently this morning. You knew that yesterday. You had all yesterday afternoon to photocopy them, and I arrived in the office this morning to find that you hadn't even taken them off the file. I had to copy them myself. I had to get Doris to type the letters to go with them. God knows, I don't regard photocopying as beneath me, Felicity – but I have better things to do.'

'I'm sorry,' mumbled Felicity.

'And I have to cover for you when you're late. That's the pathetic part. How do you think I feel making excuses for you to Mr Lamb? Excuses! I don't like the man any more than you do, but I have to tell you it makes me feel quite small covering for you all the time. I do it because I like you, Felicity – and because I think you could be better at this job than you pretend. Your administration's excellent, you sort my appointments out, you keep track of things – but your typing's sloppy and your timekeeping is non-existent.' Rachel paused and sighed; Felicity said nothing. 'Look, I know that working for me is something of a second chance for you, so why don't you make the most of it? My good nature is not inexhaustible, you know.' She leaned back, weary of the subject. 'Anyway, you seem to have quite a backlog of my tapes, so I've asked Simon if Doris can take a couple.'

This was humiliating, to have Doris helping her keep up with her work. 'Yes, all right. I'm ever so sorry, Rachel.'

'That's okay,' Rachel sighed. Felicity ran her eyes over Rachel's lavender silk blouse and the little gold bar pin that fastened it at the throat. So neat, so perfect. Her life must be like that, thought Felicity, serene, ordered, all colour-coordinated. Why can't my life be nice? she wondered. Well, it's not, and that's all there is to it. She left Rachel's room, buzzing slightly now, and decided to have a cup of coffee before starting on the tapes.

Mr Nikolaos had thought that his life could not get any worse. Apart from the grounding of the *Valeo Trader*, he had just been informed by the shipping agents in Brisbane that the *Valeo Pennant*, which had arrived from West Africa with a cargo of soya-bean oil, was being blacked by the ITF.

'I don't believe this thing!' wailed Mr Nikolaos to the agents. 'Why are they doing this? Tell me!'

'They seem to have got wind of the fact that you've been underpaying your crew. The stevedores are refusing to unload the cargo.'

'This is only cash-flow problem! You understand?' The shipowner's round face was creased with worry. One vessel in dock in Almirante awaiting repairs to its propeller – expensive repairs – with an entire reefer cargo jettisoned and large claims from the cargo owners about to come in at any moment, and now a second vessel blacked in Australia, while the cargo receivers fretted and the berthing charges mounted. It could not get any worse.

It got very much worse that same afternoon, when a fire and explosion in the engine room of the *Valeo Dawn* in Bombay harbour killed eight crewmen and blacked out the entire vessel, causing the breakdown of the refrigeration system on a consignment of frozen squid. Mr Nikolaos actually cried for three minutes before ringing Rachel to tell her of the two latest tragedies in his shipowning career.

Rachel leaned against the filing cabinet in Simon MacBride's room, recounting the latest disaster to have befallen Mr Nikolaos. Simon was a fellow partner, some nine years her senior, and she felt that she liked and trusted him rather more than the others. Besides, she had known him before joining the firm, having been at university with his wife. She found she went to him most days just to exchange gossip or to take soundings on whatever current problems she had.

'Poor Mr Nikolaos,' said Rachel. 'He's been running this shoestring operation for years, carrying general bulk cargoes, and then he decides to get a couple of reefer vessels in hopes of building up business. So much for his hopes.'

'What caused the fire? Do they have any idea?' asked Simon.

Rachel shook her head. 'It's impossible to say, yet. The engine room is gutted – they're just lucky the whole ship didn't go up. Possibly one of the engines started it. I don't know.'

'But I thought there was an explosion?'

'Well, quite. Anyway, I've got Finlayson's to instruct a surveyor first thing. I've already had the solicitors for the cargo interests on the phone. They didn't hang about.' She sighed and plucked at the silk-covered button of her cuff. Simon noticed how white the cuticles of her delicately shaped nails were. She always seemed so clean, he thought, so utterly immaculate and cool. He was aware that most of his colleagues fancied her from afar, but for Simon there was something chilly about her slender, fine-boned loveliness. He could never imagine anyone mussing up that sleek black hair. She probably wore white underwear. Too clinical and perfect for him. He wondered if there was a man . . . No, he would have heard. Roger would have been sloping around telling everyone. Roger was one of the ones who occasionally referred to her in unspeakably crude terms. But then Roger referred to most women that way.

'So I can foresee a long, protracted argument ahead,' Rachel was saying. Simon roused himself from his speculations to concentrate on what she was saying. 'I know it's early days, but I can see us having to instruct counsel and I'd like to have someone lined up.'

'What about Bernard Kelly?'

'No. I've gone off him lately. I'd like someone new.'

Simon considered. 'How about that young bloke at 5 Caper Court? I've forgotten his name. Anthony something. Alistair uses him a lot. Says he's extremely good. Very keen.'

'I've never used anyone from that set,' said Rachel. 'My old firm had a down on them. I think the senior partner had a row with one of the leaders there. No, that's not true – I did instruct Cameron Renshaw once on a reinsurance case.'

'Well, he's someone new, if that's what you want.'

'I'll bear that in mind. Thanks.'

Simon lowered his feet from his desk and swung round in his chair. 'I'm meeting Sally for a drink in Leadenhall Market tonight. Fancy joining us?'

'No, thanks,' said Rachel with a smile. 'I've got a load of household chores to catch up on. Bye.'

When she got home, it seemed very quiet in the flat. She had

36

told Simon she had chores to do, and he had assumed she was meeting a man somewhere. But Rachel had been telling the truth. She set down her briefcase in the hall, then took off her coat. It was past seven o'clock, so she made herself a small vodka and tonic and switched on the compact black television set that stood discreetly in the corner of the living room. She left it tuned into the Channel 4 news while she went into the kitchen to make her supper. She made herself a salad of ham and avocado and lettuce hearts, a wholewheat roll with low-fat spread, poured a glass of milk, and took it all back into the living room on a tray.

When she had finished supper she washed up, rinsing the cutlery carefully, and then went to change. When she was changed into what she thought of as comfy old clothes, Rachel looked as immaculate and tasteful as something from a page in *Vogue*. She got out a tin of beeswax from the cupboard below the sink, a duster, some Jif spray and a J-cloth. She cleaned all the surfaces and cupboards in the kitchen. She spread wax polish on the kitchen table and polished it gently, then replaced the vase of freesias that had been standing there. Rachel liked fresh flowers. Elegant little arrangements with faint fragrances, not opulent, imposing blooms with over-powering, sensuous scents. Those would have troubled her. When she had finished in the kitchen, she went into the living room and carefully dusted all the surfaces. Then she waxed and polished the wooden tables that stood by each sofa, and passed a duster over the glass of the framed watercolours on either side of the fireplace, and over the shining mirrors, and straightened the rugs. She stood back to admire her work. Then she stepped forward again to tidy the pile of magazines lying on one of the tables – the *Law Society Gazette*, *Tatler* and *The Economist*.

No need to do the bathroom – she had done that last night. Tomorrow night she would hoover and clean her bedroom. She washed her hands in the kitchen and gently rubbed handcream into them; she always remembered to push back her cuticles with the soft edge of a towel when she did this. Then she put what little washing she had into the washing machine and set it off. In the morning she would hang it on the clothes rack which was left standing in the kitchen during the day. Rachel never hung clothing over radiators.

When she had finished in the kitchen, she fetched her briefcase from the hallway and went to her bedroom to do some work at her word processor. At ten she switched off her desk lamp and went back to the kitchen to make herself a cup of Ovaltine. She listened to *The World Tonight* as she drank it, flicking through the back of *The Times* to see if there was anything worth watching on television. When she saw that there wasn't, she washed her mug, switched off the radio, and went to the bathroom to take off what little make-up she wore and clean her teeth.

In bed, she switched on her clock radio to *The Financial World Tonight*, and opened her book at the place where she had stopped reading the night before.

When she at last switched off her bedside light, Rachel fell quickly asleep, her arms curved protectively around her breast, her legs tucked in.

In her Brixton flat, Felicity lay back on a cushion with her eyes closed. The Guns 'n' Roses tape that Vince had put on was competing with the sound of 'Buffalo Soldiers' from the Rastafarians' flat next door.

'Come on,' said Vince, 'try it.' He leaned over, his long hair touching Felicity's cheek as he spoke. Felicity shook her head and did not open her eyes. 'Go on,' urged Vince, 'it's good.'

'No,' said Felicity firmly. She opened her eyes to look at him as she said this, then closed them again. 'No,' she repeated. 'I've had half that joint and I'm not doing anything else.'

'It's not a joint – that's so old-fashioned. It's a spliff. You call it a spliff.'

'Call it what you like,' said Felicity. 'That's all I want. I'm getting up in time tomorrow. And you're going home.'

'Oh, Fliss, baby . . .' Vince slid his hand quickly inside her bra and tried to kiss her.

'I meant it.' Felicity's voice was muffled. She tried, not very hard, to remove his hand.

'Why, Fliss? Come on, you've done everything else I've suggested, and liked it.'

'That was sex,' replied Felicity. She took his hand out and stood up. 'And anyway, I've made some resolutions. I'm going to get this place really cleaned up' – she stared around through the haze of smoke at the dirty carpet, the tatty curtains, the sagging sofa, the empty glasses and cans, the pile of videos and dog-eared paperbacks stacked on a wooden shelf balanced on bricks – 'and I'm going to get my life together. No more drugs, not so much drinking – and you can go home tonight.'

Vince, lying back against the split cushions with their stained batik covers, legacies of some hippy era, rocked one knee from side to side and laughed.

'I think you must come out with this stuff once a week just to make yourself feel better.' He took a deep drag of what remained of the joint smouldering in the ashtray. 'Fliss, you're always making resolutions. None of them come to nothing. Why don't you just sit back down here and try some of this?'

'I told you, Vince,' she replied, as he reached up and tugged her hand, 'I'm tired of doing all this stuff. My head can't stand it. Neither can my job. I've got to get some sleep so's I'm up in time in the morning.'

'A little tab of this and you wouldn't even need to go to sleep. You'll be flying for a fortnight.' She allowed herself to be pulled back down next to him. 'Go on.' He gave her his best, beautiful smile, the one that made him look like Tom Cruise with long hair, and handed her the silver foil.

'I've never done acid before,' she said doubtfully.

'It's beautiful,' he said, and leaned back, closing his eyes. 'Makes you want to make love all night.'

'Honest?' She gave him a sideways look and giggled.

'And then you won't be afraid to do all those interesting things I've been wanting us to do.'

'That's all you think about, isn't it? Sex.' She stared at the silver foil. 'And drugs.'

'And rock and roll,' added Vince. And they both laughed. Just this once, thought Felicity. It'll be all right with Vince.

The next day, the first of October, was bright and mild. Mr Slee, head clerk at 5 Caper Court, came back well satisfied after lunch. He had spent a profitable morning persuading the clerk of the Commercial Court to shuffle the lists in his favour, and had followed it with two pints in the Suffolk Arms with fellow senior clerks. He felt serene and benevolent. He smiled upon the typists, he whistled as he opened the lunchtime mail, and he delivered only the mildest of reproofs to Henry, the junior clerk, for negligently arranging a conference with solicitors for Mr Hayter on a day when he was already due in court.

As he made his way to Leo's room with some papers which had just come in, Mr Slee felt like a king in his kingdom. He often felt this way. To hold the reins of power in such an illustrious set of chambers was a thing of great pride to him. Without him, the barristers would be lost. He it was who organised their cases, arranged their conferences, negotiated their fees. He liked, too, to feel that he acted as the spirit of tolerance and harmony within chambers. Not that he ever displayed his pride. Discretion and humility were all. Mr Slee was well schooled in this; his father had been a barrister's clerk, and his father before him.

But as soon as he entered Léo's room, Mr Slee could tell that Leo did not share his equable frame of mind that day. He sat behind his desk, some papers spread out before him, leaning back and chewing on a paperclip. Mr Slee didn't know how Leo could do that, he really didn't; it set his teeth on edge just to watch him.

Leo leaned forward and frowned as Mr Slee put the papers on his desk, murmuring some pleasantry about the weather.

'William, what's happened to the money on that letter of credit case? I should have had it weeks ago.' It suited Leo to be peevish with William. He seemed to be in a perpetually bad mood these days and found it useful to take it out on his clerk. He'd spent all last weekend brooding over his application for silk, and that business of Sarah and James had been preying on his mind. Thank God he'd got rid of them – but how had he been such a fool as to let it start? He had only meant to pick up James in that club that night. Sarah had been James's idea. 'If you like it both ways, you'll like Sarah,' he had said. And Leo had. He had found the entire situation such a novelty that he allowed them to stay. They'd been useful, too – cleaning and cooking for him, looking after the house and the garden, as well as sharing his bed, driving back the loneliness. But nothing could drive that back for long. All this morning he had been chewing paperclips and wondering how he could have let his desires get the better of him, to the point of what now seemed like nauseating folly. Even though it was unlikely that anyone of any importance should learn details of his personal life, it was vital, now that he was applying to take silk, that his conduct should be utterly blameless. Vexation and guilt fuelled his irritation with his clerk.

'Well,' said Mr Slee in answer to Leo's question, 'I gather the solicitors are having a bit of trouble with their clients. You know how it is.'

'Bloody Church and Moylan are always having trouble with their clients,' retorted Leo sharply. 'Can't you chivvy them a bit?'

Mr Slee folded his arms above his broad stomach. 'Naturally I'm doing my best, sir, but we don't want to go upsetting them too much. Might start taking their work elsewhere, otherwise.'

'We shouldn't be taking work without money up-front. You know what these bloody Iranians are like. Quite frankly,' added Leo, 'I wish they *would* take their work elsewhere.'

He snapped the paperclip in two and leaned back. Mr Slee waited. He had known Leo for twenty-two years and was aware that a storm of minor irrelevancies always preceded some more important issue.

'William,' said Leo after a pause, 'how do you think it would be if I applied to take silk?' Mr Slee looked at him attentively, concealing his surprise. 'I mean, how do you think the work would stand?'

Mr Slee pursed his lips and tried to look nonchalant. He had not expected this. When Stephen Bishop had confided in him, two weeks ago, his own intention to apply for silk, Mr Slee had regarded it as a sensible and timely move. One that might have been made two or three years earlier, but still, better late than never. There were already four silks at 5 Caper Court – Sir Basil, Roderick Hayter, Cameron Renshaw, and Michael Gibbon, who had taken silk only last year – and that was quite a lot for a chambers of their size, but Mr Slee had thought the thing would work. He was confident that Leo, Jeremy Vine, and the younger tenants, William Cooper, David Liphook and Anthony Cross, would generate enough work to keep five QCs busy. But now Leo was thinking of applying, too. This altered the picture entirely. Mr Slee leaned back against the bookshelves and said nothing for a few seconds. Leo raised his eyebrows enquiringly.

'Well,' said Mr Slee, shifting his weight, 'I would hope that there would be enough work to go round. Anthony is bringing in a good deal, and Sir Basil is thinking of taking on another two juniors . . .' He ran his thumb along his lower lip. As a matter of confidentiality, he could not tell Leo about Stephen's application, but it was regrettable that they should both choose to apply in the same year. He did not like this. He did not like it at all. It was always possible that the Lord Chancellor's Office might give preference to Stephen, as being the more senior in chambers, but he felt in his heart of hearts that, of the two, Leo was more likely to succeed. Mr Slee had spent years talking to lawyers, clerks and judges, had spent the better part of his life immersed in the grey mysteries of the courts and their workings, from the minutiae of the daily grind to the cogitations of the highest law officers in the land, and he felt this in his bones. Leo would succeed, and Stephen's nose would be put badly out of joint. Tensions would inevitably arise in chambers. That one member should leapfrog another in the matter of taking silk would not be well regarded. Still, Leo must have his own reasons. Mr Slee eyed him. For all his dapper good looks, for all his careless charm and good humour, he knew Leo to be flint-hearted in his ambition. Not that Mr Slee liked him the less for it. That was just the way Leo was.

'You don't sound very certain,' remarked Leo, swivelling from side to side in his chair, his eyes fastened on the clerk's face. It was very important, he knew, that William should support him in this.

'No – I was just thinking,' replied Mr Slee quickly. 'Just thinking about figures. No, I'm sure enough work would come your way. Not a doubt of it.'

Leo nodded. 'Let's talk about those figures, then.'

When Mr Slee left his room fifteen minutes later, Leo sat back with some satisfaction. At least William seemed to foresee no particular problems with his application. Nor had any mention been made of the fact that he might be seen to be overstepping Stephen. He felt more cheerful as he resumed his work. He would put that sordid episode of the summer behind him and concentrate on the matter in hand. He must succeed in this – it was a matter touching his vanity, as well as his ambition. The names of the new silks would not be announced until the following Easter. That gave him a good six months in which to live the saintliest of existences, just in case the Lord Chancellor's Office turned its attentive eye upon him, as no doubt it would.

Mr Slee left Leo's room in a less happy frame of mind. Leo's application raised all kinds of new possibilities. A thought suddenly occurred to him. What if both men were successful? It was possible; the Lord Chancellor's Office moved in mysterious ways. If that were to happen, it would put the squeeze on Sir Basil's practice, which was not so fertile as it had once been. And that could cause problems for Mr Slee. His heart contracted at the thought. He came to a halt on the second-floor landing and gazed out at the fading leaves on the autumn trees. He and Sir Basil were of a generation. He had been the callowest of junior clerks when Sir Basil had first joined chambers. He stared down at the familiar flagstones of Caper Court; he could remember vividly the very first day he had walked across those very stones and through the door of number 5. If Sir Basil were forced to retire, what would that mean for Mr Slee? Perhaps, with Sir Basil gone, the other members of chambers might feel it was time for him, too, to give way to a younger man. He was finding it difficult, he knew, to keep up with a lot of this new technology, and sometimes he felt the pace of chambers pushing him a bit. And there was Henry, spry as you like, nearly twenty-nine, ready to step into his shoes any day.

Mr Slee leaned the tips of his fingers on the wooden windowsill. He did not wish to retire. The Temple was his life, his second home. No, in many ways his real home. He felt that the Inns of Court, and all the lawyers and clerks that worked and lived there, were the very lifeblood of the City. Even the most commonplace, everyday workings of the law courts possessed a drama and significance which existed nowhere else for him. He loved everything, from the sonorous majesty of the bench to the scuttling ordinariness of the lowliest clerk. He could not leave it.

Revolving all this in his mind, Mr Slee went back to the clerks' room in a frame of mind very different from that in which he had left it. He was conscious now of the importance of his unspoken power weighing heavily upon him. He knew that there was much he could do to affect matters. He had not lived and breathed the air of the Temple and the law courts for forty years for nothing. His influence was great, his contacts extensive. The risk of both men succeeding in their applications might be slight, but it was one he could eliminate entirely, merely by a few timely conversations with the right people, a little well-placed information in the hands of the wrong ones. He had watched and worked with Leo for many years, and knew much. If he chose to, it was within his power to stop Leo's application dead in its tracks.

He glanced up as Henry came in and sat down at the computer, watching him as he tapped the keyboard, his eyes on the screen, young and confident. Yes, thought Mr Slee, he was going to have to think carefully about all of this. Very carefully indeed.

Chapter four

In her Majesty's High Court of Justice, Chancery Division, court number eleven, Michael Gibbon QC shifted his spindly frame on the hard wooden bench and watched musingly as Anthony made his closing submissions. It was extraordinary, really, how the boy had matured. He had a self-possession now that no one would ever have guessed at two years ago, when he had been Michael's pupil. Yet his voice still possessed a certain diffidence, and his handsome face that quality of openness, which seemed to give him a peculiarly modest charm – it appeared to work especially well on older people, judging from the benign way in which Mr Justice Howe was nodding as he listened to Anthony.

'Well, Mr Cross, what do you say about costs?' asked the judge.

'We would respectfully ask for costs on the basis that, as my Lord has seen, this was a lengthy and costly matter, and one in which the plaintiff has succeeded.'

'That is only because, for the purposes of the motion, Miss Llewellyn and I have to accept that your case is right.' Michael could have sworn Mr Justice Howe almost smiled at Anthony. Anthony cast a glance at their opponent, a horsey and energetic woman who had, Michael felt, done her best in difficult circumstances. She caught the glance. Not even Miss Llewellyn can resist our junior tenant's charms, thought Michael with amusement. He had never seen the keen features of that notoriously able lady counsel soften quite so perceptibly.

'As an alternative to an outright costs order in favour of the plaintiff, might I suggest the plaintiff's costs in cause – which is a customary order to make?' replied Anthony. He might have been an eight-year-old boy asking for his ball back. Miss

Llewellyn rose and rested her bony red knuckles on the ledge before her. 'I would not challenge an order for the plaintiff's costs in cause, my Lord,' she barked graciously.

Anthony adjusted his wig as she sat down, and cast a glance at Mr Justice Howe, who nodded.

'This has been a hotly contested motion, and the usual order in such cases is the plaintiff's costs in the cause. I so order.'

'Thank you, my Lord,' murmured Anthony, and sat down.

The judge wrote for a moment, then looked up. 'Thank you, ladies and gentlemen,' he said. The court rose.

As Michael and Anthony made their way out of the law courts and across the Strand, Anthony tapped the red velvet bag slung over Michael's slightly stooped shoulders, in which he carried his silk's robes.

'I give myself another fifteen years,' he said, and smiled with a touch of arrogance.

Michael smiled back. Anthony would never have made such a guileless remark to any other member of chambers; there still existed traces of their master-and-pupil relationship, despite the fact that Michael often felt that Anthony had drifted off into his own little world of success and maturity.

'I rather think,' he replied archly, 'that only the most exceptional juniors take silk at thirty-eight.'

'Makes you wonder why Leo's left it till now,' said Anthony unthinkingly. He stopped at the entrance to Caper Court, his face slightly flushed. 'Oh, God – forget I said that.'

Michael glanced at him. 'I already have.' But that, of course, was just one of those things one said. He pondered Anthony's slip of the tongue as he mounted the stairs to his room. It was one thing that Leo should be leapfrogging Stephen in applying for silk – that, Michael supposed, was Leo's business – but he was surprised that Anthony should know of it. He had been aware that Anthony had once been rather a protégé of Leo's for a month or two when he was still a pupil, but he had not thought that they had remained especially friendly since then. But one knew so little of Leo, and of his personal relationships. Oh, he was a charming, witty man, and Michael was one of the first to seek out his company for a drink in El Vino's after a hard day, but there was an elusive side to Leo's nature, as though

46

part of his personality lay somewhere like a hidden pool in a forest. It bemused Michael to think that Anthony was in some way privy to Leo's most confidential affairs. Things were not always what they seemed.

Anthony was standing in the clerks' room going through his mail as Michael came downstairs on his way to lunch.

'More instructions from some woman solicitor,' remarked Henry, jerking his head in Anthony's direction.

Anthony was standing flipping through the instructions, and swatted absently at Henry's head with the envelope. Catching sight of Michael, he said, 'Who's Rachel Dean? I've never heard of her.'

Michael glanced at the letter-heading. 'Nichols and Co. I don't know. Yet another poor creature who's fallen prey to your ruthless charms, perhaps.'

'Get lost,' said Anthony with a smile. Dismissive though he might be of the good-humoured taunts regarding his popularity with women solicitors, Anthony was not without his vanity. He had almost begun to believe that his good looks assisted his exceptional intelligence in securing a steady stream of work.

Feeling that the air of general levity should not rise any further, Mr Slee distracted Michael's attention with a discussion regarding a fee note, and Anthony took the instructions back to his room.

He did not get round to reading them until three days later and when he did he was intrigued. This was potentially a big case. Any disaster such as this was bound to be. Grateful though he was for the instructions, Anthony loftily told himself that he was not especially impressed by the fact that Rachel Dean, whoever she might be, had omitted to send all the relevant documents with her instructions. As he picked up the phone to call her, he wondered what she was like. He could not, at his age, help wondering what any unknown woman might be like.

'Hello? Is that Rachel Dean?' he asked, when he was put through.

'Yes, speaking. Who is this?' Her voice was light and cool.

'This is Anthony Cross,' said Anthony. 'You sent round some instructions the other day – the *Valeo Dawn*, the explosion in Bombay.'

'Oh, *yes*.' Her voice was not so chilly as it had first sounded. 'It's an interesting case, isn't it?'

'It is,' agreed Anthony. 'Very. The reason I'm ringing is that there are some documents I need which you don't seem to have sent.'

Rachel was surprised; she was quite sure that she had given Felicity all the relevant enclosures. In fact, she had been particularly careful to do so. She was always meticulous about enclosures. 'Really? I can't imagine what they might be.' Her voice was cool again. 'I'm quite sure I sent you everything you need.' This young man had a rather languid, arrogant tone, she thought. She knew the type. Rachel wasn't especially fond of barristers, particularly the self-satisfied public-school types to be found in successful commercial practices.

'Well,' said Anthony, smiling slightly to himself – he rather liked to hear women on the defensive – 'the charterparty for a start. And the surveyor's report.' He paused. At the other end Rachel rolled her eyes in disbelief, then leaned sideways to look out of her doorway in the direction of Felicity's chair. It was empty. 'And the master's note of protest,' added Anthony. 'I think they're all probably of some importance to me.' He had already formed an impression of a somewhat inept creature handling a case that was beyond her capabilities.

'Yes, I can see that,' replied Rachel tartly. Her mouth tightened. 'I'm afraid I can't understand how this can have happened. I distinctly told my secretary which documents to send.'

She sounded a little icy now, thought Anthony. Was she annoyed with herself or with him? He wondered what she looked like. This was a brunette's voice, he would say. Fat? Thin? Short? Tall? He was quite enjoying baiting her, even though he was aware that it wasn't perhaps the best policy. But he had unshakeable faith in his own charming ability to bring her round.

'I'll have them sent round to you – as soon as I – ah – as soon as I can lay hands on them,' Rachel was saying. She would murder that girl. This pompous prig of a junior barrister was making her feel like a complete incompetent.

'Oh, no need,' said Anthony, leaning back in his chair and snapping an elastic band between his fingers. 'I have to come up your way at the end of the afternoon, anyway. I'll drop by and pick them up.' He paused. 'I suppose that will give you enough time to find them?'

'Yes, Mr Cross. Plenty of time. I do hope this isn't taking you out of your way?' Distinctly frosty.

'No trouble at all. Goodbye.'

He gave a little laugh as he hung up. Nice voice. Probably fat and over forty. Ah, well. He would see.

When she had put the phone down, Rachel went out to Felicity's desk. She looked down at the jumble of work, the copy of *Bella*, and at the empty chair.

'Doris, do you happen to know where Felicity is?' she asked.

Doris took off her earphones and opened her small eyes wide. 'Ooh, no, I don't, Miss Dean. Was it something urgent? I can always fit it into Mr MacBride's work, if you like. I'm sure he wouldn't mind.' She gave Rachel her marshmallow smile, her little eyes fastened inquisitively, helpfully, on Rachel's face. Rachel returned the smile sweetly; she did not like Doris.

'No, thank you, Doris. I just wish to speak to her.'

'Right you are, Miss Dean.' Doris gave a simper, then added, 'She's a little bit scatterbrained, Felicity. You know.' At this Louise gave a snort, her eyes fastened on the screen in front of her, fingers flashing over the keys.

Rachel thought she had a pretty good idea where Felicity might be. And indeed, there she was, relaxing in the Ladies with a cigarette, chatting to two of the filing clerks. She had her shoes off and was leaning against the cubicles. When she saw Rachel, she put her cigarette out with a stubbing hiss in one of the basins, slipped on her shoes, and with a breathless 'See you, girls!' followed Rachel back to her office. Rachel said nothing until they were in her room with the door closed. Doris's eyes peeped over the top of her word processor and then she ducked down out of sight.

'Felicity,' said Rachel in a normal sort of voice, 'do you remember those documents that were to go out with the instructions to counsel on the *Valeo Dawn*?'

Felicity nodded, then hesitated, and then shook her head. 'Yes, I remember them. But it wasn't the *Valeo Dawn*, it was the *Valeo Trader*.'

'No, Felicity,' replied Rachel, her voice still kindly. 'The documents belonged to the *Valeo Dawn*.'

'Oh.' Felicity looked thoughtful, then contrite. She wound a curl of brown hair round her finger. 'Oh. I sent them to Richards Butler. I thought they were on the *Valeo Trader*.'

'Felicity, you may have sent some of them to Richards Butler, but not all of them. You have, whatever you have done, made a real mess of things. You realise those were original documents, don't you?' Rachel was angry now.

Felicity looked at her questioningly, and Rachel sighed. Why did she, of all people, have to be lumbered with Felicity? 'And now I shall have to ring round trying to track them down. *Please*,' she looked beseechingly at Felicity, 'when I give you documents to send out, double-check that you're sending them to the right people. You only had to *look* at them to see which vessel they referred to! honestly . . .' If Felicity were Simon's secretary, or any of the other partners', she'd have been given her marching orders weeks ago. As it was, Rachel knew she didn't have the guts. And, anyway, there were some things at which Felicity wasn't completely hopeless. She looked sadly at her for a moment, and then said, 'Felicity, why have you got coloured string tied round your wrists?'

Felicity glanced down, then beamed a smile at Rachel. 'That's for my driving lesson after work. So's I remember which way I'm going. Red for left, blue for right. I'm not very good at left and right.'

'I see,' murmured Rachel. She gazed after Felicity as she went back to her word processor, sighed, and picked up the telephone.

Anthony reached Nichols & Co at six thirty. The traffic had been slow, but he had whiled away the minutes in the taxi wondering whether he should ring up that Harriet girl this evening. She'd left messages twice on the answerphone, and he supposed he was vaguely interested. He wasn't sure if he could be bothered. She was a bit keen, and he preferred to have more of a challenge. Perhaps that business with Julia had made him cynical, but at least the approach he now adopted towards women meant that there was no danger of being hurt again, of becoming involved. Leo had taught him that you should simply enjoy whatever was on offer.

He gave his name to the porter who had come on duty for the evening, and the porter rang up to Rachel's room. Yes, she was still there, and would he please go up.

Anthony felt a pang of guilt as he walked through the deserted offices, past the cleaners with their black plastic bin bags. Perhaps it was rather rude of him to leave it so late. Still, she'd waited.

Rachel, as she sat in her office, was not quite sure why she had waited. She had tracked down the missing documents, which Felicity had erroneously enclosed with some other piece of mail to a different firm, but she had been unable to get them back that day. When she'd rung up Mr Cross to tell him so, he was out. It was only courteous to wait. And she was curious to see what kind of person she was instructing, this young man of whom everyone seemed to think so highly. He certainly hadn't made much of an impression on her that afternoon, beyond one of overweening arrogance.

She thought she detected the same arrogance in the smile he gave her as he stopped in her doorway. She was mistaken in this. Anthony was merely trying to suppress his amusement at realising how far adrift his speculations had been. The girl he was looking at fitted her voice entirely – and yet he had never imagined anyone like this.

'Hello. Anthony Cross,' he murmured, and leaned forward to shake her hand.

'How do you do? I was about to leave. I had begun to think you weren't coming. Fortunately I had some work to finish.'

Anthony slipped into a chair and gazed at her. 'I'm very sorry,' he said, sounding not in the least penitent. 'The traffic was bad.'

She nodded. She was conscious of a certain cold stiffness that had taken possession of her limbs. She knew this feeling, knew what it meant. There was a pause.

'Anyway,' said Anthony, and smiled, leaning one elbow on the arm of his chair and stroking his chin with his fingers. God, what a beautiful girl. He wondered if she ever took that frozen-fish expression off her face.

'I'm very sorry,' she said, rousing herself. 'I couldn't get hold of those documents this afternoon. I know where they are – my secretary sent them to Richards Butler by mistake – but I won't have them until tomorrow.'

'Not to worry,' said Anthony easily. He shifted in his chair, taking in the pale, soft curve of her face, the dark brows and slender nose, the sleek black hair falling to her shoulders. And her mouth – such a mouth. He would like to see it smile. She didn't look like she smiled a lot. And why did she have that wary expression in her eyes? He wanted to make her stand up, see what the rest of her was like. He glanced at his watch. 'Why don't we improve the hour and go for a glass of wine?'

She lifted her chin. 'I'm afraid I have a few things to do at home –'

He waved this aside. 'Come on. We have to discuss this case, anyway. Forget about whatever it is you have to do.'

She looked down uncertainly, wishing this tension would pass from her limbs, wishing he wouldn't smile in that way. She *must* try and get over this thing. She must make the effort. This would be safe enough. Just a drink. He was only counsel in a case, that was all. This was purely business. Don't be afraid, she told herself. This is so stupid!

'All right,' she said, giving him a quick, bright smile. 'Why not?'

That was more like it, thought Anthony, delighted to see her expression warm for a few, brief seconds. They went out into the fading light of the early October evening, walking together down Bishopsgate and into Leadenhall Market. Rachel felt more relaxed. There were lots of people around. She needn't feel threatened by the directness of his interested smile. Not for the time being.

'I love Leadenhall Market,' she said, glancing around the cobbled alleyways beneath the high vaulted roof.

Anthony nodded. 'It's nice. It reminds me a bit of Spitalfields Market. Only it's a lot cleaner. I used to work in

Spitalfields,' he added ruminatively.

'Did you?' She glanced up at him in surprise as they crossed the cobbles to the wine bar entrance. 'What did you do there?'

'I was a porter. Real low life.' He smiled, his face losing its hauteur and looking momentarily boyish. 'It was just a holiday job.'

Rachel thought about this in silence as they went into the smoky throng of the wine bar. While Anthony went to the bar, she sat on a stool next to a wooden ledge backed by a high mirror, nibbling at a bowl of crisps and glancing covertly at his reflection as he stood waiting to be served. In an odd way his reflected person seemed less threatening; it put him at a distance, his tall, dark figure, his rather feminine good looks. She watched him as he paid for their drinks. How odd, to think of him working as a market porter. She would have put him down for the usual Oxbridge double first, everything on a plate, taking from life exactly what he expected it to give him.

He came back with a bottle of white wine and two glasses and set them down on the ledge. Rachel looked at the bottle in dismay.

'You shouldn't have got all that! A glass would have been fine.'

'You only get rubbish if you buy it by the glass,' replied Anthony. As he drew up a stool and sat down near to her, his knee brushed the edge of hers, and she stiffened and inched it away. Anthony pretended not to notice and poured the wine. He gave her a glass and smiled at her, noticing that nervous, watchful look of hers before she returned the smile briefly and took the glass from him.

'Cheers,' he said, and she murmured in reply.

'So – when were you a porter at Spitalfields?' she asked. She wore a bright, opaque expression of interest.

'Oh, a couple of years ago. In the summer holidays after Bar School.'

Now her expression of interest and surprise was genuine. 'You're only – what, twenty-three, then?' She gazed at him. 'I'm sorry. That sounded rude.'

He laughed. 'No, no – that's right. But I'll be twenty-four in February. I'm really twenty-three and three-quarters.'

She laughed, too. He enjoyed seeing her laugh, felt that it was a tiny achievement. He found her interesting for all the wrong reasons – or rather, not simply for the usual ones.

There was a silence in which she sipped her wine, uncomfortably aware that he was looking at her in a considering fashion. How sure of himself he seemed. And only twenty-three. Rachel herself was twenty-seven. The realisation that he was really no more than a boy lessened her tension.

'From first appearances, I wouldn't have judged you to be the type to work in a fruit market in the holidays,' she remarked.

'No? What type would you think me?' asked Anthony, flattered by her interest.

Rachel suddenly wished she had not allowed the conversation to take this personal turn. 'Oh, I don't know,' she replied vaguely, and glanced away.

'What, public school, Oxbridge, money at home, holidays spent skiing in winter, Italy and Greece in the summer – that kind of thing?'

He had made her laugh again, but a trifle uncomfortably. She swallowed the rest of her wine and he poured some more. 'Well, you said it – not me,' she answered.

'How do Herne Hill Comprehensive and Bristol University sound?' he said. His brown eyes still held a faint expression of arrogance.

'You do astonish me,' said Rachel coolly, then added, 'I'll bet you got a first.'

Anthony drained his glass. 'You're right.' He nodded. 'I did get a first.' And he grinned at her. This time, when she smiled back, it was a soft, curving smile, not like the brief, reserved smiles of before. God, she was lovely, he thought. He felt a surge of excitement and pleasure at the thought that, because of this case, he would be seeing more of her, regularly. Why should he be so pleased? After all, he'd only spent ten minutes talking to her, and pretty banal stuff it had been. Perhaps it was simply that she was so good to look at – beautiful in a remote, hands-off way which he had never encountered before. That was it. It was the pleasure of melting that chilly reserve. Yet each time he did it, he felt the frost creeping

54

quickly back over the surface. Even now, her smile had faded and she was studying her wine glass seriously.

'Do you want to know what I imagined you would look like from hearing your voice on the phone?' he asked her. His voice was lazily intimate.

She looked up swiftly. 'No, I don't think I do,' she replied, giving him a brief, polite smile. 'I think we should talk about the *Valeo Dawn*. It's a good deal more important.'

Anthony was a little taken aback. He was accustomed to making easy headway with women. He had forgotten that she must regard him as no more than counsel whom she had happened to instruct in a case. She was looking at him as though he were no more than that. And he wasn't anything more than that, when he came to think of it. He felt a bit of a berk.

'Yes,' he said. 'Absolutely right.' And so they talked about the case for a while, Anthony doing his best to forget about the way she looked and treat her as he would any other lawyer. Rachel felt better, relieved that he had eased up on the intent, admiring glances. It was those that made her stiffen up, that ravelled up her insides into a little ball of anxiety. As her attention wandered from what he was saying, she glanced round and saw someone coming over to them. It was Roger Williams. Her heart sank.

Anthony looked up at the heavy, slightly red-faced man who had joined them.

'Hello there, Rachel,' said Roger. 'Thought it was you. Haven't seen you in here before, have we?' He laid a hand on her back and slid it round to her shoulder as he stood next to her, surveying Anthony. 'You and your – ah – friend care to join us over there?' Roger gave Anthony a boozy smile and held out his free hand. 'Roger Williams,' he said.

Anthony shook his hand. 'Anthony Cross.' He looked back at Rachel, disturbed by her face, which was frozen into an expression – not of distaste, but almost of contained panic. The muscles of her back and shoulders seemed to have gone rigid, and he could tell that she was steeling herself not to draw away from Roger's hand. Anthony was suddenly aware of an instinct of protectiveness. He looked up quickly at Roger and said, 'Actually, we're just off. Thanks, anyway.'

'What – not going to finish this off?' Roger indicated the half-full bottle of wine. 'Still,' he added, grinning at them and sliding his hand away from Rachel's shoulder, 'if you've got better things to do . . . '

Anthony gave him a tight smile and got up. Rachel rose, too, and Anthony helped her on with her coat. Roger had drunk too much wine to be aware of any undercurrent of tension. As she buttoned her coat, Rachel turned and said clearly, 'Goodnight, Roger.' Anthony was surprised at the sudden change in her, from rigid fearfulness to calm carelessness.

''night,' said Roger. And he nodded a farewell to Anthony before making his way back to his colleagues to regale them with information about Anthony, who he had decided must be Rachel's bloke.

As they walked back out of the market, Anthony remarked, 'You didn't seem to like him very much.'

Rachel glanced up at him. 'No, not much,' she replied. 'Actually, I don't really know him very well yet. I've only been with the firm six weeks, you know.'

They came out into Gracechurch Street and stopped on the pavement. 'Well,' said Anthony; he turned to look at her. She was staring straight ahead, clearly thinking about something which had nothing to do with him. He was not accustomed to feeling so shut out from any woman's attention. He was uncertain what to do or say.

After a pause, he said, 'Which way do you go? London Bridge?' He rather hoped he could walk a while with her, try to melt this cold, aloof exterior. The slight warmth of their conversation in the wine bar seemed to have faded entirely.

She shook her head. 'My car is parked near the office. Anyway' – she held out her hand – 'that was a very pleasant start to our case. Thank you.' Her voice held just the correct blend of informality and politeness. She wasn't the least bit interested in him, he thought. She might as well be looking right through him. Well, why should she be interested in him? This was purely a professional relationship. It was his habit, he knew, always to reduce encounters with women to sexual terms, and it was a ridiculous, adolescent habit, he told himself. Anyway, she was obviously a few years older than he was. He shook her hand, and her fingers felt slender and cold.

He said goodnight, and walked down towards the Monument and London Bridge, conscious of a sense of flatness. She was obviously a bit of a cold fish, and yet he couldn't help feeling his heart lift slightly at the thought that he was bound to see her again before long.

As she drove home, Rachel tried to steel her mind to concentrate on the books programme on Radio 4. But her thoughts kept drifting back to Anthony, to his face and his dark eyes. So sure of himself. She gripped the wheel tightly. She had not wanted this. She had not wanted to meet anyone to whom she felt in any way attracted. Why? She sighed as she slowed down at a red light. She knew why. To be so afraid of men, of all men, was absurd. No one was likely to harm her, or hurt her as she had been hurt before. Each time she met someone she liked, she told herself that it would be all right, that this time she would be able to make some return of their interest and affection. But each time she was wrong. Nothing changed. Not the rigidity of fear at the warmth of an interested smile, an intent gaze, nor the clammy coldness of her limbs if anyone tried to touch her.

She changed gear and moved forward as the lights turned to green. It amounted to nothing but pain, over and over again. Yet he had been so nice, so charming and boyish and handsome. And so innocent. What right had she to have anything to do with innocence? Put him out of your mind, she thought. There was nothing for her in any relationship with any man. There was nowhere for it to go. She could not give anything back.

She turned the corner into the terrace where she lived and stopped the car. She sat there for a moment, thinking, maybe it doesn't matter. Perhaps I am being entirely foolish. I've only just met him and he can't be interested in me. You're paranoid – and conceited, she told herself. But she knew it was not that. She remembered the way he had looked at her, the compelling gaze of his brown eyes. He was too young to conceal much. Rachel suddenly wished with all her heart that she had never sent Anthony Cross the instructions on the *Valeo Dawn*.

Chapter five

Over the days that followed, Anthony found himself thinking a good deal about Rachel. He spent idle moments – and others not so idle – conjuring up her image, dwelling on the recollection of her face. Sometimes he succeeded in bringing that soft, illuminating smile vividly to mind, but at other times her image would elude him entirely, irritating him. He even found himself, during an application for an interlocutory injunction, so lost in contemplation of when he might see her again that the judge had to ask him the same question twice.

Something about all of this troubled him. He was accustomed to the occasional infatuation, to meeting some unusually attractive girl at a party or a friend's house, and wanting to see her again. But then the attraction was invariably mutual, and he was able to build his romantic fancies upon the probability that his interest was reciprocated. Such relationships normally followed a pattern, one in which he would take the girl out several times, then eventually to bed, and all the while the enchantment of the initial infatuation would be fading, until at last he got bored and let it drift off into nowhere. That had happened with Lizzie. The insubstantiality of these relationships did not trouble him unduly. In a way, he was relieved each time when the thing petered out. He had no real wish, since his love affair with Julia two years ago, to become involved with anyone. He had been painfully and deeply in love with Julia – lovely, amoral, hedonistic Julia – over a period of several months. He had landed himself in debt in an attempt to keep up with her expensive habits and friends, to the point where Leo had had to bail him out, and ultimately she had deserted him for someone else.

And there had been the business with Leo, too, and all the

emotional confusion which that had engendered. No, he was happy to keep his relationships with women on an easy, physical level. He didn't mind falling in love, as long as it didn't last.

He supposed that the amount of time he spent thinking about Rachel could be put down to plain physical attraction. The problem was, his instinct told him that she hadn't felt the same way. Still, he told himself, he could probably remedy that. Anthony had few doubts about himself. He had changed more than a little since the days when he had been Michael Gibbon's gauche, nervous pupil, living at home with his brother and schoolteacher mother, scraping coins together for bus fares and sandwiches, dogged by self-doubt in all aspects of his life. Then he had had only his good looks and intellectual brilliance to keep him afloat. These days, those were merely the basic qualities upon which he capitalised. He felt that he could, if he wanted, turn his strictly professional relationship with Rachel into something infinitely more interesting.

But once he had sent back his initial opinion on the *Valeo Dawn*, he realised that he was unlikely to see her again for some time. There was no need. The case could hang fire for months, and he could do nothing but wait.

The potency of her image began to fade, and he had almost decided to dismiss her from his life, for the time being at least, when he met her by chance in Middle Temple.

He was passing through Fountain Court on his way to Hare Buildings when he saw her coming up the steps from Temple Place. She was wearing a dark suit and a striped shirt, the severity of their cut emphasising her femininity. She wore her silky black hair loose, and her face was preoccupied. She would have passed straight by him if he had not stopped her.

'Oh, hello,' she said, her smile uncertain as she returned his greeting. They were standing under the trees, close to the fountain.

'So,' he said, searching for something to say, something with which to detain her, 'any more news on the *Valeo Dawn*?'

'No, not much,' replied Rachel. 'Well, that is, the other side seem to be sticking to their line that the explosion was caused by some defect in the auxiliary engine.'

'How do they arrive at that conclusion?' Anthony's mind was not even on his words. The attentive expression on his face had nothing to do with his question, and everything to do with the fact that he was trying to absorb every detail of her features, quite lost in her loveliness. The reality of it made his imperfect recollection of the past weeks seem quite threadbare. His eyes traced the line of her cheekbones, the movement of her mouth, the slight frown in her eyes as she spoke.

'Well, we haven't seen their survey report, of course. But they seem to be suggesting that either there was something wrong with the oiler cap on the tank, or else it was the auxiliary engine itself which ignited.'

Anthony managed to skim the surface of this to come up with a coherent response. 'But what evidence could they possibly have to support that?'

'I don't know.' A brisk October breeze swept the court, scuttering dead leaves across the surface of the fountain, whipping shining strands of Rachel's hair across her face. She raised a hand to brush them back, away from her mouth, as she spoke; Anthony noticed that her cuffs were fastened with men's cuff links, enhancing the slenderness of her wrists. He wondered to what man the cuff links belonged. 'There's a possibility I may have to go out to look at the ship. The master's going to be in Bombay for the next few weeks, helping with the investigation. I need to take a statement from him.'

Anthony nodded. 'I see.' The breeze persisted, and Rachel pulled her jacket around her and shivered. Anthony wanted more than anything he could think of to put his arms around her and make her warm. He smiled at the absurdity of the thought.

'Well,' she said, and hesitated. He had run out of things to say, and she was about to go. In a minute she would have said goodbye and be walking away from him. He put a sudden detaining hand on her arm.

'Look,' he said, 'I really enjoyed our drink together a couple of weeks ago. Could we do it again? I mean, some evening when you're free.'

Rachel shivered again. 'I don't know,' she said, glancing away. Don't do it, she told herself. Don't be unfair to him.

Oh, please, he thought. Please. The sound of the water splashing in the fountain seemed suddenly loud, insistent.

'It just seems like a good idea,' he found himself saying. What the hell did *that* mean? He was making a mess of this. Normally the girl in question was only too happy to say yes. Having to handle reluctance was a novelty. 'Don't you think?' he added feebly.

'I suppose so.' She looked up at him hesitantly. 'I'm not sure if it's strictly professional, though.' And she smiled. Why not? It wouldn't matter, just an hour or two.

Thank you, he thought. Thank you. He adored moments of capitulation, even on this most prosaic level, and could not help betraying this. His smile in reply was radiant, so that Rachel was quite touched by his pleasure.

'Good,' he said. 'Excellent. Why don't I meet you somewhere after work? Tonight?'

Rachel was a little startled. 'Oh, I don't think so. That's rather short notice. Perhaps Friday would be better.'

'All right. Do you know Gregory's? Just off Chancery Lane? About seven?'

She nodded. 'Yes. All right. I'll see you then.' And she raised a hand and carried on across Fountain Court, while Anthony stood for a moment under the trees. Then he laughed to himself and went cheerfully into Hare Buildings.

Leo, standing by the postbox in Middle Temple Lane, looked at the girl as she walked past him, then glanced at Anthony walking off from under the trees. She was very beautiful, thought Leo. He wondered if this was some new woman in Anthony's life. He was aware, with irritation, of a faint flicker of jealousy. Everything was going well for Anthony. He was young, his work was good, he was liked in chambers, he was earning decent money, and beautiful women stopped to talk and smile. And the smiles stayed on their faces even after they had left him, reflected Leo, as he watched Rachel's figure disappear through the archway into Pump Court.

He stood there for a moment in the chilly air, watching the

61

barristers and clerks going up and down the lane, suddenly visited by one of those occasional flashes of alienation, a feeling that he stood in the middle of a world which was entirely foreign to him. He did not understand why these moments should occur. He was one of them, was he not? Good God, he had even come down to the postbox to post his application for silk. Of course he was part of it. He had lived and worked in the Temple for twenty-three years. The patterns of the flagstones, the shadows of the trees in summer, the scent of polish in the libraries, the hush of the courtyards and the echoes of the cloisters – all these things were dear and familiar in his life. And yet there were days when he felt as though he were looking at it all from a distance, with the eyes of a stranger.

I have learned to speak their language, he thought, I know all the correct moves to make, I perform my work as though it were second nature. Second to what – what other nature? They know nothing of me. What would they say, what would my worthy fellow members of chambers say if they knew about my life away from here? Perhaps they would say nothing. Perhaps their own lives possess equally absurd moral dichotomies. Perhaps morality has nothing to do with it. What do I know of their minds? What do they know of mine? Only Anthony has glimpsed it, but even he knows nothing of the truth. I may inhabit their world, thought Leo, I may have assumed the appearance and habits of the type, but I am not really of their kind.

As he toyed with his thoughts, Leo watched a car come slowly up the lane, watched the porter raise the barrier and salute the occupant of the car as it turned slowly into Crown Office Row. Leo smiled to himself. Now there was someone who possessed no doubts about himself, who was as sure of his own importance in the scheme of things as he was that God had placed the mighty machinery of the English legal system, full-scale and in working order, on earth on the very first day of creation. The Right Honourable Sir Mungo Stephenson, TC, KCVD, FSA, CBE, QC, Lord Justice of Appeal, had been brought up from his earliest days, his father having been a judge before him, to believe in the greatness of his country's institutions, and in the pre-eminence of the judicial system as the shining star in Great Britain's crown of constitutional perfection. He had unshakeable faith in the law and its traditions, he thought it right and proper that the Inns of Court should be impregnable bastions of male dominance, self-regulating, their affairs ordered by men of the right type and background. Men who instinctively knew one another. Men such as himself. Leo knew all this about Sir Mungo Stephenson, and knew, too, that the views of such a man might be influential in deciding whether or not Leo would be allowed to take silk.

Musing on this, Leo turned to walk back to chambers. He wondered what Sir Mungo would make of his other world, of the pretty boys and occasional strange young women, of the gay bars and clubs, of weekends and evenings spent in ways which Sir Mungo could not begin to imagine. A cold hand laid itself momentarily on Leo's heart, and he stopped to look up at the overcast sky. What if some of it, the merest trace of it, had found its way into the Lord Chancellor's confidential file, that file marked 'Leo Davies', which had been carefully built up over the years since Leo's very first beginnings at the Bar? But he shook the hand away. The same fears had occurred to him often over the past few weeks, as he had been preparing his application. No one knew how much hearsay, how many trivial reported incidents and chance mistakes were filed away in those reports. No one ever saw them. They belonged to the quiet world of judicial secrecy which even the officious statutes of the Data Protection Act were not allowed to penetrate.

No, he told himself, it was all very unlikely. He had been utterly circumspect over the years, even to the point of duplicity. The closest he had come to committing any act of folly had been in the matter of Anthony. Leo stopped again, this time beneath the archway of Caper Court, as he thought of Anthony. But then he had lost his heart, ridiculously, humiliatingly, and nothing like that would ever be permitted to happen in his life again. That could have destroyed everything, if he had let it – or if Anthony had not got his tenancy.

Leo sighed and walked on into chambers, trying to shake his black mood from him. But he knew that this anxiety would be hanging over him for the next few months, until Easter, until it had all been decided.

Back in his room, he decided to take stock of things. He should take soundings, have a chat with those judges with whom he was friendly, those who knew him well on a personal level. Winding a length of pink ribbon round his fingers, Leo leaned back in his chair, a frown sharpening the angles of his handsome, gaunt face as he drew up a mental list.

There was Sir Mungo, of course; they'd always got on well enough. He abhorred Sir Mungo's chauvinistic bombast, but he had always smiled in his company, never betrayed his feelings. He would simply have to trust to luck there. Anyway, Sir Mungo was a great one for sheer proficiency and ability, and on that level he should score well.

Then there was Michael Winstanley. He knew he could count on him. They were sufficiently good friends for Leo to know that there was no need even to canvass him.

Then there was Frank Chamberlin – he was a good old boy, definitely someone whose backing he could expect. He had known Frank for years, had been led by him in countless cases before he was made a judge, and now appeared regularly before him. He knew Frank liked him, and always sought him out at legal gatherings, preferring Leo's amusing conversation to the dry murmurings of his own contemporaries. Frank would be a useful fellow to speak to, someone honest enough to tell him how the land lay, and what was going on in the minds of the likes of Sir Mungo and Sir Mostyn Smith. Two diehards, two reactionaries who, if even the faintest shadows of scandal were found to darken the pages of his file, might hum and haw and make difficulties over his appointment. Yes, he would sound out Frank. Who else was there? John Rushworth – he was a decent enough fellow, and Leo often appeared before him, but he didn't really know him well. He was a relatively new judge and came from an Admiralty background. Nothing to be guessed at there.

Lionel Rawden – he might be worth having a word with. And Alan Still. That left Roger Ware, the Honourable Sir. Leo grimaced as he unwound the ribbon from his fingers and leaned forward thoughtfully. Well, he certainly knew Roger well enough to take him out for a drink and do a little lobbying, but he wasn't entirely sure of the man. He was always friendly enough – he was one of the younger judges, easy-going on the bench, and he and Leo had a cordial relationship – but there was a sharpness about the Honourable Sir Roger's glance which Leo did not find comfortable. He was not always easy in the company of those as keenly intelligent as himself. It made him feel vulnerable.

As for the appeal judges – well, they were beyond his reach. He would simply have to hope for the best there.

Leo rose and went to the window. Looking down, he saw Anthony, his bag containing his robes slung over his shoulder, on his way to court. He looked cheerful. He had that blissful, boyish expression that Leo recalled from months and months ago, when he had first taken Anthony to dinner. He wondered what it was that made Anthony's heart sing these days. Certainly not Leo. Not any more.

Anthony ploughed impatiently through his work until Friday arrived. The morning passed quickly enough in court, but in the afternoon, as he sat trying to draft an opinion on sub-freights, time dragged interminably. The worst – but in some ways the best – hour was between six and seven. Most people had left chambers by then, so there was no impetus to work and merely time to mark. But there was also the delight of anticipation, of wondering what she would wear, what they would talk about. He had booked a table for dinner at Le Café du Jardin. He hoped she wouldn't make some excuse after their drink at Gregory's and just leave. There was always that possibility. They hadn't planned anything more definite than just meeting for a drink. He wondered if his tie was all right.

At last he left chambers at ten to seven, and hurried through the darkness up Chancery Lane. She was there when he arrived, hanging her coat up, and she smiled when she saw him.

'Hi,' he said as he came towards her. 'Look, shall we just have a quick drink here? I've booked a table for dinner.'

She looked slightly surprised. 'Oh, fine. Yes. Yes, I'll have a gin and tonic, thanks.'

His heart was bathed in relief as he made his way to the bar. He would have her to himself for the whole evening. He loved this feeling, loved being swept away by someone. The first evening was, in many ways, always the best. Except for the first time you took them to bed, of course. He turned to glance at Rachel as he waited for his change, and felt suddenly overwhelmed at the thought of taking her to bed, of making love to her. And then he stopped himself. Don't be absurd, he thought. She probably doesn't think it's anything like that. You're merely professional colleagues. Remember how it was last time. This is all in your own mind. Don't get ahead of yourself.

He took the drinks back to the table and they sat for an hour or so, talking. They talked about people they both knew, about other barristers and solicitors, about the events of the day. There was nothing remotely personal in it. In fact, Anthony got the impression that she was wary of allowing the conversation to take any sort of personal turn.

The effort of keeping the conversation commonplace, however, could not last, and they lapsed into a long and oddly strained silence on the way to the restaurant. Once there, however, she began gradually to open up a little about herself.

'No, I'm an only child,' she said in reply to a question of Anthony's. Then she put down her menu and rested her elbows on it, cupping her face in her hands so that her hair swung forward and the light from the candle lit her cheekbones. 'My mother lives in Bath. She's wonderful. She's everything I'm not.' She smiled.

'And what's that?' said Anthony. He wanted to reach out and trace the line of her face with his finger, right down to her mouth.

'Oh, energetic, amusing – always dashing about, seeing things and people, doing everything there is to do.'

'Aren't you like that?'

'No. I'm a bit of a stay-at-home, I'm afraid. Not very good with people. Don't have my mother's social dynamism.'

'We'll order in a couple of minutes,' said Anthony to the

waiter hovering next to them. He turned back to Rachel.

'Do you share a flat, live with friends?' he asked.

'No. No. I live alone,' said Rachel. Wonderful, thought Anthony.

'What about your father?' He picked up a breadstick and snapped it.

Rachel sat back away from the candlelight and shadow fell upon her face. She looked down at her lap. 'I don't see him. That is, he and my mother split up.'

Anthony nodded and ate some of his breadstick. He sensed that she didn't want to talk about this. The faint, cold reserve had returned. He could think of nothing to say until the waiter returned to take their order.

After two glasses of wine, the chilly edge to her manner dropped away. She even laughed so much at Anthony's description of his father and his doings that she dropped her knife on the floor.

'Honestly,' said Anthony, as the waiter brought her another, 'he's the most incredible fraud. I mean, there's no getting away from the fact that people buy his paintings, but I don't believe there's a shred of intrinsic merit in them.'

'Your father's behaviour may be a bit bizarre, but I don't think his paintings are,' replied Rachel.

'Do you know them?'

'Of course I do. Anyone who likes modern art has heard of Chay Cross.'

'Well, not vice versa, I can tell you,' said Anthony. He was about to pour out more wine for her, but she placed a hand over her glass. He put the bottle down.

'I saw him on a Channel 4 arts programme,' said Rachel thoughtfully, 'the one that's on on Friday nights. I thought he was very interesting.' She turned her gaze to Anthony. 'You look rather like him.' She smiled. 'I wonder if that's the way you're going to look in twenty years' time.'

'God, I hope not,' murmured Anthony.

'You're really well on the way to being a stuffed shirt, aren't you?' she said teasingly. 'And only twenty-three.'

He smiled. God, he loved it when she did that thing of dipping her head and then looking up at him. He wanted to run his hands over that long white throat and on to her shoulders, over her breasts. He wondered fleetingly what her breasts were like. Small. Small and soft. He swallowed. Think of something else.

'I think if you'd seen my father three years ago, after he'd just been done for possession and let out on police bail, you might have thought differently. He must be the luckiest old hippy in the Western world. And I still think his paintings are a con.'

'Well, you can take me to his new exhibition,' Rachel said. 'I would quite like to meet him.' This was a mistake, she told herself. But it was too late.

His heart slipped. She wanted to see him again. No, no, she didn't. She just wanted to meet his father. Oh, well. At least it would mean another evening in her company.

'Yes. Yes, we'll do that,' he said.

It seemed to him that there were too many people around as they walked from Covent Garden down to the Strand. They walked slowly, lingeringly, and she said nothing when he slipped his hand into hers. They were quite silent as they walked. She glanced up at him, wondering what he was thinking about. It was all right. He had touched her, he was holding her hand, and she hadn't done anything stupid. It was all right. But she was aware of a tension in her chest as they walked, a tension that made her unable to say anything.

She took her hand away as they reached the Strand. 'I left my car at home today. I can get a bus from over there,' she said. He stood uncertainly. He didn't want her to go home. He didn't want the evening to end. But he could think of nothing to do.

'You don't want to go on anywhere? A club, or – '

She shook her head. 'I don't really like clubs. And I've had a pretty long week. I'd better go home.'

'All right.' Things to say were fighting one another in his head. When can I see you again? Shall I call you next week? Are you busy tomorrow night? What's your phone number? All of it sounded gauche. Anthony didn't want to be gauche. He wanted to behave with casual assurance. He already suspected, since he'd discovered over dinner how old she was, that she regarded him as no more than an amusing boy. The tables were turned. For once, he wanted someone more than they wanted him. Or possibly they didn't want him at all. He glanced up and down the street.

'We'd better cross over,' he said at last.

When they reached the other side, she said, 'Thank you for a lovely evening. I did enjoy it.'

'So did I,' said Anthony. His glance wandered over her face, and she watched his eyes. How very, very nice he is, she thought.

The pavement was still busy with people heading for Charing Cross station. Behind them, two youngsters were bedding down in the doorway of Saxone for the night. He felt a sense of urgency and frustration. 'You know,' he said, and paused. 'You know – ' And he put up a hand to touch her hair lightly. ' – I . . . '

'What?' Her face held only a blank look of curiosity; there was not a shadow of reciprocation of his own desires and feelings. He felt confused, horribly wrong-footed. He dropped his hand.

'Nothing,' he said.

'Well,' she said, 'goodnight, and thank you.' As she walked away, she turned and gave a little wave, relief and guilt in her heart.

Chapter six

When Felicity stumbled into the office one morning two weeks later, in early November, puffing from her run from the station, she felt a small glow of triumph at having arrived on time for the fifth day running. Although there was still something of a backlog of Rachel's work on her desk, she felt that she was getting somewhere with her resolution to prove herself capable and efficient. All she had to do now was improve her spelling and typing.

As she made her way to her desk, pulling off her woollen gloves, Felicity was aware that the Menopausals were huddled together like so many twittering birds. They drew apart at her approach, and she knew they had been talking about her. Despite a sour little sense of ostracism, she managed a cheerful smile and called 'Good morning!' to them.

Without even pausing for her morning coffee, Felicity set straight to work, clattering away at Rachel's tapes, and felt by the time eleven o'clock came that she was breaking the back of it. She would just grab a sandwich at twelve and spend her lunch hour photocopying those charts on the *Valeo Trader*. As she worked, however, Felicity was aware of the glances of Louise and Alma straying in her direction; there was an atmosphere of secrecy and tension. When her phone rang at eleven thirty and Mr Lamb's voice summoned her to his office, she knew, with a sinking heart, that trouble was coming.

She took the tapes and letters she had completed to Rachel's room. Rachel, she thought, was looking as serene and lovely as she usually did; it almost broke Felicity's heart that someone should look as good as that. Maybe some day they could sit down, just girls together, and talk, and she could ask her how she did it. Maybe I could find out how to get my life straight, thought Felicity wistfully.

Mr Lamb had an office on the eighth floor, right at the end, in a remote corner of the accounts department. Quite what he did there all day, unless it was to shuffle round the holiday rotas and count out luncheon vouchers, no one knew. He wore a sour, officious expression as Felicity entered the room; she knew he was relishing this.

He did not ask Felicity to sit down, but let her stand. 'I expected you to come as soon as I asked to see you,' he said.

'I had some letters to take to Miss Dean,' replied Felicity. Where did he get off with all this stuff? she thought. He was only an office manager, not the senior partner. Still, let's try to keep him sweet. 'Sorry,' she added, and smiled.

'I imagine you know the reason why I asked to see you,' said Mr Lamb. He ran a hand over his head, smoothing down the sparse black hairs on his pink, shining skull.

'No, I don't, as a matter of fact,' said Felicity brightly.

'I've received complaints.'

'From Miss Dean?' asked Felicity, lifting her chin and swallowing.

'No, not from Miss Dean,' said Mr Lamb. 'It seems Miss Dean is rather stupidly good-natured where you are concerned. No, I'm afraid that your fellow secretaries are the ones who have complained.' He clasped his hands together on the desk in front of him. They were stubby white hands, with coarse black hairs on the backs of his fingers. What a mean, horrible little man you are, thought Felicity, in your nasty little office, hating your own inadequacy, getting your own back by picking on people like me.

'What kind of complaints?' she asked.

'Mainly that they are being forced to take on extra work – work that you should be doing – because you are habitually late, slow, sloppy and generally incompetent.' Now he smiled. 'That about sums it up. It's really just a question of what I am to do about it. As Louise has pointed out, it's hardly fair that they should pay the price for your inability to keep up with your work.' He paused. 'Is it now?'

She was forced to make some reply. 'No,' she said. Oh, please just make this a telling-off and get it over with. It was so unfair. She'd really been trying hard recently – none of the other girls had had to help her out with her stuff for a while now.

'So it may be that we shall have to let you go.'

Fear rose up in Felicity's throat. She stared straight at him and said, 'You can't sack me. It isn't up to you.'

He smiled again and rose from his desk. 'No, but I can have a word with those who can.' He could, she knew; this had been her last chance.

Felicity clenched her fingers; her palms felt damp. 'Come on, Mr Lamb, you're not going to get me sacked just because of this?' Maybe there was a way of talking him round. He was probably just enjoying flexing his administrative muscle here.

'Not necessarily.' He walked to the door and turned the key. Felicity looked at him in astonishment. He came over to her, putting his face very near hers. 'It's really a question of – I scratch your back, you scratch mine.'

'What?' said Felicity.

'I mean, before you do anything, or say anything, think very hard about the situation. You're not likely to get another job in a hurry. We won't give you any references. Now, I've an idea that your home life isn't all that easy.' He laid a hand on her breast, and she jumped at the touch. 'You just give me one little kiss, Felicity, and we won't say anything more about it.' He was breathing quickly now, and she felt his fingers tighten on her breast. She was about to raise an arm and shake his hand off, step away from him and unlock the door, when she thought of Sandy, of the flat, of a life that was teetering on the edge of disaster. He was right. She wouldn't get another job in a hurry. She said nothing, merely stood rigid, looking away at his desk, her eyes fixed on the sharp steel letter opener that lay there. I'd like to slide that right between your ribs, she thought. She felt his other hand on her back and then his face against hers, his lips pushing on her mouth, his tongue forcing it open. She closed her eyes in disgust, trying to squirm away, and as she opened them again she saw the black hairs in his nostrils, the suety flesh of his face close against hers. His mouth was rubbery, and the sensation of his saliva in her mouth was nauseating. His hand kneaded her left breast frantically as he kissed her, pressing his body against hers. At last she pushed him away and stood glaring at him, eyes wide, jumper disordered. He smiled, lifted his chin, straightened his tie, and looked at her. He licked his mouth as he passed a hand over his head.

'Maybe we can do that again some time, Felicity. In the meantime' – he paused, still regaining his breath – 'I don't see the need to take the matter of your work any further. Not for the present, anyhow.' He moved over to the door and unlocked it. Felicity stood motionless. 'Thank you for coming to see me,' added Mr Lamb, and he opened the door, indicating to Felicity that she might leave.

Felicity went out in a daze, went straight to the Ladies, and rubbed at the inside of her mouth with liquid soap, rinsing and spitting until she had washed away the taste and feel of him. Still shocked, she stared at herself in the mirror. She was uncertain what she felt. Part of her told her that she should go to someone, tell them about this. But whom would she tell? And what would happen then? She'd be forced to leave, in any event. Another part of her said, forget it, you've still got your job. He's just another sexist shit who wanted a quick fumble in return for you not losing your job. Count yourself lucky that was all it was. She ran a hand through her ragged curls. That was all it was. She would make sure he never got the chance to lay a hand on her again. But that was all it was. She still had her job.

Try as she might to rationalise it, she was aware all the rest of that day of a tight knot in the pit of her stomach, a feeling of shock and nausea. She needed something to get rid of this, she thought. She'd get something from Vince this evening. She'd promised herself to ease up on the drug thing, but a little couldn't hurt, and she needed it. She couldn't bring herself to look at the other secretaries. The atmosphere in the office was one of wordless malice. When Doris approached her, touched her lightly on the arm, and asked sweetly, 'Everything all right, dear?' it was all Felicity could do not to strike her. But she managed to smile shakily and reply, 'Everything's fine, thanks, Doris.' You had to hand it to her, she had real hypocritic gall, did Doris. Felicity only wished she could have the satisfaction of telling them then and there that she hadn't been sacked. They'd find out soon enough. That would disappoint them. But as she remembered the reason why she still had her job, her face burned with self-disgust.

By the time five thirty came, she could take no more. I'm going to tell Rachel, she thought. She'll know what to do. He can't treat me like that. She went to the Ladies to have a pee and prepare herself, staring at herself in the mirror as she washed her hands and tried to think of the right words.

But when she went back to Rachel's office and knocked on the door to go in, there was someone with her. Some bloke, really nicely dressed, dark and slim, stood up.

'Oh, Felicity, I thought you'd gone home,' said Rachel. 'This is Anthony Cross, counsel in the *Valeo Dawn*. Anthony, this is Felicity, my secretary.'

'How do you do?' said Anthony, and held out his hand. Felicity shook it limply. Gordon Bennett, he was drop-dead gorgeous. I couldn't half do *him* some damage, thought Felicity, gazing at Anthony's brown eyes and boyish smile.

'Oh, yeah,' she said brightly. 'I remember your name from the file. Well . . . ' She glanced at Rachel. Rachel's face was soft and pleased, watching Anthony.

'We're just off to an exhibition of some paintings,' said Rachel, ready to share her pleasure with the world. 'Chay Cross. He's Anthony's father.'

'Oh, nice,' said Felicity, and tucked a curl behind her ear. Well, bang went her chance of telling Rachel. Probably just as well. She wouldn't want to know. Best just forget the whole thing. She glanced from Rachel to Anthony. They were perfect for each other, she thought. So clean and nice and lovely. Oh, shit, she thought. 'Right, well, have a nice time, then,' she said. 'See you tomorrow, Rachel.'

She closed the door and went to get her coat. All the way home on the tube she kept trying to push the thought of Mr Lamb's sloppy mouth and eager hands out of her mind, but the memory refused to go. I'll tell Vince, she said to herself as she got out at Clapham North. She felt better as she walked through the frosty darkness to the flat. Yes, she would tell Vince, at least get it off her chest, let him comfort her and tell her what she should do about it. She was sure there must be something she could do about it.

In the empty flat the smell of stale cigarette smoke seemed accentuated by the chilly air. They must have been out all day, she thought. She fumbled in her purse for some coins for the gas meter, then sat crouched in front of the gas fire, her coat still clutched around her, waiting for the room to get warmer. She glanced down; the threadbare carpet by the grate was gritty with dirt. She should clean the place up, but she felt too tired and dispirited.

At last she got up, took her coat off and went into the kitchen. In the sink lay a jumble of dirty dishes; some empty lager cans stood by the side. The cooker was so filthy it depressed her. She wondered if Vince and Sandy were at the pub. She'd go to McDonald's and look in on the way.

But they weren't in the pub. Felicity bought herself a quarter-pounder with cheese and small fries, and ate it in the silence of the kitchen. Then she went into the living room and switched on the television. She sat morosely, alternately jiggling the indoor aerial and picking at the chipped varnish on her nails, and watched a soap, a situation comedy and a Channel 4 programme about the roots of African music. She switched that off and read for a while, but by the time 11 o'clock came, they still weren't back. She felt dreadful. Everything inside her felt tight and weird, and her head seemed to be bursting. Maybe I'm having a panic attack, she thought. She'd often wondered what they were like. She went into the room she shared nowadays with Vince, and rooted around in the pockets of one of his jackets. Eventually she found two Valium in the cupboard beside her bed. That was something, at any rate. She was in the hallway on the way to the bathroom for a glass of water when she heard a key in the door.

Sandy came in, alone. 'Hi,' he said. He looked tired.

'Hi,' said Felicity. 'Where've you been? Where's Vince?'

'Vince?' Sandy scratched at the back of his head, then took off his leather jacket. 'Dunno.' He ducked his head and went into the living room, switched on the television, and flopped into a chair.

'Well, hasn't he been with you today?' asked Felicity.

'Oh, yeah . . . yeah.' Sandy's voice sounded absent.

'Well, I looked for you in the pub. So when's he coming back, then?'

'Who?'

'Vince! I need to talk to him.'

Sandy sighed. 'Look, Felicity, I don't think you should bother with Vince. He's bad news, you know.'

She walked round to stand between her brother and the television. '*You're* telling *me* he's bad news? Who brought him round here in the first place? Anyway, what is all this? *Why* shouldn't I bother?'

Sandy shifted in his chair, glanced up at her and then back at the television. 'You know where he is, don't you?' she asked suddenly, her eyes on his face. 'You've been with him. Where have you been all evening?'

Sandy scratched his head. He got up and went back into the hallway and fished a half-bottle of whisky from his jacket pocket. 'Carol's,' he said shortly. He went into the kitchen, and took two glasses from the sink and washed them. Felicity followed him through.

'Carol's?' she said, eyes wide.

'Yeah, that's right. He told me to tell you he was staying there tonight. So.' He poured some whisky into a glass and handed it to her. He hated to see her hurt, hated to be the one who had to do it, but she'd been mad to get mixed up with someone like Vince. He didn't care about anyone.

Felicity drank the whisky and burst into tears. Sandy handed her the half-bottle. 'You have it,' he said, patted her awkwardly on the shoulder and went back into the living room. She stood there in the kitchen, sobbing. This was all she needed. She felt all the shock, anger, frustration and despair of the day roll up into one great black ball of misery. Still crying, she went back to her room, stumbled out of her clothes and into a nightdress. Then she swallowed the Valium down with some of Sandy's whisky and lay huddled beneath the duvet, shivering and crying, little black streaks of mascara staining the pillow. At least, she thought, I'm getting an early night, with nothing and no one to interrupt it. And she began to cry in earnest again.

*

In the gallery in Cork Street, people drifted around admiring the paintings, sipping wine and talking in low voices. Anthony stood with his father and Rachel near the gallery door, impatient to leave. He listened absently to their conversation, thinking how much his father had changed over the past three years. All his life Anthony had known him as a superannuated hippy, living in various squats around London, moving from one fad to another, chemical, religious and artistic, without any apparent aim in life. He'd just been a long-haired, penniless embarrassment. Now look at him, thought Anthony. He eyed his father, a lean, angular figure clad in a pair of Gap denims, nubuck boots, and a hand-painted silk jacket bought on the Maximilienstrasse. He made Anthony feel stuffy in his City suit. Chay's hair was cropped, his chin silvery-grey with designer stubble, and he wore a silver earring in one ear. Two years ago he had jumped bail on a drugs charge, gone into 'spiritual retreat' in California, begun work again on his paintings, and emerged into the LA sunshine hailed as a genius among postmodernists.

Anthony couldn't decide whether luck, talent or lack of critical discernment in the art world was more responsible for his father's success. Still, even if he was not entirely admiring of Chay's work, he was ungrudgingly pleased for him. The poor guy had had a lifetime of failure – mainly through his own fault – and it was good to see him successful. And though he would never have admitted it, Anthony was not averse to basking a little in the reflected glory of his father's cultural acclaim.

He and Rachel were getting along pretty well; she seemed to know somethng about modern art and was discussing Mark Rothko's work earnestly with Chay. Perhaps I'm a bit of a philistine, thought Anthony, as he wandered a few feet away to inspect a very large exhibit, described in the catalogue as '"Nostalgia" (fibre glass, epoxy resin, acrylic paint)'. It looked to Anthony like nothing more than three badly painted clouds and a tree-house. Yet he had read reviews of this work in the Sunday papers, one of which had described it as 'massively confrontational' and another as 'perhaps under motivated, but wonderfully uncompromising'. Even Rachel had thought it marvellous. Perhaps I should try and learn more about it all, if Rachel likes it, thought Anthony. Leo, he recalled musingly, collected modern art.

He turned to look at Rachel and smiled; though still talking to Chay, her slender body seemed poised to move in Anthony's direction, as though drawn to him. She and Chay walked slowly over to join him.

'Anthony, I've had a wonderful evening. I've just been telling your father that I think the exhibition is stunning.' Her eyes were shining with genuine warmth and pleasure. Anthony smiled at her, then at Chay.

'Not bad, Dad,' he said, aware that it sounded childish and slightly ungracious, but unable to find anything else to say. He just wanted to get her away, have her to himself.

'I'm glad you came,' said Chay. He turned to Rachel. 'Anthony doesn't generally take much of an interest in my work,' he added, 'but I'm glad he managed to bring someone a little more appreciative along this evening.'

Oh, get you, Dad, thought Anthony. What a class act, and all because he obviously fancied Rachel. Looking at his father's fashionable person, set against the backdrop of a chic London gallery, Anthony felt a little spurt of jealousy. 'Perhaps you'd both like to come to supper one evening?' Chay asked, still looking at Rachel.

'Yes – we'll see. Great. Thanks,' said Anthony, and glanced at his watch.

'Well, goodnight,' said Rachel, and shook Chay's hand; Anthony could have sworn he held it for longer than was absolutely necessary.

'Goodnight,' said Chay.

'I'll call you, Dad.'

When they were out in the cold air of Cork Street, Anthony took a deep breath. 'At last,' he murmured.

'Didn't you enjoy it?' asked Rachel in surprise. She tucked her chin into the collar of her coat and dug her hands deep into her pockets. Anthony was annoyed that he couldn't even take her hand.

'Yes, I suppose so,' he replied. 'Well, I mean, it's all right, that sort of thing. But I can't say it does a lot for me.'

'Philistine,' said Rachel.

'Just what I was thinking,' replied Anthony, and smiled.

'Anyway,' added Rachel, 'I thought it was heaven.'

'Honestly?' Anthony stopped and turned to look at her.

'Honestly what?'

'Was it honestly heaven standing around looking at meaningless pictures with titles like "Puffin Number 8" and "Still Life in Exodus" and saying how wonderful they were?'

She stared at him. 'I wouldn't say a thing was good if I didn't think so. It's not all some kind of joke, you know.' Her look of icy reserve had returned.

'Isn't it?' said Anthony, wishing he'd never spoken. He felt suddenly far away from her. He sighed, stepped towards her and ran his hands down the sleeves of her coat and into her pockets, where he clasped her hands. 'I'm sorry. I've just spent the whole evening wanting to be alone with you.'

Rachel stiffened at his proximity. She should not have suggested this evening. It was not fair to go on seeing him. He would want a closeness she could not provide. She sensed he wanted it now.

Stiffly she pulled her hands from her pockets, his with them, and turned to walk slowly on.

'Would you like to go for a drink?' he asked, anxious to prolong the evening, not to let it end on this note.

'I don't think so, thanks. I had more than enough wine at the gallery.'

'Can I see you home, then?' He felt about fourteen, trying to work out this coldness in her. She behaved as though he were a cipher – not even a trace of physical understanding between them. How could she fail to read his behaviour, his words?

'No, it's all right, thanks.' Her voice was bright, but distant. 'I'll just find a taxi.'

'Rachel – ' He stopped and held her by her arms, looking into her face. The street was deserted. Her eyes were defensive. There was an unresponsiveness about her that disarmed him utterly. He thought of similar situations with other girls, their warm eagerness, and wondered whether he wasn't just entirely mistaken in all this. He leaned towards her; her features were so still that he put his hands gently on either side of her face. Her body was completely motionless.

When he kissed her, she was saying to herself, it's all right. Don't be stupid. It's absolutely all right. But she felt her muscles tightening, her mouth shrinking away from his. Still his lips sought hers. In an attempt to steady herself, prevent herself from falling backwards, she grasped his arms just above the elbows with both hands.

For Anthony, the whole thing was beyond comprehension, as with frustrated longing his mouth tried to find hers. He could feel her shudder faintly, and taking his face from hers, he let her go abruptly. Her arms fell to her sides.

'I'm sorry,' he said. 'I didn't realise.'

'What?' Her voice was faint, her head cast down, the street light shining on the blackness of her hair.

'That I offend you.' His voice was cold, hurt.

She gave a little laugh, still not looking up. How could she laugh? God, he felt a fool.

'You don't – offend me,' she replied, and lifted her head. In spite of her laughter, her face was serious, her eyes studying his. How beautiful and hurt and childish he looked. This was such a mistake. She wanted so much to be what he wanted. She drew in her breath. 'Here,' she said. And she reached up and kissed him lightly, hoveringly. He put his arms around her and kissed her back hungrily, but all he could feel was a complete stillness, right to the core of her being. It was as though there was nothing there.

She stood rigid as he released her. When he stopped kissing her, it was as though it was, for her, an utter relief. He gazed at her. There is something here that I do not understand, he thought. The almond eyes, their blue brightness very still, gazed back at him; her lips were slightly parted, and tendrils of dark hair blew about her cheeks. The light carved her face into soft planes of shadow and ivory.

'Rachel – ' he began. Don't ask me, she thought. But he merely sighed, picked up her hand and kissed it. This is not worth going on with, he was thinking. At that moment a taxi swung round the corner from Burlington Gardens, and Rachel looked up with relief.

'Thank you for this evening,' she said to Anthony as she

raised her hand to the taxi; then, before turning away, she added, 'I'm sorry.'

'Me too,' murmured Anthony to the shadows, as he watched the taxi purr off up the street.

Chapter seven

A nthony was standing in the clerks' room a week later, fiddling with the computer and trying to work out how his fees stood, when Mr Slee put the phone down and turned to look up at him.

'That was Miss Dean from Nichols and Co,' he said, 'fixing a con with you for herself and a Mr Nikolaos. *Valeo Dawn.*' He turned to make a note of it in Anthony's diary. 'Four o'clock on Friday.' He glanced back round. 'I wish you wouldn't do that with the computer,' he added reprovingly. 'It doesn't help.'

Anthony walked to the window and looked morosely out across the courtyard at the driving rain. He had no special wish to see Rachel again; he wanted to try to forget about her, wishing the thing had never begun. Still, she had instructed him, and that meant he had to see her. Why did he have to go about starting things up with every attractive woman he met? It only complicated life.

Leo came into the clerks' room in his shirtsleeves, his new half-moon spectacles perched at the end of his nose. He really thought they made him look rather distinguished.

'Here you go, William,' he said, passing some papers to Mr Slee. He glanced at Anthony. 'Cheer up,' he said. 'Don't tell me you're worried about meeting me in court next week, eh?'

Anthony looked at him. Good God, those new glasses of Leo's really made him look his age. Anthony was rather taken aback. 'Don't worry,' he replied with a smile. 'I happen to know we're going to win. Lewis is bound to uphold the award.' For the first time, he and Leo were on opposite sides in a case, and Anthony found it an enjoyable novelty. It gave them a common interest that seemed to set their relationship back on its old amiable footing.

'Ha!' said Leo. 'I admire your optimism. But,' he added

ruefully, as he joined Anthony at the window to inspect the weather, 'I rather suspect you're right.'

There was a pause, and then Anthony said, 'Tell me – how do you get out of a case once you've been instructed in it? I mean, can you?'

'Don't they teach you that sort of thing at Bar School?' asked Leo. Then he added, 'I don't know. The situation has never arisen with me. I think the answer is – you can't. Not unless you have some formidable, really earth-shattering excuse. Anyway, you'd make sure William got you out of it – isn't that right, William?' Leo turned and grinned at Mr Slee.

Mr Slee looked grimly at Anthony and sighed. 'I don't think it's something we want to start thinking about,' he said. 'Not quite at this stage.'

'No, I was only joking, really,' said Anthony. 'Just something that's turning into a bit of a drag.'

'Hmmm,' said Leo. 'How nice to feel you can pick and choose. I must go and do some work.' He left Anthony staring out at the rain, cursing himself for the fact that, despite everything, he was very much looking forward to seeing Rachel again. Try as he might to suppress the feeling, he was now impatient for Friday to arrive.

When Mr Slee showed Rachel and Mr Nikolaos into Anthony's room that Friday, Anthony was uncomfortably aware of his own nervousness. It seemed to him that it had been tacitly accepted, at their last meeting, that whatever he had tried to start with her had been an utter failure. As a result, he felt stiff and awkward at the prospect of meeting her. But when he saw her, saw her calm, lovely face and gentle smile as he said hello, it all receded. He was more than glad to see her, just to look at her. She was wearing some suit of pale grey, and a high-necked white shirt that made her neck look very slender. Her black hair was swept back into a knot, and she looked infinitely more elegant than he had ever seen her. But it didn't matter what she looked like, he reminded himself – she was not for him. He only wished she didn't have to look so bloody wonderful.

They sat down opposite Anthony's desk, where the papers

in the case were neatly arranged, Mr Nikolaos perching nervously on the edge of his chair. Anthony gave him a brief, reassuring smile as he surveyed him. He was a small, stout Greek in his mid-fifties, not very well dressed, and seemingly full of pent-up agitation. Poor guy, thought Anthony, as he began to expound to Mr Nikolaos how things stood for him – Rachel had already told him about Mr Nikolaos's other minor disasters.

' . . . so the main difficulty that we face, as Miss Dean has no doubt already explained to you' – he put this in just as an excuse to glance in her direction, let his eyes rest for a moment on her mouth, slightly pursed as she inspected some document, and on the soft darkness of her eyelashes and brow – 'is in establishing that the vessel was not unseaworthy, but that the explosion was caused by some act or default in the navigation or management of the ship.'

Mr Nikolaos was nodding attentively, listening carefully to everything Anthony was saying.

'Which will give us,' continued Anthony, 'a defence under the Hague Rules. So it really is an evidential issue.'

'But how can they say this vessel is unseaworthy?' demanded Mr Nikolaos. 'You see the surveyor's report – ' He rose and half-crouched over Anthony's desk, grubbing the report out excitedly from among Anthony's papers, flicking through the pages and muttering. 'There! You see?' He stabbed a stubby finger at the page and read aloud: ' "The fire, which started at the aft end of the number two generator, had involved a massive release of oil. Analysis of the oil in the bilge showed that the majority of the oil there was lube-oil. In addition, the number two generator had lost three hundred litres or so of lube-oil." ' He looked up excitedly into Anthony's face. 'There! You see? It must have been the mistake of someone working with the generator! Is not my vessel was unseaworthy!' Mr Nikolaos's breath smelled strongly of garlic, and Anthony sat back slightly.

'Yes, but the problem, Mr Nikolaos, is in showing that it was in fact an error by one of the crew, and not, say, some defect in the filters.'

Mr Nikolaos sat back down and looked at Anthony with a

mixture of hope and impatience. 'But you will get the evidence to show this was so?'

Anthony hesitated and glanced at Rachel. 'If it is there, then I hope we shall.'

They debated the surveyor's preliminary findings for another twenty minutes or so, Mr Nikolaos becoming more and more agitated, until Rachel laid a hand on his arm.

'I think you're right, and Mr Cross thinks you're right,' she said, 'but we have some further way to go before we can establish it conclusively. I'm going to Bombay to see the master shortly, and maybe we can get a clearer picture then. We have another surveyor making a more thorough examination while I'm out there, and I'm sure his report will clarify things.'

Mr Nikolaos subsided. He looked at Rachel and shook his head sadly. 'Okay.' He glanced up at Anthony. 'But we must prove this thing! I cannot afford to lose this! I have big problems already, Mr Cross, and I'm relying on you – '

'I understand, Mr Nikolaos,' interrupted Anthony. 'I promise we shall do our best.'

When the conference ended, Rachel and Mr Nikolaos rose. As Anthony was seeing them to the door, Rachel turned to Mr Nikolaos. 'Would you mind if I had a word with Mr Cross? Perhaps you would wait for me downstairs.'

Mr Nikolaos, preoccupied, nodded and left them. Anthony felt his heart beat a little faster as the door closed; she looked at him and said, 'I'd like to return your kindness in taking me to your father's exhibition last week. Would you like to come to supper tomorrow night?'

Anthony was mildly astonished. 'Look,' he said uncomfortably, 'don't you think this is best kept on a – um – professional footing? I mean, I'm clearly not your cup of tea – ' Best to come clean, he thought, though he wished he could find a more appropriate way of putting it.

'Anthony, this is just a friendly gesture. Please.'

Anthony wasn't quite sure he knew what this meant, but if she wanted to be with him, then . . .

'Yes, all right,' he said. 'Thanks.'

'I'll give you the address.' And she wrote it down and left it on the corner of his desk. 'There.' She smiled at him. It was a smile of such promise that Anthony felt confused. 'I'll see you about eight,' she added.

He sat back down behind his desk after she had gone. David Liphook, with whom he shared the room, came back from court a few minutes later and glanced in Anthony's direction as he slung his bag into a corner.

'You look a bit dazed,' he said.

Anthony raised his eyebrows, still gazing vacantly ahead of him. 'I am. I'm trying to work out what makes women tick.'

'I've been doing that for ten years,' said David, from the lofty heights of twenty-six. 'It's a waste of time. Come on,' he said, 'it's Friday, it's nearly five thirty, and the weekend is full of promise. I'll buy the first round.'

Anthony sighed and rose, wondering just how full of promise his weekend was.

That evening, Rachel stood before the mirror and stared at her reflection. She dragged one finger across her pale skin, down from her brow and past her mouth; her eyes looked blankly back. There has to come a point, she told herself, when you must make the effort to find your way back to normality. What normality? How could she possibly reach back into her life and find a place where things had been normal? It was a state belonging to others, a condition to be attained. 'Your healing has to come from within,' her analyst had said. What did *she* know? How could you heal someone who had never been well or whole to begin with? But you had to make the attempt, you had to climb up, step by step, towards the real world. Then, when you reached it, you would just have to stand teetering there for as long as you could, praying you didn't lose your balance.

Rachel dropped her head, looked at her hands spread out upon the dressing table, then looked back up again. She did not see the fine-boned loveliness that others saw when they looked at her. It was just her face, after all. To her, it looked as it always had – hollow and lost, with fear behind the eyes. Sometimes it seemed that her reflection belonged to another person entirely.

When she lay in bed later, she slid her hand beneath her nightdress and drew it up across her stomach to her breasts.

Her skin felt very soft. She thought of Anthony touching her thus, and in her imagination it was gentle and desirable, and she herself was pliant and unresisting. But that was not the truth, she knew. She drew her hand outside the covers. If I can just take a grip on these fears, she told herself, if I can edge the darkness away and remember that he is safe and kind, then it could be all right.

She recalled how she had let him kiss her, and how she had made her mind a black vacuum for the thing to be supportable. But it won't always be like that; it must get better. She tensed the muscles of her arms, then relaxed them, trying to remember the relaxation technique she had been taught, so that her body and mind might float away into sleep. There is nothing to be afraid of, she said to herself, and squeezed her eyes tight shut.

The next day passed smoothly and brightly, with an unexpected savour of optimism. She went to Marks & Spencer in the morning and bought wine and olive bread and salad, and pasta and cheese and ham and cream. She spent most Saturday mornings shopping, but then it was rather more mundane, unless she happened to be having one of her friends from school or university round for supper, with their boyfriend or husband. Everyone seemed to have husbands or partners these days; everyone seemed to have lives that moved in shining, kaleidoscopic patterns made up of weddings and houses and pregnancies and babies, while Rachel felt as though she were standing still, watching it all go by. Occasionally such threesomes would feel a little awkward, but Rachel preferred to entertain at home, instead of having to go to her friends' dinner parties, her heart sinking with dread at the prospect of meeting the unattached male who was inevitably roped in on her behalf. No, she felt safer at home.

As she carefully mixed wine vinegar into the salad dressing that evening, Rachel thought of those unattached males. She had learned how to deal with them, to assume the social mask of polite friendliness while turning them in her mind to wooden images, consigned to oblivion as soon as the evening was over, never to be thought of or encountered again. She had adopted a similar technique with those men who would occasionally approach her in art galleries on Sunday afternoons, friendly, hopeful, lonely. She had learned to drift unseeingly past and away, learned how not to look or feel threatened.

But Anthony was different. She could not look past him, or consign him to oblivion. She did not want to. She wanted to be able to keep him close. She had thought over and over about Anthony and this evening, telling herself that if she could do this, then she had taken the first step to overcoming the fears which made her shrink from all intimacy. There are good, kind men in the world, her analyst often reminded her. Not every man is a threat, not every man wants to hurt you. She knew that Anthony was one of those men; she recognised that. So it will be all right, she told herself. Take it moment by moment. But still her hands tightened spasmodically on the side of the salad bowl she was holding as she thought of his hands upon her face. She thrust the thought away.

Anthony got to Rachel's a little after eight, bearing wine and some flowers. 'These were a last-minute thought, I'm afraid,' admitted Anthony, as he gave them to her. 'The flowers, I mean. They're from the garage down the road. You see the way they wrap them in this foil stuff to make them look more and better? Sorry.'

'They're very nice,' said Rachel, 'wherever they come from.'

He followed her through to the kitchen, glancing around with interest at the meticulous feminine order of her flat. He watched her as she reached up to a shelf to fetch a vase for the flowers. She was wearing jeans and a simple black sweater, which clung to her body. Her hair hung loose about her shoulders. Anthony had never seen her in anything but business suits, and he found the sight of her in jeans girlish and touching.

'It's nothing special, I'm afraid – just spaghetti,' she said, and handed him the wine and a corkscrew. You could divide women into two types, thought Anthony: those who opened wine themselves and those who gave it to men to do.

'I think we'd better stop apologising to each other,' he said, smiling as he twisted in the corkscrew. 'You like the flowers and I love spaghetti. In fact, I believe my own spaghetti bolognese is the envy of all Kensington.'

Rachel laughed; she could feel her nervousness ebbing a little. 'Well, this is carbonara, so that lets me out of the competition.'

'Far too sophisticated for me to attempt,' said Anthony. He poured them each a glass of wine and they talked as she cooked. She seemed very bright and jokey, a little nervy, Anthony thought, as he leaned back against the fridge and took a sip of his wine. But it was wonderful just to be with her, just to watch her and talk to her. He liked to feel that, once he had managed to bring down a little of that wary resistance of hers, a real affinity existed between them; warmth, amusement, an unspoken understanding. If only he could bring down that physical resistance, too. If everything had gone the way it should have last time, he thought, then I should be able to walk over to her and kiss her, just hug her. But watching her back as she stood at the cooker, he could almost sense how she would tense if he were to approach her. It puzzled him. There is so much affection between us, he thought, but this great physical barrier. He brushed against her shoulder with his arm as he leaned across to pick up the wine and take it into the next room, and felt her jerk nervously away. Then she smiled awkwardly at him, trying to move away more naturally from him as though simply to pick up some plates. Oh Lord, he thought – so it's still going to be like that. Irritation swept him. Very well, then – she won't have a thing to worry about, he told himself. I won't lay a finger on her.

Rachel watched him nervously throughout the meal, examining the lines of his face as he talked and his hands as they stroked the base of his wine glass absently. She looked for a long time at his hands, watching their movements almost with fascination. Then she looked back up at his face and smiled. She liked him so much. She wanted so much to want him that maybe, if she tried very hard, then she could do it. She could let him touch her without turning to ice. Then he would come here often, and the hours would be less lonely, and life might gradually become safe. When he had touched her in the kitchen, she simply hadn't been expecting it, that was all. Next time she would be ready. Better.

'I can't believe how wonderfully tidy your flat is,' remarked Anthony, as he finished his salad. 'Adam and I just lurch from one scene of domestic chaos to another.'

She smiled and tucked her hair behind her ear with slender fingers, then glanced around. 'I tidied up especially for you,' she lied. 'It doesn't always look like this.'

'So,' said Anthony, leaning forward, 'what do you usually do with your weekends?'

'Oh, not much.' Her voice was flat, transparent. 'Shop. Go to a film. See friends. I like to go to art galleries. I think I might go back to look at your father's exhibition again tomorrow afternoon, if it's open.'

'You're a glutton for punishment,' he said with a laugh. 'But you did say you liked modern art.'

He watched her speculatively as she began to gather the plates up. He had been wondering if there had been some man – some relationship that had recently broken up. That might account for a lot. But he thought he recognised, as he looked at her, that her arid manner, her watchful aloofness, were a result of not having been in the company of any man for a long time. Not intimately.

He helped her to clear the dishes away, and was conscious, as they moved past one another in the kitchen, that she kept her body at a careful distance.

Rachel was conscious of this, too. Don't be absurd, she told herself. You must let him touch you if he wants to. You mustn't be afraid.

When she brought the coffee cups through and set them down on one of the little low tables, Anthony was standing flipping through one of her magazines. As she straightened up, he looked towards her, then put down the magazine. There was a pause. 'Come here,' he said gently, his earlier resolution quite forgotten.

His eyes were fixed on hers as she moved towards him, her limbs feeling like water, slack and without sensation. Walking into his embrace was like walking into a cage; she stiffened at the clasp of his hands upon her back, as he moved one hand up to her neck to lay her head gently upon his shoulder. He held her for a moment as though she were a child, and she stood, arms at her side, trying not to tremble. When he pulled his head back to look at her face she could feel every atom of her concentration focused upon what he would do next. It will be all right, she told herself. It happened once before, and – just let it happen again. As he put his mouth to hers she did tremble, but there was a sweet liquidity about the sensation that allowed her to put her arms around him. She felt as though she were clinging to a rock, and the kiss was like a wave which must cease, eventually, to beat against her. Remember who it is, she thought, remember you are safe.

For Anthony, the feeling of her arms around him, the little surge of response to his kiss, filled him with relief and affection. He lifted his mouth from hers; he looked at her eyes, still closed, and at her parted lips, her tilted head, and smiled. He murmured her name and unthinkingly traced a line with his hand from the curve of her neck over her breast. She suddenly took a deep, shuddering breath, and pushed him away. Her eyes were open, cold and terrified. 'Don't!' she whispered.

Anthony stared at her. 'I'm sorry,' he said; he felt chastised, foolish. Her expression was fierce and rigid. Again he was aware of a sense of confusion, of proportions slipping. He tried to draw her back into his embrace, but her body seemed to be half-crouched in resistance. He lowered his mouth to hers, but she shook her head frantically from side to side and began to struggle and push herself away. 'Don't! Don't!' she said, her voice hoarse and high. He took his arms from her and watched her back away, trembling.

Suddenly anger and frustration seized him. He walked forward and put his hands on her arms; they felt hard and tense, like the sinews of some animal poised to fight.

'Rachel, what is the matter with you?' he muttered, and his gaze travelled across her face, across her body, which was heaving with the effort of containing her fear. He suddenly wanted her very much, and without thinking he pulled her to him and kissed her over and over, heedless of her struggles as

91

she tried to twist her mouth away. 'Please,' he whispered as he covered her throat with kisses, 'I don't want to hurt you. I just want to hold you . . .' And he spoke her name over and over again, his hands upon her back, pressing her body against his. Rachel could feel, through her panic, the stiffness of his erection, and a new fear mounted higher and higher from her stomach to her throat. 'Stop it!' she managed to scream.

And suddenly there was silence, and they stood apart, Anthony breathing heavily, Rachel tense and shuddering. Anthony stared at her for a few seconds, then sat down on the arm of one of the sofas.

'I'm sorry,' he said. 'I'm sorry. Look, what I – ' He rubbed a hand across the back of his neck. 'Rachel,' he said after a long moment, 'why did you ask me here tonight?' His voice was genuinely curious.

'Not for that,' she replied levelly, her voice dead, her eyes turned away from his.

'Not for what?' he asked in exasperation. 'I kissed you. I'm sorry. That was all. I find you very – very desirable.' He looked at her, and she slowly turned her eyes to meet his. 'Anyone would. But it's more than that. I just want us to be close. Everything is so good – ' He gazed at her expressionless face and haunted eyes, the tension between them almost palpable, and wondered what was so good. 'I just want it to be more than – than talking, looking at one another. I can't look at you for long without wanting to touch you,' he finished.

Rachel clasped herself defensively and took a deep breath. 'It's not your fault,' she said. 'It's – ' No, she could not tell him. He would feel pity, maybe distaste; it would drive him away. She must deal with it alone. 'It's just me. I'm sorry.'

'Don't you – don't you like me to kiss you?' asked Anthony hopelessly. She closed her eyes momentarily at the question. He was so touching, so naive. What was there to say?

'I – want to like it,' she answered tentatively.

Anthony pondered this. 'You want to like it,' he said. His gaze wandered away from her face and around the room, the neat, pretty, tasteful room, the table where they had eaten, their wine glasses, the gentle glow of the lamps which Rachel had switched on to light the room softly, invitingly. I must be reading the signals all wrong, he thought. I do not understand. 'You want to like it,' he repeated thoughtfully.

Then he sighed and stood up. Part of him wanted to stay here, to sit with her in the shadows and go gently over all of this, work some way towards an understanding. After all, he knew he loved her. Everything he felt for her amounted to that – except for . . . whatever it was that kept going wrong between them. And the other part of him was tired, sexually frustrated and unable to cope with all this heavy stuff on a Saturday night.

'I think,' he said, picking up his jacket from the chair next to the door, 'that I'd better wait until you've worked out what it is you *do* want from me.' He spoke as kindly and as gently as he could. She looked so beautiful, less tense now, standing in the middle of the room. He thought for a moment of going over to her and – Oh, no, he thought. No. Not again. His pride and his desire could not stand it. As he gazed at her, he suddenly thought, how alone she looks. 'Don't you think that's best?' he added.

She nodded. But how could she know what she wanted unless he helped her? Yet that was the last thing she could ask. Let him go. Let it go, she told herself.

'Okay,' he said. 'Thank you for supper. I really enjoyed it.' This was all so uncomfortable, so unnatural. He should never have come. She should never have asked him.

'I'm glad you came,' she replied. How awful it sounded. She walked slowly over to the doorway and watched as he opened the front door.

'Goodnight,' he said.

'Goodnight,' she murmured. Then the door closed, and she was left standing in the empty silence of her flat.

As he walked to his car, Anthony thought of her kiss, of the warmth of her body against his before she had pushed him away, and felt as though some pain were tearing at his heart. This relationship is pure destruction, he thought. He stood looking at his car, keys in hand. The last time he had been in love, he recalled, he had been twenty-two and happy and the greatest of his worries had been scraping together the tube fare home from Julia's. Now he almost wished that the car did not exist, so that he might be forced to let the cold night and a few miles of empty streets eat up all the misery and confusion.

Felicity sat in the noise and smoke of The Star in Coldharbour Lane, and decided to stop trying to pretend she was having a good time. The thump of the live band in the back room drifted through, and she leaned over to try to catch what her friend Lisa was saying.

'You want to go through, have a bit of a dance?' asked Lisa, her voice raised above the roar and hum of late Saturday night in a Brixton pub.

Felicity shook her head. 'No, thanks. Tell you the truth, I think I'll go home. I've got a splitting headache.' She knew she had drunk too many vodkas. She lifted her elbow from the puddle of beer in which she had placed it in leaning over to listen to Lisa, and mopped at it with a tissue. Then she glanced into her cigarette packet and saw she had only three left. She felt depressed. She only came out because she kept hoping that she might see Vince somewhere, and that he might be on his own. She couldn't believe that he'd dropped her like that, not saying anything. All she had to do was talk to him. She could fix it so it would be all right again.

She came out into the cold air, the door of the pub flapping behind her, and began to walk up the road. Twice someone called out softly to her, asking her if she wanted anything, but she just glanced away and shook her head. She didn't have the money. But, oh, for a bit of a smoke. Just something to make it all float away, bright and sweet, into the corner of the room. Maybe Sandy would have some stuff, maybe he was at home right now. She quickened her step.

She passed a couple locked in an embrace in a doorway; the girl had long dark hair, and Felicity was reminded suddenly of Rachel. She pictured Rachel, imagined her spending a sophisticated evening in some expensive restaurant – decent food and really nice wine, not a Wimpy and too many vodkas – and then going back to some clean, comfortable West End flat, all low-lit and chic, and having fantastic sex with that hunk she'd had in the office the other day.

94

Coming round the corner, Felicity glanced up at the windows of the flat and saw that they were dark. Lucky fucking Miss Dean, she thought.

Chapter eight

Anthony sat in number 14 court on a dreary Tuesday afternoon at four o'clock, and smiled to himself. It gave him a peculiar pleasure to have won this case against Leo. Not that it had been through any particular merit on his part, he had to acknowledge, since the point was an academic one which they had both rather suspected would be decided in Anthony's client's favour. But still, the thing had a dash of the sweetness of victory about it. He listened as Leo, who had been prepared for this eventuality, now sought leave to take the matter to the Court of Appeal.

'As for the jurisdiction point,' Leo was saying, 'which I think your Lordship has decided on an obiter basis, I would certainly need leave to appeal, in order to take that further . . . '

Anthony glanced up at him as he made his notes, thinking how alert and concentrated Leo's entire person seemed to be when he was on his feet in court, no matter how pedestrian the task in hand. His glance strayed to the lean, restless hands, now tugging at his robe, now twitching it aside, now adjusting his wig. Perhaps it is because I still like him so much that I take pleasure in winning against him, thought Anthony. Some sort of subjection. He suddenly remembered once telling Leo he loved him, and he turned his gaze abruptly away and back to his notes.

' . . . in my submission,' continued Leo, 'it is common ground between these parties that this provision arises very frequently, and therefore gives rise to a point of general importance.' Mr Justice Lewis was sitting with his eyes closed. They had been closed for ten minutes now, and Anthony was wondering whether he was asleep. 'Your Lordship may recall looking at the affidavit sworn on the part of my learned friend's client – ' Leo seemed to be wondering the same thing, for he paused rather pointedly in his discourse. The judge, his cheek resting lightly on the forefinger and thumb of one hand, nodded and, without opening his eyes, said, 'Yes.'

Leo coughed and continued. As he jotted down some notes, Anthony's mind tentatively fingered the events of eighteen months ago, his thoughts straying to the various encounters with Leo since then. Now that the memory had been broached, he began to recall the way his pulse had once raced at the mere sight of Leo's face or the sound of his voice. He laid down his pen and leaned back. Someone must love Leo now. Every day someone waited for his return, thought of him constantly, felt alive because of him. Anthony wondered who it might be. No doubt there were even women who had broken their hearts over Leo. Certainly he ruled the typists in chambers through sheer charisma – shouting at them one day, charming them the next. They would sooner work for Leo than for any other member of chambers. Perhaps it was merely Leo's force of personality that had made Anthony imagine he was in love with him once. Infatuation was a peculiar thing.

Mr Justice Lewis opened his eyes and interrupted Leo's flow of eloquence and Anthony's idle thoughts. 'Now, are we dealing with section one? I think I should have a look at it, because – '

Anthony roused himself, annoyed at having let his concentration slip.

'Would your Lordship like to look at my copy of Mustill and Boyd?' asked Leo, and handed his book to the usher who, with a look of infinite boredom, handed it up to the judge. 'It is page 655, my Lord, section one, sub-section seven.'

Anthony paid attention again for a few moments, but he knew in his own mind the rest of the points which Leo must make, and he took up his former train of thought again. He had, he believed, rationalised this business with Rachel. It had merely been a very forceful initial attraction, an infatuation, intensified by his own frustration at finding someone so lovely to be so physically unresponsive. And his disappointment, his sense of failure and humiliation, had all combined to make the thing seem more important than it really was. They just hadn't hit it off. A pity, but there it was. Next time he saw her, which he supposed might not be for a while, it would all have settled back into proportion. She was clearly a very confused young woman who didn't really know what she wanted. She would be nothing to him from now on.

And as he thought all this, he suddenly remembered very vividly, the way she had been that night in the restaurant, the fun they had had, the sweetness of her smile, and the heartbreaking emptiness of his attempts to make love to her. His heart filled up with a hopeless pain. He sighed. Winter afternoons in gloomy, near-empty courtrooms were death to the soul. He must just hope time would make it all better. Or perhaps there would be someone at Lawrence's dinner party on Saturday, someone new, someone to obliterate Rachel. He doubted it, and turned his attention again to Leo, who was obviously winding down.

' . . . naturally, my Lord, these other two issues may not need to be taken further, but if your Lordship would like me to address your Lordship on them – '

'Well, I do not think you need do so, Mr Davies, not at this stage. Let us hear what Mr Cross says.'

Anthony rose, with that customary surge of adrenalin which he experienced whenever he addressed a court, even one which consisted only of himself, Leo, the judge, the usher and the court reporter. He had known largely the grounds on which Leo would seek leave to appeal, and was prepared with arguments to counter Leo's, but still, certain items had been thrown up in the judgment which neither of them had expected, and he was touched with a slight thrill of nervous misgiving as he began to speak.

'My Lord, I wish to deal with a number of things. First of all, there is no doubt that this is a provision of general importance. We would not dispute that . . . '

Leo leaned back, glancing speculatively at Mr Justice Lewis. Lewis had been on the bench for eight or nine years now, and Leo had appeared as his junior in a lengthy and important salvage case some ten years ago. They didn't often meet – Lewis seemed to spend most of his spare time down at Leamington, devoted to his yacht – but they were on pretty cordial terms, nonetheless. Definitely worth sounding out. He would send a note round to his clerk once the afternoon's business was over, suggest a drink next week. He leaned forward and concentrated on what Anthony was saying.

' . . . so, for that reason, my Lord, I would submit that this is not an appropriate case for your Lordship to grant a certificate under section seven – '

'I think, Mr Cross, that we are looking at section one, are we not? I have Mr Davies's copy of Mustill and Boyd before me . . . '

Anthony reddened and looked flustered, then glanced down at his notes. 'I beg your pardon, my Lord. Section one. And so . . . ' He frowned, flicked through the pages with finger and thumb. He'd lost track of what he'd been saying. 'That is . . . Yes, I would submit that it is not appropriate under that section.'

Leo felt a stab of sympathy for Anthony. No matter how much self-confidence one had, any perceived slip in competence at that age always threw one. Leo remembered his own hesitations, his own awkward beginnings, and felt a little tender impulse towards the younger man.

'Well,' said the judge quite gently, 'even so, Mr Cross, I take it that you would not deny that it is always open to the Court of Appeal to grant leave under that section?'

Anthony paused. Why wasn't I paying attention? he thought. What a waste of time thinking about that wretched girl. His mind sped back, and recollection rescued him. 'No,' he stammered, 'naturally your Lordship can give leave or, additionally, the Court of Appeal.'

Mr Justice Lewis nodded and Anthony carried on without any further mishaps. At the end of the hearing, Anthony came over to where Leo sat scribbling in a page of his notebook.

'I wasn't sure if he was going to take that point about the certificate,' said Anthony.

'Hold on,' said Leo, as he finished writing. He tore the page out, folded it up, and handed it to the judge's clerk, who was clearing books away. 'Would you give that to the judge, please?' Then he came back to where Anthony stood. 'No, I don't think he was sure about it, either, for a moment or two. Still, there you are.'

'And on we go. I'll need a leader, if it goes to the Court of Appeal.' Anthony smiled. 'If you weren't on the other side, I'd be able to suggest you in a few months' time.'

Leo raised his eyebrows as they made their way out of court and along the echoing, sombre corridors to the robing room. 'I shouldn't like to count those particular chickens . . . ' He paused at the wooden arched doorway to the robing room. 'By the way, what were you dreaming about while I was astounding Mr Justice Lewis with my exceptional eloquence? I looked at you twice and you were miles away.'

Anthony took off his wig and gown and bundled them into his bag. He would leave his bands on, since he was just walking across the Strand to chambers. He felt his face flush slightly as he replied, 'Oh, just some problem. Something that's been troubling me.'

Leo glanced at him shrewdly as he unfastened his collar. 'For God's sake, don't let your love life get in the way of work. Always save it for later.'

Anthony shrugged and sighed, leaning back against the large oak table and watching as Leo carefully knotted his tie. Then Leo turned to Anthony, thinking that although young men on the whole did not lounge very gracefully, Anthony seemed to have the knack; he said to him, 'Take those off,' indicating Anthony's bands, 'and I'll take you for a drink.'

'It's only five,' replied Anthony, pleased but a little surprised. Then he felt a faint misgiving; Leo was always so perceptive, and he wasn't sure that he wanted to talk about Rachel. Just let it be.

'So what?' said Leo, shrugging into his jacket. 'El Vino's is open. Come on. I can give you half an hour before my little rendezvous with Roger Ware, the Hon. Sir.'

'Oh?' Anthony unfastened his bands from his collar.

'Just buttering the bench up a little in preparation for their Easter cogitations. Makes them feel good. Nothing like the feel-good factor.'

El Vino's was almost deserted when they went in. 'Remarkable,' said Leo, glancing round as they sat down in a corner. 'Not so many years ago half of Fleet Street would have been in here at this hour. Now they're all in Wapping, dry as dust.'

'Yes, I remember,' said Anthony.

'Do you?' said Leo, as a waitress came over to their table. 'Yes, I suppose you do,' he murmured. He glanced at the waitress, then at Anthony. 'A bottle?'

'Just a glass for me, thanks,' replied Anthony. 'I've still got some papers to look at. Got an arbitration next week.'

Leo ordered two glasses of house white. 'So,' he said, fishing in his pocket for his cigars, 'who or what is so troublesome that you're not paying proper attention in court?' He took out one of his little cigars and lit it, lifting his chin slightly as he did so.

Anthony sighed and sat back, thrusting his hands into his trouser pockets. In a way he was glad of the opportunity to talk about it. It wasn't really the kind of thing he could discuss with Adam. 'Well,' he began, 'I did a rather stupid thing, I suppose. I got a bit involved with this lady solicitor who instructed me in the case I told you about – the explosion in Bombay.'

'Oh, yes.' Leo nodded, blowing out a plume of smoke. There was something bright and attentive about his manner which struck Anthony for a second as being almost prurient. He knew that Leo loved gossip, the details of other people's personal lives. There was almost a sort of greed about it. But Anthony felt he didn't much mind. In a way he wanted to involve Leo; it made him feel closer to him, and that was something he wanted to recapture. Just that part of it. Just the friendship. That was all.

'Anyway, I realise now that it wasn't a very good idea, but – '

'Certainly not something I would ever recommend,' put in Leo, 'but that's not to say that I haven't been tempted. Take young Jonathon Webster at Holman's.' He chuckled, smoothing his hand over his grey hair.

Anthony felt slightly embarrassed at this. He didn't really want to know about Leo's feelings for other men. He was curiously struck by this realisation and said nothing for a moment.

'Sorry – I interrupted you,' said Leo. 'Ah!' The waitress set their wine down before them, and some water biscuits.

Anthony decided to continue. 'Well, we went out together a

few times and it was all very good. You know, we got on well together. I make her laugh, she makes me laugh, all that sort of thing.' He stopped. He suddenly felt he did not know how to say any of this, especially to Leo. He wished now he'd just gone back to chambers.

'But?' Leo sipped his wine, not looking at Anthony.

'Oh, I don't know . . . Look, I probably don't really want to talk about any of it. I thought I did, but – anyway, it doesn't matter. Let's talk about something else.' He drained half of his glass in one swallow.

'But the physical side of things is not all it should be?' said Leo, tapping a little ash from his cigar. His voice was mild and assured.

Anthony looked at him in surprise. Leo was wearing his best worldly-wise expression; he looked up, met Anthony's glance and smiled. 'Is that it? Oh, don't look so surprised. I mean, what else could it be? It's just what one would expect to be coming next.'

'Yes,' said Anthony. 'That's about it. I mean, I really like her – '

'You fancy her but she doesn't fancy you. Is that it?'

'Well, no,' replied Anthony thoughtfully. 'Not quite. If it were just that, I wouldn't give it a second thought. Just give up and go home. No, the thing is, I think she likes me as much as I like her. I think she really wants – ' He stopped, staring at his wine. His look of boyish, wistful candour was such that Leo felt a slight rush of rekindled affection for him.

'Well,' replied Leo lightly, amused at how deeply the young could be touched by life's trivia, 'perhaps she's one of those rare commodities – a blushing virgin.'

'Good God,' said Anthony, smiling a little ruefully and glancing at Leo, 'things certainly never progressed that far. No, even on the most basic level we're not hitting it off. At least . . . Well, she's just so remote, sort of frightened. Or else it's some awful sort of game. I mean, she asked me round to supper, just the two of us . . . ' He rubbed at the side of his face with his hand. 'Oh, I know you can't take that to mean anything, but – well, it was all set up as though something was meant to happen. As though she wanted – ' He sighed. 'Oh, I don't know. Anyway, I won't be seeing her again, I've decided – not in that way – so I don't suppose it really matters.'

'It sounds to me,' said Leo with a frown, 'as though the young lady has some sort of problem. That is, of course, a quite valueless opinion to offer, since I don't know her. But anyone who doesn't respond positively to your physical charms must be mad.' He raised his eyebrows and popped a fragment of water biscuit into his mouth.

Oh, don't, thought Anthony. Don't be camp. Don't refer to us, to you and me, in that way. He felt that Leo was debasing what had happened once, trivialising it.

Leo perceived something of this as he glanced at Anthony's face. How serious it all is at twenty-three, he thought. 'However,' he went on, 'it does sound as though you'd be taking a lot of trouble on board if you did get too involved. You're young, the world is full of young women. Don't get tied up in messy emotional knots, other people's hang-ups. And if you think it's some sort of a game, for God's sake don't play. It's unhealthy. Some people get a kick out of it, but I don't think you're one of them. Look, it's made you unhappy enough already.'

'Oh, I'm not unhappy,' said Anthony, as he finished his wine. 'I just find it all a bit confusing. But, no – you're right. You've just told me what I'd already told myself. Only, it seems rather a pity. You don't often meet someone with whom you feel so – so utterly right. Still.'

'I know,' murmured Leo. 'One generally has to settle either for good conversation or for good sex. They rarely go together.' He glanced at his watch. 'I'm rather afraid Sir Roger awaits me.' Leo picked up his matches from the table and put them in his pocket. 'Don't worry about it,' he added to Anthony. 'Women, in my experience, are never worth it.'

'Right. Anyway, thanks for the drink,' said Anthony, rising. He wondered what a gay forty-four-year-old's experience of women could amount to. You never could tell. Leo was a strange one.

As Leo took a cab to Brooks's and Anthony made his way back to chambers, the shades of the November evening were closing around the City. Lights twinkled in the windows of the clubs along Pall Mall and in St James's. In the smoking room of White's, Sir Mungo Stephenson sat nursing his whisky morosely, the glass resting on his broad stomach, his stumpy legs in their striped spongebag trousers stretched out before him. In the chair opposite, Sir Frank Chamberlin was toying with the *Telegraph* crossword, occasionally gazing into space and muttering to himself, pausing from time to time to take a sip of his drink. Sir Bernard Lightfoot sat in the armchair nearest to the fire, his eyes closed, his handsome narrow face serene and satisfied, listening to Sir Mungo carping about the new Lord Chancellor, Lord Steele of Strathbuchat. It was a cosy and reassuring sight, two judges of the Commercial Court and a Lord Justice of Appeal taking a well-earned rest after a hard day on the bench, in the soothing, masculine surroundings of their club.

'Naturally,' muttered Sir Mungo, 'one would expect no better from a crony of Thatcher's.'

'Wouldn't one?' enquired Sir Bernard without opening his eyes. He stirred slightly and crossed his ankles. 'I don't know about that. After all, I suppose he feels that, as he is now the Lord Chancellor, he has to make his presence felt. One can see that.'

Sir Mungo snorted and took another sip of his whisky. 'We don't need any damn-fool Scot foisting his own ridiculous legal system upon us. Fusion of the professions, indeed!'

'Oh, come,' said Sir Bernard, opening his eyes. 'It's an old chestnut. Anyway, the Green Paper hardly goes that far. It merely talks about extending greater rights of audience to solicitors. Nothing horribly drastic.' He closed his eyes again, smiling to himself in anticipation of his colleague's deliberately provoked wrath.

'Nonsense!' growled Sir Mungo. 'It's the thin end of the wedge. You allow solicitors rights of audience in the High Court and the two-tier system will disintegrate.'

Sir Frank, his eyes still fastened on his crossword, nodded. 'Indeed. You lose the critical mass.'

'Quite!' agreed Sir Mungo, wondering where on earth Frank got these peculiar expressions from, and what this particular one meant. Still. 'If it is to be opened up in that way,' he continued, 'then the Bar will eventually disappear, and we shall have a system run by a lot of grey-minded solicitors with degrees from polytechnics. Good God! The next thing you know, you'd have the likes of Carter-Ruck on the bench!'

'Well, of course,' said Sir Bernard, uncrossing his legs and pulling himself up in his chair to ring the bell on the wall next to the fireplace, 'there are those who would say that solicitors are perfectly well equipped to appear in the High Court on behalf of their clients. They do so quite adequately in the lower courts, after all.' He enjoyed playing devil's advocate to Sir Mungo, even though he agreed almost entirely with his views.

'Well, anyone who thinks *that* is a fool,' replied Sir Mungo. 'Advocacy is an exceptional skill. I wouldn't trust the senior partner of any leading City firm to defend himself on a speeding charge. They couldn't acquit themselves with even average competence.' He handed his glass to the steward who had appeared. 'Another one, please, George.'

'Small brandy, please, George,' murmured Sir Bernard.

'Moreover,' went on Sir Mungo, hoisting his portly person up in his chair and fumbling in his breast pocket for a cigar, 'in a properly regulated two-tier system – '

'Thank you!' exclaimed Sir Frank suddenly. Sir Mungo stared at him. ' "Directed characters in a great duel," ' said Sir Frank, looking up and smiling. 'Nine letters. "Regulated".' He scribbled busily.

Sir Mungo continued to stare at him. Where had he got to before Chamberlin had gone off at his usual ludicrous tangent? Oh, yes. 'As I say, in a properly regulated two-tier system, the advantage of the exclusivity of the Bar is that it consists of select advocates untainted by any close client contact. Now that, I believe, is vital to our system.'

' "In law, what plea so tainted and corrupt . . . " Thank you, George,' murmured Sir Bernard, taking his drink from the steward's tray.

'I don't know that one need worry unduly, you know,' said Sir Frank, removing his spectacles and folding up his paper. 'It will simply mean a closing of ranks. I don't believe that Lord Steele's proposals will amount to anything, at the end of the day.'

'But just imagine what it would mean if he manages to push the thing through,' growled Sir Mungo, snatching puffs at his cigar as he attempted to light it. 'Of course, the Bar would not lose out at the specialist level, but in the more general areas all the junior work would go to solicitors. The specialist High Court work would go to leaders, and the rank and file of the junior Bar would vanish within a decade.' He stared angrily at the glowing tip of his cigar.

Sir Bernard eyed him lazily. Mungo really did enjoy having something to get worked up about. But it was all nonsense. This new Lord Chancellor would see the error of his ways. As Frank said, ranks would close. 'Well, at least that would keep the QC cabal happy,' he remarked, then added, before Sir Mungo could continue a fresh harangue, 'Speaking of the QC cabal, do you see that two men in Sir Basil Bunting's chambers are applying for silk at the same time? Bit of a surprise.'

'Oh?' said Frank Chamberlin with interest.

'Yes, Leo Davies and Stephen Bishop. Odd, isn't it? I imagine neither is aware that the other has applied. Mind you, not before time in Bishop's case. But then he always seemed to me to be a bit of a plodder.'

'I like Davies,' remarked Sir Mungo. 'Got a bit of dash about him. Bit of colour. The Bar needs more like him. The junior members seem to me to be a very mundane lot these days.'

'Oh, he's colourful, all right,' said Sir Bernard with a smile, swirling his drink gently in its glass.

'Exceptionally able,' said Sir Frank. 'Very suitable.' He nodded vehemently as he thought of Leo; he was very fond of him.

There was silence for a moment.

'How do you mean – colourful?' asked Sir Mungo. He'd seen Bernard smiling in that particular way of his.

Sir Bernard stretched his legs out before him, tugging down his waistcoat. 'Oh, one hears things, you know. Rather fond of – ah – little boys, I believe.'

'Davies? Good God!' Sir Mungo stared at the fire in disbelief. 'If anything, I would have taken him for a ladies' man. But boys – how disgusting!' He puffed his cigar and took another pull at his whisky.

'Well, even if such a thing were true,' said Sir Frank mildly, but leaning forward a little anxiously, 'it's hardly so very much out of the way, is it? I mean, we all know . . . ' Here tacit and well-understood reference was made to a senior figure on the bench, infamous among his peers for his eccentric sexual proclivities.

'Well, Bishop's not a nancy boy, is he?' demanded Sir Mungo. 'There are standards, you know. Call me old-fashioned' – at this, Sir Bernard smiled and murmured something inaudible – 'but I'm sick and tired of these faggots monopolising our institutions. First the BBC, now the Bar – next thing you know, it'll be the army! I'm afraid that, for me, these things tell against a man.' He shook his head. 'Leo Davies. I am very sorry to hear it.'

'Not likely to go down too well with the Lord Chancellor, either,' remarked Sir Bernard. He took a last sip of his drink. 'Not after that débâcle with the Scottish Bar, accusations of gay intrigue, blackmail and what-not. But frankly,' he added, glancing at his watch, 'it's a matter of indifference to me. And so I shall inform our new Lord Chancellor when he asks me for my view of Davies, as I am tolerably certain he will. What a chap does in his private life can't make much difference to the way he performs his job. Anyway, I must be dashing. Wife's having a dinner party.'

He rose and bade them a smiling goodnight, then made his way out into St James's to take a taxi to Camden, to the flat of a certain twenty-four-year-old girl of his intimate acquaintance.

Sir Frank sat in his chair, staring at the fire, while Sir Mungo snarled a little more about 'damned Scots and queers', before stumping out. Poor Leo, thought Sir Frank. What Sir Bernard had said about the new Lord Chancellor was probably right. He sighed, put away his pen and picked up his newspaper. He would have to have a word with Leo. He did so want to see him do well. Perhaps if they had a bit of a talk, then they could straighten it all out.

Chapter nine

Two days later, Rachel lifted her phone in her office and heard Nora's singsong voice announcing that she had Mr Nikolaos on the line.

'Put him through,' said Rachel absently, wondering what fresh disaster had befallen him now. But fate had decided to put a decent limit on Mr Nikolaos's current crop of problems.

'Miss Dean,' he said in important, slightly defiant tones. Rachel could tell that he had an announcement to make, that he had been chewing something over privately and now wished to share it with her. It struck her as sweet, the formality with which he still addressed her, despite their working relationship over the years.

'Yes, Nr Nikolaos. Good morning.'

'Good morning to you. Miss Dean, you are going to Bombay to see the master of the *Valeo Dawn*, yes?'

'Well, yes – I haven't booked my flight yet. I'm still waiting for my visa. But, yes, I'll be going out there very shortly.'

'Yes. Good. What I wish is this. The young man who is our counsel in this case – it is Mr Cross, yes? I wish him to go, too.'

Rachel's heart sank. Oh, no – not more confrontation. Why, oh, why, had she ever instructed him? Not that he wasn't the best company in the world – she couldn't think of anyone she would rather travel with – but after the fiasco of Saturday night, she shrank from the prospect of everything else that his intimate companionship might entail.

'Oh, Mr Nikolaos,' she replied hurriedly, 'do you really think that's entirely necessary? I mean, I'm sure I can take the master's statement without Mr Cross.'

But Mr Nikolaos was a man who, having reached what he perceived to be a decision of consequence, would not be shaken. He was only too accustomed to feeling helpless in the hands of his lawyers, and an opportunity to move the pieces about in his own chess game made him feel that he was still of some importance.

'No, Miss Dean, this I have decided. Mr Cross says that the evidence is crucial in my case, and I wish him to see it himself, to inspect the ship himself.'

Rachel felt slightly patronised. 'I am sure that the surveyor and I can assess the evidence quite adequately. In fact, it is the surveyor's report which will be crucial, not what Mr Cross or I might think.'

'Still, I wish him to be there.' Rachel could tell he was not to be dissuaded. 'He will be speaking for me in court, and he must see for himself where this explosion happen. Besides, Miss Dean,' he added in paternal tones, 'these ships are not always suitable places for young ladies to visit. I think a man would feel more comfortable, perhaps.'

Rachel bridled at this – she had heard it often enough before, but never from Mr Nikolaos. Still, he was only trying to be nice about it – at least he didn't object to having a female solicitor, unlike a few former clients whom Rachel could think of. It had been more than a small impediment to her progress in her work, encountering men who did not like their business to be handled by a woman; Rachel suspected that it was because they felt that it robbed them of their authority, rendered them impotent. She sighed. 'Very well. But I have to warn you that Mr Cross may not be free. I'll have to speak to his clerk.'

When she rang Anthony's chambers, Rachel knew that there was a good chance that Anthony would already be tied up on the dates on which she had intended to travel. He was very popular and in court a good deal. But no, he was free, Mr Slee told her, consulting Anthony's diary. 'He's got a summons on the twenty-third, but I've been trying to move that back, anyway. I think he should be fine from the twenty-third to the twenty-sixth.'

'Oh, good,' said Rachel unenthusiastically. Already various small fancies and fears were playing around in her mind. She detested having to feel like this, the bunched-up, nervous dread of something – nothing – that loomed ahead of her. Oh, stop it! she told herself. It's only a business trip. He's probably lost interest completely after last time, and just as well if he has. It was a ghastly mistake, and I should have known better. 'Do you think I might speak to Mr Cross?' she asked. She might as well tell him herself, so that he didn't hear from his clerk and get the wrong end of the stick, imagine that she had somehow engineered it. That was the last thing she wanted.

'Hold on, I'll put you through,' said Mr Slee.

Anthony was not quite sure what he thought of it all, when Rachel told him.

'I told Mr Nikolaos that it was quite unnecessary for you to go,' Rachel said in distant tones, 'but he seems to think it imperative that you inspect the evidence for yourself, for some reason.'

Anthony leaned back in his chair and fixed his eyes on the glow of the gas fire. 'Didn't you tell him that it's all down to the surveyor? I'm no technical expert.'

'Of course I did,' said Rachel shortly. He caught the tone of her voice. She doesn't want me to go, he thought. He wondered whether he really wanted to go either, after all that daft business at her flat. Not that he intended to let such an incident repeat itself, but they might be uncomfortable company for one another. The ghost of that Saturday evening would hang between them. At that moment David came into the room and made 'coffee?' signals at him. Anthony nodded, then tipped his chair forward. He rather fancied a couple of days away from London in freezing November, he decided. Only business, after all. Nothing more.

'Well, I suppose if your client insists, and if William says I'm free . . . '

'Yes, apparently you are,' replied Rachel, just preventing herself from adding 'more's the pity.' She mustn't let her irritability get the better of her. After all, it was her own stupid hang-ups which were to blame. Not him. Not Mr Nikolaos, either. Anyone else would treat this as a run-of-the-mill business trip. 'You'll have to get a visa,' she added, 'but I think they can rush these things through. Here, I've got the details somewhere . . . ' She pulled her diary towards her.

As he took down the address of the Indian High Commission, Anthony's mind strayed beyond the business aspect of this trip to its further possibilities. Maybe being away with her, alone with her, would help. Help her to get rid of whatever problems she had. Whatever he had been telling himself since that Saturday night, he had to acknowledge that he was in love with her, and where there was love, there had to be hope.

'Will you book the tickets for me?' he asked. 'I mean, I assume you've got all the timetables and stuff.'

'Yes,' replied Rachel. 'And I'll book the hotel.' The hotel. Just the thought of that jolted her.

'Fine. If you don't mind doing all that, then . . . ' He wondered what to say next. She sounded so uptight about the whole thing. 'It should be fun,' he added.

'Yes,' she said, 'it should be.' As she hung up, she told herself that that was the right way to look at it. He wouldn't try – no, not after last time. He'd said 'fun', and that just meant a good time. A good time? She rubbed at her temples with her hands. She knew what Anthony's idea of a good time inevitably led to. Oh, let it alone, she told herself. You can't go on getting paranoid about these things. But she knew it was getting worse every time she saw him. She was slipping further and further. She hesitated a moment before picking up the phone again and making an appointment for the following evening with Dr Michaels.

Dr Michaels' office was an unpretentious, rectangular and rather narrow room, decorated in pastel greens that reminded Rachel of school. The contents of the room, too, from the watercolour of a canal at a barge lock to the row of four cactus plants on the windowsill, bore the same stamp of impersonality, as did Dr Michaels herself. It was as though everything had been placed in the room – desk, chairs, bookshelf, little rug, cacti, picture and window blind – to turn it into a representation of a room, a pretend room. Rachel often felt, as she sat talking to Dr Michaels, as though she were in some silent theatre, her back to the audience. She imagined Dr Michaels walking on to the stage earlier, prepared in her role as the squat, comfortable Jewish psychoanalyst, sitting down, waiting for Rachel to make her entrance. Then Rachel would come in through the door and the play would begin.

It was generally the same one-hour play, but with varying scripts. Sometimes its mood was dictated by the way in which the streets of Earl's Court affected Rachel on her walk to this room. Sometimes she found the crowds, the multiplicity of nationalities and their transitory quality quite enervating, and she would be glad of her sense of isolation and remoteness, even though it was for that sense of separation that she sought Dr Michaels' help. At other times, especially if the weather was fine, the same streets and the same people would exhilarate her, make her determined to cope with and conquer her problems, so that she could share and saunter in their sunshine without any secrets.

Today she had come by car, and the walk from the parking meter had been bleak and wet; she had turned into Culver Gardens and walked with a sense of futility towards the tall grey building which housed Dr Michaels' green room. It seemed to have become purely habitual, this business of visiting Dr Michaels. There was no longer anything she could do to help Rachel. It even seemed to Rachel that Dr Michaels' broad, impassive face conveyed the same message: I can listen, but can give you no more hope. She has heard all this a hundred, a thousand times before, thought Rachel. And not just from me. A vision flashed through her mind of all the little one-hour playlets performed in this room. Rachel wondered whether, in any one of them, Dr Michaels ever leaned forward, her customarily deadpan gaze lighting up with excitement, and said, 'I think I have the answer!' As though any analyst ever could. Maybe it will be today, in my play, thought Rachel.

But they were into the second half-hour and Dr Michaels had evinced no sign of possessing a miracle cure. They seemed to be covering old ground. But then, what else was there in Rachel's life, but dead ground? Doesn't she ever get bored? wondered Rachel. But why should she? She is earning money just by nodding and listening.

'It's not just a question of rationalising it,' Rachel was saying. 'I can do that. I can go over events and face them, in the way you taught me, and I can say – "look, there is your explanation. Now deal with the problem." But it seems very

112

artificial. I don't really *need* to go through all that. It's just mind games.'

'What do you mean when you say you don't need to go through it?' asked Dr Michaels. Her face bore no look of curiosity. It was a pale, round face, not pretty, but with a heavy intelligence, framed with dark hair in short, springy curls. She looked back now at Rachel, who wondered, as she often wondered, whether the other woman resented Rachel's slender prettiness, of which she felt inordinately conscious when in Dr Michaels' muscular, plain presence. But Dr Michaels gave nothing away.

'I mean – ' Rachel hesitated. 'I mean that when it comes to – when I have a good reason for wanting to confront and get rid of my fears, my ability to rationalise it all fails me. Or rather, it doesn't help me.'

Dr Michaels shifted her position slightly and rested her jaw on the fingers of one pudgy hand. Rachel noticed that she was wearing a bracelet of carved bone. It looked so incongruous, so little like an article of adornment, that Rachel was quite struck by the thought of Dr Michaels putting the bracelet on in the morning as she dressed, perhaps admiring it on her plump wrist. Perhaps some man had given it to her – Dr Michaels wore no wedding ring – out of love. Rachel found it difficult to think of Dr Michaels as a woman like herself.

'You mean, when you are with a man,' said Dr Michaels. It was not a question, not a statement – more in the line of a helpful hint.

'Yes,' said Rachel. Her mind flew to Anthony, and to the strength of his detaining grasp as they had struggled, absurdly, that Saturday night. She felt her muscles tighten suddenly at the recollection. 'Yes. You see, there is this one person in particular.' Rachel paused. Dr Michaels looked at her, waiting, not waiting, her expression inert. 'I know that I'm very much attracted to him.'

'You know that you are, or you feel that you are?'

This was an interesting question. The play had taken a new tack. 'I – I must feel that I am, surely, if I know that I am?' replied Rachel, considering this. Dr Michaels said nothing. 'I know that I am, in that he's the kind of man – the kind of man that I think I would like. That I *do* like. Well, he's not so much a man, more a boy, really. Then again . . . But he's very good-looking, he's very nice – ' She stopped and smiled. 'That sounds trite, I know, but he really is . . . nice. That's the only word to describe him. He's intelligent, and he's fun to be with, and I know that he's very much attracted to me . . . ' Rachel wondered if she was becoming too detailed, bringing Anthony too much to life.

'He sounds *very* nice,' said Dr Michaels, and smiled suddenly. Rachel had never heard Dr Michaels speak jokingly before. What kind of man do *you* like? she wondered, as she watched Dr Michaels' thoughtful gaze straying towards the window. Some large, loving bear of a fellow psychoanalyst, Rachel imagined, someone who makes love to you every which way five times a night. The thought of Dr Michaels in the frantic flesh. Rachel smiled. She's probably a lot luckier than I am, she thought. But then, any woman is. It's only Dr Michaels who knows it.

'Yes. So, of course, I feel attracted to him. Or know I am, whichever you like. I just can't respond to him in the way I want to. Or he wants me to.'

'You see,' replied Dr Michaels, 'what I meant about the difference between feeling and knowing is that you must be careful to distinguish between someone for whom you feel a real sexual attraction, and someone who simply represents that which you perceive is – or should be – desirable.'

'But how would you know?' asked Rachel in bewilderment. 'How would you ever know?'

'I think, in your case, that it may make all the difference, ultimately. I don't believe your problems are to do with men, as such. We have been over all of this. Your father is not all men. The man who attacked you does not represent all men. It is a question of approach. Instead of regarding sex as a barrier to closer intimacy with someone, you should let it follow the intimacy, the closeness. But you must be careful to distinguish between the kind of inchoate attraction which you feel you must tackle as the answer to the problem, and those emotions which are' – Dr Michaels hesitated – 'more enabling. Which give you scope to respond.'

'I see,' murmured Rachel, dimly perceiving some truth in this. 'But the question still remains – how would I know the difference? Do you mean that because I can't respond to this man, I can't really be attracted to him? That there's some sort of Mr Right waiting out there?' Rachel gestured with a quizzical smile in the general direction of Earl's Court station.

Dr Michaels smiled and looked down, fingering her bracelet, slowly revolving it on her wrist; Rachel noticed that the hairs on Dr Michaels' wrists were coarse and grew almost to the backs of her hands. 'I'm not saying that. It may be that you're very much attracted to him, but that this anxiety to resolve your fears sets up as a barrier between you. But you see, I think of you as someone who would respond very positively to the right person, to the right approach. I don't really think you're as afraid of it all as you might imagine. You say that this boy – or man – is good-looking, intelligent, funny. Fine. As we said, he sounds very nice. Does he turn you on?'

Rachel was struck by how curious this phrase sounded in Dr Michaels' mouth. Turn me on. She imagined Dr Michaels being turned on. Rachel suddenly realised that a lot of men might find Dr Michaels a very sexy woman. Potent. Powerful.

She stared at Dr Michaels for a moment, wondering what the answer to this was. 'I don't think,' she replied at last, 'that I know what this is like. How could I possibly know? I've only ever been used.'

'I believe, in spite of what you think, that you are capable of normal sexual response. I think you would know.' Dr Michaels, shorn of her sensible skirt and oatmeal sweater, of her bone bracelet, beneath the bedclothes, face down. Dr Michaels in her other life. How many lovers? A wild Jewish wanton, all her carefully contained desires unleashed.

Would I? wondered Rachel. 'Would I?' she said.

Dr Michaels stopped playing with her bracelet and glanced at her watch. She looked up at Rachel. 'Stop concentrating on this young man as a focus of your anxieties. Can you speak to him about any of the things in your past?'

Rachel shook her head. 'I couldn't. It's too much of a burden. Besides . . . ' She turned her head to glance out of the window. It had stopped raining. She wondered if she'd get a ticket. She'd only had enough change for fifty minutes on the meter. 'I don't think it would help. I think it might just confuse him. Worry him. He's very young. It might just – turn him off. There you are.' She smiled and looked back at Dr Michaels.

'Perhaps it says something about the nature of your attraction to him – that you feel you can't tell him. I think it would indicate a lot if you met some man to whom you felt you could talk about all this.'

'I have to go on a business trip with him,' said Rachel. She looked back at the window, at the little pots of cacti. 'In two weeks' time.'

'Well, don't look upon everything as a test. There are things you enjoy about this relationship. Try to nourish them. And if you can't explain the past to him, simply tell him that you need to keep everything on a platonic footing for the present. Feel less threatened. Just let it develop, take it for what it is. Not every man has to be seen as such, you know.'

Rachel smiled at this. 'I know. It's just that they all expect to be.'

'So enjoy the trip. Enjoy being with him. But get things clear and unequivocal. I have no real anxieties for you, you know, Rachel.'

I like it when she uses my name, thought Rachel. It makes me feel a little more special, not just another hour-long slot in her working day. I wonder if she ever thinks of me when she's not working? Rachel gazed at the square, capable hands with their plump fingers, envisaged her chopping, preparing, cooking, making food for her lover for them both to eat before they fell to their passion. She makes me feel thin and spare and dry, while she looks rich and full and – But why should I think this? Maybe all is not wonderful for her. Not all doctors are healthy, just because they cure others. But I have to believe her to be so. She has to be what I am not.

'Haven't you?' she asked.

'I think we fought through the worst of it long ago. No, it's just a question of understanding your emotions and motives a little better. Try not to confuse the significance of relationships.' She looked at her watch again.

'I know. Time to go,' said Rachel. She stood up and slipped

her coat on, lifting her dark hair clear of the collar. 'Thank you, Dr Michaels.'

'I hope I can be of help from time to time.'

'Maybe I should come more often,' murmured Rachel, thinking back hopefully to the days when time spent with Dr Michaels had been the warm haven of the week.

'I don't think you need regular therapy, Rachel. I think there are still difficulties, but – '

'Better to confront them as real issues in real life, yes? I am trying, believe me.'

She went out into the gathering gloom of late afternoon, seeing in her mind's eye the rectangular stage of Dr Michaels' room, perhaps the props requiring a little rearranging before the entrance of the next character, with Dr Michaels sitting there patiently, unmoving, waiting for another life to pass before her eyes.

Chapter ten

Although they spoke once or twice on the phone in the intervening days, Rachel did not see Anthony until the evening of their flight. She checked in, bought a magazine and a paperback, and sat down in the coffee lounge where they had agreed to meet. It was ten o'clock, and the flight was at eleven. Already the terminal had a sleepy, deserted air about it; the duty-free shops were closing down, a couple of vacant cleaners pushed their wide duster mops around the shining floors, and only a handful of travellers dotted the lounge. Rachel drank her coffee and tried to concentrate on her magazine, but time was slipping by and still Anthony had not appeared. When the flight was called at ten thirty she felt a squeeze of alarm at the thought that he might miss it, that she might have to make this trip alone. She realised that she had gradually become accustomed to the thought of travelling with him; it would be lonely otherwise.

Deciding she could wait no longer, Rachel picked up her hand luggage and made her way to the gate, yawning. She had had a long day and already felt weary at the thought of the eight-hour flight. Where on earth could Anthony have got to? She continued to scan the faces of the passengers trickling into the departure lounge, and it was only when the flight was about to board that she saw him hurrying up to the desk. The sight of his tall figure relieved and cheered her.

'What happened to you? I thought you weren't going to make it,' she said, as he strode over to her, glancing down at the seat number of his boarding card.

'What happened to *me*? I've just spent the past hour wondering where on earth you were. I've been waiting in the Club lounge.'

Her hand flew to her mouth. 'Oh, God! I forgot about the

Club lounge! I've been waiting in the ordinary one. Oh, I'm sorry.'

'Doesn't matter,' he said. 'I'm just glad to see you. I wasn't exactly looking forward to going alone.'

'Neither was I,' replied Rachel, happy that he was there. They smiled at one another. Dr Michaels had it all wrong, she thought. How could she not be attracted to him? It was a question of time, that was all. She would have to explain that to him. It would be all right.

'Come on,' he said, as the last few passengers dawdled past the stewardess, 'we'd better get on. I don't think we can be sitting together,' he remarked, 'since we checked in separately. But maybe the flight's not full.'

The flight was only half full, and they were able to sit together in a bank of three seats, piling the flight paraphernalia of headsets, pillows, rugs and magazines into the spare seat between them.

When the hostess brought dinner, Rachel had only a coffee and some fruit, but was amused to see Anthony devour everything which was brought to him by way of food and alcohol.

'You'll starve,' he remarked, glancing at Rachel's meagre meal.

'I ate earlier in the evening. I don't care for the food on aeroplanes.'

'Don't you?' said Anthony, genuinely surprised. 'I love it. Little feasts on plastic trays. I like all the tiny bits and pieces, the little sachets of stuff, pats of butter, dinky cutlery all wrapped up. It's like being a child.'

'You don't fly very often, do you?' she asked, smiling and leaning back to look sideways at him.

He shook his head. 'I had to go to Livorno once, and I went to the States with Adam last summer, but this is real luxury,' he replied, glancing around the Club Class section.

He's like a child, she thought, quite unaffected, able to enjoy everything that is a novelty. It was odd, she supposed, that he could be so clever, so intellectually gifted – for she had come to realise that he had a natural talent as a lawyer – as to be able to deal easily with immensely complex issues of law, often involving weighty issues and vast sums of money, and yet still be so young in other ways. It was a great burden of responsibility to carry, she reflected. Still, he seemed to bear it quite easily.

Anthony enjoyed himself. He read the in-flight magazine – Rachel did not think she had ever seen anyone do this from cover to cover before – put on his headset, flipping through the radio channels with amusement, and settled back to watch the in-flight movie when it came on.

Rachel tilted her seat back, tucked the pillow beneath her head, pulled the rug over her legs, and slept. She slept only fitfully, however, and woke from time to time to glance at Anthony. He seemed to be enjoying the film, whatever it was. She glanced at the screen and saw Al Pacino mouthing soundlessly at a blonde woman in a restaurant. She wondered how Anthony could manage to stay awake. She fell asleep again, and when she woke the cabin was largely in darkness, with huddled forms shifting uneasily beneath their blankets, the businessmen having put away their laptop computers and filofaxes to dream of sales targets and earning curves.

Anthony was sleeping, too, but Rachel could see that he had not given up without a struggle; he still had his headset on, and Rachel's magazine lay on his lap. She studied his face in the half-light, the long, soft line of his cheek to his jaw, the dark hair flopping over his forehead. How long his eyelashes were. She had had no opportunity yet to speak to him about – about just letting things alone, keeping them friendly. There hadn't been an appropriate moment. He had been so eager to enjoy this journey that there had been no hint of anything beyond friendly companionship between them. Maybe it would continue like that. Good, she thought, feeling betrayal at her sense of relief. Good.

She leaned back, reflecting that being with Anthony sometimes made her feel quite old. She thought of the countless trips she had made in her working life, the hotels, the airports, the in-flight meals. Schiphol, Brussels, Paris, Genoa – faceless, tubelike corridors leading to faceless arrival lounges, then boxlike hotel rooms the same as boxlike hotel rooms all over the world. And the people, the business people, the dreary,

120

preoccupied masculine faces – even the women seemed to adopt token masculine expressions on business trips – with their briefcases and raincoats, milling past and around one another in their antlike quest for deals, for money, for contacts. She yawned, feeling on the floor for her shoes. She had achieved a sort of modus operandi for business travel, switching off and letting the blank vista of airports and taxi rides and offices and other people's secretaries smiling at you with coffee slip by like a grey dream.

But there was Anthony, stirring now in his sleep as the pilot announced their descent into Bombay, for whom it was all fresh and new and exciting. How many years, Rachel wondered sadly, until he, too, leaned back wearily and dismissively on his fiftieth flight, ignoring the in-flight magazine, eating only a little, reading through his papers instead of watching the movie, perhaps taking a pill to help him sleep through the tedium of it all. But that was a long way away, she thought, watching as he woke. He smiled at her.

'We're nearly there,' she remarked. 'I'm going to freshen up a bit.'

When she came back from brushing her teeth and splashing her face with water, she found Anthony at the window seat on the aisle opposite, gazing intently down. She slid into the empty seat next to him and peered over his shoulder. Below them a ragged brown patchwork stretched out for mile after mile, made up of the tiny square roofs of Bombay's shanty-towns, ramshackle dwellings huddled together in a sea of teeming poverty.

'I never thought slums could look romantic,' murmured Anthony.

'I shouldn't think they are, close up,' replied Rachel.

'I want to go out and have a look around as soon as we've checked into the hotel. What time is it?'

Rachel glanced at her watch. She had reset it to local time earlier. 'About midday. I know it's first thing in the morning at home, but my body tells me it's bedtime. I just want to go to the hotel and sleep.'

'You've had a sleep,' said Anthony, as they returned to their seats. 'In fact you've been asleep for most of the flight. You missed a good film.'

'I still feel exhausted. Sleeping on planes isn't the same thing, anyway.' She glanced at him. 'You need a shave.'

And they smiled at one another, childishly pleased with their adventure.

Bombay airport was shabby and crowded, the air hot and humid and laden with some hidden promise, the fragrance of a place that was foreign and vital. Brown-faced businessmen in starched, shortsleeved linen suits sauntered around with briefcases; knots of families, women in saris with clutches of children and babies-in-arms, queued at the ticket desks, and the airport police moved about with a powerful air of authority. Rachel and Anthony waited for a long time at a battered baggage carousel, and when they finally emerged on to the hot pavement outside the terminal, a dozen brown voices jabbered at them and hands leapt to take their luggage. They stood bewildered, until one man eventually singled himself out from his fellows, whom he shooed importunately away, and, taking their bags, directed them with peremptory gestures towards the taxi rank, where a queue of dilapidated Morris Oxfords stood. Having loaded their bags into the boot of one, the man stood patiently while Anthony dug out some tattered rupees. These appeared to be insufficient, and the man frowned and shook his head until Anthony produced some more. Rachel watched this performance, thinking that a masculine presence at least spared one the effort of doing it all oneself.

The taxi bumped its way along heat-laden roads, through the shantytown suburbs and into the city. It was a slow, sweat-trickling journey. The traffic, both vehicle and pedestrian, was dense. Children and chickens wandered into the road from the maze and huddle of the shanties, then sidled away at the sound of the taxi horn. The occasional cow would lumber ruminatively across the road, dogs nipped in and out of the traffic, tongues panting in the sun, and the noise of car horns, bicycle bells and scooter klaxons merged in a jangle of raucous sound.

Anthony gazed in fascination at the ramshackle huts lining the road, their roofs and walls of plywood and rusting corrugated iron, curtains of sacking covering their dark entrances, where watchful women squatted and bare-bottomed toddlers played in the dirt, their merry shouts and bright eyes flashing in the smoggy air. Everyone seemed cheerful, despite the squalor. People of all descriptions swarmed along the roadside – housewives, beggars, workmen with tools and handcarts, street vendors, tea boys carrying their gleaming cans of food and tea to offices, neat crocodiles of schoolchildren in white blouses and grey pinafores – mingling with the traffic. Some of the huts had been turned into booths and these, as well as the little one-man roadside stalls, peddled an infinite variety of sweets and nuts and fruit and fried food. The shanties stretched for ever, an endless sprawl of Indian humanity.

Suddenly a fetid stench rose into the air as they lurched across a bridge. Anthony and Rachel both sat back from the window. 'God!' said Anthony. 'What on earth is that?'

'Fish farm – is fish farm!' said their driver, waggling a brown hand in the direction of a river bank.

'Remind me not to have the fish tonight,' murmured Anthony.

The hotel was a cool and sudden contrast to the bustle of the Bombay streets. The lobby was filled with the expensive cosmopolitan calm of the five-star hotel. Anthony and Rachel felt as though they had been set down in an oasis, a quiet spot in the very hub and heart of the teeming city. The corridors of the hotel, as they walked with the porter to their rooms, could have been the discreet corridors of any hotel in the world, except for the faintly marshy, musty aroma that pervaded them.

Their rooms faced one another across the corridor. Anthony stood in the doorway of his, fingering his key, as the porter took Rachel's bag into her room.

'Well – I'll give you a knock after I've had a shower and things. Then we can have a look around. Maybe get some lunch.'

'Fine.' She nodded. She noticed his face wore a suddenly self-conscious look, as though he had only just become aware of where he was, and that she was alone there with him. I'll have to say something to him before this evening. But it wasn't going to be as easy as she had imagined.

After lunch, they stepped out into the bright afternoon heat to wander around. Rachel bought some earrings from a street stall and Anthony bought some aspirin from a chemist, whose shop was dense and tiny and flyblown, crammed to the ceiling with teetering shelves of assorted pharmaceuticals, some apparently dating back to the sixties. Every shop seemed to yield its own little enclave of hangers-on, groups of men wandering in and out, chatting among each other, or to the patron and his customers.

After an hour or so, the muggy air and the noise and the importunity of endless beggars began to weary them; even the exotic succession of colourful booths and shops began to pall.

'I'm longing for civilisation and a long, cold drink,' said Anthony. 'Aren't you?'

'Philistine,' murmured Rachel. 'I think we're almost back at the hotel, anyway. If we go up that road there . . . '

'I think you've called me that before,' remarked Anthony, and his hand, swinging at his side, caught hers. She stopped in the dusty street and looked up at him. Her pale face was lightly filmed with sweat.

'Anthony, there's something I want to say – '

'What? That I shouldn't hold your hand?' He smiled at her, raised her hand to his mouth and brushed it with his lips.

'No,' she said quietly, and disengaged her fingers from his.

He sighed and his shoulders drooped. 'What, then?'

'Let's go back to the hotel first,' she said.

They walked back in silence to the hotel, through the quiet cool of the lobby and out again into the hot air, on to the lawns that surrounded the swimming pool. They sat down at a table in the shade of one of the towering palms which filled the courtyard, and ordered lime sodas.

As the white-uniformed waiter drifted away, silence fell between Rachel and Anthony. It was broken by the sudden explosive splash of a German businessman diving into the pool. Both glanced sharply up, watching him swim sedately to the far end. Then silence and heat fell again.

'So,' said Anthony at last, 'what was it you wanted to say?' It

124

has something to do with us, he thought. It's going to be something sad and final and I don't want her to say it. Even though everything that's happened between us so far has been a disaster, I don't want to hear it. I want there always to be another chance.

He looked at her, at the soft blackness of her hair and the slenderness of her arm as she reached across to finger the little brown paper bag containing her earrings, which she had laid on the table.

'This is going to sound – well, presumptuous,' she began.

'Presume away.'

'Look, Anthony, I like you very much – I really do – ' She paused and glanced at him, then tucked a strand of hair behind one ear. 'But this is a business trip.'

'I know. I know that.' He squinted up at the shafts of sunlight falling between the palm leaves. The German had begun to swim back down the length of the pool. The chattering of birds high above tore at the air for a few seconds, then died away. 'Rachel – ' He shifted his chair so that he was directly facing her and leaned forward, resting his elbows on his knees. When he looked up at her a stripe of sunlight fell across his face, and he creased his eyes against it. 'I didn't come out here with some idea of seducing you. If that's what you're worried about.'

She sighed. 'I told you it would sound presumptuous. But you didn't really let me finish.'

He dropped his head, then plucked a blade of grass and rolled it between his fingers, saying nothing.

'What I wanted to say was – I like you, and I just need to take things slowly. There are – have been – some things in my life that I don't want to talk about, but if you give me enough space – then I think it might be all right.' I sound ridiculous, she thought, ridiculous and pretentious. Why can't I find the right words?

He lifted his head and looked past her, over her shoulder, to the waiter approaching with their drinks. She went on. 'Anthony, I'm just not ready for a relationship at the moment. Because – that is – I thought I was coping with things, and that's why I asked you over that night – ' Her voice was hurrying along and she did not look at him, until he suddenly laid his hand on her arm. She stopped and looked up to see the smiling waiter standing next to her. She started and smiled hesitantly, foolishly. The waiter placed their drinks on the table, then left them. Rachel did not go on, merely stared at the chilly droplets slipping down the side of her drink in the heat.

'So you're not telling me to push off?' he said at last. He was smiling as he took a sip of his drink. Oh, thank you, God, he was thinking. She does think there can be something – that this isn't all just doomed to failure.

She looked at his face and laughed, relieved. 'No, I'm not.'

'I thought you were going to. I thought that was what this was to be all about.'

'But you do understand?'

'I think so. Well, perhaps not entirely. You just want things to – slow down, sort of?' He put his drink down.

She nodded. 'Just give me some time.'

He hesitated for a moment, then said, 'Can you tell me why? I mean, you said something about things that had happened . . . '

'No, that's not important. Just that you understand that I want this to be a friendship. Until I'm ready for – for – whatever,' she finished, looking down.

'Okay. But there's something I want *you* to understand.' He had lowered his voice, and she looked quickly at him. 'I want you to understand' – he looked intently into her eyes – 'that I love you, that I haven't felt this way about anyone for – a long time. I wanted to tell you that. I'll do anything you say, play it any way you like. But you talked about being made love to, and that is something I want to do to you more than anything else in the world.' His voice was very quiet.

She looked away, watching the German climb dripping from the pool, sunlit drops of water showering the warm tiles by the steps, light glancing off the choppy water where he had emerged. 'So, you see, this mustn't just be a game. Please.'

She did not know what to say. The earnestness in his voice moved her, worried her. Was she playing games with him? She looked back at him, at the serious brown eyes, the anxious, gentle mouth, the way his long fingers were stroking

126

the cold glass, at the lean frame beneath the thinness of his shirt, the slight sweat stains where it touched his body. Does he turn you on? That was what Dr Michaels had asked Rachel. Of course he does, she told herself. He must do. I want him to. Only not just yet.

'It's not a game,' she said quietly.

He could think of nothing to say. I've told her now, he thought. I've said it all, and now I must wait like some hopeless swain until she bestows her favours. It struck him as rather quaint. He had never been in such a situation before. What did one say or do next? He sat back and glanced at the pool. He should let it go. Let it all go and see how things went when they got back to London. 'I feel like a swim,' he said.

Chapter eleven

Far away in London, a raw and chilly wind blustered through the courtyards and alleyways of the Temple, sending drifts of dead leaves from the garden of the Master's House into Inner Temple churchyard, forcing its way into the collars of clerks hurrying through Serjeant's Inn and Hare Court. As the early dusk crept over the grey buildings and ancient stairways, lights shone in barristers' rooms upon rows of briefs and humming computers, on high bookcases, on piles of documents, on polished tables and polished minds. In the murmuring courtrooms, judges listened and counsel soliloquised, clerks dozed and ushers yawned, witnesses fidgeted and juries daydreamed. Throughout the long winter afternoon the law and its agents toiled away endlessly, sifting and burrowing, piling up words and paper that would all be forgotten a century hence, while the world beyond the Temple and the law courts hurried on regardless.

Leo, leaning back in his chair, was yawning his way through a discussion with Michael Gibbon concerning the amendment of a writ.

'I just don't think Order Twenty can possibly cover it,' he remarked, folding his arms behind his head. 'Not only have they got the plaintiff's name wrong, they've got the country of incorporation and the place of business wrong, too. That takes it outside the slip rule, as far as I'm concerned.'

Michael leaned his thin frame on a low table and pursed his lips. 'I don't see that. Anyway, since it was a genuine mistake, and since they amended it before the writ was even served, I don't see how you can say that your people were misled.'

Leo smiled. 'Well, we shall see. I have to say I think it most unlikely that Borchard will strike out the amendment, but I have to give it a go. In all conscience.'

'Oh, yes,' Michael smilingly agreed. He glanced at his watch. Six fifteen. 'Shall we?'

At that moment Leo's phone rang, and he tipped his chair forward to answer it. 'Oh, hello, Frank. Yes, that's fine with me. Give me half an hour, would you? No, I'll come to White's. I don't see why not . . . Yes. Goodbye.' He put the phone down and glanced up at Michael, who was hovering hopefully. 'Sorry, can't do it. Frank Chamberlin has been wanting to have a word with me, and he's free this evening. Can't let the great and the good down.'

'No, I suppose not. Oh, well, another time.' And Michael went off to canvass support for a session in El Vino's among the younger members of chambers, while Leo cleared up the rest of his work and then took a taxi to St James's.

He found Sir Frank at his club, poring over the *Financial Times*. He looked up and over his spectacles as Leo greeted him. 'Ah, Leo! Hello. Just reading this piece about the ruling on stop-loss policies. That will ease the minds of a few names at Lloyd's, wouldn't you think?'

Leo settled himself into a chair and crossed his legs, smoothing a hand back over his silver hair. 'Depends upon one's policy, I'd say. I know more than one chap whose policy specifies that the money has to be paid into his premium trust fund, and not directly to him. Mind you, anyone at Lloyd's who doesn't have a stop-loss policy is a fool. It's just another damned casino, after all.'

Sir Frank nodded thoughtfully. 'Quite – well, yes, you're right, of course.' Then he brightened. 'What will you have to drink?'

Their drinks were ordered, and Sir Frank settled back in his chair, folding up his paper and tapping it nervously against one of his long legs. He was uncertain how to broach the subject which he wished to discuss with Leo. Leo, however, did it for him.

'I'm glad to get this chance to speak to you,' he said, drawing his chair a little closer to Sir Frank's. 'I've been meaning to talk to you for a few weeks.'

'Oh?'

'Yes. I – oh, yes, thank you.' He stopped as the

white-jacketed steward set his drink down on the table next to him, then waited until he had moved away. 'Yes, the fact is, I've put in my application for silk.'

'Oh. Ah. Yes. Have you? Very good.' Sir Frank frowned, then his face cleared, then he frowned again and looked at his drink.

Leo took a sip of his. 'I really just wanted to ask whether I could count on your support, all that sort of thing.'

'Oh, yes. Yes, yes, yes.' Sir Frank looked at Leo. 'I'd heard something of this from Bernard Lightfoot, actually. He mentioned it a little while ago.' He paused. 'Naturally, you have my support.'

'Thank you,' said Leo. There was a brief silence. Something's up, thought Leo, and a small, icy fear crept into his heart. Sir Frank's expressive face was alternately morose and anxious as he searched for words. Just as the silence had lengthened uncomfortably and Leo felt he should break it, Sir Frank began to speak.

'Leo,' he said, 'I feel I must be frank with you.' He paused and then smiled. 'Ha. "Frank" with you.' Leo smiled politely and shifted in his seat, then took another swallow of whisky, wondering what was coming. 'Yes, anyway,' went on Sir Frank, 'it's rather in connection with your application . . . I don't quite know how to – well, look, there are some things, Leo, which I feel – well, that I've always known about you.' His voice was low, and he glanced around to check that no other members were within earshot.

'Known about me?' said Leo.

'About your – ah – life. Your private life.' Sir Frank smiled, an encouraging but bashful smile. He really did like Leo, he did so want to help him.

Leo put his glass down slowly and looked at Sir Frank. He could not be mistaken. Frank could mean only one thing. Leo cleared his throat. 'I suspect I know what you are saying,' he replied, his voice casual. 'You mean that I – ah, as it were – have never married.'

'Yes, yes – as it were. Quite.' Sir Frank seized gratefully on this euphemism from the world of obituaries and nodded confidingly at Leo.

'And so forth,' added Leo, nodding in return. One didn't wish to embarrass poor old Frank unnecessarily.

'Indeed. And so forth.'

Leo took out one of his small cigars. 'Do you mind if I smoke?' he asked. Frank shook his head and watched as Leo lit his cigar. So far so good, he was thinking – but now that the subject was aired, albeit in a veiled way, how should he continue? Again Leo came to his rescue. 'I imagine, then, that it is less of a closely guarded secret than I had thought? My – way of life, I mean.'

Sir Frank pursed his lips and made a so-so movement with his head, his gaze straying to the carpet.

Leo blew out a little plume of smoke. He was testing his mind for a response to all this. It reminded him of situations in courtrooms where one's witness suddenly says something entirely unexpected. Collect your thoughts and consider. That was what one always did. He had not imagined that Frank – or anyone else, for that matter – knew anything of his private life. Just how much was known and how much was rumour? he wondered, tipping the ash reflectively from his cigar. Clearly he had been naive. It was such a little, little world that they lived in, after all. He smiled to himself, then looked up at Sir Frank.

'But Frank,' he said, his voice cool and thoughtful, 'you don't honestly believe that it is of any importance, the fact that I might be homosexual?' He felt that the situation now demanded a little clarity. He paused and thought of Sarah, of other women, of the various meaningless tarts who occasionally drifted into his dark and hedonistic life. They, of course, could be discounted. No point in using terms like 'bisexual' with Frank. It was the young men who mattered; they were the focus of all this. 'Do you?' He looked searchingly at Frank. He did not honestly believe that it could matter. A third of the bench were probably queer. Well, a bit lopsided. In this day and age, it could not matter, surely? But then, it was Frank's world, he knew the ways things went, the basis on which decisions were made. Leo drew on his cigar again, the fingers that held it tightening as he waited for Sir Frank to reply.

'Normally,' said Sir Frank slowly, 'I would say, no.'

'Normally?' Leo mused, nodded thoughtfully. Shuffle the papers a bit. Wait for the witness to say whatever he's got to say, even if you don't know what it might be.

'Well, you see, Leo, it was something Bernard Lightfoot said . . . ' He paused ruminatively. 'I take it you don't know the new Lord Chancellor?' He glanced at Leo.

Aha, thought Leo. 'No, I don't, as it happens.'

'No – well. He's a decent enough man, Steele, but I gather he's got something of a bee in his bonnet about – you know, this and that. There was all that fuss in Scotland, you remember, about queer advocates and blackmailing and all that sort of thing. I think it may have – um – prejudiced him in his views somewhat. I think he is anxious to avoid any similar sort of scandal – ah – anywhere else. I have spoken to others, and it seems Bernard may be right. There is prejudice to be feared from that quarter.' Sir Frank frowned and swallowed the remainder of his drink. 'So you see.'

'Are you serious?' asked Leo.

'Oh, quite. Yes, yes, quite.' He sighed. 'I'm afraid that his appointment may be something of a step back into the dark ages, so far as – as that kind of thing is concerned.'

So far as gay QCs are concerned, thought Leo.

'And you know,' added Sir Frank, 'that whereas it might not normally matter – your life away from your work, as it were – well, besides this Scottish business, in a situation where there is any kind of competition between applicants from the same set of chambers . . . However, you will appreciate that I can say no more – discretion, confidentiality, all that kind of thing . . . ' Sir Frank's voice murmured off into silence.

Leo crushed the stub of his cigar into the ashtray. Competition. That had to mean Stephen. He must have applied to take silk. Sir Frank was not going to say so outright, but that had to be the hint he was dropping. Leo put his fingers to his lips and gazed at the ceiling. So, when pitch comes to toss, he thought, the Lord Chancellor will give preference to Stephen. Stephen is safe, I am not. But this is all speculation, he reminded himself. It depends not on what Sir Frank knows, or Sir Bernard Lightfoot, come to that, but what the Lord Chancellor knows, or comes to know.

He regarded Sir Frank. 'I don't suppose,' he said, 'that you know anything about my file? My confidential file?'

'Oh, good heavens, no.' Sir Frank shook his head, scratching at a tuft of grey hair beside his ear and then nervously smoothing his hand over his bald pate. 'No, not a thing.'

'I was just wondering,' said Leo, 'whether it was necessarily a matter of common knowledge, the business of my private life.'

'Oh, ah, that I can't say. As for the file, that is quite another matter. But these things do get about, I'm afraid. I heard Bernard Lightfoot mention it to Sir Mungo, for instance.'

'Sir Mungo Stephenson?' Leo stared at Frank. If Sir Mungo knew, if Bernard Lightfoot knew, then there was little chance of the Lord Chancellor's Office not hearing about it. But why the hell should it matter? He felt angry at the bad luck and injustice of it. Bad luck that Stephen should have applied to take silk as well, and injustice in that the thing would probably never have mattered under the previous Lord Chancellor. Now he was to be the subject of some sort of witch hunt. He said as much, in terse tones, to Sir Frank.

'Oh, no. Oh, no, I wouldn't see it in that light, Leo. It's just that . . . well, anyway, I felt it better that you should know about this. Forewarned, and so forth.'

Why? Leo wondered. Why? There was nothing to be done about it. It just meant that the next few months were now poisoned – more than that, the next few years. The rest of his life. Oh, he could always apply next year, but the damage would have been done, the seeds sown. Short of a new Lord Chancellor with more enlightened views, there was little he could hope for. He suddenly felt as though all the brilliance of his career had been blighted by this one conversation. All that he had hoped and worked for – his practice, his success, then the natural progression to silk, to further success and greater esteem, then ultimately to the bench, to sit among the great and good – all this was finished. God, he had always wanted to belong – wanted it passionately. And now he must stop short, his career stunted. Leo Davies would gradually become that most pitiful of creatures, an ageing junior, inhabiting a static, twilight world, while others rose past and beyond him. He would continue, year after year, to watch the ascent of people half his age, perhaps eventually be led by them in cases. He clenched his fists upon his knees until the knuckles were white. And kind Sir Frank had brought him to a premature understanding of all this, through whatever misguided motives.

He looked candidly at Sir Frank, who had motioned to the steward to bring them each another drink. What was the point of all this? He would rather have remained in ignorance, enjoyed a few optimistic, untroubled months until Easter and the shock of disappointment.

'Well,' he said lightly, and, lifting a hand, he unclenched it and let it fall back into his lap. 'At least I know the worst. I must thank you for that.' His voice was cool and level.

'Oh, please!' exclaimed Sir Frank, leaning slightly forward in his chair, his eyes earnest. 'Don't think that I told you any of this simply to upset you. No, no!' He leaned back, watched as the steward set down their drinks and whisked their empty glasses away, then lifted his gaze and let it wander over the dark panelled room, the heavy curtains drawn against the dank November evening. He looked back at last to Leo. 'What I was wondering, Leo,' he said thoughtfully, 'was whether there might not be something one could do about all this.'

'Do?' echoed Leo. His heart felt heavy, injured, as he absorbed the full reality of what Frank had revealed to him. He was being excluded by narrow prejudice from the upper ranks of the profession which he had always striven to serve with every talent at his command; he was among the best, he knew. And yet, rather than be rewarded for it, advanced, he might be punished for leading a life which the Lord Chancellor thought could expose him and the profession to some nameless threat. The very institutions which upheld the rights of ordinary citizens to regulate their own sexual and private lives as they saw fit, without the fear of prejudice and harassment, were to turn on him and deny him that same equality. It was a bitter irony.

'Do?' he repeated. 'What is there to do? What can I possibly do?' He stared at his fresh drink, but did not pick it up.

134

'Well,' said Sir Frank tentatively, leaning forward again, 'you know, life is not all black and white, Leo. Not by any manner of means. You are a very personable young man.' Leo told himself that he did not feel very young at that moment; he felt grim and middle-aged and bitter. 'And, you know,' went on Sir Frank, 'the thing is not unheard of. I have a nephew – admittedly, the marriage did not last, but there . . . They had two children. Not the happiest of situations, I admit, but the thing can be done. I wondered if there was not a possibility . . . some arrangement? After all . . . ' Leo stared at him as he went on. 'I imagine any woman would appreciate the stability, the financial status which you could . . . It would scotch what is, after all, only a rumour. But if you were to – I mean, if you could find some suitable young woman . . . then I think that would put paid to it all. It would have to.' He glanced up at Leo. 'Wouldn't it?'

Leo had listened to this rambling, hesitant speech with mild amazement. He picked up his glass and took a drink. Then he set it down again, and regarded Sir Frank. When he spoke, it was almost with amusement. 'You're suggesting that I should marry?'

Sir Frank was disarmed by Leo's mocking half-smile. 'Yes, well, as I say, this nephew of mine knew he was queer and all that sort of thing when he got married – hoped it might cure him, or some such thing. Anyway . . . ' He scratched at his ear. 'Anyway, it's a drastic sort of notion, I admit, if one isn't too keen on women, and so forth . . .' His eyes met Leo's. 'But, dammit, you're a good-looking man, and I can't think why, when it would surely be a fairly easy thing to accomplish, your career has to be – to be messed up in this way!' He felt vexed, vexed at himself and at Leo and at Lord Steele of Strathbuchat, at the whole situation. 'If you got married – why, the whole issue simply wouldn't arise. It would all have to be dismissed as idle rumour.' He sat back, feeling he could say no more.

Leo slowly unbuttoned his jacket, uncrossed and recrossed his legs. 'Frank,' he said at last, not unkindly, 'I don't know if you realise how – how unlikely it is that such a thing might happen.' He smiled again at the thought of it.

'Then make it happen!' exclaimed Sir Frank with unexpected vehemence. 'Good God, man, we're talking about your career here! Your entire future, everything you have worked for, everything you deserve! Don't imagine if the Lord Chancellor turns you down this year, that there will be other chances for you. I know these men. I know the way prejudice reinforces itself, year after year, like concrete hardening! This is a tight, narrow world we work in, Leo. You will have to watch your chances slip away from you, one after the other, if you don't take the opportunity to change things. I *know* you, Leo. I know you and I like you and I want to see you get on. I want to see all able people get on.' He stopped, his eloquence spent, his vehemence draining away at the sight of Leo's sad, quiet smile.

Leo gazed at the carpet for a moment, then lifted his head. 'Frank, I thank you for your thoughtfulness – and, well, for thinking so much about it all, about me. For wanting to help. But I think I just have to take my chance. If what you say is true – well, there it is. But, for a variety of reasons, I don't think the solution you suggest is – well, feasible.'

Sir Frank nodded sadly. 'Yes, well, it was just an idea.' He sighed. There was a pause as Leo rose, buttoning his jacket. 'Won't you stay for another?'

'That's kind of you, Frank, but there are a few things I must attend to. You know.' He simply wanted to get away, to think about all this, to see if Frank was right, if attitudes and understandings were as he had said.

Sir Frank nodded. Both men felt slightly awkward as they said goodnight, and Leo left Sir Frank to ruminate alone.

Leo went out into St James's Street and stood for a moment, the cold air enveloping him.

'Shall I call a cab for you, sir?' asked the doorman. Leo considered a moment; he had left his overcoat in chambers, but he wanted to walk and think. He shook his head and set off towards Piccadilly, then across into Berkeley Street and up to the square. As he walked, he went over in his mind everything Frank had told him. He did not doubt for a moment what Frank had said about Lord Steele; he was already known to be a hardliner. If Bernard Lightfoot had got wind of the fact that this new Lord Chancellor feared a homosexual cabal at the Bar, then there must be something in it. How ludicrous! It wasn't even as though he could lay his hand on his heart and say he was well and truly homosexual. That was the irony. But that was the part of his nature which could finish him.

Leo stopped and leaned against the railings of Berkeley Square, feeling the freezing air penetrating to his bones, the slight, raw wind lifting strands of his grey hair. He thought again of the discreet canvassing he had done over the past few weeks. Not once had anyone betrayed a hint of any knowledge . . . Michael Winstanley had been quite confident, anticipating the thing as a *fait accompli*. Sir Bernard Lightfoot, when the thing had come up casually at that benchers' cocktail party, had murmured that it was an excellent thing, every success, my full support, and so forth. But Frank had said that Bernard had told Sir Mungo Stephenson the rumours about Leo. That either meant that Bernard dissembled very easily, or that he was not aware of the Lord Chancellor's views.

He pushed himself away from the railings, confused. Sir Mungo – well, he hadn't spoken to Sir Mungo yet, and would now take care not to. Either Sir Mungo would take the Lord Chancellor's line or he wouldn't. That went for more or less the entire Commercial bench. Much would depend upon what had been said, how much was mere rumour, or whether someone had got hold of something more concrete about Leo's private affairs. Yes, that was what it came down to. How much was known, and how much believed. Yet he had no way of knowing what information was in circulation, or how damaging it might be. As he made his way slowly along Hill Street towards his mews house, Leo recalled the hour he had spent with Roger Ware. There had been, he now told himself, a certain watchfulness in Roger's glance as they talked. The more he considered it and their conversation, the more convinced he became. Roger must know. He must have heard the rumours, and that must have been why he was so guarded. Leo had noticed it at the time.

He walked along the cobbled mews to his house, then paused as he put the key in the lock. How had the rumour got around? How had anyone come to know? Perhaps he was deceiving himself. Perhaps it had been known for years. But he was sure it had not. He was sure he had been the model of discretion over the years. Except in the case of Anthony. Anthony . . . He wondered for the briefest of moments, as he stepped into the darkness of his hallway, whether Anthony . . . But he dismissed the thought almost immediately. Of course he could not be the source.

You have been a fool, Leo, he told himself, as he snapped on the lights and went into the kitchen. A fool to think that anyone could live as you do without others coming to hear of it. Who knew how information, little snatches of gossip and conjecture, came to be blown upon the air? He sighed and rubbed his hands across his face. How appallingly naive he had been. As he stood in the middle of his kitchen, Leo felt quite powerless, and knew himself and his fate to be directed by forces that were now utterly beyond his control.

Chapter twelve

Anthony woke from a deep, unbroken sleep. The edges of the heavy curtains were rimmed with white light, and he suddenly remembered where he was. He got quickly out of bed and pulled back the curtains. The window opened on to a little marble balcony and he stepped out, marvelling at the gentle freshness of the heat reflected from the white walls of the hotel. He looked down at the sparkling blue water of the pool, still and unbroken, and traced the little flashing, darting movements of the birds in the tall palm trees.

It should have been perfection, he knew, to be in such a place when one was in love. But there was nothing tangible in his love, no reassurance he could seek. Only uncertainty, imponderability. He must simply let time take care of it, he told himself, and went to dress.

After breakfast, Rachel and Anthony were met in the lobby by Mr Gillespie, the surveyor, who was to go out to the ship with them. He was a rangy Scot with wispy reddish hair, wearing a blue linen suit already stained with sweat. They travelled together in an Ambassador car to the docks, Anthony and Rachel in the back, and Mr Gillespie towering beside the driver, who rattled and honked his car at terrific speed through the streets, while a little ivory statue of Ganesh, the elephant god, swayed on top of the dashboard.

The scene at the docks was one of frantic clamour. Brown-skinned workmen swarmed everywhere, hauling sacks, tallying containers, heaving at water pipes to replenish the ships' tanks, all shouting orders to each other at once. The air was filled with the rank smell of rotting vegetation and fruit, mingling with the odour of gasoline. Trucks careered slowly among the workers, their battered cabs gaudily painted and hung with strange, faded garlands of flowers, and tubby, sweating officials from the various shipping lines would emerge with clipboards fluttering with wads of paper, to holler and direct matters. Rachel could not imagine how anything ever got done in anything like an organised manner. She said as much to Mr Gillespie.

'Oh, they're organised, after a fashion,' he said, as he jostled his way through the crowd of chattering dockers, holding his briefcase aloft, his face red and perspiring. 'It's just that they take a good deal longer to get things done. They love bureaucracy, the Indians – love nothing better than a load of official paperwork, everything in triplicate, stamped and signed. You might say it's our legacy to them, from the days of the Empire.'

They reached the place where the *Valeo Dawn* was docked and, after a good deal of official haggling and gesticulation between Mr Gillespie and a harbour official, were allowed to board and shown by a crewman to the master's cabin.

The master, Captain Craddock, was a weary, resigned man from Tynemouth who, along with his crew, had just about had enough of hanging around in Bombay waiting for things to be done that never got done, and was longing daily for repairs to be finished so that they could get away.

He greeted his three visitors civilly, but eyed Rachel's white cotton sleeveless dress unenthusiastically. 'I think you might need something a bit more practical for the engine room,' he remarked, 'unless, of course, you'd rather just wait here in my cabin.' He did not entirely approve of women on board his ship, and felt that this one, with her striking face and slender figure, might not exactly be good for his Greek crew.

'No,' said Rachel, 'I'll go down with Mr Cross and Mr Gillespie. I'm not particularly bothered about my dress getting a little dirty.'

'That wasn't quite what I was thinking about,' said Captain Craddock. 'I'll get someone to find a pair of overalls for you.'

Overalls were duly found, and the master, Mr Gillespie and Anthony all waited outside the cabin while Rachel changed. She emerged encased in voluminous canvas overalls which must have belonged to a seaman of considerable dimensions. Anthony smiled broadly, and Rachel, a little pink, lifted her chin and followed the men to the engine room. How can anyone manage to look sexy and beautiful even in those? wondered Anthony, as he watched her descend the first staircase down to the bowels of the ship.

They climbed down, deeper and deeper, through clanging metal walkways and along gantries, until at last they reached the engine room.

'Right,' said Captain Craddock, 'here we are on the bottom platform. There's the engine control room, and along here' – he walked along and the others followed – 'is the number two generator, which is where the fire started.'

They gazed around the vast metallic vault, at the massive piping, the gauges, dials, levers, lengths of blackened cable, and finally at the generator itself. Its shell was encrusted with the flaking, silvery debris of a burnt-out fire, and the smell of burnt fuel oil still hung in the close air. Rachel felt stifled.

'The engine control room was where my men were killed,' said Captain Craddock. 'They died of smoke inhalation. The fire crew tried to rescue them a few times with BA, but the heat and the smoke in the engine room made it impossible. The air in their BA kept running out before they could reach them.'

Mr Gillespie knelt down and began his slow and careful inspection of the generator and its valves, pausing to take notes with difficulty in his squatting position, the sweat trickling down his beef-red neck and into the soaked collar of his shirt. Rachel and Anthony followed his discussions with the master as he went on to examine the smoke-blackened banks of insulation cables and shell plating, but after half an hour or so of listening attentively to what was being said, the conversation became so technically involved that Rachel and Anthony could follow none of it.

They walked back along the clanking metal corridor to the engine room. A couple of crewmen watched them impassively. Even in that rig-out, thought Anthony, they can't take their eyes off her. He felt possessive, wanting in some way, by word or gesture, to assert control over her. But she walked ahead of him, heedless and detached, utterly remote.

They looked around the control room in silence, gazing at the sooty walls, the blackened dials and equipment, at the pathos of the plastic seating burnt off a chair, the charred papers lying on a desk. The temperature of the fire had been so great that the bulb of an alcohol-filled thermometer on the control panel had burst. Separately, they imagined the horror of the choking, airless deaths of the seamen entombed in that place.

When they went back along the corridor, they found Mr Gillespie busily taking photographs of the generator and the surrounding equipment.

'See here,' he said to Anthony and Rachel, pulling a finished roll of film from his camera. They bent over as he pointed to an innocuous-looking stub of metal with a nut at one end rising from the oily, blackened shell. 'That's one of the lube-oil filters. There was a socket spanner attached to the release nut of the aft filter' – he shifted and pointed further over – 'which means the oil flow was through the outboard filters. In number four generator the inner pair would have been in use. My guess is that the oiler, when he was cleaning the oil filters, released the nut holding down the top of the outboard filter, but forgot to change the oil flow to the inboard filters.'

'Which would mean,' said Rachel, 'that when he released the top of the filter, there would be quite some pressure on it.'

'That's right,' said Mr Gillespie, and both he and the master glanced at her in surprise. 'About thirty pounds per square inch, possibly more. Result – the rubber sealing gasket was pushed from its seat and you got this massive spray of oil. The oil filters are immediately below the auxiliary engine's exhaust system, and the surface of that would be in excess of three hundred degrees centigrade.'

'And since the flashpoint of lube-oil is something between a hundred and fifty and two hundred and thirty degrees,' said Rachel, 'it would ignite on the hot surface.'

Mr Gillespie nodded. 'Lube-oil is a bitch when it burns. Produces all this dense black smoke. Cable insulation will do the same. It would have taken less than a minute before the engine room and control room were choked with it.'

'That looks pretty conclusive,' said Anthony, running a finger along the grimy surface of the oil filter. Such a little mistake, he thought, such an easy thing to forget, changing the flow before turning that spanner. Poor guy. He sighed.

'You think we can pretty well rule out any defect in the system?' he asked Mr Gillespie.

'I've checked everything thoroughly, twice. No defects. This has to be the answer. Human error, pure and simple.'

'Well, that should cheer Mr Nikolaos up,' said Anthony to Rachel. She stared at the little stub of metal and said nothing.

The four of them made their way up and along the clanging gantries, out of the engine room and back to the upper reaches of the ship.

'Well, I'll have my report ready in a couple of weeks or so,' said Mr Gillespie, 'plus the photos. I have to drop in at one of the agents' offices, so I'll say goodbye here.'

They shook hands with Mr Gillespie and he left. Rachel and Anthony stayed and had lunch with Captain Craddock, which was a strangely formal affair in his rather cramped quarters, with a couple of silent crewmen, spruced-up, helping every-one to cold ham and smoked cheese and bread and beer.

When lunch was over, Rachel said, 'I think I'd better get down to taking your statement now, Captain Craddock. We only have this afternoon, as Mr Cross and I leave tomorrow. I'd also like to see the fourth engineer and the first mate, if I may.'

'I'll be getting back to the hotel, then,' said Anthony, and he left the master and Rachel to their business. He sauntered along the quayside towards the customs sheds, away from where their car was waiting, and watched a ferry taking on passengers for a trip down the coast. The decks teemed with people, and as the ferry hooted its departure, it listed heavily to one side with the sudden rush of passengers waving to relatives. At last the mooring ropes were untied and the vessel throbbed away. Anthony watched its progress across the harbour, out into the heat haze that lay like a shroud across the Arabian Sea, blurring the horizon, so that the tankers which lay at anchor far out in the bay, awaiting their berth, looked like the dim ghosts of ships.

Anthony was suddenly seized by the wish that he could stay here, that he and Rachel could take a boat far down the coast, away from everything, to some place where they could just be together and where everything would come right. At that

143

moment, in the heat and bustle of the Bombay docks, he felt that he didn't care if he never saw London again, or the cold old stones of the Inns of Court, or the grimy grey splendour of the law courts, or that toiling world of briefs and opinions and fees and judges, just so long as he could stay with Rachel in this warm, strange haven. I want her to myself, he thought. I want to be with her away from all of that, from all the people we know. Then everything would work. As it was, he felt as though he were emotionally suspended in mid-air, waiting for some signal, some clue as to what came next.

Sadly he turned away from the docks and made his way back to the waiting car, and to the hotel. There he swam and read until late afternoon, watching the shadows lengthen on the lawn around the pool, waiting impatiently for Rachel to return. Time seemed to drag without her, and he was conscious of drinking one large gin and tonic too many to beguile the time. A whole hour passed between five and six, in which he reread page 103 of *The Old Devils* several times, unable to concentrate for thoughts of her, expecting every time he looked up to see her coming towards him in the late sunshine.

When the sun had begun to go down, he left the poolside and went back into the hotel. He stopped at reception, but Rachel's room key was still in its pigeonhole. He scribbled a note telling her he was in the coffee bar, and left it for her. He ate alone and tried to read, then to study the other people in the coffee bar, and finally he ordered a beer.

When it was seven thirty and she had still not appeared, he went back up to his room. The beer on top of the gin had been a mistake, he realised. He flung himself on to the bed and closed his eyes, and within five minutes he was asleep.

When he woke to a tapping at his door, it was dark. 'Yes?' he murmured. 'Rachel?' He felt groggy. The door opened, and Rachel came in. He could see the glow of her white dress in the dimness of the room. He rolled over and lay on his back.

'What time is it?' he asked. His head felt muzzy and his limbs heavy.

'It's eight thirty. I'm sorry. It all took longer than I thought. Have you eaten?'

He nodded. Then he closed his eyes and laid a hand over them. He did not feel well. She sat down next to him on the bed, and he opened his eyes and looked up at her.

'I'm sorry,' he muttered. 'I really feel terrible. I think I sat too long in the sun. And I drank too much. Waiting for you.'

'Don't worry. Go back to sleep. We have an early flight, anyway. I'll get something from room service.'

'Don't eat the local fish,' he said, and smiled. He lay looking up at her, imagining how it would be if she bent to kiss him, how her soft hair would swing forward, how her mouth would feel. Remember what she said, he thought.

'Rachel?' he murmured.

'Yes?' He looked like a child lying there, she thought, fuzzy from sleep, his features barely discernible in the dark room.

'Will you lie down next to me?'

It was a simple request. She looked at him for a long moment. Of course you can do this, she told herself. Why not? He can't have forgotten what was said yesterday. There is no harm.

She swung her legs up and lay down hesitantly, a little way away from him. He turned slightly to face her, looked at her for a few seconds, then closed his eyes. She lay next to him in the gloom for a while – she did not know how long – watching his sleeping face. If she could stay there throughout the night, she thought, next to him, perhaps she would feel safer and safer. But when he woke and found her still there, there would be no safety. She inched herself off the bed and stood looking down at him for a moment, then went quietly to her own room.

They met next morning in the lobby at five. Bills were paid, their bags loaded into the taxi, tips handed out, and the long ride back to the airport began. They spoke little on the way there.

'My grandfather had a Morris Oxford,' Anthony remarked at one point. He still didn't feel too good. The aspirin he'd taken didn't seem to have begun to work. Later on he said, yawning, 'That was a long way to come just to look at an oil filter. At least you had some real work to do.'

Rachel just smiled and said, 'It'll keep Mr Nikolaos happy.

He likes his lawyers to have a hands-on approach.'

'Oh, is that what it is?' replied Anthony.

The first streaks of dawn had touched the sky as they set off from the hotel, and by the time they reached the airport day had broken and the air was freshly warm and humid. After they had checked in, Anthony went back outside to savour the heat and colour of the Bombay day for the last time, even though the vista was only an unappealing stretch of road, a low concrete wall and a far-off drift of dusty trees. To him it was still magical.

'It was good,' he said to Rachel on the flight back. 'Only a day or so, but it was still good.'

'You'll go back there some day, won't you?' she asked.

'God, yes. I'd really like to.' He fingered the book lying in his lap. 'Would you come with me?'

'I don't know,' she answered. 'Please don't say things like that. I don't want to – to disappoint you. Please let's just be friends for now.'

'Only for now,' he replied, still looking at her. She felt a little cold at his words, at his look. That was what she had said, wasn't it? It had been like some kind of promise, something she would have to fulfil sooner or later. That was how he saw it, at any rate. A little of the old apprehension touched her. 'Anyway,' he continued lightly, 'strictly as a friend, will you come with me to this thing at the Guildhall tomorrow night?'

'What thing?' she asked, glad he had changed the subject.

'It's some enormous bash that Sinclair's are holding to celebrate their jubilee. Just champagne and speeches and free food. Half the City will be there.'

'Won't I be regarded as a member of the opposition, coming from a rival firm?'

'I doubt it. I'll bet you find your senior partner's going.'

'All right,' she said, and smiled. 'I'll go with you.'

'Good. I'll pick you up from work.'

It was left at that. Just a friendly invitation to a City do. But the more I go on seeing him, she thought, the more time goes by, the more he will expect . . . The thought made her panicky. But that is what I said, didn't I? Give me time. How much time? She thought of what he had said as he looked at

146

her. Only for now. And then – what then? It will all work itself out, she told herself. But she did not sleep at all during the flight, and by the time they got to London she felt tired, tired and cold.

Chapter thirteen

They shared a cab all the way back to West London, both too weary to face the struggle of the tube.

'See you tomorrow,' called Anthony from the taxi as she got out. 'Between six thirty and seven.'

She raised her hand in acknowledgment as the taxi pulled away.

Her flat seemed very warm and peaceful after her long journey. She dumped her bag in the hall, kicked off her shoes, and went into the bathroom to splash her face with cold water. She glanced at her reflection in the mirror; it was white and strained. Sleep, she thought, oh, God, sleep. She padded through to her bedroom, drew her curtains against the cold, grey November morning, undressed to her underwear and slid gratefully beneath the duvet.

But sleep was not easy; brittle, jarring thoughts kept rising to the surface of her mind, in which aeroplane engines still throbbed and hummed. The skin of her hands and face felt taut and dried out. When at last she slept, she dreamed that Anthony was lying next to her, and she woke with a shivering start, every muscle of her body tense, ready to scramble away.

She switched on the radio and dozed a little to Radio 3, but she could not sleep properly. When the eleven o'clock news came on, she felt so out of joint, lying in bed at such an hour, conscious of the day outside, that she rose and had a bath. As she lay in the soothing hot water, staring at the taps, trying to assemble disparate thoughts in her mind, she was aware that her eyes felt hot and gritty. I'm too tired to sleep, she thought. I might as well go into work.

She left her car at home and took the tube. Somehow, travelling outside the rush hour made her feel even more disorientated, among the little knots of foreign students and tourists. The pace of everything seemed all wrong. The feeling was heightened when she reached Nichols & Co at the beginning of the lunch hour. The second floor had a stranded air; a couple of the typists were eating sandwiches at their word processors, their eyes fastened on their magazines, and the chairs of the others stood empty; the offices of her fellow partners were silent and deserted. Somewhere a phone rang unanswered, then stopped.

Rachel made herself some coffee and went into her room. I must make a start on that letter of credit case, she thought, but her mind wilted at the prospect. Anything, she told herself, pulling the papers from the file, to stop the dragging, accusing thoughts that plagued her. Dr Michaels had been wrong. It would not just be a question of time. She had seen that; seen it the moment that Anthony had picked up on the promise which lay, implicit, in her words. So what do I do now? she wondered, as she began to separate the correspondence from the rest of the documents. Where do we go from here? Oh, this is ridiculous, she thought – I said, give me time, and I'm not even prepared to give the thing two days. Because I know. I know. There is not time enough in all eternity for things to get better.

Suddenly, unbidden and unexpected, tears welled up. She watched them spill on to the documents that lay before her, feeling her body shake uncontrollably with sobs.

Come on! This won't do! she told herself angrily. It's just jet lag, pressure of work. She wiped away her tears with the back of her hand, rummaging in the pocket of her jacket for a tissue. I do so want to be whole, she thought, snuffling into the tissue; I do so want to find some peace, be able to give myself to someone. And if Anthony cannot be the one, then there can't be anyone. Anyone. What would Dr Michaels say to all this self-pity? She would say, don't force these issues, don't think ahead. Just let things occur, moment by moment. That is right, she told herself, sniffing and ramming her tissue back into her pocket. She took a deep breath, pushed her black hair back from her face with trembling hands, and began in earnest to read Mr Lai Kew's letter of 2 April 1986 to Bank Negra, Indonesia, concerning the opening of a transferrable irrevocable sight letter of credit, as payment for 5,000 tonnes of crude palm-oil in bulk.

Felicity was not expecting Rachel to come into the office that day, and had taken the opportunity to extend her lunch hour in celebration of Nora's thirty-third birthday at the King's Head. She returned to the office at two thirty, four vodka and tonics (one of them large) the worse for wear, and gave an apprehensive grimace when she saw Rachel hunched over some papers in her office. Crumbs, she thought, I'd better get those *Valeo Trader* charts photocopied. Felicity's natural difficulties with machines were not helped by her condition, nor by the sardonic and flirtatious attentions of the new office boy, who, although only seventeen, rather fancied his chances with Felicity. But Rachel was too tired and depressed to notice that Felicity had copied all the charts at the wrong size. Or if she did, she didn't care. Felicity, as she laid the copies on Rachel's desk before popping off to the loo for a quick fag, thought that Rachel didn't look her usual self, but said nothing. She wasn't confident of being tremendously coherent, anyway.

By the time five thirty arrived, however, Felicity was feeling a good deal less tipsy, and her concern at Rachel's depressed and withdrawn appearance returned. She went into Rachel's room.

'If you don't mind my saying so, Rachel, you oughtn't to have come in today. You look like you could do with a good, long sleep.'

Rachel raised her tired eyes to Felicity's pretty, anxious face and tried to smile. 'I've tried that. I never was much good at air travel. Probably best for me to keep going until it's my usual bedtime.' Something in Felicity's worried, kindly expression made Rachel feel suddenly frail, longing for confidences, for comfort. 'I've got things on my mind, too. Just worries, you know. Stupid preoccupations that won't leave me alone,' she added, then abruptly returned her gaze to her papers.

Felicity regarded her thoughtfully for a moment. 'What you need,' she said, 'is to be taken out of yourself for a bit.'

Rachel smiled and looked back up. 'I've always wondered what that expression meant, exactly.'

'Look, Mr Rothwell's secretary, Isobel, is having a do in City

Limits this evening. She's off on maternity leave. Why don't you come and have a glass of wine or two, cheer yourself up?'

Rachel hesitated. The prospect of going back to her empty flat, back to her usual routine – routine which struck her forcefully, at that moment, as sterile and sad – had been looming before her all afternoon. It would only mean more thinking, more screwing up her mind, more useless introspection. Anything but that.

Seeing her hesitation, Felicity stepped over to Rachel's desk and took the pen she was holding gently from her fingers. Then she flipped closed the file of correspondence. 'Come on. You work too hard. You can't just go shooting off to India and back again and then bury yourself in work. I'm taking you for a drink.'

Rachel sighed and then smiled. 'You're right,' she said and stood up, fetching her coat from the peg on the back of the door.

In the crowded wine bar, gossiping and chatting with the other women from Nichols & Co, Rachel was glad that Felicity had suggested this. After the first two glasses of wine, the edges of anxiety melted away and her preoccupations were forgotten. Her glass was refilled several times without her really noticing.

Then Roger Williams, who had been drinking with friends at the other end of the wine bar, sauntered over, smirking.

'Girls' night out, eh?' he said, his gaze warm and intrusive as he ran his eyes over Rachel. 'Just let us boys know if you want any company, all right?'

'Drop dead, Roger,' replied Rachel, and took another swig of her wine.

The remark was made in a smiling, offhand manner, but that the cool and lovely Rachel should speak to him in so dismissive a fashion galled Roger. She was only twenty-seven, after all, and he was her senior in the firm. He felt he should be permitted the odd sexual innuendo towards the female juniors; it was what power and the pecking order existed for.

'You should be careful who you're seen drinking with, Rachel,' he replied unpleasantly, glancing at Felicity. 'People might get the wrong idea about you.' And he headed for the

Gents before either girl could say anything.

But Felicity merely broke into a splutter of laughter. 'He really fancies you, you know! He didn't much like being told to drop dead.' She took an appreciative drink.

'If he fancies anyone, it's himself,' remarked Rachel. Suddenly she realised that she must have drunk more than she had intended to. She put down her glass. 'I think I'd best be going,' she said.

'I'll come with you,' said Felicity, getting their coats. She glanced at Rachel, whose eyes were very brilliant from the wine; two faint spots of colour stood on her cheeks and her dark hair fell across her face. She pushed it back with one hand as she took her coat from Felicity, murmuring, 'Thanks.' I wish I looked that good getting pissed, thought Felicity.

Outside, they stood together on the cold pavement. Rachel shivered inside her coat. 'Maybe I should be getting home,' she said doubtfully; she didn't feel like going home. She wanted to escape somewhere, anywhere.

'No way,' said Felicity, taking her elbow. 'We've only just started! Come on!' And they trotted together down to the traffic lights and hailed a cab.

'Where are we going?' asked Rachel, as Felicity leaned forward to give some instructions to the driver, then settled back in her seat. It was wonderful to surrender the evening to someone, let them take your life over for a few hours. She felt distinctly drunk, and she didn't care.

'Just somewhere,' replied Felicity mysteriously. They gossiped throughout the journey, dissecting the various personalities in the office, Rachel picking up fascinating scraps of history and little-known information about certain of her fellow partners which she felt sure would horrify them to hear repeated. All this was probably very indiscreet and unprofessional, Rachel supposed, talking to one's secretary like this, but she didn't care. She liked Felicity, she liked feeling a little drunk and out of control for a change. It helped her not to have to think about things.

The cab took them all the way to Brixton and stopped outside a shabby, brightly lit café.

'I'll get this,' said Rachel, eyeing the meter. She knew she could afford it, and that Felicity probably couldn't.

'I'm buying dinner, then,' said Felicity. She led Rachel into the café, a steamy, snug place with a scattering of chairs and tables and a handful of customers, mostly black, sitting around, some talking, some reading over their food. Felicity and Rachel sat at a corner table. The chairs were rickety and the walls splashed with posters for plays and concerts and local events, all of them West Indian. Sounds of Yellow Man came from a speaker somewhere.

'There's the menu,' said Felicity, pointing to a blackboard above the counter, where a large West Indian woman was calling orders into the back kitchen. 'I'm having the brown chicken and rice and peas. It's really good.'

'What kind of food is it?' asked Rachel, gazing around. She had never been in a place like it before, never smelled smells such as the spicy, exotic, faintly sweet aromas emanating from the kitchen.

'Caribbean. It's brilliant and it's really cheap. Sandy and I come here a lot.'

Rachel decided that goat curry didn't sound too promising, and she didn't know what callaloo or ackee were. 'I'll have what you're having,' she said to Felicity. 'Who's Sandy?' she asked, after they had given their order.

'My brother,' said Felicity. She paused. 'Did you think he was my bloke?'

'I thought he might be.'

Felicity looked morose. 'I haven't got one at the moment. Want a fag?' She offered Rachel her packet of Silk Cut Mild. Rachel shook her head. 'Anyway,' went on Felicity, lighting her cigarette, 'I did have one until not long ago. Vince. But he went back to his old girlfriend.' And she told Rachel all about Vince and how lovely he had been, and some of the good times they'd had together. 'I mean, we hadn't been together long, like, and it was nothing really heavy or anything, but I did – well, I did think it was a bit special. You know.' She blew out some smoke, glancing past Rachel's head at a poster for the Brixton Academy. How soothing it was, thought Rachel, just to lean back and listen to someone else's problems, everyday problems, women's-page problems, blokes leaving you, heartache, lonely nights. 'Thing is,' went on Felicity, 'he's a mate of my brother's, and I keep thinking, like, that I'll see him around. That we could get back together. Know what I mean?' There was a pause. 'Daft, really, I suppose.'

'Maybe you'll meet someone else,' suggested Rachel.

'Oh, yeah. Plenty of blokes around,' replied Felicity lightly, leaning back and tipping the ash from her cigarette into the little foil dish that served as an ashtray. 'No problem there. It's just,' she smiled ruefully at Rachel, 'that I don't want anyone but Vince. You know how it is.'

Do I? thought Rachel. Oh, how wrong you are. I just wish there was someone, anyone, that I wanted the way you want your Vince. 'All you need is a little time,' she told Felicity. And there's another lie, she thought. One that I keep telling.

'Yeah, well,' murmured Felicity, unconvinced.

Their food arrived, steaming and appetising. Rachel found it surprisingly good, and said so.

'Great, isn't it?' agreed Felicity. 'Want a beer?'

'Do they sell beer?' asked Rachel, glancing around. It didn't look like the kind of place to have a liquor licence.

'Not exactly,' replied Felicity. Then she turned to the large West Indian woman at the counter. 'Leila?'

'What you want, mi darlin'?' called Leila, counting change into the till.

'Any chance of a beer?'

'Jes' you wait, now,' replied Leila and vanished into the kitchen. She returned with two bottles and glasses and set them down. 'Straight from mi own fridge, nah,' she said with a smile. 'I don' sell this. Mi hospitality.' And she went off chuckling.

'It's true,' said Felicity, grinning at Rachel. 'She doesn't sell them. She keeps them in her own fridge upstairs and gives them away. Just tops up the cost of the meal, that's all.'

The beer was warm and strong, and gave another little lift to Rachel's mood. She had needed the food, she realised. She felt warm and expansive, and watched, sipping her beer, as Felicity went over to speak to Leila.

'Benjy in?' she asked. Leila nodded, wiping the counter with a cloth and not looking at Felicity. 'Can I go up?'

'You can, darlin'. Only I never see you.'

Felicity disappeared into the kitchen and came back a few moments later.

'What was that all about?' asked Rachel as Felicity sat down, slipping a glance at Leila as she did so.

'Oh, just a little something to round off a good evening,' said Felicity, and gave Rachel a wide-eyed, guileless look.

After they left the café, Rachel allowed herself to be taken to Felicity's local. There she had two gin and tonics, and then decided she'd better not have any more. She was already feeling extremely heady, losing all sense of her customary fastidiousness in her new surroundings, closing her eyes to the music, opening them to smile around at the chattering, clinking pub. What an easy, untroubled life Felicity has, she thought. Even her problems are easy.

'Oh, my God!' uttered Felicity suddenly, and dropped her glance to the table.

'What?' said Rachel.

'It's Vince,' said Felicity, casting little sideways glances up from the table without moving her head.

Rachel looked up with interest at the man approaching their table. She could see, she supposed, why Felicity was stuck on him. He was big and cheerful-looking and very attractive, in an unkempt way. He stood over their table for a moment, looking down at the top of Felicity's curly head. She was staring into her drink, her mouth pursed tight.

''allo, Fliss,' he said tentatively.

'Hello,' she replied, then sat back and regarded him coolly.

Vince looked at Rachel, then shifted uneasily, glancing back to Felicity.

'This is my friend, Rachel,' said Felicity. 'We're just having a quiet drink together.' Her voice was pinched.

'Yeah, yeah, I can see that. 'allo, Rachel.' He nodded at her, then looked back at Felicity. 'I just wanted a word, sort of.'

'Well, "a word, sort of" will have to wait,' replied Felicity. Rachel laid a hand on her arm.

'No, look,' said Rachel, 'I have to be going, anyway –'

'No,' said Felicity, 'we haven't finished our natter. You want to see me,' she said, addressing Vince, 'you can come

155

round later.'

Vince hesitated for a moment, then nodded. He moved off without another word, shooting Rachel an interested glance as he went.

'There. You see?' said Rachel, delighted for Felicity. 'He wants to see you.'

'Yeah, well. He wants a lot of things, doesn't he? It could be anything. Doesn't mean anything.' But her heart was thudding. He did want to see her, talk to her. It must mean something. But she was out having a good time with her boss, and he would just have to wait. 'Come on,' she said, 'let's go back to mine for some coffee.'

Felicity kept apologising for the state of the flat, moving crockery hastily into the kitchen, throwing books and videos back on to shelves, plumping up cushions and emptying ashtrays. But to Rachel it was all wonderful, liberating. She thought with mild distaste of her pristine, quiet flat. This was real, she thought, not some made-up world where nothing happened. The muffled beat of 'No Woman, No Cry' suddenly came through the thin walls from the flat next door.

'Yeah, well, we can compete with that,' said Felicity, and put on an Eric Clapton tape. The flat next door got the message and the volume dropped, and Felicity turned her own music down. 'There,' she said to Rachel. 'Nice, neighbourly understanding.'

Rachel sat down on one of the tattered, fat batik cushions and leaned her head back against the wall. Felicity switched on a small lamp which stood on the floor in the corner of the room and switched off the overhead light. Then she pulled over another cushion and sat down next to Rachel.

'Cosy,' remarked Rachel with a smile, looking round at the soft shadows. It reminded her of people's flats at university. She was in another world, in someone else's hands, her problems far away. Tonight she was nowhere.

Felicity had spread a few objects out on the floor between them, and Rachel watched with interest as she licked and stuck together two cigarette papers, carefully spread on to them a length of shredded tobacco from a Sun Valley tin, and then crumbled something that looked like an Oxo cube on to it.

She wrapped the remainder of the cube up carefully in a piece of silver foil.

'This is what I got from Benjy,' she said to Rachel, as she licked the edge of the paper and rolled it carefully into a long, fat cigarette. 'You're going to like this.'

'You're joking!' said Rachel. 'I'm a solicitor of the Supreme Court,' she added self-mockingly, then laughed and leaned her head back again.

'Yeah, yeah,' said Felicity mildly, twisting the end of the joint. 'Take it from me, this is just what you need. Loosen you up a bit.' She glanced at Rachel, who was looking dubiously at what Felicity was doing. 'Don't worry,' she added, 'the police aren't suddenly going to burst into 86B Evelina Road and bust us. They'd be rounding up all of Brixton, at that rate.'

'I've never smoked dope before,' said Rachel. Why was she even contemplating this? Perhaps because of those wonderful words, 'loosen up'. They sounded so good, so promising. Or perhaps it was just that she was tired of being herself, living always in her right little, tight little code. Anyway, she reflected, it was true. Who was going to find out? What was going to happen? Nothing.

Rachel watched as Felicity inserted a little cylinder of cardboard into the joint, then lit the twisted end. She took a deep drag and the tip glowed red. She swallowed the smoke and leaned back. 'There,' she said, handing it to Rachel, 'now you'll find out what it means to be taken out of yourself.'

Rachel took the joint precariously between finger and thumb and took a little puff. She tried to do as Felicity had done, but started coughing. Felicity fell about giggling.

'Sorry,' she said through her giggles. 'You just looked really funny. Here, try again. Only take a deep, slow breath and hold it in.'

'It's all right for you,' said Rachel. 'You smoke. I don't.'

'Yeah, well, you'll learn. Here.'

This time Rachel did as Felicity had told her, and tried to hold in the sweetish smoke. As she let it out at last, she felt a warm, expanding sensation in her brain. She took another drag, and the feeling came again, exquisitely pleasurable and soothing.

'Here, hold on!' said Felicity, as Rachel was about to take a third drag. 'Don't hog the joint! You don't want to get so stoned that you miss it.' She took the joint away from Rachel.

Rachel leaned her head back, feeling languorous and happy.

'So, anyway,' said Felicity, settling back against her cushion, 'tell me about your bloke. You know, the nice one with the dark hair that came round to the office that day.'

'What makes you think he's my boyfriend?' asked Rachel. Her limbs were beginning to feel deliciously light. She wished Felicity would pass the joint back. Her mind had strayed to Anthony, and she realised she didn't want to think about him. He was intruding into her world of escape. She did not want him there.

'Well, he looked at you like he was. I just had that feeling. Anyway, if he's not, he should be.'

'Yes,' sighed Rachel, closing her eyes, 'he should be.'

'What – you mean he's not made a move, then?' She looked at Rachel in surprise, admiring for the hundredth time those fine cheekbones and that translucent, pale skin that didn't need make-up, the black hair falling back from her face on to the old cushion.

Before she realised it, Rachel began to talk about Anthony. She told Felicity exactly what had happened – or hadn't happened – between them. Felicity handed her the joint from time to time as she listened, and Rachel took it and smoked, almost heedlessly. Her eyes became dark, deep pools, and she gazed abstractedly at the lamp as she talked. She could see little spheres of light drifting from it and rising to the corners of the room. Then it seemed as though her own words, as they fell from her mouth, melted into the spheres of light and floated upwards with them. She found, at last, that she was weeping as she talked – soundless weeping, tears that simply flowed from her eyes as easily as words from her mouth. Felicity watched and listened. It could have that effect on some people, she knew, but she hadn't quite expected this.

'I know why it is,' Rachel was saying. 'I know why it is.' She rocked her head back and forth against the cushion. 'I haven't been able to trust any man since my father. I can't get close.'

Felicity spoke at last. 'What did your father do?' Mere

cessation of speech after talking for fifteen minutes broke something of the spell for Rachel. She looked at Felicity, and drew some of her defences instinctively back down.

'Oh, not much,' she muttered. She pushed the tears away with the flats of both hands. 'He – he was just a bit hard on me. More than a bit hard.'

She looked away, dreading the next question. But Felicity didn't ask it: she merely said, 'Yeah, well, my old man used to knock me about something rotten,' and gazed at the carpet. 'In fact, the only bleeding thing he didn't knock about was the budgie.' She laughed without amusement. 'It's my mum I feel sorry for. Me and Sandy just got out as soon as we were old enough. It was worse for Sandy than me, really. I think it is, if you're a boy.'

Rachel thought this a curious remark, but she did not question it. She was simply relieved at having to say no more about her father. But isn't now the time? she wondered. Now, when you're feeling like this, when you're a million miles away from it all and there's this – she closed her eyes and tried to find the words – this warm light shining inside of you. That was it. She felt illuminated from within. Her tears had vanished as quickly as they had come, cleansing something from her. She felt untethered, as though speaking of Anthony had loosened something inside her and it was drifting away, part of her, not part of her. But no, she could not tell Felicity about her father, nor about the rest of it. Felicity was not the right person. God, where was the right person?

'Well, if you ask me,' said Felicity in a businesslike fashion, drawing greedily on the very last tiny millimetre of the joint, feeling the heat on her lips, 'this Anthony bloke just isn't the one for you. Don't go blaming your dad for everything, though. He's not all men, you know.'

'That's what my analyst said,' remarked Rachel.

This made Felicity feel profound. 'Well,' she said with an airy touch of pride, 'it's right, isn't it? You don't need qualifications to see that. But I don't think you want to worry about Anthony any more. Tell him it's no go.'

'He says he's in love with me,' said Rachel sadly.

'Doesn't mean you owe him anything,' retorted Felicity.

'I wish, I really wish, it were as simple as all that,' said Rachel, and sighed. 'I want it to be right between us.'

'If it was going to be, it would be. Find someone else.' Felicity reflected for a moment on what she'd seen of Anthony. 'Bit of a waste, mind,' she added, then said, 'but don't get the idea that you can't stand all men.'

It's not an idea, thought Rachel, it's a certainty. But she did not say this.

Felicity changed the music and they listened and talked, and the mood lightened, time stretched. The music and the dope made Rachel feel as though she were living on some other plane, one she didn't want to leave. The thought of Nichols & Co, of work, of everything that was real, seemed far, far away.

'Look, d'you want to kip here tonight?' asked Felicity.

Rachel looked at her watch and got stiffly to her feet. 'Oh, God,' she moaned, 'look at the time. It's half one.' She registered Felicity's question and shook her head. 'No, thanks. I must get back. I've got clients in the morning. I can't turn up like this.' She looked down at her crumpled skirt, at the long ladder in one of her stockings.

'Well, you can always have the sleeping bag and the couch, you know.'

Rachel glanced at the sofa, and suddenly the thought of her own fresh, sweet bed seemed very welcoming. She felt enormously tired. 'No, honestly. That's sweet, but I'll get a taxi.'

They rang for a taxi, and when it came and Rachel went down to the street, she passed Vince on the stairs. He didn't recognise her, and she smiled, yawning, to herself. Lucky old Felicity. At least she knew what she wanted, even if he was unreliable and a heartbreaker.

All the way home to Fulham she thought of what she had told Felicity, and of her soundless, easy tears, and was glad it had happened.

Back in the clean, sober reality of her flat, Rachel realised that her clothes and hair smelled of smoke, and that her head, which had felt so deliciously light and expansive a few hours ago, was now aching profoundly.

She thought of having a shower, but it was now after two,

and she knew she must get some sleep before the next day. She suddenly remembered Anthony and her promise to go with him to the Guildhall, and wondered briefly whether she should put it off. Tomorrow, she thought. She would take care of everything tomorrow.

Chapter fourteen

She felt better the next day, but still weary from lack of proper sleep. In her mind there was an odd sense of distraction, as though she had visited some place in the past few hours and was still haunted by its imperfect recollection. It must have been the joint she and Felicity had smoked, she decided – what on earth had possessed her to do that? Too much alcohol and the desire to be, literally, out of her mind. And she had been. Something had been trapped within her, in those hours at Felicity's flat. Like a valve, like that stubby, sinister piece of metal sticking up from the number two generator in the engine room of the *Valeo Dawn*, she felt something had been loosened, little bits of her past seeping out . . .

The blurred image of the generator valve reminded her, as she yawned her way through her tea and grapefruit, that she must get that statement from Captain Craddock typed up. She thought about the Bombay trip as she sat in the Embankment traffic; it seemed as though it had happened weeks and not days ago. She was struck by an odd new sense of serenity as she thought of Anthony and all that had been said. Her mind no longer jarred with apprehension at the thought of seeing him. She smiled to herself, fiddling with the buttons on the car radio, pleased with the realisation. That was a start. That was something. No, she wouldn't put him off this evening. In a way, she was rather looking forward to it.

When Rachel reached the office, she smiled a conspiratorial smile at Felicity as she passed her desk and, glancing briefly at the watchful faces of Doris and Louise, murmured, 'I've got that Bombay tape to be typed up, Felicity – do you want to pop in and get it?'

Felicity rose and followed Rachel to her room, and closed the door gently behind her as Rachel hung up her coat.

'Well?' asked Rachel with a smile of curiosity, turning to Felicity, who looked somewhat worn-out but perceptibly chirpy.

'Yeah, it was all right,' said Felicity with a sheepish grin. 'I mean, he wanted to make up and everything.'

'So everything's fine?' It gave Rachel a sense of vicarious pleasure to think that at least Felicity's love life had taken a turn for the better.

Felicity picked at the corner of Rachel's desk with her thumbnail. 'Yes, I guess so. It's just that – well, I feel I am being really weak about all this. I mean, I gave him an earful and everything, but I still let him stay . . . ' She glanced sadly at Rachel. 'Now that I've let him get away with it, forgiven him and that, I know it'll happen again. It's bound to. He knows how soft I am.'

'Not necessarily,' said Rachel, opening her briefcase and taking out some papers.

'Don't you believe it. He knows he's got it made.' Felicity sighed. 'Maybe it would have been better if I'd told him to get lost. Thing is –'

'I know. You love him.'

'Yeah.' Felicity looked down at the carpet and folded her arms. 'Yeah. I'd do anything for him. That's the way it gets you. You feel like you're losing all your pride, all your self-respect. But you can't help it. At least I can't,' she added wanly.

As she lifted the tiny cassette from her handheld recording machine, Rachel wondered what such a feeling could be like. She could not imagine herself in that dilemma, robbed of all self-possession, ready to do anything, just for someone's love, just to keep them near. Would it make one feel utterly abased, or would one be beyond caring about such things? I'll probably never know, she thought, gazing at the minute spool of brown cassette ribbon in its transparent cartridge.

'Anyway,' said Felicity, stretching out her hand for the tape, 'this won't get the baby bathed. I'd better be getting on with this.'

'Thanks,' said Rachel. 'I'll want four copies – one for the file, one for the master, one for counsel – '

'That's that chap, isn't it? The one you were talking about last night.'

'Yes,' replied Rachel. 'That's Anthony.' She suddenly remembered everything she had told Felicity, all the unstoppable words, the easy tears brought on by the night and Felicity's dope, and felt oddly compromised, embarrassed. Last night's sense of liberation had vanished. It occurred to her now that she should not have told Felicity so much. That had been a mistake, though one she could not have helped making. Felicity would expect more confidences, would expect to be able to ask after Anthony in the way that she, Rachel, had asked about Vince just a few moments ago. Much as she liked Felicity, Rachel did not want that.

'You know,' she added awkwardly as Felicity turned away with the tape in her hand, 'all those things I said last night. About Anthony, I mean.' She hesitated. 'Well, it's not as bad as it sounds. I mean, you can forget it all. I was just being stupid. Out of my head, if you like.' She smiled at Felicity, her expression frank and careless.

It seemed to Felicity that the little pocket of confidence which had opened up between them both last night had suddenly closed. She wishes she'd never told me, thought Felicity. She thinks it's all right for her to know all about me and Vince, but she doesn't want me knowing her stuff. She thinks she can treat me familiarly and keep herself distant. She returned Rachel's smile a little sadly.

'Yeah, well, sometimes the old ganja does that to you. Brings it all to the surface. Don't you worry about it, though. You tuck it all back safely out of sight.'

Rachel sat, stung, after Felicity had left the room. She was right, of course. It had embarrassed her to allow her feelings and fears to be known, and now she wanted to pretend that none of it was true. But it was true. She stared at the backs of her hands. I can't be honest with Felicity, so how can I be honest with myself? she wondered.

As the day progressed, Rachel found herself growing more tired and depressed, the cumulative lack of sleep draining

164

away her energy. I can't go tonight, she told herself at five o'clock. She rang Anthony's chambers, but Henry told her that Anthony was at an arbitration at the Baltic Exchange and wouldn't be coming back to chambers that evening. Rachel sat there after she had put the phone down, feeling grey and washed-out. She would just have to wait for him, that was all. It crossed her mind to go straight home and leave a message for Anthony at reception, but somehow, since her return from India, the prospect of solitude in her flat repelled her. Time spent on her own seemed to have lost its contained, safe quality. She felt that the routine of life cocooned in her pretty flat would no longer protect her, that hinges somewhere in her were becoming unfastened, parts of her flapping about in an unsteady wind. She did not want to be alone.

Felicity passed her door and stopped to say goodnight. She noticed Rachel's drawn, thoughtful face, and thought of all the things Rachel had told her last night. It seemed so sad, thought Felicity. She was so lost and mixed up, and yet Felicity had thought her totally in control, her life wonderful, matching the perfection of her outward appearance. She did not, at that moment, envy her boss.

'You ought to go home and get some kip,' she told Rachel, pausing in the doorway as the rest of the secretaries packed their belongings up and headed for the lift.

Rachel sighed. 'I'm meant to be going out with Anthony tonight. I don't feel up to it, but he's not in chambers and he said he would pick me up here. I'll have to wait.' She passed her slender white hands over her face. 'I don't suppose you've got any aspirin, or anything like that, have you? Last night's just beginning to catch up with me.'

Felicity, eyeing her, hesitated for a moment. 'I think I've got something somewhere. Hold on.' She went away, then reappeared a moment later. She laid two white tablets on Rachel's desk and a little paper cup of water from the water cooler. 'There you go. They should do the trick.'

Rachel thanked her and swallowed them with the water. Felicity said goodnight, and left.

By the time Anthony arrived, Rachel thought she was feeling distinctly better. She would be able to get through the

165

evening without too much trouble. Just so long as she got home at a decent time. She would leave this Guildhall thing at nine, not let Anthony persuade her to go to dinner afterwards.

'How are you?' asked Anthony, as they stood together in the lift. She looked bright, he thought, but a little strained. Perhaps she was still jet-lagged.

'Good,' she replied cheerfully. 'Better than I felt this time last night.' And she did. Her mouth felt slightly dry, but she felt animated, alert. The lights along Bishopsgate, the traffic lights, the car lights, the shop lights – so many lights – all crowded in upon her vision. Yes, she felt good. She felt really good.

As she drove through the traffic on London Wall, Rachel tried to fasten her concentration on what Anthony was saying, but it seemed as though her own thoughts were rushing ahead of his words, jumping lightly from one thing to another, so that it was all she could do to nod and smile brightly at the right junctures. Anthony thought her preoccupied, but was glad she was so carelessly cheerful. It was a change from her usual watchful, slow-smiling reserve.

When they entered Guildhall, Rachel was struck by the way the great cathedral-like hall seemed to well up with sound, like a radio suddenly turned to full volume. Voices seemed to clash and rise, swooping notes of noise, and the faces that turned to her in the vast crowd of faces shone like discs. She was aware of a mild buzzing sensation in her limbs.

'I've never been here before,' she said wonderingly. She thought she had spoken to Anthony, but realised she must have been speaking to herself, that no words had come out.

They had reached some point in the hall and had stopped. Anthony was talking to people. Fred was there, Fred Fenton, and she spoke to him for a few moments before the crowd and the tide of conversation eased them away from one another. She lifted her eyes and looked up at the high vaulted roof, at the trembling rows of guild insignia. Or at least they seemed to tremble. She looked around slowly; the rigid forms and folds of the stone drapery on the Victorian statues and plaques ranging the walls seemed liquid with motion. How absurd, she thought, and smiled. She gazed ahead at the minstrels' gallery, and it seemed to her that the music which floated from the unseen musicians filled the air with a charming swarm of notes, a carpet of sound floating above the heads of the crowd and into the lofty grey corners of the Guildhall roof. She wanted to touch people on the arm and say, 'Listen! You're not listening – listen to that!'

A sudden unsteadiness shook her and she looked away, staring down at the floor, and the dancing in her heart ceased and settled. Her vision steadied. Someone to whom Anthony had introduced her was speaking, and she was able to focus her attention. She managed to make conversation, and her brain became a little clearer. She spoke to more people, felt smiling and animated, and drank some of the champagne she had been given.

A High Court judge made a speech, full of jocular topical references to the firm of Sinclair, Roche & Temperley on the occasion of their jubilee, and everyone laughed and felt cosy. Rachel could not follow much of it. Tables along the side of the hall were laid out with food, and she discovered herself to be ravenously hungry. She ate quickly and nervously, glancing from time to time back to Anthony, who was talking to some new people. She knew them, she thought – they were from 5 Caper Court. The big man with the moustache was Cameron Renshaw, whom she had instructed once. She must go and speak to him. She felt bright and eager and nervous, and swallowed back the remainder of her champagne before walking over to Anthony.

Leo had not wanted to come that evening. He had spent the past two days in sullen fury, unable to concentrate properly on his work, his talk with Frank Chamberlin gnawing away at his thoughts. For hours together he remained stolidly convinced that the thing was over, that he had lost the high moral ground and had now no hope of recovery. His application must fail, particularly in the light of the competition from Stephen. Then moments of cold clarity would occur, in which he told himself that the Lord Chancellor's Office could not be so ludicrous, so bigoted, as to care about anyone's sexual peccadilloes. In those brief intervals he had been able to reassure himself that Frank had gauged the temperature of the thing entirely wrongly, that merit alone would be the criterion. Good God, these were the eighties, after all.

But then the doubts would creep back, the imagined contents of that unread report, the possibility of parts of his past having come to the ears of such as Sir Mungo, or Sir Mostyn Smith. Perhaps someone had, somehow, found out about that boy who had once been Leo's lover, and who had finished up dead in some bedsit in Balham. That had been long after Leo had lost touch with him, and he had not felt remotely touched by the tragedy then, but now it returned to gnaw at his conscience. All it took was one wrong connection, rumour imperfectly attached to fact, and he could be finished.

Not knowing what was known – that was the worst of it. Perhaps the business of Sarah and James – that tacky domestic arrangement which he had imagined to be so discreetly tucked away in its rural fastness, far from the City or anyone who knew him – had reached someone's ears. Not heinous, but sordid enough to tarnish his reputation at this most critical of junctures. It was when he dwelt on these dark and tormenting possibilities that Leo felt staggered by his own past naivety, by his years of calm assurance and the constant belief that things could be kept secret.

But berating himself for his own folly could do no good. Neither, he had told himself, gazing in his room at the engraved oblong invitation from Sinclair's, could it do any good to shuffle oneself out of sight, letting the uncertainty of the next few months eat away at one. After all, it could still be that Sir Frank was worrying about nothing – in which case it behoved Leo to act with his usual ease and brilliance, to be seen among the multitude of the great and good who would throng the Guildhall that evening, to conduct himself with his customary confidence and charm. Appearances were all, he knew. There was much that thinking could make so. If he were to behave as though such rumour as floated about neither troubled nor touched him, perhaps others could be persuaded that it simply had no basis, or was so slight in substance as to be easily dismissed. It was important to brave this storm, imagined or otherwise.

And so he stood near the entrance to the Guildhall, an easy, attractive figure, impeccably dressed, surveying the crowd with cool nonchalance. He made his way among them, murmuring a greeting here, nodding and smiling to an acquaintance there. He picked up a glass of champagne and drifted over to where Michael Winstanley, one of the Commercial Court judges, was chatting with Lewis Tree, a Lloyd's arbitrator, and a couple of solicitors. Leo felt that his own conversation was as polished as ever, that the general laughter which greeted his wit was warm and appreciative, but then – or did he imagine it? – he thought he detected the narrowest of glances from Michael as he spoke, that the faintest breath of unease orchestrated the slight body movements of the other men. It was nothing, and yet it was everything.

Making an excuse, Leo moved off, his face relaxed and reflective, his heart grinding away at the suspicion that the manner of those men towards him had shifted in some minute degree, that something known yet unspoken hovered in the air. He told himself that it was all paranoia, nonsense, that his faculties were alert to find that which did not exist. In an effort to smooth away the tensions he felt, Leo drank several glasses of champagne. He attached himself to a rowdy and amusing little knot of the more jovial and urbane of Sinclair's partners, but somehow his mood could not support itself for long, and he detached himself again, glancing at his watch and telling himself that it was time he left, sick of keeping up the front.

Then he saw Anthony and Cameron with a couple of people, and he strolled over to join them, thankful at the sight of Anthony's young, kind face. Anthony would not judge him. Nor would Cameron. With them he could relax, feel more like himself, shake off this dog of self-doubt, if only for a little time.

At the same moment, Rachel was walking towards Anthony and Cameron, and as she approached them, she was struck by the appearance of the man who had just joined them. His head was turned away from hers, his handsome face grim and distracted as he sipped his champagne and stood, one hand in his pocket, detached from the chattering crowd around him. She noticed his silver hair, the rapidity of his blue gaze as he scanned the room impatiently, the fine, restless fingers that held his glass. Then he turned to look at her, and as his eyes met hers, Rachel felt as though jolted by some force. But his glance merely brushed hers and he looked away, his expression faintly troubled and bored.

Leo was wondering whether he knew this woman, and whether the manner in which she had looked at him meant that he should smile and say hello as though he remembered her. This kind of thing annoyed him. He liked to think that he had an unfailing memory for names and faces, that it was one of his social excellences. She was familiar, certainly. Damn, damn . . . He ran his mind back, glanced at her face again, and then realised that Anthony was introducing them.

'How do you do?' he said politely, and took her hand, which felt thin and cold. Then he remembered. This was the girl to whom Anthony had been talking in Fountain Court a few weeks ago, and who had passed him as he stood at the postbox. That dark-haired beauty. He made his customary, detached assessment of her charms as they made small talk, his eyes straying across the fine-boned, delicate face with its wide mouth and almond-shaped blue eyes. Rather bright eyes – possibly she had had too much champagne. He felt confirmed in this as he began to realise that her conversation was somewhat out of the ordinary. It was neither the mannish, robust line normally taken by women who found him attractive but were damned if they were going to show it, nor was it the flirtatious, intelligently inviting approach favoured by women more sure of their own good looks. This was something else entirely – really rather sweet and unusual. She was talking to him very seriously about the measurements cast in brass lettering and figures in the stones at their feet, which interspersed metal crosses and fleur-de-lis set in the marble floor.

'You see,' she was saying, 'it says a hundred links. Now to what do you suppose that refers? Is it the distance from here to there – and if so, where?'

He smiled at her. 'I haven't a clue,' he admitted.

'Now, did you know,' she went on seriously, 'that a chain is sixty-six feet? I don't think many people here would know that. Everyone's forgotten about roods, poles and perches, things like that.'

Leo picked up the train of discussion with some amusement. She must be on something, he thought as he listened to her and scanned her intent, glowing eyes. Yes – though he couldn't guess what. Certainly more than champagne. He wondered if Anthony knew about it. At that moment Anthony said something to him. The talk became more general; she began to talk to Cameron, then someone accosted Leo, and so they drifted apart in the eddies of conversation and people that swirled around the hall.

As she saw Leo moving away, talking to someone else, Rachel excused herself from Cameron and went over to one of the tables and put her glass down. She could not believe she had babbled so incoherently to that man, Leo. Something about him had made her so nervous, so self-conscious, that she had just said the first things that came into her head. What a fool he must think her. She felt most peculiar, she realised. Her mind felt as though it were ablaze, dancing with tiny, fiery imps of thought, yet at the same time she felt giddy and weak.

I must go, she thought, and lifted her tongue to the parched roof of her mouth. She looked back to where Anthony stood and could not face the thought of speaking to him, of explaining, of trying to get away into the night without him. She had to leave now.

She retrieved her coat and made her way out into the freezing air. Someone in a peaked cap gave her a little salute and said something; she gave him a wandering gaze and a tremulous smile. She walked across the cobbled square towards Gresham Street, where she had parked her car, and wondered whether she was capable of driving home. She had had only two glasses of champagne, and yet she felt so strange. She heard a voice behind her and turned. Someone loomed up through the semi-darkness.

'Oh, hello, Roger,' she said faintly. Roger caught up with her, his soft, interested eyes taking in her unsteady, smiling features. Dear dear, so Miss Dean was capable of having one too many after all. And where was that boyfriend of hers? This was something of a fortunate occurrence.

171

'Everything all right?' he asked.

She stood uncertainly for a moment. 'Do you know, Roger, I think I'd better take a taxi home. The thing is, I've left my car in Gresham Street – it's all right there at this time of night, but . . . ' Her voice trailed off. She wasn't quite sure what she was saying. 'I have to get my briefcase from it. Do you – ' She looked at him, trying to concentrate. 'Would you mind finding me a taxi, Roger?'

'Certainly,' replied Roger easily. 'No trouble at all. Let's just get that briefcase of yours first. Wouldn't do to leave it in the car overnight.'

'No,' she agreed. And she walked down the deserted street with him, glad that there was someone who could at least see her safely into a cab.

When they reached her car and he made his slow pass at her, it was as though all the loose, untidy ends of her mind flew together. His hands clutched her arms and he pushed his mouth against hers so that she fell back against the side of the car; the keys fell from her fingers into the gutter as she tried to push him away from her.

'Just a little goodnight kiss, Rachel,' he was saying, his voice soft but intent, and his grip utterly immovable.

At the smell of his breath and the forcefulness of his mouth and body, a wave of fear broke over Rachel and she began to shudder and tremble violently in his grasp. She felt totally unable to struggle free from him, and as she wrenched her face away from his she brought her hand up and raked the side of his face with her nails. He stepped back and cried out with pain, but as she took a couple of staggering steps away and bent to fumble for her keys, her heart hammering, her only desire to get into her car and away from him, he grabbed her by one wrist and pulled her upright. He began to say something, and she had no idea what was about to happen next, when she heard a voice say, 'Hey, hey. Come on.' Roger turned to look at the figure approaching them in the dimly lit street. He dropped her wrist and flexed his body, tugging at his jacket and stepping nervously back as Leo walked up. Then he turned abruptly on his heel and strode away, his steps loud and hasty in the empty street.

She leaned back against the car, clutching her keys in her fingers, looking away from Leo. He was standing, head on one side, hands in pockets, surveying her curiously. She was about to say something, she did not know what, but felt her chest begin to heave, dry sobs rising to the surface. She turned away, shaking, and leaned against the car, dry, croaking sounds of misery and fear breaking from her throat. The metal frame of the car window felt like ice beneath her trembling hand.

Leo stepped forward and put a hand on her shoulder, and felt the shaking of her body.

'Hey,' he said again. 'Come on, come on. What's all this about?' He knew Roger Williams of old and could see that Roger, as usual, had been attempting to force his unwelcome but trivial attentions on this girl, but she seemed more than averagely upset about the whole thing. He turned her round and put his hands on her shoulders. Her whole body was convulsed with these dry sobs, and her head was bowed. This was not good, he told himself. He stood uncertainly for a moment, then glanced at his watch. Ten past nine. Here we go again, he thought, Leo the Good Samaritan. A distressed lady with too much champagne inside her and a little of something else, besides. He took the car keys from her fingers.

'In you get,' he said. He opened the passenger door and she slid inside. He got into the driver's seat, searched for the ignition and surveyed the unfamiliar dashboard. Then he glanced at her, watching her fasten her seat belt, seeing the visible trembling of her whole arm as she did so.

'Shall I take you home?' he asked.

She whispered something, her head turned away.

'Sorry?'

She lifted her head, but still did not look at him. 'No. No, please. I don't think I could . . . ' And the crying began in earnest, racking her completely.

Oh, hell, thought Leo. He wondered whether he should go and fetch Anthony. Then he turned to look at her again, and some instinct told him that was not a good idea. He sighed.

'Okay,' he said, and started the engine. 'I'll take you back to mine for some coffee. I could do with the company of someone in a worse state than myself.'

Chapter fifteen

Rachel stared out unseeingly at the dark streets, the people, the lights, her head leaning heavily against the seat. The sobs fell away from her and gradually ceased, but still tears flowed, sliding down her cheeks. She wondered that anyone could have so many tears inside them, thinking of last night in Felicity's flat. She turned her head away from the window and watched, through the dancing blur of her tears, Leo's hands upon the steering wheel, changing gear, his elbow leaning on the door and his chin resting on one hand as they drew up to some traffic lights. She lifted her eyes to his face; he was staring straight ahead, his face a blank.

Rachel's body felt inert, and the dizzying patterns which had swum in her brain in the Guildhall had now subsided. There was a slackness in her mind which would scarcely admit sensible thought. She knew dimly that she should feel wretched and embarrassed at what had happened, her hysteria, but nothing in her was capable of proper feeling. She realised now that whatever Felicity had given her in the office had not been aspirin, but she could not even feel angry about that. She just wanted time to wash it away, for normality to return – but above all, she did not want to be alone.

She looked at Leo's face again, closed her eyes and then opened them. He must think that I am a nuisance and an embarrassment, she thought – but it did not trouble her. He had rescued her, and he would stay with her. That was all that mattered, until this thing inside her went away.

In fact, Leo was thinking about his case the following day, an application to set aside the arrest of a ship in Falmouth. He had ceased to think about Rachel, whom he intended to send home in a taxi after a couple of cups of black coffee and a brief lecture on the folly of drinking on top of drugs.

When they reached Mayfair, it took Leo some time and trouble to find a parking place near to the mews.

'You can't drive home tonight,' he remarked. 'If I leave it here you can get a taxi later and pick it up tomorrow.' He turned off the engine.

They got out and she followed him up the cobbled mews to the door of his house. He went in ahead of her, switching on lights, and she followed him up into a long, low room, sparsely furnished, with deep leather sofas and pale, muted lighting. Rachel stood awkwardly in the middle of the room, near to a low square table. Leo switched on a lamp that stood on the table, tugged off his tie and threw it with his jacket on to one of the sofas.

'Sit down,' he said to Rachel, as he walked past her to the kitchen. 'Or lie down,' he added. 'You probably need to.'

She was struck by the casual chill of his voice. I'm just being a bore, a nuisance, she thought. I should have let him take me home, or find me a taxi. But she felt so odd, so alienated, that the idea of returning home alone was impossible.

She edged towards the kitchen door, watching him spoon coffee into a cafetière, his movements brisk, as though he wanted to give her coffee and get rid of her. 'May I wash my face, please?' she asked. 'I feel a bit of a mess.'

'Certainly,' he replied. 'Second door on the left.'

She went into the bathroom, as clinical and impersonal as the living room, and splashed water on to her face and rubbed it dry. She glanced up into the mirror. Her face looked very pale, but her eyes were hardly red at all; instead they looked dark and luminous. She wondered what it was that wretched girl had given her. Whatever it had been, it was still working within her, not with the heightened euphoria of an hour ago, but as a soporific, fuzzing her consciousness. She took a comb from her bag and combed her hair over and over again, the sensation clearing her brain slightly, then lifted her hair back from her face with both hands, letting it fall over her shoulders.

When she went back through, Leo had laid two cups and the pot of coffee on the little table. 'Sugar?' he asked.

'No. No, thank you,' she murmured, and stared vacantly at

the steam rising from the pot into the dimly lit air of the room.

'You still have your coat on,' remarked Leo, bending to fetch something from a cupboard.

She glanced down, then slowly unbuttoned her coat and laid it on top of his jacket. She sat down stiffly next to it, her limbs feeling heavy and chilled. Leo came back over with a bottle of brandy and a glass.

'Not for you,' he said, sitting down on the edge of the sofa opposite. 'You've had more than enough interesting things for one evening, I'd say.'

She watched as he poured coffee into each cup, then slopped some brandy into his glass. The light from the lamp cut his face into angles, throwing shadows beneath his brow and cheekbones and in the hollow of his neck where he had unbuttoned his shirt. Rachel felt quite tranquil now, mesmerised, happy just to let each moment follow the next in a steady, neat progression.

He unbuttoned his cuffs and rolled them back, then drank some brandy and looked up at her. 'Drink your coffee,' he said. 'You need it. Then tell me what all that was about.' He paused, and added, 'You're not the first person Roger's made a pass at, you know. He wasn't exactly trying to rape you. Or maybe it was whatever you'd been taking earlier in the evening.' His voice was caustic, impatient.

'What do you mean?' she asked, lifting her cup to her lips and staring straight at him.

'I have been around long enough to know the signs,' he replied. 'You're as high as a kite. Not very sensible to go drinking champagne on top of it. No wonder you overreacted to Roger.'

She set down her cup. 'It was . . . ' she began. Then she suddenly felt very tired; was it even worth the bother of explaining to him? 'It was something my secretary gave me before she went home. I thought it was aspirin.'

'Your secretary?' exclaimed Leo.

'I think she did it with good intentions. I think she thought it would help me . . . ' And the tears began again; she could not help them, but simply sat, watching the outline of her coffee cup swim. 'I know I was stupid to react to Roger like that,' she whispered, feeling something brimming up inside her, the feeling that if she did not speak, if she did not let it all spill out to someone's ears, then she would suffocate or choke on it. 'But you know, people use words so carelessly. When you've been raped once, you keep – you keep thinking – ' She stopped and cupped her hands over her mouth, stifling her sobs.

Leo stared at her in alarm. Oh, God, this was that girl Anthony had told him about. He hadn't made the connection. The one who couldn't let anyone near her. He thought of what he'd said a moment ago, and cursed himself.

He stood up and came round the table and stood over her. Then he reached down, bundled his jacket and her coat together and gently made her lie back on the sofa, pillowing them beneath her head, stroking her hair softly with one hand as she wept. Then he knelt down next to her and looked at her thoughtfully. Eventually the crying stopped and she lay there, her face wet, staring up at the ceiling, her eyes deep and dark from whatever drug it was she had taken.

I can't send her home like this, he thought. Not in this state. He remembered what Anthony had told him that day in El Vino's, and his curiosity was aroused. There was something going on here that was well beyond Anthony's handling.

'Tell me,' he said softly after a moment. 'Come on. You're safe here, and you've got things inside you that you want to get out.' She turned to look at him. 'Haven't you?' She said nothing. 'So start at the beginning and tell me. I promise it will make you feel better. I promise.'

She looked trustingly into his face, then a faint frown of anxiety touched her features. 'Has Anthony told you anything about me?' she asked, her voice very soft. 'I know you're quite close to one another,' she added. Leo gave a wry smile. 'He talks a lot about you . . . '

He hesitated, and then nodded, stroking the line of his jaw with one finger. 'He's told me a little. That you seem – afraid of him, perhaps. That's all.'

She sighed and looked away. 'I think you're right,' she said. 'I think I do have to tell someone.' She glanced back at him. 'I thought that telling psychiatrists and all those people I used to see . . . ' Her voice trailed away. There was a pause. 'I was going to talk to Felicity about it last night. That's my secretary,' she added.

'The one with the line in useful pills.'

Rachel smiled in spite of herself. 'Yes. I think she's a great believer in drugs.' Her fingers fiddled with the buttons on the front of her dress. She felt foolish lying down with Leo kneeling next to her, listening to her, but somehow she had neither the desire nor the strength to move. Just to talk. 'We smoked some stuff she had last night, and it made me sort of want to talk about it . . . '

'My, you do get around,' murmured Leo, pulling a cushion from the end of the sofa and making himself more comfortable. He felt it important that he should stay near to her. Sexuality in all its forms fascinated him, and here was some well-repressed experience that he thought might be very interesting.

'. . . but I couldn't. Maybe I should have.'

'Tell me now,' said Leo quietly. 'Tell me what makes you so afraid.'

There was a long, deep silence, and then Rachel, her blurred black eyes searching the farthest shadows of the room, began to talk.

'It goes back a long way, I suppose. To my father. I think it must have begun when I was about eight or so. Just coming to my room at night, touching me, telling me things. And then, as I got older, I began to realise that he shouldn't be doing those things. That it was wrong. But it went on, and the things he did got worse. I couldn't tell my mother – how could I? Then eventually – I don't think I really meant to – I told a teacher at school. I was fourteen. And then – then the very worst part of it began.' She took a deep breath. 'They took my father away – I really did love him, you know, in a way, even though he did those things to me – and the days just began to get awful. My mother screaming the most awful, hateful things at me, that I was a liar, that I'd destroyed our family and my father – ' Rachel put her hands over her eyes, tears trickling between her fingers. 'I didn't know what they would do to my father. And this woman – I don't know what she was, a social worker, or a policewoman, or something . . . ' She stopped, sniffing back

179

her tears. Leo pulled the silk handkerchief from the pocket of his jacket beneath her head and handed it to her.

'Here,' he said. Then he picked up his brandy and sipped it, watching her.

She took the handkerchief and mopped her eyes, then went on. 'This woman told me I would have to go to court, give evidence. And I couldn't face the thought of that. I couldn't.' She shook her head and stared at Leo's dark blue handkerchief, stained with her tears. 'So I ran away. But they found me, and they – I suppose they took me into care for a little while. I don't know. There was an assessment centre, and I used to have to talk to these child psychiatrists every day. Counsellors, they're called now. My mother came to visit me, and she didn't yell and shout any more. She was very withdrawn and quiet. I don't think she really wanted to have to see me, to think about what my father had done . . . '

Leo regarded her gravely, saying nothing.

'So then,' she sighed, folding the handkerchief into a neat square and dabbing at her eyes, 'they told me that my father was going to plead guilty, and that I wouldn't have to go to court . . . And in the end my father went to prison, and I went home to my mother. I had to face everyone at school. They weren't meant to know, but they all did, of course. I never went out. I was taboo. Tainted. The three years after that were a nightmare. I just wanted them to be over so I could get away from home. I knew there wasn't any point in running away again. There wasn't anywhere to go. The worst part was the constant feeling that my mother blamed me, that she thought I'd made him do those things, that I wanted them.' She drew a shuddering breath. 'It was as though she was thinking about it every time she looked at me. They got divorced, and I haven't seen my father since. I don't think my mother has, either. I don't see her much. She moved to Bath, got a job there. She's become very bright and extrovert, the way she used to be. I think she's had a few boyfriends. But she doesn't want me there. I remind her of – of all that.' She sighed and unfolded the handkerchief. 'I spoil the mood. Anyway, at the end of those three years I got away, went to university to study law.' She stopped, and there was silence for a while.

Leo reached behind him and picked up his brandy again, and took a sip. 'And?'

She put a hand up to her forehead and stared at the ceiling. Her pupils were still dilated, velvet black centres to her blue eyes. Leo wondered whether she would be telling him this if she were completely in control.

'And – I thought I had put it all behind me. I thought I could just be a normal human being. There wasn't any damage, after all . . . none that you could see.' Her voice was very quiet. 'But I gradually discovered that there was something not right with me. Boys used to ask me out – they never did at school, only later – but when it came to – when they wanted to touch me, I would just freeze. I didn't want them to. I don't know why, but I didn't want them anywhere near me. I hadn't really hated my father until then – I'd just felt sorry for him. But I began to see what he'd done, how he'd ruined part of me . . . ' Rachel ran her tongue over her lips, her mouth dry.

'Your coffee's gone cold,' said Leo. 'Here, have a little of this.' And he handed her the brandy glass. 'I don't think it can do much harm.' If anything, he wanted to keep her suspended in this blank, talkative state, desiring more and more of the details of her past, scraps of her darkness.

Rachel took a swallow of the brandy and lay back again.

'You would have thought that that would be enough, that God would let it go at that . . . ' She closed her eyes, little sweet drifts of alcohol coursing through her limbs and her brain. She was glad to be talking, glad to let it empty out of her like liquid from a vessel, the past flowing into nowhere. 'Actually, it seemed to be getting better after a while. I went to see a psychiatrist again, I began to come to terms with what had happened, to look at it, think about it.' She paused. 'A kind of exorcism, I suppose. And then I met this boy. He was in the year above me at university. He was very quiet, very much his own person. I met him at a Union debate. He was sitting next to me. I didn't usually go to those things, but . . . ' Her gaze wandered round the room, lighting on pictures and pieces of sculpture. It was as though everything in the room was poised, listening. 'Anyway, we began to go out together. Not as – just as friends, you know. We liked the same things,

181

films, books. I think he was a bit shy of girls . . . I hadn't really had a close friend, ever. Not since childhood . . . I had girlfriends at university, of course, but they must have – well, I suppose I kept at a distance, because I couldn't do any of the things they did. So Alan was my friend, my closest friend, and I thought things were getting better for me, because I liked him being near me. I think I wanted something to happen. A love affair. Someone of my own. I know I did . . . '

Leo studied her face, the way the lamplight shone on the curve of her cheekbones and the dark depths of her eyes, the movement of her lips as she spoke. He watched with fascination as tears came shimmering, unspilled, to the surface of her eyes, then slid down across the fine skin of her cheeks. Her mouth trembled. He waited. She breathed deeply again, stroked away the tears with the backs of her fingers, lifted his handkerchief to her face.

'There had been someone – there had been a man around the campus, attacking people. Girls. We were all told – oh, you know. We were all told not to go out alone, not to be on the campus after dark, to be on the look-out.' She turned her face to look at him, her dark eyes fastened on his. 'But I wasn't the kind who went around with other girls, in pairs. And I didn't think it could happen to me. I didn't think I could go on being hurt . . . ' Her voice was no more than a whisper. To his surprise her mouth tilted into something like a smile. 'But, of course, who better to choose than someone who was already a victim? So, to add to it all, I was raped – and there was this nightmare starting all over again, police and people talking at me, those soothing voices going on and on, prodding at me, uncovering everything . . . ' She put her hands over her eyes again and cried without speaking for a few moments. Then eventually she took her hands away. She turned to look at the brandy glass which Leo held. 'Do you think I could have some more, please? Just a little.' Leo handed her the glass and she finished it.

'What happened to you?' asked Leo, breaking the silence.

'Afterwards? Oh, I suppose I went completely to pieces. Poor Alan tried to comfort me, to stay near, but it couldn't go back to the way it had been. I drove him away. Couldn't handle it – not even having him as a friend. And there I was. Just a wreck. The university were very good. They let me take time off, stay back a year.' She sighed. 'I think my studying, my work, was the only thing that helped me survive.' She gave a shaky little laugh and glanced at the handkerchief, crushing it into a damp ball. 'Not that I did, really. I just exist. That's all I've ever done since. Which is why I was so stupid this evening, and why I've made such a mess of this thing with Anthony . . . '

Leo suddenly thought of Anthony, remembering a time when Anthony, too, had sat in this room. When Leo had sought to make him his lover. The memory was oddly disturbing.

'How – how did this man rape you?' asked Leo.

She stared at him. 'You want me to tell you?' Her voice was very soft, lightened by surprise. Her eyes were still very dark and far away.

'Yes.'

'Why?' she wondered.

'In case it helps,' replied Leo, lying. 'To get rid of everything, I mean.'

Rachel had never imagined she could recount to anyone what had happened. Even for the police she had dragged out only the barest facts. They had never caught him, anyway. She had only sketched the event for Dr Michaels, leaning instead on an account of her own subsequent feelings, making that the important thing. But now she told Leo, running back in her mind over every moment. It seemed to her as though she heard her own voice coming from a distance as she spoke. And Leo listened, scanning her face, saying nothing, his blue gaze mesmeric, a muscle in his cheek flickering. Why am I telling him this? she wondered suddenly. We don't even know one another. Why does he want to hear? She stopped.

'So,' she said, looking away. 'So now you know.'

'And do you think,' he said, putting the empty glass he had been holding back on the table, 'that it's helped?'

She stared at the backs of her hands, then shook her head against the pillow of coat and jacket. 'I doubt it. Why should it?' She glanced at him, thinking how fine his face was, how oddly expressive, patient. She studied his light blue eyes for a moment, suddenly remembering the feeling she had had on first seeing him. 'I've been going over everything with my analyst – except for what I've just told you. Good God,' she sighed, and turned her gaze back to the ceiling, 'we've done the thing to death. It hasn't taken me anywhere. I'm still rigid with fear any time a man comes near me.' She laughed, then sniffed, suddenly a little sad at the thought of dear Dr Michaels, sitting solid and healthy in her green, helpful room. 'She thinks it's just a question of finding the right person. Somewhere out there.' And Rachel gestured slightly into the far shadows of the room and beyond.

Leo thought about this. 'Perhaps she's right. Perhaps if you stop seeing men as men . . . '

Rachel gave a short laugh. 'How do I do that? They are, after all, aren't they?'

'I mean, not as these dreadful, penetrative, plundering creatures –' He rubbed his chin, cast his glance away. 'I know that's all you've ever known, but they're not all like that.'

Rachel noticed he said 'they', not 'we', and looked at him curiously. Then she sighed. 'I know. I know. Don't you think I've tried to tell myself that about Anthony?'

'Don't talk about Anthony,' said Leo. 'This has nothing to do with Anthony.' The tone of his voice made her turn to look at him again. 'This is between you and me.' At the words, she felt a sudden current of intimacy between them, and a recollection of the force that had touched her earlier, on first seeing him; then it ebbed away, leaving her feeling warm and inert.

'Now,' he said gently, 'you have told me everything, and there is nothing more to know. Not about all that. Now there is only you left. You can't keep the pain with you for ever. Let it go. It's part of the past, it only lives in your mind. And the past is gone.'

As he spoke, her gaze darted from his bright blue eyes to the silver of his hair, then back again, back and forth. He watched, as he spoke, the movement of her eyes, her mesmerised stare fastening on his face, then flitting away again. As he talked to her gently, insistently, his voice low and idle, the movement of her eyes gradually ceased, and at last her gaze was fixed only upon his face. She looked at his mouth as he talked, at the fine lines, either from pain or laughter, or both, that creased the flesh on either side. She stared at the angular jaw, the skin against the bone slightly soft and slack with incipient middle age, and at the lines of his nose, his cheekbones, the faint shadows beneath. She felt as though she had known this face for a long, long time.

Such a wonderful face, she thought, as her body relaxed with the cadence of his words. She had liked his face from the first moment she had seen it, when he had turned to look at her. For a moment she struggled with the idea of telling him this, of talking about that moment, but her mind would not move words to her mouth. She simply lay there and listened, drugged with kindness.

When he lifted his hand to the first of the buttons on her dress, she clasped it in both of hers and rocked her head from side to side. But her hands did not stop his; they merely remained fastened to his wrist as he undid the button. Then the second and the third, all the way down. She followed his hand, watching the sinews sliding beneath the skin of his wrist where the unbuttoned cuff of his shirt sleeve had fallen away.

Her hands dropped from his as he opened her dress, pushing it to either side of her body. She did not wonder at her lack of fear; she was only aware that there was no fear there. Her mind seemed to be floating, incapable of fixed thought. Her gaze remained fastened on the fine covering of hair on the back of his hand as he stroked his fingers lightly across her stomach, then, as his hand moved slowly downwards, easing her pants past her hips, down her legs, slipping them to the floor, she looked back to his face. It was expressionless, meditative, and he looked into her eyes as though thinking of something far away. At the first touch of his fingers between her legs, she drew in a soft breath, and her hands clutched convulsively at his wrist. He paused only for a second and then carried on caressing, stroking, gazing at her face as she closed her eyes and drew in sudden breaths at each movement of his fingers. His whole being was impassive, except for the slight quickening of his breath in time with hers. He watched with detachment the pale, slender fingers holding his wrist as his hand moved, over and over. They did not release their grip until her last, shuddering sigh had died away and her arched back relaxed.

He leaned his chin upon the edge of the sofa, watching her, his damp fingers stroking her stomach softly, until the last small, shocking waves of pleasure died away within her, and she opened her eyes. They gazed at one another with a naked intimacy that seemed to spread fire through her limbs. She did not want to move. She wanted to stay there for ever, gazing at him, lost in him.

Why have I done this thing? wondered Leo. Perhaps to help her, because the moment was there, although she didn't know it, and because if I hadn't taken it, it might have vanished for ever. But he knew himself better. If that had been part of it, he knew also that he had become aroused listening to her, that her pain and her isolation had excited him. It had been experimental, he had enjoyed that sense of power in taking her beyond herself, watching her come.

'You see,' he murmured, his chin still resting on the edge of the sofa, 'we are not all monsters. We do give, occasionally.'

He raised himself up in his kneeling position, conscious of the tingling stiffness of his legs. I am getting old, he thought. He buttoned her dress gently to the top, and she simply lay there, looking at him. Impossible to send her home, he thought, looking down at her. But how would it be in the morning? Well, that must take care of itself.

'Come on,' he said, his voice as kind and persuasive as he could make it, 'don't keep thinking about it. You need some sleep. A lot of sleep, I'd say. You can sleep in the spare room.'

He got up, flexing his knees, and went through to the spare room, pulling open a cupboard and taking out a duvet and a pillow. He arranged them on the bed. When he turned round she was standing in the doorway, her shoes in her hand. She did not look at him. Her face was blurred and beautiful, and he felt suddenly quite touched by what had just happened.

'Thank you,' she said, and went past him to the bed.

He paused in the doorway. 'Goodnight,' he said.

He went back into the living room and stood there. All very

peculiar, he thought. All very unexpected. He rubbed at the back of his neck with his hand, then glanced at his watch. Nearly eleven. He picked up the coffee cups and took them into the kitchen, then returned for the brandy glass and the coffee pot. Then he locked up and went to bed.

As Rachel sat on the bed after he had gone, thoughts and feelings moved like slow, giddy birds in her brain. Each time she thought about what had happened, what he had done, his hands upon her body, it seemed that it could not have happened. Yet each time the recollection repeated itself a warm wave of desire eddied up in her, and she knew it had. She sat listening for a while, a long while, until he had gone to bed. Then she undressed and stood up in the darkness. She felt her way out of her room and along to where his bedroom must be. She opened the door and her eyes grew accustomed to the half-darkness, the room faintly lit through the blind from the lamp out in the mews.

When she slid beneath the sheets, Leo was almost asleep. He turned over instinctively, and the drowsy shock of her closeness, as he felt her gentle, tentative hands slide across his skin, sent a current of pleasure through his half-awake body. He woke, gathered her to him without a word, stroked her face, then kissed her for a long, long time, and when he entered her, she gave only the smallest whimper of absolute relief.

Chapter sixteen

When Leo's radio alarm began to buzz, he reached out and fumblingly switched it off. He lay face down, listening to the sound of rain upon the window, and then remembered. He turned his head. She was still deeply asleep, her dark, silken hair over her face, one hand upon the edge of his pillow. He lifted locks of her hair gently away from her face with his fingers, and studied her features. Then he sighed, and got out of bed quietly, fetched his robe and went through to the bathroom to shower and shave.

He dressed, made some coffee, and still she slept. Leo looked at the clock. Twenty to nine. If she didn't wake soon, it would be time for him to go. He didn't see how he could decently leave without speaking to her. He would have to wake her in half an hour; he was due in court at ten. But what was he to say to her? The situation was not straightforward.

Rachel woke to the sound of rain and the smell of coffee, realised where she was, and knew suddenly that the sound of rain and the smell of coffee together would always take her back to this moment. Her mind was instantly flooded with him, with everything that had happened, with complete and unconditional love. She turned over and lay on her back, recalling it all – talking to him, watching him, then listening to him, the hypnotic charm of his voice, the touch of his hands, their lovemaking. It had been, she told herself, the most important night of her life. She suddenly wanted very badly to see him, to see his face, have him before her.

She sat up slowly, listened, and could hear nothing. A small wave of panic swept her; suppose he had gone, and she was here alone? She got out of bed and picked up Leo's shirt from the chair where he had flung it last night. She held it to her face for a moment, breathing the scent of him, then slipped it on, buttoning it carefully.

Leo was eating oatcakes and marmalade in the kitchen when she appeared in the doorway.

'Very pretty,' he murmured, getting up and taking his coffee cup and plate to the sink. She was swept with relief at the sight of him, the wonderful, absolutely perfect sight of him.

'Coffee?' he asked, lifting a cup from the shelf without waiting for her reply.

She sat down at the table and watched him, uncertain what was to unfold between them now. She did not care. She could not care; she was entirely in his control, without freedom of will or action. She simply waited.

'There we go,' he said, and set the cup down in front of her. 'Milk,' he added, pointing, 'sugar,' pointing again. Then he looked at her face, calm and lovely. Possibly still a bit groggy, he told himself. He smiled encouragingly. 'Oatcakes.' He lifted the packet, then set it down again. 'And marmalade. Not the most conventional combination, I know, but I've run out of bread.'

'I'm not hungry, thanks,' she replied, with something like a smile. This was not true, but she could not have eaten at that moment. She scarcely wanted the coffee. She simply wanted to know where all this was to be taken, this precarious, tipping feeling of happiness, of suddenly finding herself in love.

Leo moved around the kitchen for a few moments, ostensibly clearing up, humming to himself, but wondering how best to bring this to a tidy conclusion. Remembering all that she had told him last night, and subsequent events, one had to be careful.

'I think I have time for one more cup before I go,' he said at last, glancing at his watch, deciding that something had to be said. He sat down opposite her with his coffee.

'So,' he said, then paused. 'I suppose we have to sort this out a bit.' She said nothing, simply looked at him with those marvellously clear blue eyes. She looked astonishingly good, he thought, for someone who had just woken up. 'I think we have to be clear about why last night happened,' he went on, his voice light and decisive. 'For Anthony's sake, as much as for anyone else's.'

Anthony? she thought wonderingly. What did Anthony have to do with any of this? In the realm where Leo spoke and moved, Anthony simply did not exist for her.

'Why do you say that?' she asked slowly.

Leo sat back in his chair, opened his mouth to speak, and then hesitated. He wondered why his legendary eloquence had to desert him at this juncture. Not that he felt guilty about Anthony. If anything, he'd probably done the boy a favour. But he could hardly say this.

'Because – well, aren't you – aren't you seeing one another, as it were?' As it were? He could hardly believe he'd said anything so fatuous.

Rachel looked down at her coffee. There were several meanings to be read into what Leo had just said, but only one reply that she could possibly make.

'He isn't – he couldn't be – anything more than a friend.'

'I think,' replied Leo carefully, 'that he sees it as a little more than that.' He was worried by the turn this conversation seemed to be taking.

She looked up quickly. 'I don't care. Do you honestly think that I could? Now?'

He met her candid gaze, then leaned forward. He could not be mistaken as to what her words implied. 'Rachel,' he said. She watched his hands twisting his coffee cup, loving the way her name sounded when he said it. 'Rachel, what happened last night – ' She waited, watching, conscious of breathing in light, slow, suspenseful breaths. He looked up. 'It was not something I had intended. It was – well – ' He spread his hands; she had to restrain an urge to stretch out her own and place them in his. She squeezed her hands together between her thighs, out of sight below the table. 'Just look on it as – as giving one another comfort. Just an exchange of kindness.'

'Kindness?' She echoed his word softly, gazing at him. He looked away. 'Was there nothing more to it than that?' There was wonderment in her voice.

'Rachel – it happened because – because I wanted to help, because things seemed to be very bad for you, and you needed – ' He sighed, rumpling his grey hair with his fingers. 'Oh, hell, you didn't need this, at any rate, did you?'

She put out her hand and laid it over his. He looked down, thinking that this was getting difficult, and that he was going to be late.

'Yes, I did. Leo, I did.' Her voice was gentle but urgent. She was conscious of the distance between them, that whatever extraordinary emotion she felt for him, it was not returned. He was being as honest as he could when he said that he had only meant to show her kindness. But she thought about their lovemaking, how it had obliterated all her tensions and fears, dissolving the anxieties of the past years, and she could not believe that there was to be nothing more. There would be more love, and love of a different kind. Not now, but eventually. Everything she felt for Leo at that moment made her serenely sure of it.

He sighed. He wanted to have a chance to read through that affidavit before going into court; time was slipping away.

'Look, Rachel, I don't know how we both got into this, but I think we must just put it behind us.' He slid his hand from beneath hers and rose. 'There's nothing to me. I don't go the distance. A non-starter. What has happened has to be the extent of it. If it has helped you, I'm glad. If it's messed you and Anthony up, I'm – well, I don't think you should let it. Look on what happened between us as – oh, some kind of catharsis.' He looked down at his hands, then thrust them into his pockets. 'I'm sorry.'

'It's all right,' she replied, feeling as though her soul were shrivelling up inside her at the impatient finality of his voice. 'I suppose it's the kind of thing that happens to you all the time,' she added sadly.

Leo did not know what reply to make. He could hardly say that yes, it was, only it was usually some young man, and only very rarely a woman. Certainly not Rachel's type of woman, he thought, surveying her fine beauty, her tumbled black hair, the slender body that looked so charming and vulnerable in his shirt of yesterday.

'Come here,' he said softly. She got up and came round the table to him. He laid his hands on her shoulders and looked into her eyes, which searched his own face trustingly. 'Last night was wonderful,' he said gently. Tiring, though, he thought. 'I'm very glad it happened. Very. You are a lovely and most special creature. Please just go on from here. Forget everything in the past. I hope we shall see one another from time to time. Now' – he paused, kissed her lightly on the forehead – 'I have to go or I shall be late for court.'

He took his hands from her shoulders and moved away into the living room to fetch his jacket. She stood very still in the kitchen. He reappeared in the doorway. 'Help yourself to anything you want. There's plenty of hot water for a shower, or whatever.' He shrugged his shoulders into his jacket, patting his pockets for wallet and keys, and stood looking at her. 'Just give the door a good slam when you leave for work.'

'Oh, I shan't go into work today,' she said, and gave him a faint smile. 'I'll work at home. It's Friday, after all, and I'm going to spend the weekend with friends in the country. I'll just go down a few hours earlier.' She wanted to keep her voice, her words, casual and friendly, as though none of it mattered, as though she could treat it in his sensible, dismissive way. She thought she knew now, as she stood looking at him, what it meant to have an aching heart. Heavy as lead, and aching. There was no other word to describe it.

'Good. Fine,' said Leo. Well, that all seemed to have gone off without a problem. There had been a moment when he had thought things were going to get out of hand and emotional. But she seemed to be approaching it sensibly. No tears, at any rate. 'I'll be off, then,' he added. 'Goodbye.'

Although he had imagined that he had parted from Rachel on a rational note of mutual understanding, the thought of her haunted him throughout his morning in court. She had taken it very well, he knew, but the realisation grew upon him that he had treated her as he might treat the averagely promiscuous, worldly thirty-five-year-old. In fact, he told himself savagely, as he watched Angus Hooper, counsel for the other side, making his sonorous submissions, he had behaved abominably. But what was he to have done? How did one behave in such a situation? It wasn't as though he'd set out to seduce her. The thing had been totally unpremeditated. It was she who had come to *his* bed, not the other way around. Although the events which had preceded that might fairly be seen as encouragement. Still, he had not expected it.

'. . . and, my Lord, the defendants do not dispute,' Angus Hooper was saying, his over-refined vowels rolling out into the blank air of the courtroom, 'that the person who would be liable on the plaintiffs' claim in an action *in personam* was, when the cause of action arose, the owner of the charterer of the *Ara Fidelis*. That is not in dispute. What my clients contend, however . . . '

Leo tapped his teeth with his pen. He should just steer clear of sex with women; he did not handle them well. They expected things, they took lovemaking as a prelude to great emotional entanglements, instead of just taking it for what it was. He should simply have told her, without any fuss, to go back to her own bed. Ha! He made a face at this thought, and his instructing solicitor glanced momentarily at him. All very well to say that in the cold light of day, but at the time he had drawn a kind of comfort from her soft presence.

'. . . and I would submit that the words "damage done by a ship" must, as a matter of language, my Lord, clearly refer to physical damage alone – '

'But Mr Hooper, the court has already accepted that the words in the paragraph are "done by", and not "caused by",' interrupted Mr Justice Appleby with a sigh. He was growing more and more irascible by the half-hour. Leo snapped to attention as the judge glanced in his direction. 'No doubt Mr Davies would agree with me that such a submission begs the question.'

Leo rose. 'My Lord, that is indeed our view. The words "done by" import the concept of physical damage. But I would submit that it is clearly beyond doubt that there is no need to establish any physical contact by the ship which does the damage. Your Lordship is familiar, of course, with the dictum of Lord Diplock in *The Echersheim* . . . ' That'll do, thought Leo, and let his voice drift away.

Mr Justice Appleby nodded. 'Quite so, Mr Davies. That, I think, is your obstacle, is it not, Mr Hooper?' He looked to Hooper, then glanced back briefly, approvingly, at Leo.

Good enough, thought Leo. Appleby was a notoriously impatient judge, but Leo felt he had his measure – it was simply a case of knowing your stuff inside out and not being too repetitive. Leo eyed the judge's small, jowly face beneath the too-large wig, which made him look like a bespectacled, ill-tempered baby, and thought with gratification that Appleby, too, could be counted on to support him. At this, the recollection of Sir Frank Chamberlin's fears struck him coldly. And when Appleby heard whatever rumours were drifting around – what then? Would he discount them, disbelieve them, continue to regard Leo as an excellent and obvious choice for silk? Would he regard the fact that Leo had been known to take male lovers as an irrelevance? Perhaps he would. He was a man who liked to think himself free from the taint of bigotry. But what exactly were the things which might come to his ear, and to the rest of the Commercial bench? Leo thought again of what Frank had said. Perhaps he should go back to him, ask him the exact nature of the conjecture.

And then, as his mind summoned up what it could recall of their conversation in the smoking room at White's, an extraordinary and not unconnected notion occurred to him. Counsel's voice rose again.

'. . . my clients contend that it is inappropriate to claim an injunction in an action *in rem*, because the action is against a ship, and there are no defendants unless the owners of the ship acknowledge service of the writ, thereby submitting to the jurisdiction . . . '

Leo stared unseeingly at Hooper as he continued his tortuous verbal meanderings. Of course, Frank's suggestion for scotching the rumour was preposterous. The last thing Leo ever wished to contemplate was marriage, to either sex, in whatever form. But the thing need not necessarily be taken to such extremes. There were half-measures. Might he not achieve the same results by appearing, for a few months at least, to be quite markedly attached to some woman? That might have the effect, if not of giving the lie to such rumours as existed, at least of defusing them of immediate impact, of rendering them harmless, of making him a person of no obvious risk in the eyes of the Lord Chancellor's Office? If he could engineer it so that it was widely reported that he was seeing someone, and that it was serious . . . it might just swing the thing. There were women he knew, friends, who might co-operate – but no, that would not be convincing. There had to be a large degree of sincerity, at least on one side, for the thing to work – and he could think of just the person. The fact that Rachel was a lawyer was even more helpful. When the likes of Roger Williams and others got wind of it, half the city would believe that Leo Davies had capitulated at last. Leo was well aware that most of his fellow lawyers enviously believed that he was footloose and fancy-free by choice, probably bedding half the attractive women who worked within the square mile. It was a belief which he had done nothing in the past to discourage, since it served his private purposes very well.

He smiled to himself as the notion took root and developed. There was Anthony, of course – but he could be discounted. There were plenty of other young women around for him, and with fewer problems. He would be better off without Rachel. Anthony was a minor consideration. And Rachel? Well, Rachel would benefit from the experience. Last night was evidence that he could help her out of the awful emotional and sexual hole she had been living in for the past several years. He would merely be continuing the therapy.

Leo glanced down at the notes he had been making, still listening with half an ear to the interminable drift of his learned friend's discourse as the rest of his mind raced with this developing idea. Hooper was winding up. Besides, he would make sure that they were the most wonderful, pleasurable months for her. That would be her reward. That, at least, was within his gift.

Angus Hooper sat down, Mr Justice Appleby turned his head to look invitingly at Leo, and Leo rose, handsome and assured.

'My Lord,' he began, uplifted by the realisation that the game was far from over, 'I shall deal first of all with what I perceive to be the weakest part of my learned friend's argument – namely, that loss suffered by way of financial loss cannot fall within the ambit of the words "damage done by a ship" under Section 20(2)(e) of the Supreme Court Act, 1981 . . . '

Anthony had been puzzled and annoyed by Rachel's disappearance the previous evening. He had spent some time combing the crowd in the Guildhall before finally concluding that she had gone, and allowing himself to be taken by David Liphook and William Cooper to a spaghetti house in Covent Garden, where he had drunk far too much wine. His head still ached vaguely that morning as he rang Rachel's office.

'Good morning, Nichols and Co! How can I help you?' sang out Nora's voice. 'No, Mr Cross, Miss Dean won't be coming in today. She's working from home. Can her secretary help? I see. Thank you for calling!'

Anthony put the phone down and hesitated before picking it up again. If she hadn't gone in to work today, maybe she'd felt unwell last night and just gone home. She'd been behaving rather peculiarly before they got to the Guildhall, with a nervy talkativeness quite unlike her usual manner. Perhaps he should just leave it – wait for her to call him. But since he was in love with her and would take any opportunity to speak to her, he seized upon his legitimate excuse and rang her flat.

Rachel was sitting at her kitchen table working out laytime calculations for a tedious demurrage claim when the phone rang. She was still in a sufficient state of nervous apprehension for the sound to make her start. She listened to the insistent, rhythmic ringing for a few seconds, and wondered, hoped . . . But she knew that was impossible. He didn't have her number. Anyway, he would not get in touch with her. That much had been clear. Yet, despite his words, she still felt, as she walked from the table to the phone, as though she were carrying her newly discovered love like a fragile burden.

She set the burden down gently when she heard Anthony's voice.

'Oh, hello,' she said, disappointed in spite of everything she had just told herself. She walked back into the kitchen with the phone and sat down.

'Hi,' said Anthony. 'I'm just ringing to see how you are. They said you wouldn't be in to work today, and I wondered where you'd got to last night.' He had already decided that there was no point in sounding annoyed about her disappearance, even if he was.

'Oh . . . ' Rachel let out her breath in a sigh. 'I'm sorry, Anthony. I was beginning to feel a little unwell, and I just went home. I know I should have looked for you to tell you, but I really did feel quite ghastly . . . ' She paused for a second, conscious of her nervousness at the deception. Anthony was the last person who should find out that she'd spent last night at Leo's. He thought so much of both of them – he would find it hard to deal with, to say the least. 'To tell you the truth,' she went on, trying to sound bright and casual, 'I asked my secretary for some aspirin before I left work last night, and I don't know what she gave me, but it made me feel most peculiar. I'm still getting over it.'

'Oh. Right,' said Anthony. 'I wonder what it was?'

'I don't know,' replied Rachel. 'Not aspirin, that's for certain. But I'm sure it was a mistake.'

'Well, look,' said Anthony, 'if you're feeling a bit better tomorrow, why don't we go to that film at the ICA?'

'Oh, Anthony, I can't. I'm going to my friend Marsha's in Winchester for the weekend. Sorry.' She felt utterly relieved at having a valid excuse, but she knew what was coming next.

'Okay. How about some time next week?'

She closed her eyes. No, now was not the time to try to end the thing once and for all. She opened them again, staring down at her calculator, idly punching in numbers. 'I'm honestly not sure what I'm doing next week, Anthony. Can I give you a call in a week or so?'

'Yes. Yes, okay,' replied Anthony, glancing up at Mr Slee's portly figure standing in the doorway as he waited for Anthony to finish. He badly wanted to see her, but he would just have to wait, count the days. 'Look, I have to go now. Don't forget to call. Bye.'

'Bye,' murmured Rachel, and clicked the phone off thoughtfully.

'Sorry to interrupt,' said Mr Slee, 'but there's a fee note in from Coward Chance on that tanker sale case, and I don't think it tallies with what's entered on the computer. If you wouldn't mind having a look . . . '

'Sure,' said Anthony, and followed Mr Slee to the clerks' room.

Rachel sat at the kitchen table, staring at her calculations; then she lifted her gaze to the window and to the garden of the church opposite, where the gardener was raking the debris of dead leaves into heaps. A steady wind scudded rain clouds across the grey sky. What next? she wondered. Even if there was to be no more of Leo for her, even if she had fallen violently in love to no purpose except that of waiting for time to take it all back again, she knew she could not go on seeing Anthony, could not even spend time with him. Not for the present. There was no point. She had made him believe that it was possible their relationship could develop in ways which she now knew it never would. Not now there was Leo.

She closed her eyes and leaned back. She had not meant to deceive him – everything she had said had sprung honestly from hope. But everything she had – every feeling, every impulse of affection, every desire – was Leo's. And he did not want it. She opened her eyes, sighed, and watched the bare black branches of the plane trees swaying against the sky. It was nearly December. How many months would she go on feeling like this? How long would there be this unfilled longing inside her? And how often in every day would she recall his body, the strong pliant feel of it, the sense of complete fusion, utter absorption, one in another, as they made love? She hoped it would not be many months, not very long, not very often. And yet she wanted to keep it, let none of it go stale, so that she could relive the precious moments over and over.

And in the meantime? She turned from the window and gazed around her. Back to her slow, silent routine, her shadow of a life away from work. There was not even the slim hope of making something work with Anthony now. Anthony. She would have to speak to him, explain to him that she did not want to see him, unless it was in connection with Mr Nikolaos's case. And that wouldn't be for some time. Maybe she would feel better by then. What was it Leo had said? – a catharsis. Perhaps he had done something for her. Maybe he had helped to resolve her fears, shown her that it was possible for her to love and give herself just as any other woman could. She smiled wryly. He had given and taken away in the same instant. She sat forward and picked up her pen again, determined to finish this calculation before setting off for Marsha's. She would have the whole journey to Winchester in which to think about last night, to refresh her love and her pain.

Leo called at the clerks' room on his way back from the law courts later that morning, still wearing his bands, drops of rain upon his jacket shoulders, panting slightly from having trotted across Fleet Street and down Middle Temple Lane.

'William,' he called, leaning on the door jamb, 'can you chase up those papers from Walter Fry's office today, please?' He saw Anthony standing at the computer and was about to turn and go up to his room, not wishing to encounter Anthony at that particular moment. Leo was not one given to guilt, but this business unpleasantly resembled an incident which had occurred once between Leo and Anthony's old girlfriend, Julia. Different, but sufficiently reminiscent to make him feel uneasy.

'I've got them here,' replied Mr Slee, turning to the heap of papers on his table.

Leo hesitated, then went into the room. Anthony turned and smiled, then glanced back at the computer.

'William, am I doing this right?' he asked, tapping at the keys.

Mr Slee said no, he wasn't, and moved him gently aside to attend to it himself. Anthony put his hands in his pockets and came over to where Leo was gathering bundles of documents from the table.

'What did you think of last night?' he asked Leo.

Leo paused, took out his half-moon spectacles and placed them on the end of his nose, and scanned the documents.

'Very good,' he replied, and looked up briefly at Anthony.

'Very enjoyable indeed.'

'Apparently Simon Stokes walked out with four bottles of champagne. Just took them away,' said Anthony with amusement, settling himself against the table. 'Not that they'd be missed, mind you. The place was groaning with the stuff.' There was a pause, in which Anthony glanced at Mr Slee, then back to Leo. He lowered his voice slightly. 'I noticed you talked to Rachel for a bit. She was the girl I told you about. What did you think?'

'Think?' Leo looked up at him. 'Well, let me see. Distinctly beautiful. Quite remarkably so.' Anthony smiled. 'But rather – um – odd. Quirky.'

'Yes, well,' replied Anthony, still smiling, 'there were reasons for that.'

'If I were you,' went on Leo, remembering to behave exactly in part, as though he were still speaking on the basis of their conversation in El Vino's, as though none of the events of last night had happened, 'I'd find someone a little more straightforward. Easier.'

'Sorry,' murmured Anthony in reply, 'but this is definitely love.' And he strolled back to where Mr Slee was still tapping the computer and muttering.

Leo stood, a sheaf of documents in his hand, gazing at Anthony over the tops of his spectacles. Love? Oh dear, oh dear. Poor Anthony was in for a sad surprise. But there was too much at stake here for him to be overly concerned at the state of Anthony's feelings. The object of his love was, unfortunately, going to be far too useful in swaying some hefty moral judicial opinion in Leo's favour. Besides, from what the girl had said this morning, it would have been uphill work for Anthony. The irony of it was, thought Leo as he gathered his papers together, that he would probably rather have had Anthony in his bed than Rachel for the next few months. But then, that had always been his feeling about Anthony, and he had learned to live with it, just as Anthony must now learn to live without Rachel.

Sir Basil Bunting, head of chambers, came into the clerks' room just as Leo was about to leave.

'Ah, Leo,' he said, 'I was hoping to have a word with you.

One moment while I speak to William.'

Leo waited dutifully, watching as Sir Basil, tall, dignified, white-haired, conferred briefly with Mr Slee. They must be of an age, thought Leo, musing on the contrast of Mr Slee's stocky figure and rosy face. They had come together and would go together, he and Sir Basil. Possibly Sir Basil would go sooner than he expected, if there were to be two new silks in chambers next year. His thoughts moved to Rachel, and he wondered, as he gave Anthony a dismissive glance, how soon he should ring her. She was away over the weekend and, anyway, he didn't have her home number. He would ring her at work early next week.

Sir Basil came back over to him. 'Come up to my room, Leo, if you would.'

Leo followed Sir Basil to his room, which was large and stately, reflecting the importance of Sir Basil and his distinguished practice.

'Do sit down,' said Sir Basil, as he closed the door. Leo sat down, placing the bundles of documents, which were rather heavy, on the floor beside him.

'Now,' said Sir Basil, 'I am having a little party in three weeks or so.' He rubbed his hands together cheerfully and sat down behind his vast polished desk. 'A largely informal affair, but quite a – ah – distinguished gathering. Mainly senior members of the judiciary, that kind of thing, and' – he paused proudly – 'our new Lord Chancellor. Now I understand that you have applied to take silk' – This direct shot surprised Leo, reminding him suddenly of Sir Basil's reputation as one whose genteel, delicately formal manner masked disarming forthrightness. – 'and, apart from the fact that I always think it pleasant for there to be some younger people to lighten these affairs, I imagine it would be useful for you to meet Lord Steele socially, as well as some of the more senior judges before whom you may not have appeared. A little visibility always helps. You will find that they remember you later.' He sat back and surveyed Leo. 'So I hope you will come.'

'Thank you very much, Basil,' replied Leo. 'I shall be delighted.' He couldn't have heard about Stephen's application. Or could he? Was this simple favouritism? It was not unknown for Sir Basil's partisanship to sway his judgment. It had almost cost Anthony his tenancy a couple of years ago, when Sir Basil had sought to give a place in chambers to his nephew, Edward, instead.

'I like to think, Leo,' continued Sir Basil with thoughtful self-satisfaction, 'that you embody many of the qualities which I have striven to maintain in these chambers over the years.' Little do you know, thought Leo, a smile flickering at the corner of his mouth; he placed his thumb and forefinger at either side of his mouth to smooth the smile away. Sir Basil placed the tips of his fingers together. 'If I can assist your advancement in any small way, then, of course, it is all to the good. So' – he tapped the edge of his desk lightly with the fingers of one hand – 'I shall look forward to seeing you on December the fourteenth, at seven o'clock. You know my house, do you? No, well, you will receive a formal invitation in due course, naturally – I merely wished to indicate to you personally the interest which I take in your career.'

Leo rose and thanked Sir Basil again, bending to gather up his documents. As he opened the door, Sir Basil said, 'Oh, and Leo – ' Leo paused in the doorway, smoothing down his bands with his free hand, glancing enquiringly at his head of chambers. 'If there is anyone whom you would care to bring as a guest, I should be delighted to meet them.'

'Thank you,' said Leo and, smiling, he closed the door. He made his way slowly back down to his own room.

This was more than auspicious. Not only was it a chance, heaven-sent, to meet those very people whose acquaintance and favourable opinion would enhance his prospects of obtaining silk, it also gave him the opportunity of being seen with Rachel, beautiful, head-turning Rachel, and of creating a climate in which those rumours which had taken root in people's minds would begin to shrivel and, ultimately, die.

So fixed in his mind was the idea that a liaison with Rachel must sweep away the only obstacle in his path that Leo felt impatient and annoyed at having to wait a few days before speaking to her. But he was, with his customary self-confidence, quite sure that when he did so, she would react with the same ardent willingness which had brought her so fortuitously to his bed last night.

Chapter seventeen

Rachel stood in Marsha's tiny kitchen on Sunday afternoon, hugging one arm with her other hand as she drank her second glass of wine. Marsha, small, blonde and pregnant with her second child, glanced at her friend as she slid the basted chicken back into the oven. Rachel, she thought, always had a defensive, held-back look, as though hugging herself away from the world.

'You're miles away,' she said, straightening up and wiping her hands on her apron, running her fingers absently over the swell of her stomach.

Rachel smiled and took another sip of her wine. 'I know. I'm trying to drink too much, in the hope that it might make me feel better.'

'It's worth a try,' replied Marsha, picking up the bottle of red wine and splashing some more into Rachel's glass. 'You can have my share. I'm not drinking at the moment.' She put the bottle down and folded her arms, looking squarely at Rachel. 'But it might help to talk about it. You've been staring vacantly into space ever since you got here. What is it?'

'Love, I guess,' said Rachel.

Marsha supposed that it should have come as less of a surprise, but over the years she had not associated Rachel with affairs of the heart. Perhaps it had something to do with that awful business at university, the rapist, but Rachel always kept men at a distance, never let herself get involved with anyone. And now she was gazing wistfully out of the window and talking of love.

'At last!' she said sardonically. 'Mind you, I'm surprised you actually let any man get near enough.' Marsha did not know enough about Rachel to realise the import of her words. But Rachel simply glanced from her wine to Marsha's face and back again.

'Oh, he got close enough, all right,' she sighed, and drank some more. 'In a way, it's quite wonderful,' she went on, the alcohol allowing her to open up. 'I've never been in love before. Unlike you,' she added, smiling at Marsha.

Marsha rolled her eyes to the ceiling, tucking back her coarse blonde hair behind her ears.

'Oh, heavens! I'm never out of love.' She smiled musingly at the kitchen floor. 'Think of all those blokes at university, one after the other . . . ' She glanced out of the window to where her husband, Phil, was putting together a wooden wire and mesh run for their five-year-old son's rabbit, her face a little wistful. 'Even when it was all utterly hopeless, it was still the most delectable feeling. One was simply more alive.'

'You sound as though you miss it,' remarked Rachel.

'Far from it,' laughed Marsha; she picked up a knife and began to chop the carrots. 'There was the most divine foreign language student lodging with the Hendersons for six months recently. I fed off little fantasies about him for a while.' She popped a piece of raw carrot into her mouth and crunched it. 'And presently I've got a most satisfying crush on Mel Gibson.'

'Oh, you can have him,' said Rachel. 'But not Jeremy Paxman.'

'Jeremy Paxman?' exclaimed Marsha, turning to look at Rachel in disbelief. 'You must be joking!' They both giggled for a moment. 'So,' went on Marsha, 'this person you're in love with has tiny ears and no neck?'

'Jeremy Paxman *has* got a neck,' said Rachel, and drank some more wine. She paused, staring at the sink. 'No, Leo looks quite, quite wonderful. Even you would think so,' she added.

'What's that supposed to mean?'

'Well, anyone whose taste runs to Mel Gibson . . . But Leo – I don't believe any woman could look at him without finding him utterly desirable.'

Marsha had never heard Rachel speak about any man in these terms before; she smiled to herself, liking it.

'It's beyond me how he's managed to remain single,' added Rachel. A small question wandered across her mind as she said this, but then she thought of Leo's mews house, its feeling of completely solitary occupancy. No, married was the last thing Leo was, or ever likely to be.

'So, tell me about this paragon,' said Marsha. At that moment the kitchen door banged open, letting in a gust of freezing air and a small figure in mittens, anorak and wellingtons.

'Mum!' he shouted. 'Dad's finished it! Come and see! It's really good!'

'Mega,' replied Marsha, glancing at her son critically. 'I told you to put a hat on. Here.' She picked a woollen hat from the peg on the back door and handed it to him, and he turned to race back out again. 'I'll come in a minute,' she called.

'Mega?' said Rachel enquiringly.

'Very much the in word. I use it all the time. Love it. A year ago it was "wicked". I enjoyed that, too. Anyway, about this man . . .'

Rachel's smile faded, then grew again. 'Well, he's a barrister, he's about – he must be about forty or so, only he looks older at first because his hair is completely grey. He's – well, he's wonderfully handsome, in a lean sort of way. Perhaps handsome's not the word.' She frowned. 'There's something charismatic about him. Electric.'

'Sounds cute. Have you known him long?'

Rachel drank some more wine, threw back her head and swallowed. 'Not very. About a couple of days.'

Marsha gave a hoot of laughter. '"No sooner met but they looked; no sooner looked than they loved,"' she chanted gently, heaping the chopped carrots into a pan.

'Something like that,' murmured Rachel, 'from my side, at least.'

'Well, you say you've only known the poor man for two days. Give him a chance.'

'I don't think he wants the chance,' replied Rachel. 'In fact,' she added, draining the last of her wine, 'I know he doesn't.' Her voice was flat, final. Marsha looked at her. How could anyone lucky enough to be loved by Rachel not love her instantly back? She was so sweet, so beautiful – Marsha had long ago accepted that Phil was mad about her. What man wouldn't be? Possibly a little on the thin side for some tastes, reflected Marsha, who herself was plumply pretty, but still beautiful. Haunting.

'That's a defeatist attitude,' she replied. 'Can you pass me that colander?' Rachel passed it to her and surveyed her empty glass unhappily. 'Have some more,' said Marsha, nodding in the direction of the wine.

Rachel shook her head. 'I've had too much already.'

'Anyway,' went on Marsha, breaking cauliflower florets into the colander, 'what makes you so sure he's not wild about you, too?'

Rachel sighed. 'It's not exactly a conventional situation, Marsha.' She hesitated, then decided to tell her. What difference would it make? Marsha would be the last person to judge her. 'The fact is, we met, we went to bed together the same night, and the next morning he told me that – well, that he'd had a nice time, but that that was it. End of story.' Just saying the words, 'we went to bed together', suddenly conjured up the recollection of his touch, his mouth against her breast as he moved inside her. A warm wave of desire welled up within her. It was wonderful, she knew, just to have been there with him, to have let someone near enough, and now to be able, like any other woman confiding in her friend, to stand in Marsha's steamy little kitchen in Winchester recounting her humdrum tale. Whatever misery it had brought, at least she felt real, part of humanity, sharing its conventional griefs and pains.

'Well,' said Marsha, 'you may think you're in love with him, but he sounds like a complete shit to me.'

'Why?'

'Hopping into bed with you at the first opportunity, then just dropping you the next day. Talk about "wham, bam, thank you, ma'am!"'

'I hopped into his bed, actually,' said Rachel happily nursing her empty glass against her cheek.

'Mmm, I see,' said Marsha.

It was true, thought Rachel. She had gone to him – gone because she could not bear to let the moment pass, to have nothing more of him than those few extraordinary moments, the touch of his fingers, and the memory of his eyes afterwards, searching her face. What else could she have done, with that hunger awoken in her? Perhaps if she had not gone to his bed – perhaps it was true, all that old stuff about men losing respect for girls who were easy . . . But she didn't think Leo was a man for whom respect had anything to do with sex. Anyway, it was done now. Done and gone.

'Well, if I were you, I wouldn't let a one-night stand affect me so badly.'

'I can't help it,' replied Rachel. 'And I can't look at it in that way. It wasn't like that. He – oh, it's all too complicated to explain. Anyway, I'm rather luxuriating in the misery of unrequited love,' she added. At least I'm human, she thought; at least I know it can happen to me. 'What was that dreadful poem you used to recite when we were at university? – you know, whenever you were languishing with love for someone?'

'Ah, "Give me more love or more disdain . . . "'

'That's it,' said Rachel with a smile, as Marsha struck a declamatory pose next to the cooker.

> '. . . The torrid or the frozen zone
> Bring equal ease unto my pain;
> The temperate affords me none.'

She laughed, sighed and turned back to the cauliflower.

Rachel laughed, too. Thank God for friends, she thought. What was Leo to her compared with someone like Marsha, who had known and cared for her over the years, with whom she had giggled and wept and shared hopes, hours and ambitions? He was someone who had entered her life briefly, abruptly, and left it – but he had changed her irrevocably, and now he illuminated her life entirely. If Leo had asked her to go to him, and never see Marsha again, she would have gone in an instant, without one thought or hesitation.

On Monday morning Rachel sat in her office, gazing at the envelope that lay before her and wondering how best to approach Felicity. Her mood of melancholy euphoria had evaporated when she left Winchester yesterday afternoon; the evening spent alone, with the blank probability that she would not see Leo again, that day after day must pass until her feelings dwindled and were forgotten, had depressed her dreadfully. What was the point, she asked herself, of finding that you could give yourself to someone, blot out all the fears of several years, when that someone simply dismissed you from their life? She had woken this morning with a feeling something like happiness, and then recollection and emptiness had descended, deadening her day. In a way, she was glad that she had at that moment the minor – no, the major matter of Felicity's boneheadedness to contend with as a diversion from her own thoughts of Leo. She sat for a moment, then got up, went to her door and called over to where the secretaries were working, 'Felicity, may I see you for a moment?'

Felicity shuffled to her feet. Her heart dropped like a stone at the sound of Rachel's voice. When Rachel hadn't come in on Friday, Felicity had been consumed with guilt. She should never have given her those pills. God knows what had happened. Rachel wasn't used to anything like that. What had she been thinking of? Now she trotted apprehensively into Rachel's room, her steps short and hurried in her tight skirt.

'Close the door and sit down,' said Rachel. Felicity glanced at Rachel's face; it was calm and lovely, but about as chilly as she had ever seen it. Something awful was coming. Perhaps she should take the initiative, get her apology in first.

'Rachel, I think I know what this may be about –' she began.

'I doubt it,' interrupted Rachel.

'I mean, if it's – look, I'm really sorry I gave you those pills on Thursday. I think I must have got them mixed up or something.' She paused; Rachel was looking impassively at the desk. 'That's what this is about, isn't it?'

'No,' said Rachel thoughtfully. 'No, as it happens, it's not, but now that you mention it, we might as well talk about that.'

There was a brief silence. 'Were you all right?' asked Felicity hesitantly.

'No, Felicity, I wasn't. I don't know what I was, but I was not all right.' She glanced up at Felicity. 'Why do you say you got them mixed up when you know perfectly well you meant to give them to me?'

Felicity picked at her nail varnish and looked sheepish. 'I thought it would help. Lift you a bit. Help you.' Then she added, 'Sorry.'

Rachel sighed. 'In a funny way, perhaps it did help. Or possibly not. Anyway, don't do anything so irresponsible again, right?'

'Right,' replied Felicity, nodding contritely.

'There's something a little worse than that, I'm afraid,' continued Rachel, 'and this makes me bloody furious.' She picked up the buff envelope lying on her desk. 'I've just received this letter from Payne Loftus today. Returning a document which was sent to them. A document sent by you.'

Felicity tried to look intelligent and concerned, but wasn't really sure what was coming.

'The document,' continued Rachel, 'is a statement taken from Mr Sukuraman in the Indo Suisse Bank fraud case. It is a statement containing evidence which is crucial to our clients' case. You were meant to send it to our clients. You, Felicity, sent it to the other side's solicitors. They have sent it back to me today. I shall read you their covering letter. "Dear Sirs, we have today received from your offices the enclosed document relating to the above case. We are herewith returning the document to you unread. Yours, etc, Payne Loftus."' Rachel laid down the letter and the envelope. There was a silence.

'But – but they've said they haven't read it,' said Felicity hopefully. Even she appreciated the potentially damaging repercussions of what she had done.

'Felicity,' said Rachel, 'they have not only read it, they have studied it sentence by sentence, they have photocopied it, and even as we speak, a copy, which will be read and then destroyed without trace, is winging its way to their clients in Switzerland.'

'Oh, God,' said Felicity.

'There's nothing I can do about it. It's happened. But it happened because you don't pay attention, Felicity, because you never get any of the simplest clerical work right. Because you're too busy gossiping with Nora or smoking in the Ladies!' Rachel was angrier than Felicity had ever seen her. 'Every day there is something – something that has to be retyped, or

210

rephotocopied, or found because you've lost it. It's all very irritating, and up to now I've tried not to mind, because there are some things you *are* good at. But when you start sabotaging my cases with your incompetence, then something has to be done.'

They stared at one another; it was as though the evening they had spent together had never been, all the gossip and laughter and the feeling that they were on the same level, girls together. When the chips are down, thought Felicity, none of that counts. She's my boss, and I'm her idiot secretary.

'Now, I don't mean,' said Rachel after a pause, her tone quieter, 'that I want to see you get the sack, or anything like that. I'm just going to suggest that it might be better if you didn't go on working in the litigation department, where little slips can cost us a lot. As in this case. This is a very large firm, and I'm sure Mr Lamb can find you a more suitable job.' Felicity looked so miserable that Rachel felt touched, momentarily, with guilt. They'd been so friendly that Wednesday night, too. Well, that had probably been a mistake, socialising with one's secretary, to say nothing of smoking her dope. I must have been out of my brain with tiredness and jet lag, thought Rachel, to have done such a thing. 'I'm sorry, Felicity,' she said gently. 'I do like you – very much. But this has got nothing to do with liking. It has to do with efficiency and getting the job done. You do see that, don't you?'

At that moment the phone rang. Felicity just sat there, stricken, wondering which was worse – another encounter with Mr Lamb or the prospect of the pleasure the Menopausals would derive from all this.

Getting hold of Rachel had not been a straightforward affair for Leo. When he rang Nichols & Co, he suddenly realised that he did not know, or had forgotten, Rachel's last name.

'Hello, can I help you?' said Nora.

'Yes. I'd like – I'd like to speak to Rachel, please.' He felt perfectly absurd saying this.

'Dean or Maxwell?' enquired Nora pertly.

'I – well, I'm not sure, really.'

'We have a Rachel Dean, one of our partners, and a Rachel Maxwell in accounts,' announced Nora patiently, crimson-tipped finger poised to flip the switch. 'Which would you like?'

'The first one,' replied Leo helplessly. He felt he was already losing his grip on the suavity with which he had intended to handle this.

'Who shall I say is calling?'

'Mr Davies.'

Nora flicked the switch and Rachel picked up the phone, still looking at the miserable Felicity. 'Hello?'

'Rachel, I have a Mr Davies for you.'

Rachel could think of no one she knew called Davies. Whoever it was would have to wait while she dealt with this business of Felicity. 'I'm sorry,' she replied, 'you'll have to tell him to call back. I'm busy. Tell him I'm in a meeting.'

Nora flipped the switch back. 'I'm sorry, Mr Davies, but Miss Dean is in a meeting. Would you care to leave your number?'

Leo had not anticipated this. Annoyed, he replied, 'No. No, that's all right.' And he hung up.

Rachel put the phone down and regarded Felicity impassively. 'To go back to what I was saying, Felicity,' she went on, 'I'll have to speak to Mr Lamb today. We'll see what he can find for you. I'll explain to him that I don't want this to go to the other partners, because I know – well, I know your track record isn't that good, and I don't want this to be more difficult for you than it has to be.' As she was speaking, the name of that caller was still lurking in the back of her mind. Who did she know called Davies? Why was it vaguely familiar? Suddenly she realised, and her heart felt as though it had dropped to her stomach. She stopped talking for a moment and stared vacantly. Oh God, he had called, and she had said she was busy. He might never call again. Oh, stupid, stupid cow that you are, Rachel, she cursed herself. She hesitated, then carried on. 'Anyway – yes, well, let's just try to keep the thing – low-key, shall we? I'm sure Mr Lamb will understand, if I explain . . . ' Her voice trailed away and she began to fiddle with the pen lying on the desk before her. Why had he called? Oh, the mere fact that he had called – that was enough. She could feel a smile rising unbidden to her lips, and managed to suppress it. 'I'll have another word with you later, Felicity, after I've spoken to him. In the meantime, could you run off five copies of the affidavit you typed up yesterday, please? The Flight Shipping one.'

Felicity nodded and rose. 'I'm really sorry about that mix-up,' she murmured. All she could think of was having to go and see Mr Lamb again. He'd probably just been waiting for an excuse like this – and she'd been trying so hard to keep her nose clean for the past few weeks, to get things right for a change. She left Rachel's office, sick at heart, and went back to her desk. It was Doris's birthday that day and she had bought cream cakes for all the girls. Now she thrust the box at Felicity.

'Like a cake, dear?'

Felicity shook her head and mumbled, 'No, thanks.' She could feel tears not very far away and rose quickly and headed for the Ladies. Behind her she could hear Doris murmuring, concern and gratification mingled in her marshmallow voice, ' . . . she looks ever so upset about something . . .'

As soon as Felicity had left her room, Rachel grabbed the phone and pressed zero. 'Nora,' she said anxiously, 'that man who called a moment ago – did he leave a number?'

'No, dear. Sorry.'

'I see. Thanks.' Rachel put the phone down. Of course he hadn't. And even if he had, would she have rung him back? No. That wasn't form. Girls don't chase boys. They might jump into their beds, but they don't thereafter chase them. She put her hands over her face. Please let him ring back, she prayed. Oh, please. She wondered how she would get through the day until he did ring again. If he ever did.

Leo spent the entire day in court and forgot about Rachel until he got back to chambers late in the afternoon. He was tired and irritable; his case was not going well. He had not handled that cross-examination as smoothly as he should have. Then, as he closed his door and flung his papers on to his desk, he remembered that abortive phone call of the morning. Should he try again? He was almost inclined to forget the whole idea. He felt suddenly low-spirited, the business of his application and the possibility of its failure preying on his mind. The whole thing seemed rather futile. Ridiculous, even. To have to spend several weeks in the apparently devoted

213

pursuit of some woman whom he hardly knew and scarcely cared for, merely to try to furnish himself with some sexual respectability – how absurd.

He sat down and drew a sharp crease with his thumbnail in the whiteness of his blotter. Outside on the landing he could hear Stephen Bishop's voice, then Roderick Hayter's, a brief chuckle of laughter, their footsteps dying away on the wooden staircase. Stephen. Portly, plodding Stephen stood to gain, and he to lose, merely through the vagaries of the specious morality of the Lord Chancellor. He suddenly saw the life that would stretch ahead of him, if he were to fail now, and it was a blank and unrelieved picture of mediocrity, a steady plateau of unspectacular success, no brilliant heights to be scaled, no further glories. It was a dead prospect. He must seize whatever chances existed.

He thought of Sir Basil's cocktail party in a few weeks' time, of the people who would be there, of how fleeting impressions and minute understandings could tip the balance in all things. And he picked up the phone.

Rachel was just coming out of the lift as she heard the phone ring, and she sped to her room, praying for it not to stop before she got there. Her heart was racing, as it had every time she had picked up the phone that day, bracing hope against the possibility of disappointment.

'Hello?' She sat down, trying to catch her breath.

'I have Mr Davies for you,' said Nora's matter-of-fact voice as she answered Rachel's prayer.

'Put him through, please.' She waited.

'Hello – Rachel?' The sound of his voice filled her with happiness. She gripped the receiver tightly, smoothing the smile out of her voice.

'Yes. Yes, hello.'

'It's Leo,' he said, leaning back in his chair and swinging his feet up on to the desk. 'I tried to call this morning, but you were busy.' He paused. 'How was your weekend?'

'Oh,' she replied, her heart still thudding, 'it was good, thanks. Some long, brisk walks, Sunday lunch, that kind of thing. Good.' She hesitated. 'How was yours?' She couldn't think of anything else to say.

214

Leo, feeling he could hardly tell her that it had been tedious beyond belief, since all his activities were now morally circumscribed, replied, 'Oh, so-so. Dull, really.' Then he said, getting down to business, 'I'd rather like to see you.'

Rachel was uncertain how to respond; happiness soared in her, and she could not help smiling. 'Fine,' she said faintly.

He took his feet off the desk and swivelled round, gazing at the faint blur of his reflection in the darkened window. He heard the smile in her voice as she said that one word; she was pleased to hear from him. He had supposed she might be. As he stared at the window, someone switched a light on in a room on the other side of Caper Court.

'Shall we have dinner?' he asked.

'I should like that,' she replied. Please, she thought, please don't say that it's because you want to apologise for Thursday. Don't say that. But Leo did not say that.

'Excellent. I'll pick you up from your office at half six,' was what he said. Best to get the thing up and running, he thought.

'Tonight?' she said, dizzy with happiness. 'But I've – '

'Don't say that you're not dressed to go out. If you look as good as you did in my shirt on Friday morning, you'll look wonderful.'

'But – ' she began again.

'And if you had something else arranged, cancel it.' He paused for just the correct few seconds before adding quietly, 'Please.'

A dozen questions crowded her head: Why? What about all the things you said? Have you been thinking about me? Did you realise you were wrong? – oh, tell me, tell me, just say it again. But all she said was, 'Fine. I'll see you at six thirty,' and put the phone down.

Leo buzzed through to Henry. 'Book me a table for this evening at Le Caprice, would you, Henry? Eight o'clock.' Important to start the thing properly, a little cheerful sophistication, nothing too intense. If the affair were to go the distance, it had to be properly paced. The months between now and Easter stretched in his mind like a broad, curving ribbon; where it all ended, he did not speculate. Time would take care of that. What was essential at the moment was the careful staging of a most important piece of romantic theatre.

In her office, Rachel felt too elated to do anything for a few moments. Then she glanced at her watch. Twenty to five. Nearly two hours to wait. She must fill it up, do something, make the time speed by. She remembered her talk with Felicity that morning. She should go and see Mr Lamb now, arrange to have Felicity transferred to another department and a new secretary brought in to take her place as soon as possible. If she left it any longer, she might find herself relenting.

As she took the lift to the eighth floor, Rachel found herself wondering whether, apart from the disaster of the Payne Loftus business, she didn't subconsciously have some other reason for wanting Felicity transferred. Unease, guilt at the events of Wednesday night, the realisation that once the formal divide between boss and secretary had been breached, then respect must crumble? Possibly. Well, whatever it was, things simply weren't going right. Felicity would probably be relieved, too.

She tried to explain the matter to Mr Lamb in the most general of terms only, without levelling any direct criticism at Felicity, but it was difficult.

'You see, I don't want this to be taken as any indication of – well, real dissatisfation on my part with Felicity. She's very good at many aspects of the work – dealing with clients, arranging things. It's just that I don't think she's entirely suited to the kind of work we do in the litigation department.'

'Well,' said Mr Lamb, who seemed to be deriving a certain amount of satisfaction from what he was hearing, 'I don't see that her slipshod ways as a secretary are going to make her an asset to the conveyancing department either, do you?'

Rachel eyed him coldly. She disliked the man's overweening attitude, his knowing eyes, his consciousness of his own power over the lowlier employees of Nichols & Co.

'Surely,' she said, 'there must be work for her within the firm where she would be less . . . ' Rachel hesitated.

' – of a liability?' supplied Mr Lamb. He laid down his pen. 'With the greatest respect, Miss Dean, Nichols and Co is not a charitable institution. Felicity was aware that this was her last opportunity to prove she was adequate for the work of the firm. This might be a case of misplaced loyalty on your part.'

'Don't speak to me about my loyalties, Mr Lamb,' retorted Rachel frostily. 'They are none of your concern. I simply feel that Felicity has a good deal to offer, but that she is not suited to being a partner's secretary. I don't wish to see her leave the firm because of this.'

Mr Lamb sighed. It delighted him to have Miss Dean asking him a favour. Effectively, that was what it was. He savoured the moment as he deliberated.

'Well,' he said at last, 'I suppose it might be possible to move her to another department. As a favour to you, of course, Miss Dean.' He smiled at her. 'I'll have a word with Felicity in the morning. It'll take me two or three weeks to find someone to replace her, you understand.'

'Thank you,' said Rachel, hating to have to say it.

'Oh, not at all,' he replied, and sprang from his desk to hold the door open for her as she left.

When Rachel got back to her room, Felicity was there, fastening a copy of the affidavit on to its file. She did not look round as Rachel sat down at her desk. The tension in the air was dismal to Rachel, particularly since she felt so light-hearted at the prospect of the evening.

'Felicity,' she said. Felicity put the file back on its shelf and turned round. 'I've seen Mr Lamb, and he thinks he can get you transferred to another department without any fuss. You won't be losing your job – you know I wouldn't let that happen. It's just – ' she sighed. 'Look, Wednesday night was really good fun, and I still want us to be friends. But this is my job, and it's really important that things are done properly. You do see that, don't you?'

Felicity folded her arms across her generous bosom and nodded sadly, her curls bobbing. 'Yeah, yeah, I know. I'm just not that good at – well, some things, I suppose.' She chewed thoughtfully on her thumbnail. 'I'm sorry it hasn't worked out.'

'So am I,' said Rachel, relieved that the thing appeared to be accepted without rancour. It had been pretty clear from the start that, dear girl though she was, Felicity was not a clerical asset to any solicitor. 'Mr Lamb says he'll have a word with you tomorrow,' she added.

And what else'll he have besides? wondered Felicity gloomily as she wandered back to her desk. A bit more pawing in return for being allowed to carry on working at Nichols & Co, no doubt. She slumped into her chair. Mind you, she thought, aware of the furtive glances of Louise and Doris, at least she'd be away from these old cows. It might even be fun in another department. If only there wasn't Mr Lamb to be faced in the morning.

At six twenty, Felicity came into the Ladies and was surprised to find Rachel there, carefully putting on make-up. She murmured hello.

'I thought you would have gone home long ago,' remarked Rachel, giving her a smile in the mirror.

'I'm meeting Vince up town,' said Felicity, 'so I thought I might as well finish that report thing.' She disappeared into a cubicle.

'You didn't have to, you know,' said Rachel, raising her voice to reach Felicity. She gazed at her reflection. She didn't normally wear much make-up to work, but she didn't want to look completely insipid for Leo. He was probably the kind of man who liked his women well groomed. Was this too much lipstick?

Felicity flushed the loo and emerged. 'I thought I might as well try to end on a good note,' she said cheerfully. She began to wash her hands, then glanced up at Rachel. 'You going out?'

Rachel nodded; her smile was radiant as she combed her hair.

'Well,' said Felicity awkwardly, 'have a nice time, then.'

'Thanks,' replied Rachel. 'You, too.' They looked at one another for a moment in the mirror, neither saying anything.

'You look really nice,' added Felicity. 'Goodnight.'

'Goodnight,' said Rachel, feeling, she did not know why, faintly ashamed.

Felicity put on her coat and went down in the lift to reception. Nora had gone home and Ted, the night porter, was on duty, talking to a grey-haired man at the desk. Very snazzy, thought Felicity, eyeing the elegant suit and dark cashmere coat.

'I'll just check with Miss Dean,' said Ted, as Felicity walked past, twinkling her fingers at him in farewell.

Christ, how does she do it? wondered Felicity, glancing back over her shoulder at Leo's lean, preoccupied face before pushing through the revolving doors into the cold night air. Mind you, she thought, ramming her hands deep into her pockets as she headed for the tube, Rachel's men all seemed far too neat and tidy for her taste. She thought with longing and affection of Vince's tousled, unkempt cheerfulness, and did not envy Rachel a thing.

Chapter eighteen

How can anyone be this happy? thought Rachel, watching Leo's face in the restaurant as he talked. They seemed to have done nothing but talk – incessantly, wonderfully, all evening. She had never met anyone who knew so much, who was so amusing and perceptive, with the ability to be funny and grave in the same moment. It delighted her to find that they shared common interests, too. He had been talking about sculpture, and she had mentioned a bronze he had in his house in Mayfair. 'Dennis Mitchell, isn't it?' she had said. And he had looked surprised and pleased and said, yes, it was. And they had talked for a while about that.

Now he was telling her about a case he had, and as he spoke her eyes wandered across his face, a little tired now at the end of the day, shadows below the eyes. She wanted to be able to reach out and stroke a hand across his features, touching them lovingly. Instead, she sat listening, wishing the evening didn't have to end, sipping at her wine. Not once had he referred to Friday morning, nor to the possibility that this evening was purely by way of atonement for that. From his very first smile when she had emerged from the lift at six thirty, he had behaved as though being with her was the simplest, most natural thing in the world. He talked to her as though from some different beginning, as though everything he already knew about her was an irrelevance. But it seemed to her impossible that the events of the recent past should not be touched upon.

She gazed thoughtfully down at the table as Leo asked the waiter to bring more coffee, then lifted her eyes to meet his. There was a brief silence.

'You look thoughtful,' said Leo, clasping his hands together and resting his chin on them. He gritted his teeth together to suppress a yawn. Not that she wasn't good company, but he was weary after his day in court, and he still had to go over his notes before the cross-examination of that export manager continued tomorrow. She smiled a slow smile, and he thought that perhaps he didn't want to hear what was on her mind. It might go on a bit. When women got that look in their eye, it meant that they wanted to dissect something in a lingering fashion.

'You know – ' she began, and leaned forward, still smiling, her dark, soft hair swinging against her face. I was right, thought Leo. Here we go. My mistake for ordering more coffee instead of the bill. 'You know, I was wondering,' she went on, 'why you called today. Why we're here now.' Her pulse had quickened as she spoke, aware that she might not receive the answer she hoped for. 'When you left on Friday morning – '

'Don't you know the golden rule?' interrupted Leo with a smile. 'Never ask a question in examination-in-chief unless you know what the answer's going to be.' There was a pause as the waiter poured more coffee. Then Leo glanced up at her. She's still waiting for an answer, he thought. Well, now – what should it be?

'I suppose,' he said thoughtfully, 'that Friday morning wasn't the best time to make decisions.' His eyes held hers. Tell her what she wants to hear, he thought. But just a little, not too much. 'I found I was thinking about you over the weekend – more than I expected. And I – wanted to see you again. As simple as that.' He gave her his best candid gaze, then lowered his eyes. 'As a matter of fact,' he lied, 'I was afraid you might not want to see me.'

Oh, how could you think that? thought Rachel. How could you possibly imagine that for one moment? She wanted to tell him how much she was in love with him, that the interval between his phone calls today had been hell, and that the thought of this evening ending was misery itself. But she could say none of that. She simply smiled and said, 'Well, you were wrong.'

Her smile, gentle as it was, was so pure and radiant that Leo decided she deserved a little more. He leaned forward, too, and placed the tips of his fingers upon her hands.

'I want us to forget about Thursday night,' he said, his voice low. 'It was the wrong way to start. I don't know what I feel,' he went on, feeling that what he actually wanted was to be home and asleep within the hour, 'but I do know that I want us to begin here, now, as though none of that ever happened.' He covered her hands with his and looked at her. 'Can we do that?'

'Yes,' murmured Rachel. She nodded and looked away, her heart brimming with happiness.

Enough of that, thought Leo, and, gently drawing his hands away, leaned back and called for the bill. Her hands still rested on the table and she sat mute, smiling faintly.

Leo drove her back to Fulham, feeling that he had set the thing tolerably well in motion. She sat beside him, not saying anything, lost in her own thoughts as she gazed at the passing traffic. He glanced at her profile, remembering the gratifying glances of admiration she had received in the restaurant. There was a certain self-reflecting satisfaction in being seen with a beautiful girl. Most men of his age would envy him. It had been an agreeable surprise, too, to find that she knew something about the things which interested him. No one, not a single one of his lovers, male or female, had ever shown the slightest interest in the little bronze spiral sculpture which stood on the bookcase in the corner of his living room, let alone known the artist. Perhaps the next few months would not prove excessively tedious. There was always sex, too, and the prospect of exploring her faculty for experiment, but he was keeping that well in reserve for the moment.

'Right here,' said Rachel, interrupting his train of thought. He indicated and turned the wheel obediently. 'It's the second road on the right down here. The corner house.'

He brought the car to a halt beside the church opposite her flat.

'Would you like a coffee, or something?' asked Rachel, uncertain whether she should ask or not, but longing, as she had longed all evening, to be alone with him, to hold him, feel him against her.

He turned to her, the light from the street lamp etching shadows beneath his brow and cheekbones. She suddenly

222

wished, with a wistful tenderness, that he was twenty years younger, that she could have known him as a young man. It was almost as though something precious and irretrievable had been lost to her.

'I don't think I should, you know,' he replied. 'This case goes on tomorrow, and I have to look at a few things . . . ' He studied her features in the half-light, then drew his finger gently from her brow down across her cheek, his mouth moving towards hers. He kissed her gently at first, and then more fiercely, and she clung to him, a little murmur coming from the back of her throat as he deftly unfastened the top button of her blouse and slid his hand across the warm flesh of her breast. He remembered that small whimper of longing from Thursday night, and was suddenly possessed with a lunatic urge to make love to her then and there in the car. It was the kind of dangerous, imbecile thing which turned him on, the illicit and uncontrollable. That was what Leo liked.

But he did not. He lowered his head and kissed her breast for a moment between the folds of her coat; she arched her head back, her throat white in the glow from the street light. Then he raised his head and pulled her mouth to his again.

'You see,' he muttered, as their kiss ended, 'I don't think coffee would be enough. And I want us to take things slowly . . . this time.' He could feel her trembling slightly. He raised both hands to fasten her blouse, conscious of her dark gaze resting on his face. There was silence for a moment. 'When can I see you again?' he asked. 'Later this week?'

She nodded, too weak with love and desire to reply.

'I'll call you at work,' he said, and kissed her softly again as she reached for the door handle.

'Thank you for a wonderful evening,' she said, and smiled the slow, curving smile which Leo thought he really quite liked.

He said nothing, merely smiled in return and watched as she stepped from the car. Then, as she was about to close the door, he said, 'By the way, I've just thought of something. Are you busy on the sixteenth?'

'Of December?' She leaned down.

'Mmm.'

'I don't think so.'

'Good. Keep it free.'

She nodded, and he glanced at the car clock. Another minute or so, what was the difference? 'And come here,' he added softly, leaning across to her. She crouched down and let him kiss her again, then rose and went across the road and up to her flat.

He watched her go, waited for a light to appear in the upstairs window, then started the car. That, he thought, as he turned his Porsche round carefully in the narrow side street, had gone very well. Next time, however, the venue must be a little more public, somewhere he could guarantee to be seen with her. Public dalliance. He smiled to himself as he drove down Brompton Road. He couldn't remember terribly much about making love to her last Thursday night, partly because it had been dark, but he recalled that it had been generally enjoyable. She had such a nice, slender, boyish body. He wondered what she would look like with all that dark hair cut short . . .

Mr Lamb waited until lunchtime the following day before summoning Felicity to his office. When she went in, he was sitting well back from his desk, his legs crossed, the light shining waxily on his bald spot as he cleaned his nails with the edge of a piece of index card.

'Close the door, please, Felicity,' he said, glancing up and giving her a smile. She closed it and then sat down opposite him. Less easy for him to make a pass at her, she reckoned, if she was seated. She waited.

Mr Lamb chucked the piece of card aside and wheeled his chair swiftly forward on its castors to the desk, on which he rested his forearms.

'Well, I think you know why you're here,' he said smugly. 'I think you know that Miss Dean has asked to dispense with your services, such as they are. Even she has clearly had enough of your incompetence. It simply surprises me that it's taken her so long to realise what the rest of us have known for a very long time.'

Felicity, in a state of acute self-pity, felt her eyes prickling as she listened to him. She mustn't cry, she told herself. He would just love that. He'd probably have an orgasm just to see her in tears. This happy thought had the effect of banishing the incipient tears, and she tried to freeze the rest of his words from her mind as he went on. Just get it over with so's I can get out of here, she thought.

Mr Lamb examined his now clean nails. 'So I'll be finding someone to take your place. For some reason which is quite beyond me, she's asked me to try and find you some other work in the firm. Preferably somewhere where your general uselessness won't be so much in evidence. So, just this once, I've decided to give you another chance. I'm transferring you to the computer department, where you'll be doing general filing and typing up order sheets. You'll move there after Christmas. It'll take me till then to find Miss Dean a replacement.'

The *computer* department? God, thought Felicity, that was in the basement. No one went there. No one knew anyone who worked in there. The Land That Time Forgot. When the computer department fielded a team for the firm's darts tournament, no one knew their names. Still, it was a job. Her friend Maureen was only two floors up. She supposed this was an appropriate juncture at which to thank this bald-headed bastard.

'Thank you, Mr Lamb,' she murmured, her eyes fastened on the carpet tiles.

'Oh, don't thank me,' replied Mr Lamb in his Ken Livingstone twang, leaning back. 'If I'd had my way, you'd have been out on your ear in Mr O'Connell's day. What a pair you were. An old drunk and someone who couldn't do more than smoke and do her nails half the day.'

He was a bleeding sight nicer than you, pissed or sober, thought Felicity fiercely.

'As it is, you have Miss Dean to thank. Of course,' he added, 'it is true that I merely have to mention the matter to a few of the other partners – Mr Rothwell, for instance, and John Parr – and you might find yourself without a job. But I won't do that – not for the moment.' He swivelled from side to side in his chair, eyeing her. 'I think you'll find you'll have to improve your standard of dress somewhat for the computer department. Miss Luce isn't very keen on skirts that length, nor quite such revealing blouses.' His eyes were fixed on Felicity's low-cut blouse, one of her favourites. Vince liked it. 'Are you wearing a bra, Felicity?' asked Mr Lamb suddenly, softly.

She stared at him. 'Of course I am!' she replied.

'Hmm.' He continued to swivel in his chair, staring at her cleavage. 'Well, I suggest that one day next week – I'll let you know when – you could leave it off. Then maybe you can – pop up here in your lunch hour. Let me have a little look. There'll be no one about. Just as a little thank-you for being kept on at Nichols and Co.' He got up and came round the desk. 'I'm sure they're well worth looking at, Felicity, aren't they?' He moved in front of her, seating himself on the edge of his desk, folding his arms and looking down at her.

If he comes any nearer, I'm going to knee him in the balls, thought Felicity, amazed by what he was saying. But just then a light knock sounded at the door, and Mr Lamb leapt to his feet. His mousey-haired secretary put her head round the door.

'I thought you were on your lunch hour, Sandra,' he snapped irritably, putting his hands in his pockets and moving away from Felicity's chair.

'Well, I was,' said Sandra, coming tentatively into the room, a sheaf of papers in her hand, giving Felicity a quick glance. 'But you said yesterday that you wanted me to get out the pay sheets for last month, so I thought I'd get it done now. Here they are.'

Felicity took this opportunity to slide nervously out of her seat. Mr Lamb stepped forward to take the documents and saw Felicity from the corner of his eyes.

'I'll just be off, then, Mr Lamb,' murmured Felicity.

As Mr Lamb replied, 'I don't think we'd quite finished yet, Felicity,' Sandra began to say, 'There's just this one that seems a bit funny . . . ' and Mr Lamb was forced to attend to what she was saying and look at the sheet she was sorting out from the rest.

He glanced up quickly in annoyance as Felicity made her escape. He'd just been starting to enjoy himself, getting nicely worked up at the thought of getting his hands on those amazing breasts of hers, just a feel, then maybe a look next week. Still, he told himself, sighing with impatience as Sandra droned on at him about these print-outs, it would wait. He liked the idea of telling her to go and take her bra off, then come to his office, start unbuttoning her blouse slowly . . .

Felicity took the stairs instead of the lift, pounding down the echoing stairway to relieve her anger. He was beyond belief, that one! Had she heard him properly? Did he seriously believe she was going to start taking her clothes off for him, in return for him not telling the partners that she should be given the elbow? She stopped on the second-floor landing. He could stick his ruddy job, in that case, she told herself, leaning on the windowsill and looking out across the back streets and goods entrances of neighbouring offices. She didn't care any more about getting a rotten reference, not finding another job. There was a limit. But it seemed so unfair. Okay, she wasn't that great a secretary, but why should she lose her job just because she wouldn't flash her tits at the office manager?

At that moment Dee, one of the filing girls, came out of the Ladies.

'Hello, Fliss,' she said, swinging her bag over her shoulder. 'You coming down the Pindar? Melanie's having a birthday drink. She said to tell you if I saw you.'

'Yeah,' replied Felicity, turning round from the window. 'Yeah, you go on and I'll see you in reception. I'll just get my bag.'

Dee clicked off downstairs in her high-heeled boots, and Felicity pushed open the fire doors into the deserted second floor. Everyone was out except Doris and Louise, who sat hunched over their sandwiches and copies of *Woman's Realm* and *Prima*.

'Everything all right with Mr Lamb, dear?' enquired Doris through a mouthful of Nimble and Philadelphia Cream Cheese, her small eyes scanning Felicity's face.

They all knew something was up. Well, thought Felicity savagely, zipping up her bag and putting on her lilac fake fur jacket, they can have their little gossip about me. I don't care. I'll be glad to see the back of this lot.

'Yes, Doris,' replied Felicity brightly. 'Only you won't have me working with you much longer. I'm moving to the computer department after Christmas. Won't that be nice?'

'Oh, Felicity,' murmured Doris sadly, 'that is a pity. We'll really miss you – won't we, Louise?'

'Oh, yeah – yeah, we will.' Louise, not looking up from her magazine, poked a finger in her mouth to loosen a tomato pip from between her back teeth.

'We'll all have to go out for a little Christmas drink together, dear, before you go,' said Doris cosily, and took another bite of her sandwich. 'Just girls together.'

'Mmm. Something like that,' muttered Felicity.

I'd sooner have a cervical smear that sit in the pub with you, Doris, she thought, as she left them. As she went down to where Dee was waiting, she felt a bit calmer. That stuff Mr Lamb had come out with was just fantasy land. He was just getting his rocks off, talking dirty to her. It would be all right. She still had a job, hadn't she? Anyway, if he tried anything with her again, she might just have a word with Vince. Then he'd see.

Leo continued his campaign the following day. He spotted David Liphook, the most junior tenant in chambers next to Anthony, coming out of Middle Temple Hall after lunch, and fell in step with him on the way to Caper Court.

'You don't still lunch there every day, do you?' Leo asked David.

'Course I do,' replied David. 'It's quick and it's cheap. We're not all fabulously rich.' He grinned at Leo.

'Just the smell of the place depresses me – reminds me of all those endless dinners one had to eat before being called.'

'Oh, I still dine there occasionally,' said David. 'Just to keep my hand in. The benchers like to see one's face there from time to time.'

'That's true,' murmured Leo thoughtfully, making a mental note to dine there a couple of times before Easter. 'Anyway, how's that girlfriend of yours? Catherine, isn't it?'

They had stopped at the foot of the stairs to 5 Caper Court. David, small, blond and stocky, lifted his head and squinted against the pale December sunshine.

'Yes, that's right. Oh, she's fine. Great as ever. She'll be in raptures just to think that you remember her – she didn't stop talking about you for two weeks after she met you.'

'Lovely girl,' said Leo easily, hands in pockets. 'Give her my regards.'

They turned and went into chambers.

'Look,' said David, pausing on the stairs as Leo was about to go into the clerks' room, 'why don't you come over for dinner some evening? I know Catherine would love to see you. In fact, why not make it next Wednesday? William's coming, and a couple of other people. Nothing special, of course . . . '

'Thanks,' said Leo, and flashed him a smile. 'Love to. I'll bring someone, if I may.'

'Yes, do that. Good. Make it about eight.'

Leo went into the clerks' room, sighing inwardly. An evening in the company of the plump, boisterous Catherine, with her irrepressible laugh and pink cheeks. Still, all in a good cause.

Later that evening, after supper at Bucks, Leo sat in his mews house, with a large brandy before him and Brahms's Fourth Symphony in the background, and began to flick through the little sheaf of cards in his hand. They were invitations, some gilt-edged, some embossed, some square and plain – all bearing his name in various hands, some long and flowing some square and upright, some confidently scrawling, and all requesting the pleasure of his company, whenever and wherever. Every week or so he would go through his most recent pile of invitations, notepaper and fountain pen on the table before him, rejecting some, accepting others. Now the task had a novel aspect to it. It was no longer merely a question of which functions he could bear to attend, but also of which ones would be most useful in advertising his new liaison to the chattering, fashionable circle of his superficial acquaintance.

He picked up the first and read it as he wandered over to his jacket to fetch a cigar. 'Viscountess Brankin and the Committee of the Holland Park Branch of the NSPCC request the pleasure of Leo Davies's company at a private view of recent paintings at the Corcoran Gallery, Draycott Avenue . . . ' he read as he lit his cigar.

He walked back over to the table and sat down. Yes, that would do. Carrie Brankin had been trying for years to pair him off with every good-looking girl in every season. He smiled as he looked at the card. To his certain knowledge he had never taken a woman to any of her functions. The sight of Rachel would certainly get her going. Not only was she beautiful, she also, as Leo was well aware, had a way of looking at him that seemed to lay her sweet soul bare. Women noticed these things. Viscountess Brankin, and others, would notice. Love undisguised, mused Leo, blowing a little cloud of smoke into the air, suppressing the slight touch of guilt he felt at the thought that Rachel must ultimately come to grief in all this.

He picked up the next of the cards and took a drink of brandy as he surveyed it. Gilt-edged, with embossed gold lettering. Too, too much, he thought, reading it. No, not that. He picked up his pen and wrote a brief, polite note declining Mr and Mrs Ronnie Cosnansky's invitation to a charity auction in aid of Ethiopian famine relief.

The next was square and stark, decidedly reserved. This has to involve someone under twenty-five, thought Leo. He was right. He read it, smiling, pondering its possibilities. A party to celebrate the twenty-third birthdays of Tatiana and Sooty Dewes-Potter at La Poubelle in the King's Road. Why on earth had they invited him? Possibly Sooty Dewes-Potter still fancied her chances after that bash at the Cadogan Hall, where she'd had far too much champagne and had insisted on sitting, giggling, on his lap. Her blusher had come off on the front of his shirt – another perfectly good dress shirt completely ruined. Mrs Grant, his daily, had said not even the laundry would get that out. He tapped his chin with the card reflectively, then reread it as he drank some more of his brandy. Yes, why not? Not worth wasting a whole evening over – apart from which, he did not think he could bear the company of assorted twenty-three-year-olds and middle-aged hangers-on for more than half an hour – but they could look in for a while after dinner. Keep a high profile among the Sloanes.

Now, the next one looked interesting. A twenty-first-birthday drinks party for the daughter of Mr and Mrs Archie Revel, sponsored by the MP for South Reading, Mr Charles Poole. No – not more young people, and certainly not the House of Commons. He glanced again at the card. Anyway, it clashed with Sir Basil's drinks party. He scribbled a hasty note of polite thanks and regret, then picked up the last two invitations.

One was to a retrospective of the works of Richard Diebenkorn at the Wattis Gallery, and the other to a performance of *Don Giovanni* in Lincoln's Inn Great Hall in aid of the Prison Reform Trust (£50 a head). He sighed and picked up his cigar again. On the one hand, and under normal circumstances, he would have dismissed the latter out of hand and accepted the former with relish. On the other, half the judiciary would be at Lincoln's Inn, wives as well. Women were important – they saw and remembered so much. An ideal opportunity, one he could not afford to turn down.

Oh, hell, he thought, dropping both invitations on to the pile of those he intended to accept, if he had to sit out Mozart in the draughty grey gloom of Lincoln's Inn Great Hall, he deserved the Diebenkorn retrospective by way of reward, if nothing else. Anyway, Rachel would enjoy it.

He finished his cigar, then drew a few sheets of his thick, ivory-coloured notepaper towards him. He answered all four invitations, then opened his diary and filled in the dates. He surveyed December with good-humoured resignation. What a nice, frothy social confection of a month it was going to be. He closed his diary, yawned, and finished his brandy. It would be quite a relief when Christmas came, and he could make his solitary way to Wales and his mother, a momentary escape from the pretence, the reality. He scarcely knew which was which any longer.

Chapter nineteen

Thereafter, Leo devoted as much spare time and attention to Rachel as he could. He rang her at the end of that week and took her to the theatre on Saturday and to supper afterwards. On Sunday he picked her up from her flat and they spent a long, lazy Sunday lunch together with the newspapers in a restaurant tucked away in the back streets of Chelsea, a warm, scruffy, informal haunt where Leo was obviously known and liked. In fact, it seemed to Rachel that Leo was known and liked everywhere he went. She marvelled at his urbanity, his easy charm and effortlessly amusing conversation, but above all, she marvelled that he had chosen her, out of all the women in his obviously large social circle, to spend his time with. For once in her life she did not look ahead, she did not hedge her life around with domestic chores and work from the office to keep the spectres of the past and the future at bay. She simply lived for the moment, content to be in his company whenever she could, to watch and listen to him, to talk with him and see him smile.

Leo was careful to try to keep the sexual temperature down. Making love to the girl was, of course, an inevitable part of the whole affair, but he felt there was no point in expending excessive energy until one absolutely had to. Sex of the everyday, pedestrian variety, as Leo saw it, was not his strong suit and, pleasant though she had been to make love to, he felt she was unlikely to turn out to possess the outrageous and imaginative libido of someone like Sarah. So although he kissed her when he saw her and when he left her, and occasionally in between, if she looked as though she needed it, he took things no further.

This got a little difficult the following Wednesday night, after they had been to David Liphook's for dinner. Leo found the evening interesting. Catherine, David's girlfriend, was one of those impressionable girls who take their colour, chameleon-like, from the surrounding company, and she was sufficiently struck by Rachel's beauty and attractive hesitancy of movement and speech to adopt a little of it herself. Leo spent an amusing couple of hours watching the normally gregarious Catherine unconsciously aping Rachel's slow smiles and tentative gestures, even down to the faint hesitation before replying to a question. Although in his heart he slightly despised women, Leo loved to watch them, to divine their petty motivations and intrigues.

He felt it was useful, too, that David and William Cooper, another member of chambers, should bear initial witness to his relationship with Rachel. David was one of the most notorious gossips in the Temple and, like all good gossips, had an excellent eye and ear for emotional intrigue. And so Leo was careful, in his own discreet fashion, to behave as one who loved and was loved. He needed to strike only the very smallest spark, he realised, for her response to him was so obviously charged with affection. It was so prettily done, her smiles so sweet and open, that Leo was almost touched by it.

So much so that when he kissed her goodnight in the car outside her flat, he found himself responding completely to the fervour of her kiss and the warmth of her embrace. She was too loving, too abandoned for it to be otherwise. He sat back in the shadows and looked at her, his breathing rapid.

'Please, Leo,' she said, 'please come in. I don't want you to go yet,' she whispered, twisting the lapels of his coat in her fingers, then leaning forward to dab kisses on his chin and cheeks before fastening her mouth hungrily to his again.

He considered the matter as they kissed. If he slept with her tonight, then it was the start of that part of the affair which would demand most of him, in terms of performance, in bed and out of it. He would rather that didn't happen just yet, for once the going got heavy, all kinds of things could start to go wrong. And he didn't want that. This had far too important a purpose to serve.

She pulled herself gently away from him and murmured again, 'Please.'

'Rachel,' he said, looking into her eyes, which were soft with desire, 'there's something I want you to understand.' He timed his pause carefully, then spoke again, as if with some difficulty. 'When we slept together last time, it was – well, the circumstances that evening were very peculiar. But it was as though we'd started this relationship at the wrong end. I know a lot about you' – he reached out a hand and stroked her hair, his eyes scanning her features – 'but I still don't know all the small and wonderful things that people should learn about one another. Me about you. You about me. That takes time. I want us to have that time. I want this relationship to be based on something enduring.' I can hardly believe I'm saying this, thought Leo, continuing to stroke her hair. She picked up his other hand between hers and kissed the back of it lightly as he went on. 'I'm a bit old-fashioned, I suppose,' he said, astonishing himself, 'but I think that's the way it should be. Between us, at least. I want to woo you.' He leaned forward and kissed her briefly, softly. 'Win you.'

She said nothing, merely gazed back at him. You don't have to do any of that, she thought. You have me. I'm won, utterly and completely. But his words made her feel so safe, as though whatever future they might have together was assured, that she simply nodded. Then, after a moment, she said, 'Yes, I understand. If that's what you want.'

'It's what I want,' he said softly, and kissed her again.

Well, he thought, as he watched her walk to her flat, then turned his car round, he may have lied his head off, but at least it meant less of a chance of the thing going wrong. As long as it remained on its present level, those dangerous little seeds of intimate passion could not be sown. Leo knew only too well the kind of monstrous, unexpected weeds they could grow into.

Rachel smiled to herself as she got ready for bed. He *was* being old-fashioned about it, particularly after that other night, but she rather liked it. It meant he set some store by their relationship. She paused as she pulled her nightdress from beneath her pillow. The odd thing was, there was absolutely nothing about Leo that made you feel he was at all old-fashioned. Not in any way . . .

*

234

So entirely absorbed had Leo become in his own affairs that he had forgotten about Anthony. From the very first evening that he had taken Rachel to dinner, he had dismissed Anthony from the picture altogether. It was typical of his character that, in serving his own interests, Leo concentrated only on those people and things which were of immediate relevance to him. That Rachel had been seeing Anthony, albeit on some tentative and uncertain basis, was no longer important.

It was unfortunate, therefore, that Anthony should have been in El Vino's with Michael Gibbon and David Liphook on the Friday following David's dinner party.

'Yes,' David was saying in reply to a question from Michael, 'it went very well, actually. I cook rather a neat coq-au-vin, if I say so myself. And, amazingly enough, I actually managed to persuade Leo to join us.'

'Really?' said Michael, taking a sip of his wine.

'Well, quite – I wouldn't have thought that Catherine and I were sufficiently socially elevated for him to bother with. I mean, you know what he's like. He seems to go to every smart party in London. Catherine even found a picture of him in *Harper's and Queen* once, grinning away, with some horse-faced woman gazing at him adoringly.'

Anthony laughed delightedly. 'I hope you've still got it. I should love to see it.'

'Oh, I tell you, he's everywhere,' said David cheerfully, his face pink from the wine and the exertions of the week. David believed in maximising everything, from his consumption of food and wine to his capacity for hard and relentless work. 'And you should have seen the girl he brought with him. I've never met any of his girlfriends before, but this one was an absolute stunner. No wonder he seemed a bit dippy about her. I mean, Leo's not one to wear his heart on his sleeve, but you could tell from the way he looked at her and spoke to her that it's a big thing.' He drained his glass. 'Shall we have another bottle? Your shout, I think, Michael.'

Anthony looked bemusedly at David as Michael went off to order another bottle. He supposed that David didn't know Leo was gay; as far as Anthony was aware, no one in chambers did, apart from himself. Leo was the kind of man who lived an entirely private life away from work. No one knew Leo as Anthony had known him. Nonetheless, he was intrigued by what David had said. And he remembered, too, the attractive woman Leo had brought to that May Ball a couple of years ago. Maybe it was the same woman. Maybe there was more to Leo's infintely complex personality than even he, Anthony, had guessed.

'Tell me some more about this woman of Leo's,' he said. 'Did she have blonde, sort of shortish hair – '

David shook his head by way of interruption. 'No, I know who you're thinking of. That woman he brought to the do in Inner Temple. No, it wasn't her – anyway, she was just a friend, so far as one could tell. Ah, good!' He glanced up as Michael arrived with another bottle. 'This girl was dark – a lot younger than him. About my age, I'd say. Long hair – really good-looking. She's a solicitor.'

'What's her name?' asked Anthony, into whose mind a tiny, freezing doubt had crept.

David took a sip from his fresh glass of wine. 'Rachel. Can't remember her second name, offhand. Anyway, Rachel. Cracking girl. I reckon, believe it or not, that it could be serious.'

'I – ah – don't somehow think,' said Michael in his nervous, rather distant voice, the voice of infinite tact and courtesy which had beguiled so many unsuspecting witnesses during many a devastating cross-examination, 'that Leo is likely, at his time of life, to be thinking of settling down. I've known him for some time, and his interests are too peripatetic, I would say, for anything, or anyone, to hold him for long.' There was a gleam of something like irony in Michael's bespectacled eyes.

But Anthony was listening to none of this. He was aware of David's mouth moving in reply, as his own fingers tightened around the stem of his glass. Rachel. No – it had to be someone different. It couldn't be her. But how many solicitors were there in the City of London called Rachel, beautiful (even allowing for David's notoriously indiscriminate enthusiasm for the opposite sex) and with long dark hair?

'It wasn't Dean, was it?' Anthony interrupted David, his

voice even and calm. 'Her name wasn't Rachel Dean?'

'What? Yes, yes it was. Do you know her?' asked David, seizing avidly on the possibility of more gossip.

With as much self-possession as he could muster, Anthony sat back in his chair, took a sip of his wine and said, 'Yes. She instructed me on a case not long ago. I've met her a few times.'

'Isn't she amazing?' pursued David. 'If it weren't for the fact that she's obviously stuck on our dear Mr Davies, I'd recommend you to move in there and do a spot of poaching. As it is, I don't think you'd stand a chance.'

A pain seemed to have gripped Anthony's heart, and to be tightening with every word he heard. She must have been lying to him, all this time – all that stuff about give me time, I'm not ready for a relationship . . . Christ, what a fool he'd been. And Leo – Leo with his wordly-wise advice, standing smiling at him over the top of his glasses in the clerks' room, as Anthony had told him he loved her. Just a light-hearted remark, but how it must have amused Leo.

Then another voice, chasing the last, told him that it was all nonsense. It could just be coincidence. Maybe they knew one another, maybe . . . No, he had mentioned Leo's name too often; she'd had every opportunity of saying that she knew him. Anyway, surely they hadn't met until recently, when he had introduced them at the Guildhall. He suddenly recalled the moment vividly.

Now he was confused. If it was true, then why? Why would Leo – Leo who had tried to make Anthony his lover not so long ago – want to do this? To make him jealous, to hurt him? No, there was none of that left between them. That was all history. This was something new and incomprehensible.

He swallowed the contents of his glass, pushed his chair back and smiled at his friends. 'I have to be going. Sorry.'

'What about this second bottle?' asked David in surprise.

Anthony shook his head. 'No more for me, thanks. Got to go. Have a good weekend.' And he picked up his coat and left quickly, before he had to hear any more about this impossible thing. Leo and Rachel.

Their names kept repeating themselves in his head, marching in step with him as he strode through Clifford's Inn and

237

through Inner Temple, down the lane to the Embankment. By the time he had got on to the tube for South Ken, he had calmed down somewhat. He would ring her. It probably hadn't been as David had said. Anyway, he would ring her. No doubt it was all fine, just a coincidence. But doubt and jealousy flickered up like flames inside him each time he told himself this.

Adam was in when he got home. 'Hello,' he said, 'your mother rang.' He glanced at Anthony's grim face as Anthony flung his coat over a kitchen chair. 'I'm making some chilli. You want some? Debbie and John are coming over.'

'No thanks,' replied Anthony. He stood for a moment, wondering whether to ring her now or later. He felt his heartbeat quicken at the thought of that phone call. Something told him that he was going to hear the worst. His limbs felt stiff with tension, with nervousness.

'I'm just going to make a phone call,' he muttered, leaving the kitchen and going into the living room.

There he sat on the arm of one of the armchairs, chin resting on his hands, staring at the telephone. It had to be true, he told himself. It was why she hadn't rung for two weeks. She'd said she would, but she hadn't. Every day, when he'd come back from court, he'd asked Henry hopefully for his phone messages. Nothing. Every evening he'd waited, or asked Adam if there had been any calls for him. Nothing. Why hadn't he rung her? Because she'd asked him for some space, because he'd trusted her, thought that she just needed a little time. He remembered her face, her lovely face, the sweet seriousness of her expression that day beside the pool in Bombay.

'It can't be right,' he said aloud, and picked up the phone.

As he dialled, he thought about Leo. It was here that his belief faltered, then came to a complete standstill. What did Leo ever have to do with women? How could anyone who had tried to seduce another man, as Leo had tried to seduce Anthony, suddenly turn himself around and – and what? So he'd taken her to David's for dinner. It didn't mean anything.

At that moment Rachel answered the phone. Anthony's

mind was so preoccupied that he was momentarily taken aback.

'Hello?' At the sound of her familiar, cautious voice, his fear slackened slightly. This was all fantastic speculation on David's part. There was a rational, simple explanation.

'Hi,' he said, keeping his voice neutral. 'It's me, Anthony.'

Rachel's heart dropped like a stone. She put down the copy of *Vogue* she'd been reading. 'Hello, Anthony,' she replied.

He sat down, cradling the phone in his hand. It occurred to him that he hadn't a clue what to say to her, of how he could possibly broach the subject. 'How have you been?' he asked. 'I hoped you might have rung this week.'

Rachel, too, subsided into a chair. 'Oh, I'm sorry, Anthony. I've been rather busy.' It was now or never, she said to herself. She was a coward; she should have rung and told him, put out that light for ever. But how did one do such a thing? How could she have rung him and said, 'By the way, I don't want to see you any more because I'm in love with someone else'?

'So I gather,' replied Anthony, his heart tightening within him. 'David Liphook told me about his dinner party on Wednesday.'

Of course, she thought. Of course. She had supposed he might come to hear of it that way, but not so quickly, not before she'd had the chance to speak to him.

'Yes,' she replied. 'Yes, I was there.'

There was a silence, then Anthony said, 'With Leo.' It was not a question, but a flat statement. Go on, he thought, tell me that it was all a coincidence, that you happened to be there and so did he. Or tell me that it was just that once, and that – oh, even lie to me. Go on.

'Yes. I – well, he asked me to go with him.' Why am I hedging like this? she wondered. Why don't I just tell him?

'You seem to have got pretty intimate since I introduced you two,' said Anthony tersely. And then he thought of that night at the Guildhall. Had it been then? As simple as that? Was that why she had left? Impossible. He suddenly said, 'Have you been seeing him since then?'

She was relieved at the question. It demanded an honest

reply. It all had to come out now.

'Yes,' she replied weakly.

Anthony let out a long breath. What the hell was going on here? 'As friends, or what?' he demanded.

'What do you mean?' she answered.

'I mean' – he hesitated, hating this whole business, wretched, sick at heart, sick with love turned sour – 'I mean, is there something between you two that I shouldn't know about?'

'Anthony – ' Rachel gripped the receiver tight with both hands. 'Look, the fact is, I have been seeing him. And – I'm sorry if this hurts you, but I think I'm in love with him.' Silence. 'That's about it. I know I should have called you, but what was I to say? I didn't know any of this was going to happen. I didn't do it to hurt you. Nor did Leo.'

Leo? She said this as though he felt the same way about her. The idea was absurd, fantastic. 'Well,' he replied, hoping that he could hate her so much that he would never have to feel love for her again, and knowing he could not, 'you seem to have accomplished a lot in a short space of time. Well done.'

'Oh, Anthony, it wasn't like that at all! He called me the week after I met him, and we went to dinner – and well, he wanted to see me again. Don't talk as though I did this on purpose.'

'And are you fighting him off the way you did me? Or doesn't he bother you that much?' asked Anthony savagely. He wanted to know everything, whether they had slept together, whether Leo had managed to offer her something he could not, whether the whole thing was just one-sided . . . But if it was, why was Leo still seeing her? Why had David said that Leo seemed serious about her?

'Anthony . . . ' Rachel felt completely helpless.

'Have you slept with him?' demanded Anthony

'You have no right to ask me that,' she said.

'You mean yes.' Anthony closed his eyes. Through his bitterness, it all struck him as rather ludicrous. If anything, she was as much a victim as he was. She must think of Leo as her knight in shining armour. He laughed before he spoke.'Oh, Rachel, if you only knew . . . '

The sound of his laugh distressed and alarmed her. 'What do you mean?' she asked hesitantly.

He sighed. No, he was not the one to tell her. He felt suddenly dispassionate. 'Nothing,' he replied. 'Nothing.' There was a silence. 'I think,' he said slowly, 'that I'd better send back the papers on the *Valeo Dawn*, don't you?' That was how it had all started, and that was all it came back down to, in the end.

'If you think you want to,' said Rachel sadly. 'Anthony, I'm so sorry. I didn't know, when we were in India, that any of this was going to happen. I'm sorry.' She wanted to say more, to try to offer some comfort, but she knew that in such a situation there was no comfort to offer, only more humiliation.

'It doesn't matter,' said Anthony. 'It's not your fault.' And he put the phone down.

She told Leo the following evening about her conversation with Anthony. They were having a light supper in a wine bar before joining some friends of Leo's – carefully selected; a female barrister from 14 King's Bench Walk and her husband, and a professor of jurisprudence at King's and his wife – at the theatre.

He listened carefully, his expression not changing as she spoke, one elbow resting on the table, his hand covering his mouth. Rachel's voice was sad, perplexed.

'I felt dreadful – no, worse than that, I felt so *helpless*. Nothing I could say was of any use.' She sighed. 'You see, he told me once that he loved me. It wasn't as though I wanted him to' – she hastened to assure Leo of her own disinterest, thinking, misguidedly, that he might care – 'but when someone says that, it's as though – as though they're burdening you with some sort of responsibility. Cutting a little piece out of their soul and handing it to you.' Leo's glance flickered from the tablecloth to her face. He said nothing. 'And after I'd told him that we'd slept together – well, not directly, but he assumed it when he asked me and I said it was none of his business – when I told him, he just said, "Oh, if you only knew," or something like that. And laughed. "If you only

241

knew Leo." What do you suppose he meant?'

Leo took his hand away from his mouth. 'I don't know,' he replied, staring at his wine. 'I don't know Anthony's mind.' He paused. 'Was that all he said – about me, I mean?'

She nodded. 'He just said he would be sending back the instructions I sent him on that case, and then he hung up. That was all.' She looked at Leo. 'All of this is going to make a dreadful mess of your friendship, isn't it?'

Leo drained his glass. 'It can't be helped.' He set down his glass and looked at her, then laid a hand over hers. 'Can it?' She shook her head slowly, her eyes fixed on his, almost clouded with love. 'Anyway,' he added, 'don't worry too much about Anthony. He's very young. And the young have resilient hearts. He'll be all right.' In five years' time, thought Leo, there will still be something left of Leo and Anthony. And of Rachel? He did not know. 'Come on,' he said, 'let's go, or we'll be late.'

While Leo and Rachel and their companions sat through the opening night of the latest Tom Stoppard play, Anthony was doing his best to get very drunk at his friend Simon's dinner party. But Simon could see how things were going and managed to prevent Anthony from going completely overboard, so that by the time midnight came he was only miserable and maudlin. He stayed at the dinner table as the seven other guests made their noisy, hilarious way through to the other room for coffee and music, not in the mood to join them.

He sat, flattening out the flimsy discarded wrapper from an Amaretti biscuit, folding it carefully, thinking bitterly, drunkenly, of Rachel, of Rachel with Leo. Simon had unwisely left the decanter of port at the other end of the table. Anthony eyed it for a moment and rose a little unsteadily, then reached across successfully for it. He filled his empty wine glass very full, and drank it off, then half-filled it again. He knew he would feel dreadful in the morning, but he didn't care. He merely wanted to blot out the thought of his lovely Rachel in Leo's bed. He'd only come to Simon's this evening in the hope of distracting himself from his own misery. But, of course, it hadn't helped.

Leo Davies, he told himself, was completely without morality, without loyalty. Whatever warped appetites he had, he could only have done this to satisfy the worst of them. The man who would happily have taken Anthony into his bed two years ago could now, without any qualms, rob Anthony of something he had known – had *known* was precious to him. And what would be the end result for Rachel? What happiness could she possibly find with someone like that? When Leo turned his attention to the next pretty young man, as he had once to Anthony, what would become of her? Bastard, thought Anthony savagely, drinking off the rest of his port. Fucking bastard.

Miranda, the girl who had been sitting next to Anthony at dinner, having carefully arranged this beforehand with Simon, stood in the doorway of the dining room. She watched Anthony drain his glass and gaze moodily at the tablecloth. She was not sure how drunk he was. Not too drunk, she hoped. She crossed the empty room softly and sat down in the chair next to his. Then she slipped a hand on to his shoulder and kissed his cheek gently. He turned to look at her, his expression unchanged. He had known Miranda for a long time, in a distant, occasional sort of way. It had often crossed his mind that she was extremely attractive, that some day they might get together. The thought had always been idle. He knew she liked him. Now he looked at her, and felt nothing at all. He looked away.

'You're not exactly enjoying yourself this evening, are you?' she murmured.

'Pass me the port,' he said.

She did so, saying with a smile, 'Wrong direction.' He slopped some into his glass. 'I don't think Simon wants you to drink *too* much of that, you know,' she added lightly.

'Bugger Simon,' replied Anthony, and drank.

'Why don't we – ' Then she paused, her arm still resting on his shoulder, and ran a finger thoughtfully down his cheek. 'Why don't you let me drive you home? Mmm? I don't much want to stay, either.'

He looked at her. Oh, why the hell not? he thought. She

might take his mind off the whole sordid thing. One way or the other, he didn't much care.

'You can if you want,' he said drunkenly.

He got to his feet and she followed him out into the hallway. He didn't seem hopelessly plastered.

'Hold on,' she said. She slipped into the drawing room and told Simon she was taking Anthony home. When she came out, he was leaning against the wall next to the front door, fingering his car keys. She lifted them from his hand and dropped them into his pocket. 'We'll take my car,' she said. 'You can get yours tomorrow.'

The cold night air had something of a sobering effect on Anthony. By the time they reached South Kensington, he was so hardened in his resolve to dismiss Rachel and Leo utterly from his life that he managed to kiss Miranda quite convincingly before they got out of the car. But when they reached the second floor and Anthony put his key in the lock, he realised that he did not want to do this. Far from seeking a refuge from thoughts of Rachel, he simply wanted to lose himself in his own misery, to lie and think of her, even if it was painful. It suddenly seemed to him the only way to make the pain abate, to confront it over and over until its keen edge was blunted.

He turned to Miranda. 'I think we'd better just make this a quick coffee and then say goodnight,' he said to her, before going into the flat. 'Don't you?'

She looked at him sadly, a little reproachfully. He realised he had been very rude to her all evening.

'Maybe now's not our time,' he added.

'Anthony, darling,' she said, 'I don't really want any coffee. Let's just say goodnight.' She leaned forward and kissed him, then turned and went back downstairs.

Anthony sighed and closed the door. There would be another time with Miranda, he knew. That was the way their set did things, little weavings in and out of one another's lives, like a dance of some kind, dinner parties and love affairs, beginnings and endings, on and on, roughly the same people, the same little world, the City, the lawyers, brokers, merchant bankers, the girls and boys, the bistros, the parties, the lunches, credit cards, possessions . . . a pageant of materialism illuminated by sex and the constant, wistful search for the perfect person, the one who would set one's heart at rest.

It should have been so simple with Rachel, thought Anthony, leaning against the door, feeling drunk. She would have been the one. He closed his eyes and thought of her smile, the way she dipped her head and looked up, her dark hair, her lovely eyes. It was like a small, narrow blade twisting slowly in his insides, worse still when he thought of Leo with her, making love to her, possessing her. It would have been fine, thought Anthony, opening his eyes, gazing ahead of him at the kitchen door. With a little time, everything could have been good. Wonderful. If only Leo hadn't got in the way. Charming, irresistible Leo – Anthony knew only too well what it was like to be touched, to be seduced by Leo, his eyes, his looks, his talent for making one believe. Why had he done this? Anthony asked himself again. He had thought Leo cared for him, was concerned for him – and yet he had destroyed his relationship with Rachel, knowing how precious and fragile it was. Even after Anthony had confided in him, he had been able to do this . . .

These thoughts were simply the same ones which had been coursing through his head all evening. Alcohol had not chased them away – merely intensified and distorted them. He pulled his tie loose and went into his room, and lay face down on his bed, wishing tomorrow was any day but Sunday.

He had not intended to speak to Leo about any of it, merely to stay out of his way until his anger and unhappiness had abated a little, but as he came upstairs from the clerks' room on Monday morning, he saw Leo in his shirtsleeves, laughing in conversation with Michael, then turning to go into his room. The sight of him, the sound of his easy laughter, jarred Anthony like a blow. With his heart thudding, he ran up the last few stairs and followed Leo into his room. Leo glanced over his shoulder as he heard Anthony come in behind him. Anthony closed the door and leaned against it, and Leo turned to face him as he reached his desk.

'I want a word with you,' said Anthony, so angry that he

had no idea what he was going to say.

Leo raised his eyebrows slightly. 'Perhaps you'd better sit down,' he replied, his voice cool, but adrenalin pumping in him. He had expected, but not wanted, something like this. He picked up his glasses from the desk and put them on, scanning the papers he held in his hand, affecting a lack of concern.

From somewhere in the back of Anthony's mind came the ghost of that schoolboy rule – you didn't hit someone who was wearing glasses. How absurd. He had no intention of hitting Leo – but there was a tension, a murderous anger in him demanding some sort of resolution, some sort of confrontation.

'You know,' said Anthony, 'you're an even bigger bastard than I could have thought possible.'

'Oh?' replied Leo, looking up, quite without any resources, moral or verbal, that could help him to deal adequately with what was coming. He had nothing to say, no excuse.

'Don't say "oh?" like that, as though you don't know what I'm talking about,' said Anthony in a slow voice, his breathing made rapid by his anger. 'You know what you've done. I spoke to Rachel last week – '

'Yes, I know,' cut in Leo. 'She told me.' He took off his glasses and laid them on the desk with his papers. Then he waited.

'If you weren't twice my age, I'd want to beat you up,' said Anthony. 'It's about what you deserve. But we don't do that kind of thing, do we, Leo? We've got a code, a way of behaving. Haven't we?' Leo said nothing. 'Or maybe,' went on Anthony, 'you don't really understand that code. Maybe where you come from people do deceive and betray one another.' Leo flinched inwardly at this, but still said nothing, a muscle in his jaw flickering.

Then he looked up. 'Is that all?' he asked. 'Because I do have some work – '

Quite what Anthony had intended to do when he launched himself clumsily at Leo, he was not quite sure, but Leo, although he staggered back slightly as Anthony came at him, was fast enough to recover and grasp Anthony by the wrists.

He shoved him against the wall and held him there, his face close to Anthony's, both men breathing hard.

'Do you know what's really pathetic?' said Anthony through clenched teeth, pushing against Leo's grip but conscious of the older man's wiry strength. 'She says she's in love with you. And what are you going to give her in return, eh, Leo? Have you told her? Have you told her what's going to happen when the next little boy you fancy comes along? Does she know about your kind of love?'

This was too close to the truth, touched too finely on Leo's fears. He rammed Anthony even harder against the wall, aware that the sound shook the walls of chambers, that people must hear.

'Don't,' he hissed, his eyes glaring into Anthony's, 'don't you ever speak to me about love. You know nothing about it! You're so immature, so callow, so afraid! You want it all, yet you're prepared to give nothing in return. That's what it was like with us, wasn't it? Wasn't it?' He gave Anthony another push and then released him, letting his hands drop slowly to his sides. They stood close together, not moving. It was the only time, Leo realised, that he had ever seen passion in Anthony's eyes, and he longed for it to be directed at him, not against him. 'Don't you remember? Or don't you like to remember? There's too much fear in you, Anthony. There are things you don't want to confront – things about Rachel that you'll never understand. You're empty. You're devoid of anything that could help her, because you've never been to that part of yourself where you find out things, the best and the worst. But you're young. You'll learn.'

Leo looked into Anthony's eyes for a few more seconds, then turned and walked round behind his desk. Anthony was still leaning against the wall, a picture behind his head slightly askew where it had been knocked, his breathing growing more even.

'I don't want to learn,' he said, his voice hard, but his anger flaking off, bit by bit, into misery. 'I don't want to learn what it takes to become someone as perverted as you. And I'm not just talking about sex, Leo – that's bad enough. I'm talking about taking people's trust and then abusing it. That's the worst part. You've done it to me, and I've no doubt you'll do it to Rachel. You just want to fuck everyone, don't you, Leo?'

Leo turned and regarded Anthony. There was nothing he could say. Silence fell between them. Anthony pushed himself away from the wall, tugging down his waistcoat, aware that this had all been futile, but feeling that at least some of his anger had been drained from him.

'You'll discover,' said Leo, as Anthony turned to go, 'that none of this really matters. In time, you'll see that.' He looked sadly at the younger man, at his sullen, beautiful face. 'It won't matter – not between you and me.'

Anthony stared at him coldly. Leo's words sounded to him smug, the victor patronising the loser.

'Oh, yes, it will,' he replied, utter certainty in his tone. 'Not everyone is like you, you know. Not everyone is glib and shallow. Things matter to some people. This matters to me. Don't you ever forget it.'

He opened the door and went out, brushing past Sir Basil, who had heard sounds from his room above and come to investigate, with a muttered 'Good morning.'

Sir Basil, who had been joined on the landing by William and Jeremy Vine, stood for a moment, then turned away uncertainly as Leo quietly closed his door. He watched as Anthony clattered downstairs at a furious rate. Well, really. One might expect that any commotion in chambers would involve that young man. He might be exceptionally bright, but Sir Basil still had his doubts about him. He turned again to look at Leo's closed door, then shook his head and went back up to his room. William and Jeremy melted away.

Leo stood by his window, looking down into the courtyard. He watched as Anthony appeared below, pulling on his jacket and striding off through the archway into Pump Court. Walking it off, thought Leo, watching him until he disappeared from sight. He sighed, turned away and sat down at his desk, wishing that he could do the same, evaporate his passions by physical exertion. But that was no longer possible. It took far more than that. Everything Anthony had said was true. Every single thing. Was this all worth it? Could he really use people in this way for his own ends and hope it would leave no mark

248

on any of them? That might not be possible, he was beginning to realise. He had just witnessed the first casualty in this game of his. There would certainly be more.

Chapter twenty

Perfumed talk and laughter rose into the grey upper reaches of Lincoln's Inn Great Hall as Leo made his way through the elegantly dressed crowd with Rachel by his side. He was acutely conscious of the glances that she drew; even he, a cynic in the matter of female loveliness, had been moved to a smile of warm and genuine admiration when he picked her up from her flat.

'Do you like it?' she had asked hesitantly, plucking at a fold of the crimson silk jersey sheath which clung to her body. Her dark hair was swept up from her slender neck, and she wore only a thin gold necklace and earrings.

'Amazing,' said Leo, turning her round and inspecting the gently dipping back, the silk falling away in soft lines.

'I spent about four hours in South Molton Street trying to find something,' said Rachel, her eyes bright with childlike pleasure at his admiration of her. 'I did want to look – well, you know. I wanted to look all right for you.'

And he had kissed her, thinking sadly that she was very sweet. Far, far too sweet.

Now he realised, as he smiled at acquaintances, making his way over to where he could see Sir Mungo standing with Sir Mostyn Smith and their wives, that her beauty was a significant asset in this business. Everyone would remember her. Apart from being the loveliest woman there, she was also the youngest.

Sir Mungo turned and saw Leo approaching. Despite what Bernard had said, he was always pleased to see Leo, who lightened the tedium of this sort of occasion. Though he would never have admitted it, Sir Mungo was not overfond of Mozart, and would sooner have been at home in front of his fire with a Dick Francis novel. But as a senior member of the judiciary, it behoved him to attend these things, and to appear to enjoy them. He saw, with surprise, that Leo was with a woman.

'Mungo,' said Leo easily, 'very good to see you. And Lady Stephenson. How do you do?' Lady Stephenson shook hands with him, and then Leo introduced Rachel, taking care to let his eyes rest on her face with just the right amount of pride and affection as she shook hands and responded to Lady Stephenson's soft little twitterings.

'How lovely to see some young poeple at these gatherings!' she exclaimed, enchanted by Rachel's prettiness. 'I do think we old people rather tend to dominate them.' She turned to Leo, for whom she had always, in her secret heart, had a great weakness. 'And tell me, Leo, what interesting things have you been doing lately? You always seem to lead such a busy social life!'

Leo seized this opportunity. 'Oh, it's been fairly quiet of late,' he replied, glancing with a smile at Rachel.

Sir Mungo had been busily puffing himself up to the right pitch of confidence to speak to Rachel – Sir Mungo, the scourge of the Appeal Court, he whose very glance could make the most seasoned counsel quail, was always acutely self-conscious in the company of lovely young women. Especially the girls one met nowadays – they were so damned brisk, so full of themselves. But he found Rachel delightfully easy company. Sir Mostyn, who had been watching Sir Mungo's jovial progress with Leo's beautiful companion with some envy (Sir Mostyn rather prided himself on his way with the opposite sex, had been something of a ladies' man in his youth), sidled over to join their conversation after a while. Leo, talking to Lady Stephenson and Lady Smith, glanced at Sir Mostyn's beaming profile as he conversed with Rachel. Good girl, he thought, returning with a brief smile her fond, stray glance in his direction. Excellent.

By the time the opera was due to begin, Leo had, in a casual, desultory way, managed to introduce her to most of those present who might be in any way influential in the matter of his application for silk, and he was satisfied to think that their presence as a couple – a very distinct couple; an item, as David

Liphook would say – had been well noted.

'Look here,' said Sir Mostyn, sotto voce, detaching himself and Sir Mungo from the ladies as they made their way to their seats, 'what was all that stuff you were telling me about young Davies being queer? Eh? Doesn't look that way to me.'

Sir Mungo sighed and raised his eyebrows. 'My dear Mostyn, if you will listen to all the tittle-tattle in the Temple . . . Oh, I do beg your pardon!' he grunted, disentangling himself from the hem of an elderly woman's dress.

'But you told me yourself!' exclaimed Sir Mostyn in a whisper, sitting down next to his wife.

'Did I? Surely not,' murmured Sir Mungo, squeezing his bulk into his chair. 'Damned uncomfortable seats these.' He glanced at his watch and sighed.

'Well, I don't know . . . Anyway, that's the best-looking girl I've seen in a long time,' answered Sir Mostyn.

'What's that, dear?' murmured Lady Mostyn.

'I was just saying to Mungo what an attractive girl Leo Davies is with,' he replied to his wife, who leaned over to catch his words.

Her face lit up. 'Isn't she? And I do think it's so charming that she seems so devoted to him. I think he's a very lucky young man!'

She sat back in her seat as the orchestra began to tune their instruments. More than a few male eyes glanced in Rachel's direction, resting on the swanlike neck and pale profile, envying Leo as she turned her soft, smiling eyes to his in response to some remark.

As the murmur of voices ceased and the music began, Leo leaned back and let his thoughts drift away. There was a constant uneasiness in his mind these days. Although he had persuaded himself that Anthony's words of a few days ago had not affected him, that he had been expecting such a reaction and could dismiss it out-of-hand, he knew that this was not true. He had a deep and abiding affection for Anthony, and at the memory of the disgust and unhappiness he had seen last Monday in the boy's eyes he now felt prickings of self-detestation. Still, it could not be helped. This thing was too important. Anyway, nothing could have come

252

of Anthony's relationship with the girl. She had said as much herself. He glanced sideways at Rachel during the duet in Act 1, touched by the rapt intentness of her expression as she listened. He pressed his fingers to his lips and looked away. But Anthony had been right. What was he going to give her in return for her love? He closed his eyes momentarily. He had never intended that she should fall in love with him, had never . . . well, what had he intended?

He tried to look ahead, tried to think logically of the sequence of events. He had come to realise recently that the months between now and Easter, which had seemed such a brief time at first, stretched ahead in a pattern of inevitably deepening intimacy between himself and Rachel. A few months could be a long time in a love affair. And then what? Whether he failed or succeeded in his application for silk, would he just drop her, cast her off once she had served her purpose? He turned his head slightly to look at her again, and this time she became conscious of his gaze and returned it with a radiant smile.

Oh God, he thought, his own smile freezing on his lips as she looked away again, this could become the most unholy mess. He wondered if he had it in him to behave so badly to her, once Easter had passed, that she might simply end the thing herself. It struck him that this might be the only solution. But he genuinely liked her. He liked looking at her, even talking to her – for brief spells of time – and he took special pleasure, these days, in contemplating making love to her again. Anticipation had always been one of Leo's chief delights, the key ingredient to his particular brand of pleasure. She was so vulnerable. It would not be difficult to hurt her. But it would not be pleasant.

At the end of the evening they emerged from the warmth into the freezing air of Lincoln's Inn; Rachel shivered involuntarily, drawing herself close against Leo, huddling into her coat. 'Leo, I'm so hungry! I was sure that everyone would hear my stomach rumbling in the quiet bits.'

'They weren't exactly generous with their supper, were they?' replied Leo. 'If you could call a few canapés and a couple of glasses of white wine supper. Where would you like to eat?'

'I think I'm too tired for restaurants.' She yawned as she spoke. The clasp of her hands upon his arm, keeping herself close to him against the bitter cold, was so confident, so trusting. 'Why don't we go back to my flat and I'll make us some scrambled eggs?' she murmured, looking up at him.

He blew out a soft, silent breath of air, watching it plume in the darkness. 'All right,' he said after a moment. 'Let's do that.' This has to start some time, he told himself. Why not tonight?

How very feminine it all was, thought Leo, gazing around her living room as she went through to the kitchen and began clattering pans. Pale, clean colours, muted lighting, pretty cushions. And so very pristine – cool and cautious, just like Rachel. He walked around, examining the pictures. She has taste, he thought – perhaps too much of it. He turned back and stared at the room. There was something arid about the place. As lifeless as those dried flowers in a vase in the fireplace. She has penned herself in here, thought Leo. She has built this clean, pretty cage as a defence against all her fears, a still place where nothing can touch her. No wonder Anthony hadn't made any headway with her when he had come round to supper. No violating the sanctuary.

And what about me? wondered Leo, shedding his scarf and then his coat. He went through to the kitchen and stood in the doorway. She was breaking eggs into a bowl, and turned to glance at him.

'Shouldn't you change?' he asked. 'I don't think I'd like to see that pretty dress covered in egg yolk.'

She glanced down, tossing the last of the shells aside. Her hair was beginning to come loose at the back, and strands fell about her white shoulders. 'Oh – I suppose you're right . . . '

'I'll help you,' he murmured, dropping a kiss on her shoulder as she passed him.

Her bedroom, thought Leo, was even more awe-inspiring than the rest of the place. He was reminded of an illustration in a book he had had as a child, when Tom, the little chimney sweep in *The Water Babies*, came tumbling down the chimney into the bedroom of a girl, a room all white and soft and lovely.

And he all sooty and foul. That was like this room.

He approached her softly from behind, sliding his arms around her waist, kissing the back of her neck, pulling down her hair. Then he leaned away and looked her up and down.

'How does this thing unfasten?' he asked. She showed him, standing very still as he unfastened the dress and slid the straps from her shoulders, letting it fall to the ground.

'What about the eggs?' she asked, closing her eyes and leaning her head back as his hands drifted across her breasts and stomach with unbearable lightness.

'They can wait,' murmured Leo, pressing himself against her, kissing the side of her throat, already embarking on his own private, erotic voyage. He had no thought for her except as the instrument of his immediate pleasure, but when she turned in his embrace and drew his mouth down to hers, there was something so singleminded in her kiss, as though she were drinking him in, utterly absorbed in loving him, that he was oddly moved. Her existence as a person was suddenly recalled, touching him childishly, and for a moment he responded unequivocally, longing to blot out the lonely, intriguing part of himself. He returned her kiss hungrily, his hands exploring her body as she fumbled urgently with his tie, his shirt buttons; they clung to one another as they shed the last of their clothing, greedy for the touch of the other's flesh.

He stopped kissing her only long enough to lay her down on the unsullied whiteness of her bed, holding himself away from her as he kissed her again, fondling her, touching her lightly everywhere, conscious of the gathering longing in her movements, her murmurs. He looked down at the slender curve of her body arched towards his, her hands caressing him, urging him, and he whispered in her ear, flicking his tongue lightly over her lobe, 'Tell me what you want me to do. Everything. Tell me everything.' It was so practised, yet so potent.

When she spoke, eyes closed, features blurred with longing, the low hesitancy of her voice seemed to him unspeakably erotic. Then he forgot her instantly, carried away to his own world of sensuality, of anticipation, and ultimate gratification. She was no longer Rachel, and he was alone, wanting only to exist for ever in this realm of purest pleasure, the only place where he was really happy.

Later, after making love, she rose without speaking, kissed him and pulled on a robe. He lay for a while, pondering the satiability of human need, listening to sounds from the kitchen. Then he got up and dressed swiftly – he did not wish to spend the night in that white bower of a room – and went through to the kitchen.

He watched as she made the eggs and heated coffee. He was not sure, he realised, leaning against the kitchen table, how he was going to cope with the full-blown domesticity which this affair might involve. He loathed intimate suppers, games of Scrabble, yawning and leafing through the dregs of news-papers to the sound of the ten o'clock news. The prospect was stifling. But that would be the kind of thing Rachel wanted. Everything warm and safe. Oh God, what am I doing here? he wondered, rubbing his hands over his face.

They ate in the kitchen, he listening as she talked, watching her face. This, too, he realised – the cosy, idle conversations after lovemaking, little exploratory meanderings into one another's life and past, seeking out truths and secrets and ties to bind . . .

'What do I think is important?' he said, in response to one of her questions, one of her loving probes into his soul. 'Well, I suppose I think I am.' He laughed. How true this was. 'And chambers. And the work I do. My mother.' He glanced at her. Oh, very well. 'And you are,' he added.

She leaned her elbow on the table, head on one hand, staring into her coffee cup. 'Am I?'

'Of course you are.' He tried not to sound too brisk. 'Anyway, what I mean is, it's the things close to me which are important, the things which immediately touch my life. The rest – oh, the things that go to fill up all the column inches in the newspapers are important in a way. But not really. Only in so far as they affect me.'

'Isn't that a very selfish way of looking at life?' she asked, her voice hesitant as her eyes searched his face.

How perfect she would like me to be, he thought.

'Yes,' he replied simply. 'It is. But then, I am too busy to spend time worrying about the rest of the world.' He paused.

'What matters to you?' he asked, feeling it only courteous to turn the question around.

'Oh . . . ' She stared at her cup, then sat back and flicked her dark hair from her shoulders. 'Honesty, I think. Yes, honesty most of all. In work, in relationships . . . Don't you think that must be the most important thing?' She looked up at him.

What was this about? he wondered. Perhaps nothing. He met her gaze. 'I'm not sure,' he replied. Which was no more than the truth. 'I don't know that it's always wise to let the complete truth about oneself be known. Some things don't bear discovery. Anyway, show me a person who's totally honest with themselves, let alone the rest of the world.'

She sighed and smiled.

'And if I'm being honest,' he went on, 'there's nothing I'd like more than to take you back to bed and make love to you for the entire night' – he slid his hands into the sleeves of her robe, stroking her bare arms – 'but I have to go home and get some sleep. I have the first day of a Norwegian Sale Form case tomorrow.'

I wish it were so that he never had to go home, she thought. I want to be with him – every single hour, every single day. I want to be able to say 'I love you' right now, and hear him say it in return. That is what I meant about honesty. But I dare not. I dare not in case . . .

'All right,' she said, and smiled, drawing her hands away from his and beginning to pick up the plates.

'I think, you know, that this case is going to keep me pretty busy for the next week or so,' he said lightly, standing up and picking up his jacket. 'I may not be able to see you until Sir Basil's party on the sixteenth.'

A whole week, she thought, without him. Time in which she might as well not exist. 'What about the weekend?' she asked.

'I have to spend most of that with these wretched clients and our solicitor. It's Hugh Hoggart – you know what he's like. And the clients are the jittery types. Anyway, I'd probably be too tired to be much fun.'

She came over and slid her arms around his waist as he put on his jacket, then lifted a hand to stroke his silver hair. He shrank inwardly from the treacherous familiarity of the gesture. Closer and closer. But he kissed her beautiful face and slid a hand inside her robe.

'I'll just have to make do with thinking about this evening until then,' she said. He kissed her again, and she closed her eyes and surrendered herself to the delicious sensation of being in love, completely and unconditionally.

It was true, she thought, watching from the window as he walked to his car, his shirt open at the neck, stuffing his tie into his jacket pocket with one hand and pulling out his car keys with the other. Being in love exaggerated everything, taking the most trivial things to a pitch of drama and intensity which would be unbearable if one had to live one's life always like that. But, of course, one could not live for ever in the euphoria of love. No one could. So what, then, is there to be for Leo and me? she wondered, letting the curtain drop back and turning to face the silent room. What comes after? She suddenly realised that the prospect of life without him was virtually unthinkable, a blank wilderness. She thrust the idea aside. No, the important thing with Leo was to make the most of what happened now. She'd had enough of dreading the future. Now was enough.

Chapter twenty-one

Although he was single, Sir Basil lived in a large, grand house in Hampstead, set well back from the road in spacious grounds, in which there was room for a separate small dwelling for the couple who tended his garden, prepared his meals and kept house for him. The house, and the life which Sir Basil lived within it, might have struck others as being both gloomy and formal, but it suited Sir Basil, who liked life to be a sober and practical business.

Mrs Leece, the housekeeper, had done her best to make the house look festive for the party, and the panelled rooms filled with people, light gleaming from chandeliers and log fires on the dark, polished furniture and ornate mirrors, looked more welcoming than usual that December evening. Sir Basil had even permitted a large Christmas tree, dressed with careful good taste by his sister Cora, to be erected in the curve of the stairwell.

Sir Basil looked around himself with serene satisfaction as guest after guest arrived – he felt this was to be an evening of some distinction, particularly with the presence of the new Lord Chancellor and his wife.

Leo was careful not to arrive too early. He and Rachel made their entrance twenty minutes after the stated time, and came in just behind Sir Frank Chamberlin and his wife.

Sir Basil greeted Leo suavely – Sir B. in his element, thought Leo, as he handed his coat to the housekeeper – and bestowed his most gracious, elder-statesmanlike smile upon Rachel.

'I hope I shall have the pleasure of talking to you a little later in the evening,' he said to her, thinking what a very attractive girl she was, rather young for Davies, before turning to greet his next guest.

Leo, for his own peace of mind, thought it best to avoid

Frank Chamberlin at first, although he could see from the corner of his eye that Frank's tall, stooping figure had turned to look in their direction. But it was not long, once he and Rachel had met and begun to talk to other guests, before Frank had managed to intercept Leo near the table where drinks stood and steered him into a brief tête-à-tête.

'I see you took me at my word after all,' he said to Leo, smiling conspiratorially as he raised his glass.

Leo scratched his jaw. 'Well, Frank, things are not always what they seem . . . '

Sir Frank lifted his hand, like a policeman on point duty, and stopped him. 'No, no – no need to say any more. But a very sound move, I can assure you. Mostyn has already been talking about her. Good idea to pick such a stunner.' He nodded and sipped his drink.

'Well, Frank, I didn't pick her – ' began Leo. Then he stopped, realising this was untrue.

'The important thing is,' went on Sir Frank, tapping Leo lightly on the lapel of his dinner jacket, his voice almost a whisper, 'that she'll make enough of an impression on the Lord Chancellor and a couple of others here – did you know Lord Brabsy and the Attorney General are here as well? – well, anyway, it might help to scotch some of the rumours that have been flying about.' He nodded again. 'You know.'

Leo grasped Sir Frank firmly by the upper arm and steered him away from the table and towards the fireplace and greater privacy. 'What rumours are flying about?'

Sir Frank looked startled, dismayed, and then became resigned. 'Leo, I hear only the very vaguest things, you know. But' – he paused, regarding his glass, then shaking his head – 'I have the impression that Bernard Lightfoot's clerk is – um – well, now, I shouldn't say a scandalmonger, should I? But, oh, you know how tight those fellows are with one another. I should say that whatever has crept out is from some – how shall I say? – some underground source. Perhaps he has picked something up from – well . . . Oh, Leo, I detest saying this kind of thing to you, you know I do . . . '

'It doesn't matter,' said Leo. 'Go on.'

'Well,' Frank continued miserably, swallowing the last of his

Scotch, 'there was something about you picking up law students – you know, young men. That is to say – '

'That's a bloody lie!' said Leo under his breath. As though he would ever do anything so crass.

'Well, well, I'm not trying to distress you,' said Sir Frank, wanting now to escape. 'I have to say that they are merely the flimsiest of tales. Mostyn has already said that he regards them as rubbish. No doubt Sir Mungo feels the same. But, coming on the heels of – well, you know . . . However, all I meant to say, in the beginning, was that, well, I'm sure your young lady friend will be a great help to you in all of this. You really must, you know, introduce me . . . ' He began to edge away from Leo.

Leo let him go, and stood by the fire on his own for a few moments. It wasn't worth becoming angry about. He had nothing to fear but the truth. Lies were the least of his worries.

He attached himself to Rachel once again, and at last, by careful manipulation of the little drifting sets of people in the room, found himself in the same conversational group as that of Sir Basil and the Lord Chancellor.

Lord Steele of Strathbuchat was a large, craggy Scot with a square jaw and crinkling grey hair brushed back from a low forehead. The drink he nursed in its crystal tumbler looked small in his large hands, and his formidable appearance was heightened by a slight squint, which gave the impression to anyone speaking to him that his attention was not fully fixed on what they were saying, but rather wandering.

Sir Basil introduced Rachel and Leo to Lord Steele and to the other members of their little group. Leo noted as he listened – only listened at first – that the conversation seemed to have become locked into stilted formality over some question concerning the European Community, the women's eyes bright with feigned interest, the men's faces already bored with the subject. Gradually, but without appearing too importunate, Leo brought himself into the discussion, asserting himself with his natural charm and eventually delighting them with two very amusing stories concerning the ponderous doings of the European Court of Justice – not a subject upon which it was easy to be amusing. Everyone in that little group was conscious of a lifting of spirits, aware of a gradual relaxation of tone that this assured and witty man had brought about.

Lord Steele felt the customary stiffness of those around him unbending, and was sufficiently encouraged to launch into an anecdote of his own, which was well received. He began to enjoy himself. He had imagined that this evening, like Sir Basil himself, would be a rather difficult, formal affair – he still had only acquaintances, rather than friends, in London, and his natural Scottish gregariousness had been repressed by the dignity of his new office. He felt that he could chat amiably to this man, and he liked the fact that Leo had either the luck or the good taste to possess such a lovely companion.

As for Leo, he appeared, in spite of Lord Steele's mildly disconcerting strabismal gaze, to be thoroughly at his ease. In short, he was a success, and, more importantly, a memorable one.

Rachel watched him with all the utter serenity of love. That Leo should so charm and impress others was no more than she expected. She knew nothing of the complete concentration and effort of mental energy which went into her beloved's performance.

After a little while, the eddies and currents of the party carried its guest of honour off into other parts of the room, and as Leo glanced round he saw a familiar, bucolic face, topped by a thatch of blond hair.

'Hello, Leo!' exclaimed the young man. Leo suddenly recognised him as Edward Choke, Sir Basil's nephew, erst-while pupil at 5 Caper Court.

'Edward,' murmured Leo with a smile. 'How are you? What are you up to these days?'

'Oh, not a lot. I've given up the farming lark, you know. Missed London. Not a lot to do in Surrey, really, except go to the pub. So Father got me a place at Morgan Grenfell.' He scratched his head. 'I'm not making much of it, but it's early days.'

Leo smiled, wondering to himself if Morgan Grenfell realised what a priceless gem of complete inanity they had in their midst. Still, he thought, the City was chock-full of

Edwards, well-meaning young hoorays coasting by, heaping up the easy money of the eighties.

'Anyway, how's Anthony getting along?' asked Edward. 'D'you know, I haven't seen him since I left chambers. I'll have to look him up now I'm back in London.'

'Oh, he's well,' replied Leo, thinking how different life would be if Sir Basil had had his way and if Edward was their junior tenant instead of Anthony. 'He seems to be getting lots of work.'

'I always knew he'd be better at it than me,' said Edward. 'But listen, can I get you another drink? Uncle Bas sort of put me in charge of the drinks department.'

'Yes, thanks,' said Leo, handing his glass to Edward.

He stood on his own for a few seconds, watching Rachel on the other side of the room talking to Tony Brabsy and his wife – all to the good – when he felt the pressure of a hand upon his arm. 'Hello, Leo,' said a girl's voice, and when he turned, he found Sarah's face, with its foxy, clever smile, looking into his.

Dear God, he thought, what was she doing here? A wave of panic and disbelief shook him, but he managed to smile, raised his eyebrows and said, 'Well, well. What a surprise.'

'Isn't it?' She made an expression of mock surprise in return. Apart from the fact that she was more formally dressed than he had ever seen her, in a low-cut dress of black taffeta, she was just the same, with her silky curtain of blonde hair and her pretty, crafty face. He pursed his lips and smiled again, his glance flitting nervously around.

'You really *are* surprised to see me, aren't you?' she said with amusement, watching his face.

He took a deep breath, lifted his chin and looked straight at her. 'Yes,' he said. 'If you want to know, I am. What brings you here?'

She nodded in the direction of a plump man in his mid-fifties standing next to the fireplace. 'He does,' she said, sipping her wine, still watching him.

Leo surveyed the familiar figure of the Chief Recorder of London and then looked back at Sarah. 'Christ, you don't mean you're – '

Sarah threw back her head and laughed, a clear, silvery

263

sound, just a little too loud. A few people glanced at her, and at Leo.

'No, I'm not that hard-pushed, Leo, darling. He's my father.'

'Oh. You didn't tell me.'

'Well, I hardly thought it would interest you, did I? I mean, I didn't even know you were a barrister – everything was so secretive, wasn't it, Leo?' She smiled and sipped her drink, adding reflectively, mischievously, 'What a furtive little summer we had.' She paused. 'All three of us.'

He said nothing, but a knot of anxiety was growing in his stomach. This was a dangerous young lady, he knew, and an unscrupulous, irresponsible one, too.

'Actually,' continued Sarah, 'I've only just been finding out what a terribly clever lawyer you are. And what a very lovely girlfriend you have.' Leo glanced instinctively in Rachel's direction, and Sarah followed his gaze. 'She doesn't – well, how shall I put it?' mused Sarah, rocking her drink from one hand to the other. 'She doesn't exactly look as though she'd be into our kinds of naughtiness, does she? You know, three in a bed . . . ' A muscle flickered in Leo's jaw as he glanced to see if anyone was in earshot of this. 'Speaking of which,' added Sarah, 'you haven't asked after James yet.'

'Now, I wonder why that might be?' murmured Leo.

'But since you ask,' continued Sarah, 'I should tell you that he was extremely cut up about being booted out by you in that rather perfunctory way. I think you dented his pride.'

'That is a matter of some indifference to me,' replied Leo.

'Well, yes, I thought it might be.' She sighed. 'I've bumped into him a couple of times, and he does seem to be in something of a bad way, drifting around, doing too much of the wrong kind of drugs –'

'And what,' asked Leo, clearing his throat, 'are you doing with yourself these days?' He gave her an even, interested smile.

'Have I touched on a raw nerve, darling? I *am* sorry. What am I doing? Well, I'm doing my finals this year. And then I go to Bar School.'

'I didn't know you were reading law,' remarked Leo,

furiously casting around in his mind for any reason why this girl should do him any harm. For she could, he knew, if she chose to. Dear God above, why must fate do this to him?

'You never asked. It wasn't one of the things about me that you were particularly interested in,' replied Sarah, thinking how wonderfully attractive Leo looked this evening – the only man in the room worth going to bed with, and that included Edward Choke. He had once been hers, in a manner of speaking, and now he was the possession of that beautiful, Madonna-faced creature in the corner. Sarah had heard quite enough people that evening remarking on what a wonderful couple she and Leo made. A flame of jealousy and mischief burned bright within her. 'But we had other things on our mind then, Leo, didn't we?' He said nothing, wondering where the hell Edward had got to with that drink. Sarah lowered her voice. 'I still haven't forgotten some of the things we used to do . . . ' Her voice was velvet. 'We still could, if you wanted to . . . '

He tried to speak, but had to clear his throat again. Tension, he realised, a problem he occasionally encountered in court.

'I don't really think it would be worthwhile – do you?' He turned his level blue gaze on her, and she felt a flash of anger and spite.

'Just think,' she said, 'of all the people here' – her glance comprehended the roomful of judicial eminence – 'who would be absolutely fascinated to hear how you spent your summer. Mmm?'

'I hardly think,' replied Leo, 'that your father would be particularly edified by your part in it.'

'Ah, but I have nothing to lose – in a professional sense, I mean. Whereas you . . . '

I do not believe this, thought Leo savagely. Why is this happening to me? All the miscalculations, the mistakes, coming home to roost.

'What are you specialising in for your finals?' he asked as mildly as he could.

'International trade,' replied Sarah, slightly taken aback by the apparent irrelevance of the question.

Leo smiled. 'How very interesting,' he said. 'My field, too.

Just think – in two years' time you'll be looking for a pupillage. And just think of all the people I know. Every head of chambers in every decent set, every silk, every junior looking for a pupil. My, my.'

She glared at him, about to say something, when Edward reappeared with Leo's drink.

'Here we go, Leo. Sorry about that. My mother made me talk to some wrinklies in the other room. Oh, do you two know each other?' He glanced from Leo to Sarah.

'Only very slightly,' murmured Leo. 'Thanks for the drink, Edward. Would you excuse me?' And he nodded, smiled and left them.

'Great guy, isn't he?' said Edward to Sarah. 'I had a pupillage in his chambers. He's very brilliant. Actually, I did some rather good pleadings for him once.' He took a sip of his drink. 'Uncle Bas says he'll be applying for silk any day now. Anyway, what d'you think of his girfriend? Isn't she gorgeous?'

'A bit pure and simple for my tastes,' replied Sarah, looking thoughtfully at Rachel. 'But perhaps I'd better go and introduce myself, since we have so much in common. See you, Edward.'

Turning his head, Leo saw Sarah making her way across the room in Rachel's direction. No, he thought, anything but that. But before he could even move, the High Steward of Cambridge University and an Emeritus Professor of International Law had descended upon him, and he was helpless, could only glance from time to time, with beating heart, at Rachel and Sarah talking together.

Sarah had decided to favour the direct approach.

'Hello,' she said with a winning smile, going up to Rachel as she stood momentarily on her own, holding out her hand. 'I'm Sarah Colman, a friend of Leo's. I thought I'd come and introduce myself, because Leo's told me so much about you.'

'Oh, has he?' said Rachel, returning the girl's smile guardedly as she took her hand.

'Oh, yes,' replied Sarah, tucking her hair girlishly behind one ear and widening her eyes. 'But then we talk rather a lot, Leo and I. He's something of a hero of mine. I'm specialising in his field of law, so I hope he'll be able to help me with finding a pupillage, and things.'

'Oh, you're studying law?' asked Rachel with interest.

'Yes.' Sarah nodded, wondering whether, with that wonderfully clear skin, Rachel wore any make-up. 'What do you do?'

'I'm a solicitor.' Rachel's smile was warm and friendly now. It was good to find someone younger to talk to; the women here all looked either like dowager duchesses or terribly smart socialites.

'Gosh, is that how you and Leo met?'

'Sort of.'

'Mmm.' Sarah paused, eyes brightening. 'Don't you think Leo is wonderfully clever?' she asked, watching Rachel's face, amusing herself with the thought of how Rachel's serene, happy expression was shortly to change.

'Yes. Yes, I suppose I do.' Rachel laughed with faint embarrassment and pleasure at talking about her lover.

Sarah's glance fell to her drink, which she was nursing in one hand. 'And marvellous in bed, too, don't you think?'

'I'm sorry?' Rachel leaned forward, startled, genuinely thinking she had misheard.

Sarah repeated herself, then added, 'So inventive, sexually. We should compare notes some time. Has he told you how he spent last summer?' She laughed, throwing back her head slightly, as though at some delicious shared pleasantry. Rachel simply gazed at her, dumbstruck. 'This friend of mine, James – well, he isn't really a friend, not part of my set, you know, more an acquaintance. Anyway, James and Leo and I set up a very jolly little ménage à trois at Leo's place in the country. Have you been there? I always said it was just as well he had a big enough bed. But the fun we had! Didn't you know Leo liked boys as well? They're really his speciality, wicked man – we're something of a sideline – '

Rachel, recovering something of her self-possession, set her glass down on a nearby table, murmured, 'Excuse me,' and, white-faced, walked away from Sarah in the direction of the doorway.

Leo, trapped by the Emeritus Professor, who was regaling

him with an account of a conference in Copenhagen, saw her from the other side of the room, glimpsed her strained face and empty eyes. He ground his teeth silently, longing to get away, pursue her, find out what had been said. She and Sarah had hardly been talking for more than a moment or two. But that would be long enough for Sarah. He glanced at Sarah and saw her, an amused smile on her face, lifting her glass slightly in his direction in a mocking little toast.

Rachel found her way to a bathroom and locked the door. She leaned against the washbasin, drawing in her breath. Her forehead touched the cool glass of the mirror above the basin. She felt shock still tingling in her limbs. Of course she had supposed that there had been women in Leo's life before, many of them – but what this girl had said took things to another dimension. She had said that Leo slept with boys as well – as soon as she had said it, thoughts of Leo had flooded Rachel's mind and she had known it to be true. And he had slept with that girl and her friend, together . . . It seemed that the Leo of the past few weeks had been transformed into someone completely unknown, an alien character. It was as though her trust and love had been torn down like the flimsiest of curtains, and this new strangeness revealed.

Leo lived in another world which she, Rachel, knew nothing about – and that girl was part of it. Clearly Leo could inspire hatred as well as love in people, something she had not thought possible, for Sarah had been intent on inflicting damage. It did not occur to Rachel that Sarah's remarks had been intended largely in a spirit of mischief, for Rachel could not comprehend mischief of that kind.

After thinking for a few moments, she looked at herself in the mirror, rubbing at her cheeks to give them more colour, and opened the door. What came next, she had no idea, but she knew that she would have to talk to Leo about this. Why? Maybe it didn't matter. But, of course, it did.

She saw him waiting for her at the foot of the stairs, his face expressionless but tense. She came down slowly, and even managed a faint smile as she reached him. Whatever new things she was learning about him, he was still Leo, her lover, and she still felt her heart fill at the sight of him.

'Are you all right?' he asked. She put out a hand and leaned on the dark, polished wood of the balustrade. The hallway was empty, except for the occasional drift of people from one room to another.

'Fine, I wasn't quite prepared for your friend Sarah, though.'

Leo looked directly at her. 'What did she say?'

'I don't think we should talk about it here, do you?' she said. For the first time in their relationship, Rachel felt the control was hers, that she would decide how events were to proceed. He stood there with that dependent sense about him, the balance altered, as though what she said and did was now of the utmost consequence.

'Do you want to go?' he asked quietly.

'Leo, we've only been here for an hour. I don't think your head of chambers would be too pleased if we went so abruptly. Anyway,' she added with a chilly little smile, one he had never seen before, 'I think it'll keep.' And she left his side and took a few steps to the doorway. 'Come on,' she said, for he was still standing next to the Christmas tree, his eyes wary and uncertain as a boy's, 'you still have a few more people to impress.'

He was watchful of her for the rest of the evening, certain from her manner that she had been told something which could wreck it all. He managed to talk and laugh and eat and drink, but he was counting the minutes until he could get Rachel on her own, and find out how badly things might have been disturbed. Leo detested not knowing where he stood, in court or out of it.

At last they stood together in the hallway, Rachel with her coat about her shoulders, the chilly draught of the previous guests' departure enveloping them as they murmured their thanks and farewell to Sir Basil and his sister.

Leo hurried her out into the freezing night, questions and anxieties racing in his mind. They walked in silence down the long driveway, past banks of deep laurels and dark shrubs. Suddenly he stopped, and Rachel halted, too, turning to look enquiringly at him. He was not sure what he was thinking, but he trusted his impulse. He drew her quickly into the shadow of some trees and bushes and kissed her for a long time with as much feeling as he could muster, stifling any resistance and soothing her restless body until she gave herself up to him. Then there was silence, and he leaned back against a tree as she drew her arms from around his neck.

'What are you afraid of?' she asked, with real curiosity.

Her perspicacity touched him. 'Of losing you,' he replied, reflecting wryly on the truth which would be misunderstood in this.

'I think we have to do some talking,' she said, slowly and softly. They made their way back out on to the driveway and walked to Leo's car. There they sat in silence for a moment. Leo switched on the engine, and then the heater on full.

'Jesus, it's freezing,' he muttered, as he swung the car out into the deserted road. They drove for some time, neither speaking, until they stopped at some traffic lights. Leo turned to look at her.

'So – what did Sarah say to you?' He shifted gear, looking back at the lights, waiting for them to change, waiting for her reply.

'Well,' said Rachel, a trace of irony in her voice, 'she talked about how you spent your summer.'

Oh, thank you, Sarah, thought Leo with quiet fury. He said nothing, moved off from the lights.

'Is it true?' asked Rachel. Now her voice sounded small and unhappy.

'Is what true?' asked Leo grimly, not looking at her. Christ, maybe it didn't matter. Maybe this relationship had served its purpose, could end here and now. But then he remembered what Frank had said earlier that evening, and he knew that the thing still had to go the distance. Without Rachel, he became defenceless. She was his armour against all rumour and conjecture. The mere fact of the Lord Chancellor's enthusiastic conversation with her that night had shown him this. He waited to hear what she would say next.

'That you sleep with boys,' she replied evenly, watching his profile.

He ground the gears and swore softly under his breath. 'Did she say that?'

270

Rachel hesitated. 'She said – she – yes, that was what she said.' Now it was Rachel's turn to wait. He drove for a little way without speaking.

'I've finished with all that,' he said at last, finality in his tone.

'So you did – once?'

He said nothing, merely nodded, gazing straight ahead of him.

'And you slept with Sarah and this boy, James?'

He drew up to the traffic lights at Great Portland Street and stared at the Christmas lights in the shops. 'Yes,' he replied tonelessly. 'Yes, that's what we did. All summer.' The lights changed; they moved off again.

Rachel sat and thought about this. She could not imagine Leo making love to another man. The thing was beyond her.

They did not speak again until they reached Leo's house. She had expected him to take her home, but was glad that he wanted to be with her for a while longer. She had already begun to make decisions about all of this. He gave her the keys and she let herself in while he put the car away. She went upstairs and into the living room, switching on lights. She looked around the room which, over the past weeks, had now become familiar, and felt, oddly, as though parts of the room, certain pictures and objects, now made fresh sense in the light of what she knew.

She heard him close the door and come upstairs behind her. He crossed the room and fetched the brandy from a cupboard.

'Would you like some?' he asked, pouring himself a glass. She shook her head.

He sat down on the sofa with his glass and looked up at her. He stretched out a hand to hers and pulled her gently down next to him. Her coat slid from her shoulders. He shifted slightly, turning to look directly into her eyes, taking a sip of his brandy.

'Are you very shocked by all of this?' he asked quietly.

She looked down, running her fingers over the back of his hand, pulling it gently on to her thigh. 'A bit,' she said. Then she added, almost apologetically, 'I know I shouldn't be, I suppose – I mean, nowadays . . .'

'Nowadays has nothing to do with it,' replied Leo. 'This is

you and me we're talking about.' She said nothing, merely wound her fingers absently round his, not looking at him. 'I told you it's all in the past, that kind of thing. I don't want it to make any difference between us.'

'But, Leo, it's more than just the past,' she murmured. 'There's now, and the future. I mean, that kind of thing involves risks. Everyone knows that. What if –'

'What if I had Aids, or something?' He smiled grimly. 'Don't worry. I'm a most conscientious citizen. I don't take risks. And I have myself tested regularly. Not HIV positive so far.' She said nothing, but continued to stroke his hand. 'I want to know if it changes anything, Rachel.' Still she was silent. 'Believe me, all that's finished with,' he added, driving her to a response.

At this, she looked up. 'How can it be? How can that kind of thing ever be? You can't just switch yourself off like that, can you?' There was a note of wonder in her voice.

He did not know what to say to this. He drank some more of his brandy. Lying was becoming more and more difficult; the part he had played at the outset of this affair no longer seemed to fit. He felt awkward and weary. But he had to go on. He set his glass down on the table, and picked up both her hands in his, bringing his face nearer to hers.

'I want it to be finished with,' he said. 'Right now, there is nothing in the world I want apart from you. Do you understand that?' It seemed imperative that she should believe him.

'Yes,' she answered, believing him, wanting to.

He clenched her hands tight in his and kissed them, then looked back at her intently. 'I suppose,' she said after a moment, lifting her eyes to his and smiling faintly, 'that we're both damaged goods, in a sense. Aren't we?'

He caught the tone in her voice with relief; it was one of surrender, acceptance. The thing was safe for the moment. But her words reminded him that she was, sexually and emotionally, a fragile being. The damage could run deeper than he had supposed. Well, he would find out.

'Shall I take you home?' he asked. There was a pause. 'Or would you rather stay here?'

'Here,' she said. She put her lips softly against his, tasting the brandy, his body warm beneath her hands through the thinness of his shirt. 'I want to be here with you.'

He felt tired. Forty-four, tired and longing just to sleep. But there were needs to be filled and beliefs to be sustained.

'Come on,' he said. 'Come to bed.' He kissed her gently and she nodded, then rested her head upon his shoulder, feeling as though the past few hours had aged her by years.

Chapter twenty-two

Now was the season of the office Christmas party. All over the City of London the event was breaking out in its many and varied forms like a horrible rash. Restaurants rang at midday and in the early evening to the screeching laughter of secretaries in silly hats, and to the banter of white-socked clerks pulling crackers and drinking too much in a haze of cigarette smoke, surrounded by the remnants of overpriced turkey dinners and cheap wine. In works canteens, in office dining rooms, in boardrooms and in rented-out wine bars, sound systems belted out disco music, company bosses looked on with lofty indulgence and left after half an hour, typists got tight and had their virtue compromised by office boys and lowly computer operators, and the trains and buses were not pleasant to travel on after eight o'clock in the evening.

On the day before the Nichols & Co office party was due to take place, Felicity stumbled into the lift on the eighth floor with armfuls of documents. Balancing the pile with her chin, she jabbed at the buttons and then dumped the papers on the floor as the doors closed. A second later they opened again, and Mr Lamb got in. The doors slid shut and Felicity stood apprehensively against one wall. Mr Lamb turned to gaze at her as the lift began its slow descent. Conscious of his stare, Felicity folded her arms and feigned interest in the lift buttons.

'I notice you seem to have been keeping out of my way recently, Felicity, ' he remarked smoothly.

'Not bleeding surprising, is it?' she replied, not taking her eyes off the buttons. God, this lift was slow. He'd better not try anything.

'Maybe I'll give you a ring later this morning,' he said unperturbed by her tone of voice, 'and we can do that little thing I suggested the other week, eh?' And he reached out a swift hand and squeezed at her breast. Almost as soon as he did so she lifted her hand and whacked him as hard as she could across the cheek, and he lurched sideways a little.

'You do that one more time, you dirty old git,' she snarled at him, her chest heaving with anger, 'and I'll have you! You can't go around harassing people, you know!'

Mr Lamb had instinctively put his hand up to his cheek, which bore the flaming imprint of Felicity's fingers.

'You little bitch!' he hissed. 'I'm going to have you out of here so fast your feet won't touch the ground!'

'Good!' she retorted. 'I'll be glad to be out of this stinking place! But before I go, I'll tell them all about the little games you've been playing, you sexist pig!'

The lift had reached the basement and stopped. Mr Lamb leaned out and pressed the 'doors closed' button, and kept his finger on it. 'And I'll just tell them that you're a little troublemaker, cooking up stories out of spite at being fired. No one's going to listen to you, Felicity. Remember, you don't stand particularly high in anyone's estimation.' He took his finger off the button and the lift doors slid open. 'I'm afraid your Christmas isn't going to be a very happy one,' he added. He stepped out and the lift doors closed behind him.

Felicity leaned back against the wall, shaking slightly, and closed her eyes. Tears pricked her eyelids. She stabbed at a button, any button, and rode up a few floors, then mopped her eyes as she searched for the button for the basement again. She took her bundles of paper down and left them by the shredder, then went back up to her own floor, where she fetched some work from her desk and took it through to Rachel's room. She was just setting it down on the desk when Rachel came in behind her.

Rachel glanced at Felicity, whose face still looked tearful.

'That's the last of those letters,' said Felicity, turning to leave.

'Thanks,' said Rachel, and swung herself into her chair, tucking her legs beneath her. 'Are you all right?' she asked, as Felicity reached the door.

For a moment, Felicity thought of confiding in Rachel, telling her all about Mr Lamb and his threats – but the time when she might have told Rachel about it, sought her help, was past. They were still friendly to each other, but Rachel felt guilty about Felicity, and this tinged their relationship with uneasiness.

She looked at Rachel. 'Time of the month,' she said, with a little smile. 'Just something someone said. You know how you overreact.' And she left, closing the door behind her.

She sat down at her desk and stared unseeingly at the little array of Christmas cards sellotaped to the back of Louise's VDU. Why did they give each other Christmas cards every year, she wondered, when they sat next to each other all day, every day? God, she hated offices. So what if she didn't get a reference from this place? Maybe she could find something closer to home, something she would enjoy doing. Working with kids, or handicapped people. Then she sighed. Fat chance. You needed qualifications and, anyway, it wouldn't bring in the right kind of money. If only Sandy would get a job. Even if it was just banging out burgers at McDonald's. But she'd given up nagging him. She felt tears rising again as she thought of what Mr Lamb had said. She shielded her eyes with one hand and stared down at a memo on her desk, as though reading, as Doris padded up.

'Here, Fliss – d'you want to see what I got my little grandson in Petticoat Market? It's ever so sweet . . .'

'Yeah, in a minute, Doris,' said Felicity with an effort, not looking up, hand still shading her eyes. 'I'm just trying to concentrate on this.' She waited unti Doris had buttonholed a couple of the filing clerks and, to a background of 'Innit lovely?' and 'Ow, it's sweet!', she made her escape to the loo, locked herself in a cubicle, and wept. When she had finished, she scrumpled up the length of lavatory paper into which she had been crying and stared at it. Someone banged into the cubicle next door, and there was a rustling of skirt and knickers, then a genteel tinkling.

At least she'd be out of this prison of an office, she told herself, closing her eyes and resting her head on her fists. She'd sign on. They'd get by. Something would happen. It was just having that bastard stitch her up like this – that was the worst of it. That smug, horrible, groping bastard. And when she'd gone, he'd start on someone else. She pondered the possibility of going now to one of the partners and telling them what had happened. But it wouldn't be any use. They'd have her out, anyway. They'd just about had enough of her before Rachel came. Besides, Mr Lamb was no doubt in John Parr's room right now, selling her down the river, telling him that Miss Dean was finding Felicity too slack and that they'd have to ask her to leave.

Oh, well. She sniffed, waited for the occupant of the next cubicle to leave, and then came out and splashed cold water over her eyes. At least it wasn't all doom and gloom. She still had Vince. She brightened at the thought of Vince. She'd be able to go down the pub with him tonight and tell him all about it, get it off her chest. Yeah, she'd tell Vince, and he'd cheer her up, tell her it wasn't so bad after all. He might not have a job or any money, Vince, but at least he was optimistic.

On the other side of the City, the occupants of 5 Caper Court were in readiness for their own Christmas party. Sir Basil was, with trepidation, preparing to surrender his set of rooms to the use of the staff for the evening, trying not to think of the state the cleaners would find the carpet in afterwards. Each year it seemed to him that the thing sank to lower and lower depths. It was never rowdy or out of control, naturally, but it was no longer the exclusive, gentlemanly affair which it had been in Sir Basil's father's day, restricted to the tenants and the head clerk. Now all the staff attended and, with the unaccustomed luxury of free alcohol, some of them grew quite boisterous. Much food and drink was consumed, and the eldest of the typists, Mrs Frears, invariably got tipsy and started calling Sir Basil 'dear' and telling him about her son in the navy. That was always Sir Basil's cue to leave.

It was for these reasons that Sir Basil had held his own party at home a few days before, where he could relax in the knowledge that his guests would not have to witness the postboy being sick on the stair, or Henry overindulging in Cameron Renshaw's Glenmorangie.

Sir Basil would willingly have paid for a lavish luncheon for the staff at one of the Chancery Lane restaurants, so that the chambers party might revert to being a discreet little festivity among the barristers only, but, as Mr Slee pointed out, in these days of egalitarianism, such a thing would smack of elitism and the typists wouldn't like it. It sometimes seemed to Sir Basil that the members of his typing pool displayed all the refined temperament of thoroughbred racehorses.

Mr Slee himself oversaw the preparations for the festivities in quite a Pickwickian frame of mind, but that day he was conscious of feeling not quite so well as he should. He sat down heavily in the clerks' room after he and Henry had carried the two cases of Moët up to Sir Basil's room, trying to pace the thump and flutter of his heart. Too much carrying, he thought. That was all it was. He should have got one of the younger tenants to help Henry. He sat, recovering himself, and eyed Jeremy Vine, an arrogant man in his middle thirties who regarded himself as by far the most able man in chambers, as he came in with two briefs.

'There we go,' said Jeremy loftily, scribbling the inverted looped cross on their backs to show they were completed, and dropping them into a tray. He glanced at Mr Slee.

'Don't tell me you've been hitting the festive spirit early, William. You're looking a bit pink about the gills.'

Mr Slee stared at him indignantly. 'Certainly not! I've just been humping great crates of champagne about for the likes of you to drink this evening.'

'Oh God, the chambers party,' said Jeremy. 'Well, I can only look in for half an hour or so. I've got a frightfully heavy workload, even if it is Christmas.' Jeremy regarded his practice as one of monumental importance and dedicated more energy and attention to it than his clients or his bank balance required.

Leo came in in his shirtsleeves and grinned at Jeremy. 'Got judgment in the *Kapetan Kirios* this morning. Your amendment was struck out and the application dismissed. But I suppose you know that?'

'I was aware,' said Jeremy coldly. Try as he might, he always found himself cast in the pompous, unbending role when Leo was about. 'I still feel it was a perfectly proper case for service of a third party notice.'

'Well, well. I won't say I told you so. Win some, lose some, eh, Jeremy? By the way, the word among the secretaries is that the new typist has the hots for you. Save yourself for this evening. We know you like them young.'

Jeremy took a dim view of Leo's frivolities and said nothing for a moment. Then he smirked and remarked, 'Speaking of which, I hear your new girlfriend is rather on the – ah – young side. Young for you, that is.'

Leo only smiled. 'Twenty-seven, actually. I'm so glad you're taking an active interest in my love life, Jeremy.'

Jeremy sniffed and left the room, and Leo, after fishing out some refills for his stapler, went out, too.

'What's this about a girlfriend?' Mr Slee asked Henry, staring after Leo. Henry broke off whistling 'In the Bleak Mid-Winter' and glanced at Mr Slee.

'Didn't you know? David reckons it's love. Leo's been out everywhere with her. Even took her to the old man's bash the other night. A real looker, David says. Funny that,' added Henry, tucking a sprig of holly behind the computer, 'but in all the time I've been here I never heard he had a girlfriend. Not till now. I was beginning to wonder if he wasn't queer. I mean, the way he dresses an' all. You know?' He resumed his whistling.

Mr Slee looked at him but said nothing, merely laid a hand over his heart, testing, wondering.

The atmosphere at the chambers party was always a little uneasy to begin with, until people had had a few drinks and begun to loosen up. Anthony turned up early, at six thirty, determined to stay for only a short time and then leave; Leo, he knew, always worked late, and Anthony wanted to be gone before he showed up. It had been a few weeks since he had last seen Rachel, and the pain of loss had begun to fade, but the blow which Leo had inflicted on his pride still smarted. He picked up a glass of champagne from a tray and went over to join Cameron Renshaw, who was leaning against one of Sir Basil's ceiling-high bookcases with a glass of Glenmorangie in one hand and a chicken drumstick in the other.

'Do you think I'd make a good Father Christmas?' Cameron asked Anthony glumly.

Anthony smiled and regarded Cameron; take away the glasses and the moustache, and the basics were all there.

'Um – with the costume – and a bit of padding, of course –'

'Bugger the padding,' replied Cameron, finishing his chicken and dropping the bone into Sir Basil's wastepaper basket, then hitching at his braces with his thumb. 'I've got enough of that already. My wife has told the assorted heads of the Cubs and Brownies – Big Badgers and Brown Owls, or whatever they are – that I will be Santa Claus at their damned party this weekend.'

'I'm sure you'll be very good,' said Anthony mildly, as David Liphook came over to join them, fresh from the wine bar with William Cooper.

'What's all this?' enquired David, who didn't like to be left out of any conversation. Anthony told him. 'Oh, yes, marvellous casting, Cameron. Ho, ho, ho! You know, you could have used this evening as a dry run. Dressed up and handed out little pressies to everyone. Sir Basil would love it.'

Cameron sighed morosely and poured himself another drink. 'To think of it – I, a QC, the toast of the Commercial Bar, scourge of the Admiralty Court, in a red suit with a white cotton-wool beard. It's not as though I even volunteered. Oh God, here they come,' he added, as the typists flocked in and made their chattering way towards the trays of champagne. The heady scent of Anais Anais filled the air.

Forty minutes later, Anthony was crossing the room on his way out when Sir Basil intercepted him with a bottle of champagne and refilled his glass. Anthony accepted it, knowing that it wouldn't be diplomatic to let Sir Basil see him leaving too early. They talked together for a moment or two, Sir Basil formal but avuncular, Anthony polite but not entirely at his ease. He remembered only too well Sir Basil's opposition to his joining chambers two years ago, when the beloved Edward, before he had decided to take up farming, had been the favoured candidate.

'And how is your father?' asked Sir Basil. 'I understand he had a new exhibition recently. My sister Cora bought one of his paintings.'

'Oh, he's well, thank you,' replied Anthony, recalling the

one occasion on which Chay and Sir Basil had encountered one another, when Chay had just been busted and bailed and looking thoroughly disreputable. That had been at a chambers Christmas party, too. Sir Basil was also recalling the encounter at that moment. He had thought at the time that Chay Cross had looked a most unsuitable type to be the father of a prospective tenant at 5 Caper Court, but then artists were hardly like other people. The man was now celebrated and wealthy, and for these twin virtues Sir Basil could forgive any amount of bohemian eccentricity.

'Now, I see my secretary needs a bit of a top-up,' said Sir Basil, wagging his bottle jovially. 'Do excuse me.'

Anthony murmured something, and was about to make his escape when he saw Leo come into the room with Michael. He had been steering clear of Leo, not even going to tea in the afternoons in the Inner Temple Common Room with the others, and he had not seen him for over a week. As ever, the sudden sight of Leo had a peculiar effect upon Anthony, as though he stood out from the rest of those in the room, more alive than they, vivid and compelling. Anthony, this time, mistook the force of his feeling for deep dislike. He didn't want to be in the same room as the man.

Leo saw that Anthony was about to leave, and while Michael was fetching them both a drink, Leo stayed near the door, so that Anthony had to pass by him on the way out.

Anthony, feeling absurdly childish, tried to ignore him, but as he went through the doorway and out on to the landing, Leo followed him and gripped him by the arm. In a way, Anthony realised, he was glad to be detained by him. He turned, his face expressionless.

'Don't you think,' said Leo, glancing behind him at the crowded room, 'that this is all becoming rather ridiculous?' Anthony said nothing. 'I mean, how long is all this going to go on? We work in the same chambers, Anthony. It's bad for the whole set if you're going to go around looking sulky and avoiding me.'

'How do you expect me to behave after what you've done?' replied Anthony. 'Do you imagine I like you for it?'

'You don't have to like me,' said Leo. 'You merely have to

281

learn to behave in an adult fashion, not like some teenager.'

'Look, Leo,' said Anthony, 'if I'm fed up with you, then I'll act fed up. Okay?' He didn't have the heart to feel angry, merely defensive.

'I'm glad to hear that's all it is,' said Leo mildly. He paused. 'What have you done about the *Valeo Dawn* papers?'

'I've told Rachel I'm sending them back. I haven't got around to it yet,' replied Anthony.

'You know she doesn't want you to,' said Leo. 'Her client is hard up as it is. She doesn't want him forking out for another counsel to go over the same ground twice.'

Anthony stared at him, thinking absently that Leo was getting older, that his handsome face was becoming more drawn and lined. There was a touch of weariness about the eyes. 'Can I ask you something?' he said suddenly. His voice sounded challenging, genuinely curious.

'If you want,' replied Leo, moving away a little from Anthony and leaning on the banister. Why couldn't the boy just let it alone?

Anthony's eyes were still fastened on Leo's face. 'Explain it to me. I mean, tell me what's going on.' There was a pause as they gazed at one another, Leo saying nothing. 'Because I don't understand it. You tried to seduce me once' – his voice was soft against the growing chatter of the party behind them – 'and now Rachel. I don't understand it.'

'Nothing is ever straightforward,' answered Leo, glancing down at the brown polished wood and rubbing it with his thumb. 'Life and people – all very complicated.' He sighed. 'I'm afraid I don't have answers for you.'

'But why Rachel?' said Anthony insistently. 'I mean, why her, of all people? You don't love her, do you?'

Dear Anthony, thought Leo. You still think everything would have been all right with her, if only I hadn't butted in. How wrong you are. But I can't tell you that. What can I tell you? He looked up. How many lies was he going to have to tell in the course of this thing?

'I liked her when I met her. I asked her out. That's all.' He paused, then added, 'Perhaps I do love her.'

'I don't believe you,' answered Anthony, his voice still soft.

'Don't you, Anthony?' said Leo, straightening up, his voice flat and uninterested in contrast to the intensity of Anthony's tone.

'No,' said Anthony, 'I don't. Have you told her about your – let me get the right word – your sexual ambivalence, shall we say? I mean, is she getting the real Leo here?' Anthony's voice was light and dangerous.

'I think so. Yes. Yes, she knows, if that's what you mean.'

This took Anthony aback. She knew and she didn't care. She must feel very deeply for Leo indeed. Or was it that he simply didn't understand the way women's minds worked? He hesitated for a moment, then murmured, 'You're beyond me. It's all way beyond me.' He turned to go. From downstairs came the sound of the door to the clerks' room slamming, then Mr Slee's key in the lock. 'Merry Christmas,' added Anthony over his shoulder, aware that he felt no real animosity, no real anything. It had all been a waste of time and emotion. Let them get on with it. He didn't want to know any more.

As Anthony reached the landing below, and Leo the doorway, there was a sudden heavy thudding, as of something bumping downstairs, and then a groan. Anthony stopped, looked over the banister, then back up at Leo, who had reappeared on the landing.

'What the hell was that?' asked Leo.

'I don't know,' said Anthony, and then raced down to the bottom, where he found Mr Slee slumped outside the door to the clerks' room. 'Jesus, I think he's had a heart attack,' said Anthony to Leo, who had followed him downstairs. They bent over him. Mr Slee's eyes were closed, his face grey and his lips bluish.

'We'd better call an ambulance,' said Leo. He rattled the locked door of the clerks' room, then turned and ran up the stairs, taking them two at a time.

On the other side of the city, in Bishopsgate, the Nichols & Co party was in full spate. With an office of more than two hundred people, this was a rowdy and crowded affair. One of the conference rooms next to the boardroom on the ninth floor had been turned into a dark, cavernous disco, complete with

283

sound system and rented DJ (husband of one of the secretaries) and coloured strobe lighting. The boardroom itself heaved with people, all drinking as much as they could at the expense of their employers, forming themselves into exactly the same little cliques as they did at work – the partners at one end, already glancing at their watches and preparing to drift off, the denizens of the post room at the other, and little knots of people from various different departments in the middle.

Felicity was standing near one of the buffet tables with two of her mates. She was wearing a low-cut cerise dress which she'd bought in Petticoat Market just that afternoon, and which stopped several inches above her knees, and her curly hair was piled up on her head. She'd nearly decided not to come this evening, but, having decided she would, she thought she might at least make an effort. Anyway, she liked dressing up and showing this bunch how good she could really look. When she went out with Vince she never really had a chance to dress up. Not properly. He liked her in her black leather skirt and halter-neck blouse. This was her chance to look a bit glam.

She and Beryl and Maureen had made heavy inroads into the white wine, and had now decided to swap to vodka and tonics. No sense in not getting your money's worth, thought Felicity, as she scoffed a couple more vol-au-vents and wondered what that green stuff in the bowl with the crisps round it was. Looked like pus. She was about to dip an experimental finger into it when a voice at her ear made her jump.

'You're looking very sexy tonight, Felicity,' said Mr Lamb. His sparse black hair was combed carefully over the bald part of his skull, and he was wearing so much Paco Raban that Felicity could taste it at the back of her throat. Maureen and Beryl had instinctively moved away at Mr Lamb's approach, and now she was cornered. Well, at least they were in public, and he couldn't start groping her again. Mind you, you never knew. She was just amazed that he was speaking to her after what had happened in the lift.

'I like that dress,' murmured Mr Lamb. Felicity looked at him, wondering whether she should tell him to piss off, or

284

whether 'thank you' might be more diplomatic. She said nothing. 'And you'll be pleased to hear that I haven't spoken to Mr Rothwell yet,' he added, lowering his voice. 'I've decided to give you one more chance. I thought once you'd got a little of the party spirit, we could get together later on. Somewhere a little quieter, like my room. What do you think? Just a bit of fun, Felicity – a little Christmas fun. Then you'll have a job to come back to next year, won't you?' And she felt his hand slide across her bottom as he moved away, his oily smile still on his face, off to butter up the senior partners.

Felicity had listened to him impassively. She didn't care any more whether she got the sack or not. She wanted out of this poxy place. When she had told Vince last night, he'd said she should get out – that was after he'd calmed down a bit. She hadn't expected him to react as violently as he had done when she'd told him what Mr Lamb had been up to. He was funny like that, Vince. You never knew what would make him go berserk. Mind, she should have known that would do it. But he'd calmed down eventually. Oh, Vince . . . She wished she were with him right now, and not here. She wasn't enjoying herself. Still, maybe she'd feel better if she went and had a bop.

'Come on, Mo,' she said, rejoining her friends. 'Let's go and do a bit of damage next door.' And off they trooped to the conference room and the sounds of Prefab Sprout.

Down in reception Ted, the night porter, yawned and chucked his copy of the *Evening Standard* to one side. He ambled round the reception desk and stood staring out through the revolving doors into the dark, deserted street. They were all up having their party now. Probably all right to nip into the back office and have that drink with the cleaners. He checked the lights on the switchboard, then went out through the fire door to the back.

A few minutes later, a scruffy young man in a black leather bomber jacket, with shoulder-length hair and two-day-old stubble, came through the revolving doors, followed by a tall coloured man in jeans and a camouflage jacket. They stood for a moment at the desk, wary and watchful.

'There's no one about,' said Vince to his mate Benjy. 'I thought there'd be someone here. That's useful. Come on.'

'Which floor is it, then?' asked Benjy, as they got into the lift.

'I dunno, do I?' replied Vince, scanning the buttons. 'We'll just have to start at the first floor and work our way up. Right?'

Benjy nodded and Vince pressed the first of the buttons.

Four minutes later they emerged, looking very unlike typical office partygoers, at the ninth floor. The sounds of the disco and the swell of voices and laughter from the boardroom were unmistakable. Vince stood by the lift for a moment, raising and lowering his shoulders, psyching himself up. He'd sort this bastard Lamb out. Just a question of finding him, then having him. Careful not to look too aggressive just at first. Didn't want to be stopped before he'd even got to him.

They walked casually up the corridor towards the sound of the party. A young woman came out of the boardroom, heading for the lift. Vince thought she looked vaguely familiar, that long black hair and nice face.

"Scuse me,' he said to her, his voice that of a polite child.

'Yes?' said Rachel, glancing at them both. Didn't she know this man?

'We was just looking for Mr Lamb,' said Vince, then coughed.

They must be with the electricians who were working on the new computer terminals – that was why he was familiar. Presumably that was why they wanted Mr Lamb, though it seemed odd that they should still be working at this time in the evening.

'Yes – he's in there, in the far left-hand corner,' replied Rachel with a smile. 'At least, he was a moment ago.'

'Thanks,' said Vince, and gave her his best smile. Benjy muttered thanks and followed Vince towards the boardroom. Rachel walked on towards the lift.

Once inside the boardroom, Vince merely had to ask one other person to identify Mr Lamb, carefully picking someone who looked like he'd had a few and wouldn't ask questions. He nodded and stared as Mr Lamb was pointed out to him. That bald-headed bastard, was it? Right. As he squared his shoulders and pushed his way through the crowd, Benjy in his wake, people turned to stare. As he drew nearer, Vince began to shout at Mr Lamb.

'Oy, Mr Lamb! You Mr Lamb?' He strode on, drawing nearer, as Mr Lamb turned to stare at him in amazement. 'I'm gonna fuckin' drop you, mate!' and he grabbed the astonished Mr Lamb by his upper arms and head-butted him. Mr Lamb went down like a sack of potatoes, his drink spilling down one trouser leg, blood spurting from the bridge of his nose. Then Vince hauled him up by his necktie and struck him twice with his fist, before dropping him down and administering two heavy kicks to his stomach and ribs. 'I'd like to tear your fuckin' head off!' he panted at Mr Lamb. 'You touch my girlfriend once more, and I bloody well will!'

Then he turned and pushed his way out. While all this had been going on, Benjy had been shoving back a couple of the more daring spirits who had tried to pull Vince off – Benjy was such an intimidating prospect that, even in their numbers, none of the men felt like tackling him. The partners had already left. No one felt particularly authoritative. Anyway, whatever Lamb was getting, he probably deserved. No one liked him. So they stood there, drinks in hand, looking apprehensive and mumbling threateningly to one another as Vince and Benjy reached the door. Some of the girls were leaning over Mr Lamb and screaming.

Hearing the tumult, people began to come through from the disco room, Felicity among them. She saw Vince and Benjy, and for a second opened her mouth to say something. Then she thought better of it and melted back into the room. She heard someone murmur, 'That guy just gave Lamb a going-over!' Oh, Christ, thought Felicity. Oh, Vince.

Someone had the presence of mind to buzz down to the night porter before Vince and Benjy could reach the front door and make their escape. But they buzzed in vain. As Vince and Benjy legged it into the night, Ted and Sean, one of the cleaners, were discussing Millwall's chances in the Cup in the back office.

At 5 Caper Court, the members of chambers sat around morosely in Sir Basil's room after the ambulance had gone. Leo had slipped fifty pounds to Vi, one of the tearful group of typists, and told her to take the girls to the pub so they could drown their upset. There was no question of carrying on with the party.

Anthony sat next to Leo and poured him some more of Cameron's Scotch. He had been moved at the sight of Leo, crouched next to Mr Slee as they waited for the ambulance, murmuring, 'Poor old Bill. You're going to be okay. Don't worry,' while everyone else paced about saying where was that bloody ambulance.

'Thanks,' said Leo.

'I suppose we should just push off home,' said Michael, who had rung Mr Slee's wife ten minutes earlier. 'There's not much we can do.'

'I have to hang around,' said Leo. 'I told Rachel to drop by. I'll have to wait for her.'

As Leo knocked back his Scotch, Anthony glanced at him. Leo's voice was tired, he had spoken Rachel's name with all the familiarity of possession. Perhaps he was sincere. Perhaps Rachel had got lucky. Anyone who had Leo, thought Anthony, was lucky. Confused by his thoughts, distressed by the events of the evening, Anthony rose and said he was going. The others murmured goodnight.

As the sound of Anthony's feet on the wooden stairs died away, Leo said to Sir Basil, 'I'll lock up, if you like, Basil. If you want to get off home, that is.'

Sir Basil nodded. The long, normally serene face seemed to have slackened and aged with shock and unhappiness. The ambulancemen had been very concerned about William's condition, and had rushed him off. Now Sir Basil wondered if he should have gone in the ambulance with him. William was one of his oldest friends. He had never realised that until now. How odd it was with people. One was with them so long, day in, day out, throughout the years that it never occurred to one how close they could become, how much a part of one's life.

Sir Basil fetched his coat, said goodnight to Leo and the others, and left. The others gradually drifted off, too – Michael, Cameron and Roderick to their homes, David and William for an emergency dinner in Covent Garden with a few bottles of wine. Jeremy had left the party before any of this had happened.

Leo sat alone in the utter silence of chambers. He had often been there alone, working late, but never before had the silence closed so completely, so forcefully, around him. The settling creaks, the tiny ticks and sounds of an aged building empty of people, fell loudly upon his ears. He nursed his glass and looked around him, thinking of the history that lay within these walls, within every building in the Temple, every brick, every stairwell, every room. All the voices down the years, now silent, their words faded and forgotten; the feet upon the stairs, now silent; the names upon the board, painted out now, replaced by the lustre of fresh faces . . . He thought of these, and he thought of William. Poor Bill.

After a while, he heard feet upon the stairs, hesitant at first, then quicker. He knew it must be Rachel. He realised he did not want her to interrupt his meditations. He would rather have sat there alone, with the whisky and the shadows for company.

Rachel came slowly into the room. How clean and fresh and laundered she always looked, thought Leo with mild boredom.

'What's happened?' she asked, eyes wide.

'Party broke up early,' replied Leo. He sighed and set his glass down on the table, then rose to kiss her absently. 'Our head clerk, William, had a heart attack. They took him off to Guy's. Everybody felt pretty awful about it, so they all went home.'

'Oh, God. How dreadful. Is he going to be all right?'

'I haven't a clue. He looked pretty rough when the ambulance came. I'll ring in an hour or so's time.' He paused. 'I feel rather bad at not having gone with him. I suppose one of us should have, but . . . '

'Oh. Oh, well . . . ' She laid a sympathetic hand on his shoulder.

Why is she here? wondered Leo. Why on earth did I ask her to come round? Then he remembered – giving her a high profile, keeping her in full view of the crowds. Now there were just the two of them in this silent room, and he wished he could simply send her home. But that was not possible.

'Let's go and have dinner somewhere,' he said and, with an

effort, gave her a smile.

He lay in bed with her later, his face against the pillow, wanting only to sleep. She was still talking. She could talk for hours, it seemed, about nothing. About him. About her. About them. About nothing. All he had to do was murmur 'Mmm' occasionally. He heard her voice stop, felt her hand sliding around his back, grazing his stomach, moving downwards. God, he'd made love to her once – wasn't that enough? He rolled over on to his back and found her smiling tenderly down at him as her fingers stroked, trying to arouse him.

'Rachel,' he said gently, lifting her hand away and kissing her fingers, 'I'm an old man – '

'No, you're not,' she said, still smiling.

'I'm a middle-aged man who feels quite old, and who has to clear up some papers and drive all the way to Wales tomorrow, and I really think I need some sleep. Besides . . . ' He put a hand over his eyes and yawned hugely.

'Besides?'

He stopped yawning, took his hand away and stared at the ceiling. 'I'm a bit worried about William.' He had rung Guy's earlier and had learned nothing, except that William was in Intensive Care. He glanced at her lovely face, which now wore an expression of compassion and concern. Like those elegant suits she has, thought Leo, she always has the correct expression for every occasion. What a sod I am, he thought a moment later. Literally and figuratively. He took her suddenly in his arms and kissed her. 'Now go to sleep,' he said firmly, and rolled over.

'Think I broke his nose,' said Vince into Felicity's bare shoulder, grinning in the darkness.

Felicity gasped and then giggled. 'That's terrible! He looked dreadful when they carted him off. A right mess. Vince, you shouldn't have, you know.'

'Why not?' Vince's voice was muffled. 'Bastard deserved it. He won't go groping you again in a hurry.' There was silence for a moment. 'You should have seen Benjy. He played a stormer. Half those blokes were so shit-scared of him they couldn't move.'

'I've really had it at work now,' sighed Felicity.

'Doesn't matter,' said Vince. 'You said you were fed up there, anyway. Besides, I didn't mention any names. No one's to know it had anything to do with you.'

'That's a point,' murmured Felicity.

'Except him,' added Vince.

Chapter twenty-three

Leo's mother, Maeve, lived in Llanryn, a small, sad town near Bangor, in North Wales. Like a fly caught in amber, thought Leo, as he arrived there on Christmas Eve. The place was still redolent of the fifties – the smoky chimneys, the rows of unpretentious grey houses, the light, high calls of children playing in the empty winter streets, the corner shops. In some ways he liked to go back, liked to visit all that he had escaped, playing that childish game of haunting himself with what might have been. In other ways he hated it, depressed by the grey hopelessness of his beginnings, the drab streets and the small minds.

On Boxing Day he left his mother's house and walked down to the canal, taking the back route to his old school. He passed a dog, an old man, and two teenage girls who went past him in a giggling stumble on the towpath. The light in the sky was violet at the edges, as though threatening snow, and the ground was like iron. His breath billowing out in the air, Leo turned off the towpath and up across wasteground, picking his way through the gravel and weeds past dirty puddles, until he came to the street. On the other side stood his old school. He crossed over and stood at the railings for a while, remembering himself, remembering a classroom behind those tall windows, the boys, the teachers, the dense, clouded minds. Or so they had always seemed. He had known then – was it possible that he had been as young as nine when the knowledge had come to him? – that he must get away. That there was a bigger, brighter world somewhere, and that it was not Wales.

He moved away from the railing and walked in the direction of the Llanryn Arms. Was his world now so very different from the world of his childhood? The world of the City, the world of the law and the Temple. It was still a small, grey world, hemmed in, claustrophobic – and threatening, now. Yes, that was the true nature of the feeling which had been haunting him for the past months. He felt threatened by the very society in which he lived, by its tight rules and strict values, and he did not like it. It was an uncomfortable sensation, that of one's own charmed world turning upon one. He tried to shrug off the feeling, telling himself that a few stiff drinks would help, as he pushed open the shabby little door of the pub and let its smoky, small-town warmth envelop him.

'I met Brendan Lewis in the pub,' he said later to his mother. She was sitting in a chair next to the fire, going through notes for the WI, of which she was the local chairwoman, while Leo made tea.

'Brendan Lewis? I don't remember that name . . . ' She looked up, a small, square-set woman with Leo's prematurely white hair and a still pretty face.

'Yes, you do,' said Leo, cutting pieces of Christmas cake and setting them tidily on a plate. 'He was at primary school with me. Big lad. We always used to call him Dan.'

'Oh, God, Dan Lewis! *Diawl bach* . . . ' Maeve Davies laughed and went back to sorting out her papers. She ruminated for a moment, then grimaced. 'His brother was a bad lot. He was in prison a while back for robbery, or some such thing.'

'Well, Dan used to make me laugh,' said Leo, bringing the tray over and setting it on the low table in front of the fire. 'He wasn't afraid of any teacher. He was a funny kid.'

Leo thought of Dan supping reflectively at the drink Leo had bought him in the pub, eyeing the butter-soft leather of Leo's expensive Italian overcoat. Leo had wished, at that moment, that he had not been wearing it. Dan, out of a job for two years now, did not seem to have much to laugh about nowadays. Leo had not stayed long in the pub.

Leo and his mother sat over their tea, chatting. At length Maeve got up, taking off her spectacles.

'Right. I'm going down the road to Pat's, give her these patterns. She's got her fifth grandchild on the way now, you know.' She could not help saying such things, despite her good intentions not to get at her son. But she longed for him to marry, so that she could have grandchildren of her own to boast about. It seemed a pointless kind of thing to her, life, if your only son was just going to let the line die out like that.

But Leo just smiled up at her, not rising to the bait. There were so many of these sighing, sweet, half-chiding remarks. They had been going on for years.

'I think I'll clear some of the stuff out of my old room,' he said.

'I wish you would. I don't think it's been touched since you went to university,' replied Maeve. 'You'd be doing me a good turn if you'd get rid of some of it, give me some more cupboard space.' She shrugged her shoulders into her coat. 'Mind and show me what you're throwing out, though,' she added.

Leo took the tea tray through to the kitchen and stood looking out over the little net curtain strung across the window above the sink. It was a new piece of net, he realised, not the pattern of lacy swans through which he had seen so many dawns and dusks as a child. Of course it was new. She must have changed it countless times over the years. Still, he had expected to see the swans.

He thought suddenly of the other members of chambers, and of the different ways in which they would all be passing the day. Roderick on his Boxing Day shoot at his splendid place in the country, Sir Basil with his sister and her family, the famously dimwitted Edward included, the rest in middle-class affluence. None of them washing up the teacups in the tiny scullery of a terraced house, looking out on to a grimy back yard and rows of other houses. Except Anthony, perhaps. Only he and Anthony came from the same sorts of beginnings.

From Anthony, his thoughts moved inevitably and unwillingly to Rachel. Upstairs in his suitcase was the present she had given him before he left London. It was a book about Fauve paintings, published by the Yale University Press. She must have gone to some trouble to find it. It must have been that conversation they had had about André Derain, about whether his work was political or merely cultural. That she should remember that fleeting conversation, that she should

294

find him such an apparently impersonal gift, yet one implying such intimacy of ideas and understanding, both touched and troubled him. He had opened the gift at a service station on his way to Wales, and had sat with it in his hands, feeling its slender weight as another small burden in their relationship.

Leo was not accustomed to giving and receiving presents. He would have to buy her something when he got back to London. Or would he? A book was a small enough thing, but he knew how much love and thought lay behind it. These tokens, these slender threads that pulled people closer and closer . . .

And there was no doubt, too, that the tone of their relationship had altered since the night of Sir Basil's party. For Rachel, the enchantment and frivolity had been replaced by something deeper and more serious. Leo could feel this. It was as though she felt charged with some mission, as though Leo's sexuality were within her keeping, her responsibility. Each act of love between them seemed like a commitment to some unspoken future. Yet Rachel did not realise, did not know, that there was to be no future.

I do not want to think about any of this, Leo told himself. He rinsed the cups and plates and put them on the draining board, then went upstairs to the little back room which had been his as a child. He no longer slept there when he came to visit his mother. Now he slept in the guest room, the larger, airy room on the other side of the landing.

The room was much as it had been when he first left home, apart from a few extra boxes and bags of remnants which his mother had stacked by the bed. The bed itself looked slight and forlorn, denuded of its covers, the red striped mattress thin and shabby. There were still some RAF squadron stickers from a comic pasted to the cheap wooden headboard. A narrow wardrobe stood in one corner, next to it a chest of drawers, and by the bed a little cabinet, its varnish chipped.

Leo began to fish through drawers and boxes, trawling through the debris of his childhood and adolescence. Some of it amused him, some of it saddened him. At length, from beneath the bed he pulled out three cardboard boxes containing lecture notes and essays from university and Bar School.

He could not remember having brought these back to Wales, and wondered why he had. He thumbed through a thick slab of revenue law notes, noting how rapid and compressed his writing had been then, the blue of the fountain-pen ink faded upon the yellowing paper. It was more haphazard and arrogant these days. Then, he had been too consumed by ambition to be arrogant. Revenue law, thought Leo, marvelling at all the forgotten industry – he didn't know the first thing about it any more. So much for learning. Well, these notes could go, for a start. To think he had once imagined that they might one day come in useful.

He stacked them behind the door and pulled a fourth box from beneath the bed. He recognised the spines of some of the books protruding from it, and for a moment his hand hesitated, about to push the box back. But instead he pulled the books out and glanced at their titles. They were playscripts, thin little volumes with shiny, frayed covers. Rattigan, Shakespeare, Shaw . . . I could have been an actor, and not a barrister, mused Leo. And what would life have been like, then? He remembered playing Viola in *Twelfth Night*, remembered the peculiar pleasure with which he had dressed as a girl, then as a girl disguised as a boy.

He blushed now at the recollection of his conceit. He picked up the script and glanced through it, the annotations, the underlinings, the little directions to himself. Then he put it back in the box and picked up a copy of *The Rivals*. He knew what he would find within its pages. He slid it out between his fingers and stared at it, feeling something rise and catch in his throat, some emotion long suppressed. The pose in the head-and-shoulders photograph struck him as quaintly dated now – the slightly tumbled lock of blond hair falling over the brow, the open shirt neck, the full mouth and the Dirk Bogarde stare. But it was still Christopher, and he was still beautiful.

What a transition that had been, from the school drama group to the sophistication of the Cambridge Dramatic Society. He had first seen Christopher in their production of *The Rivals*, and then in *A Man for All Seasons* – which part had he played? The King? Not a big part, but he had been, for Leo, quite marvellous. Leo smiled to himself and turned the pages of the text. He had been the prompt; all the cues were marked in ink. He remembered sitting there in the wings, the musty wooden smell rising from the floorboards, sounds and light turned away from him in sideways projection, so that one felt adrift, cut off, not part of the cast, nor of the audience . . .

He had only seen him once after that, some years after their brief affair had ended, when he was playing Tommy in *Entertaining Mr Sloane* in an out-of-town rep, strutting his way through the part, blond, beautiful and androgynous. But seeing him had only opened up the deep wound again, and Leo had been glad, thereafter, that Christopher did not become famous – not even remotely well-known. He was spared that much. The memory of that first love made his heart ache, literally, with its pathos, its quality of irreclaimability. Where was Christopher now? And where would I be, wondered Leo, if Christopher had not taken me and changed me for ever? Who would I be?

He was about to slip the photograph into his pocket, then changed his mind and put it back into the pages of the book, which he returned to the box. That was all past. He had borne the little pain of looking on Christopher's face once again, and he did not wish to keep it with him.

In the bottom of the wardrobe he found old Kodak wallets stuffed with photographs, some from his teenage years, some from university. More of Christopher – but these, taken with groups of friends, far-off images in fields or on picnics, in pub gardens or by the river, had none of the tender intentness of that other picture. Smiling, Leo pulled out a few which included himself to show to Rachel. She was always asking him what he had been like when he was younger. These might amuse her. He quite liked the idea of her pleasure, her laughter. He stared at his own youthful image for a moment. He could scarcely remember what it had been like to look in the mirror and see a dark-haired reflection.

Sighing, he put the handful of photographs on the worn carpet next to him. He was about to stuff the others back into the wardrobe when, from the back of one of the packets, there fell out a larger photograph, black and white, a head-and-shoulders portrait of a man in uniform. He recognised it as his father – not from recollection, for he had no memory of what his father had looked like – but from the fact that he was very like Leo. A younger, softer Leo, the face slightly longer – Leo had his mother's square jaw – but the same eyes, the same brow and mouth. He must have found the picture as a boy and decided to keep it for himself with his other possessions. He could not recollect doing so, nor the impulse that had led him to it. It struck him as odd to think how many pieces of one's past – gestures, impulses, words, emotions – lay buried and obliterated. How many people one could be in a lifetime. He looked back at the photo. And where was his father now? Dead, perhaps. No, Maeve would have said. Perhaps she knew where he was. But Leo had no desire to see his father now. In Leo's mind he was merely a ghost, and Leo did not wish to conjure him up. He, too, could stay in the past.

He put the rest of the photographs back and closed the wardrobe door. Straightening up, rubbing the cramp from his thighs, Leo glanced up and saw, on top of the wardrobe, his old record player. God, what a priceless possession that had been. He remembered the Christmas when his mother had given it to him. He had been sixteen. She must have saved up religiously in the Co-op Christmas Club. He stretched up and pulled it down by its plastic handle. It was one of those record players that folded up like a boxy little suitcase. He flipped up the rusty snap fasteners, his thumbs stroking the grainy beige plastic of the lid, and opened it. How flimsy and pathetic the plastic stylus looked – even its very shape was a breath of the sixties. The sight of it brought back days of his adolescence with a rush of familiarity that was almost heady in its potency. Where were his records?

He got up again and stepped back, craning his neck to peer at the top of the wardrobe, where he could see the edge of another cardboard box. He fetched a chair and brought the box down. For another half-hour he sat on the bed, going through his records, reading sleeve notes, rediscovering his forgotten self. The Everly Brothers, Elvis, Lesley Gore . . . Then, when he had left university, the Stones, Cream, Hendrix, the Beatles, Papa John Creach . . . There were tapes, too, compilation tapes he must have made at some time in his twenties, though he could now no longer remember doing so. But there was his handwriting, bold and young and obsessed with the music of his times, listing the contents of each tape carefully on its back and front. That had been before he discovered that tastes for opera and classical music were more positive social assets. How much he had discarded of his old self, and how ruthlessly. And for what? He went through the tapes slowly, marvelling, and put one aside with his photographs.

He had heard the front door slam a while ago when his mother came in, but it was nearly eight by the time he had put everything away, snapped off the light and closed the door on his past. He went down to the little sitting room, where his mother was knitting and watching a repeat of *Fawlty Towers*.

'Oh, good,' said Leo, and settled down in an armchair in the darkened room. His mother always watched television with the lights off; she said it helped you to see better, and she could knit without even glancing at the needles.

'It's nearly finished,' remarked his mother. 'I would have called you when it came on, but I thought you must be enjoying yourself up there.'

Leo watched the closing exchanges between John Cleese and Prunella Scales with regret. He rarely watched television in London. Either he was busy, or working – anyway, it seemed rather a lonely thing to do, and not part of the self which he had constructed in London.

'Switch it off,' added his mother. 'There's only the news on, and I don't want that.' She knitted, then said, 'I haven't made you any supper because I didn't think you'd fancy much after a big lunch.'

'I'll make some cheese on toast later,' said Leo, turning off the television and switching on a lamp in the corner of the room. He sat back down and there was companionable silence for a moment or two, broken only by the tapping of his mother's needles as she worked.

'So,' she said, coming to the end of a row and turning her knitting, 'how much did you find to throw away?'

'Not a lot,' replied Leo. 'Well, that is, all my stuff from university can go – notes and things. I've put those boxes on the bed. And I can't think why you've kept half of those

299

clothes. I don't think even the jumble sales would want them now.'

'Oh, well . . . you know . . . ' murmured his mother. The firelight danced and glinted against the spectacles.

'I found some interesting bits and pieces, though. And some photos.' Leo got up and fetched them from the sideboard, where he had put them earlier. He brought them over to his mother's chair. She took them from him, laying down her knitting and preparing herself with pleasure. She loved old photographs. Leo crouched beside her and they went through them together with little absorbed murmurs.

'Oh, weren't we all thin, then? . . . That's that Llewellyn girl – been married three times, would you believe it?'

A pause.

'There you are at my graduation. I remember thinking how young and pretty you looked. I was very proud of you.'

'*Cer i chwarae*! Mind, that was a nice hat . . . Yes.'

'Oh God, look at the length of my trousers. You made me buy that suit. I hated it.'

'A very nice suit. You look very nice . . . Now, what became of that boy? I remember his mother, lived over at the Rhydoul . . . '

They came at last to the picture of Leo's father, which Leo had left in deliberately. Maeve stared at it impassively, critically. 'I remember this picture,' she said at last, in a matter-of-fact voice. 'He had it taken before we were married. Where did you find it?'

'With my things. I must have pinched it from a drawer when I was little, and kept it. I don't remember.'

Maeve nodded her head as she looked at the photograph. 'You were always asking after your dad. Always wanting to know things about him.'

'And what did you tell me?'

'Don't you remember?' Maeve glanced at him in surprise. Leo straightened up and went to sit down in the armchair. He shook his head. 'Well, you were very young, I suppose. You never asked much when you got older. It wasn't much that I used to tell you. Same as what I would tell you now, I suppose. He was a decent man, in his way. Always meant well. Just

couldn't fix on one thing for long. Not a job, not his family.'
She stared at the fire, her mind in the past. 'Mind, he was
clever. Oh, a great turn of speech, a great talker.' She glanced
at Leo. 'So you come by that honestly.' She looked back at the
picture. 'But a born philanderer. It was a temptation, I
suppose, with those looks. He was so young when we
married. *Chwerea teg*.'

'You sound as though you don't blame him,' said Leo
quietly, his chin resting on one hand.

Maeve gave an uncertain little grimace. 'Can't say as I do.
Not now. I did at the time, though.' There was a silence. 'He
broke my heart for me.'

Leo had a sudden memory of sitting on the hearthrug in that
very room, when he was seven or so, his football cards spread
out in front of him, his mother standing in the bay of the
window, watching the street, waiting, waiting. Was that the
time when he had never come back? Or was it just a random
recollection?

Maeve glanced over at him and gave a wry smile. 'No doubt
you've broken a few in your time.'

Leo smiled back at her. 'I shouldn't like to think so,' he
replied. In the past, he had often thought of telling her – telling
her what? That he would not marry, that there were to be no
sweet little grandchildren for her, no fuss to be made, no
christenings, no photos, no birthdays. But where was the
point in telling her? Just let life roll on. Everyone had their own
disappointments. That was what came of too many expec-
tations. Maeve knew that.

'I have to be getting back tomorrow,' he said, gathering the
photos together.

Maeve nodded. 'Well, it was good to see you. I was
thinking, though, that next year I might get over to see Clare
and her family at Ruthin. I haven't seen your cousins for a
while now, and they've all got families. I should like to go.
And this is a long way for you to come. The roads are bad at
this time of year.'

He appreciated the little excuses she laid out for him. She
would rather be in Ruthin with family, he knew. These
Christmas visits were labours of love on both sides.

'That's true,' he replied. There was a pause. 'I could always pop up for a couple of days in summer, when work eases off. I'm hoping I won't be quite so busy next year.' He thought for a moment of telling her of his application to take silk, but his feelings about this were now so blackened with pessimism that he did not wish to tempt fate. 'Or you could come down to London for a week or two. You'd like it, you know. I've always told you.'

Maeve wished he would not make this offer; she found the business of declining gracefully rather difficult. She had no wish to visit her son in London. She had stayed once overnight on her way to Devon to visit her brother, and she had not been comfortable. In London her son became a creature she could not fathom. She was proud of him and his success, but she did not understand his world. She detected changes in his accent and manner which lent him a falseness she did not wish to witness. She remembered the first time she had been aware of the changes in him, when he had graduated from King's and she had met all his university friends. Just like his father, she had thought, longing to be after the finer, brighter air of other worlds, new faces, connections, opportunities. That he ever came back to North Wales at all she took as a token of love for herself, and nothing else.

'Well, we'll see,' she said easily, and rose from her chair. 'Let's do something about that cheese on toast.'

The next day Leo set off early, when the sky was raw and grey. He felt unaccountably depressed at the thought of the next few months. He thought of Rachel, and of the present he ought to take her, and on an inspiration he turned off at Llangollen and headed out through the grey-green countryside towards Llynmawr. When he stopped outside Nell's cottage it had an air of blankness, of dereliction, that made him think she might no longer be there. He hadn't been in touch for three years. Why should she still be there? But there was a fastness, a solidity about Nell that made him think she would not have moved.

No one answered his knock at the door, so eventually he turned the handle and went in. The door opened straight into

302

what was Nell's sitting room, a comfortable clutter of rugs and sofas and books. A large wooden table under the window was heaped with a tangle of fabrics, sketches, skeins of thread. Leo looked around uncertainly in the silence and then walked towards the door beneath the stair that led to the kitchen. As he went through, the door at the rear of the house opened and Nell came in from the back yard, wiping her plump hands on the edge of her caftan. She saw Leo framed in the doorway, and stopped in surprise.

'Good God!' She came forward, moving a chair aside and stepping closer to him. 'Well, you're a stranger.'

He leaned forward and kissed her cheek. Like a soft, withered peach, he thought. He remembered how tight and smooth her skin had been twenty-six years ago, how sunburnt. She had been slender then, but with that fullness around the breasts and hips which promised what he saw now. Gone to seed, he thought. All that lovely, warm ripeness had swollen to fullness, to soft folds of flesh hidden beneath her caftan. Still pretty, though, with that wispy blonde hair, only faintly touched with grey, escaping from the cotton headband wound round her head. She looked like some exotic, overblown relic of the sixties. Which, of course, was what she was.

And Nell thought, how expensive he always smells. How desirable. It ached her to see how handsome he had become, how assured and elegant. Maturity became him. He had got better-looking with age, while she, she knew, was beyond reclaim. But she did not betray any of her thoughts. It was not part of the image which Nell projected to the world. Nell did not care. Nell was strong, independent, her own person. It doesn't matter what you look like, she told people, it's what's inside that counts. And people would say, isn't Nell marvellous? She's really *comfortable* with herself, she doesn't care what people think. But what Nell thought, at moments like this, was, God, give me back my youth. Just an hour of being what I once was, so that this man might want me, might undress me and I could let him look at me and love me without shame.

'You look more like something from "Man in Vogue" every time I see you, Leo,' she said, eyeing him from top to toe. 'Cup of tea?' She edged away towards the sink, her loose silk moccasins shuffling on the stone floor. 'Or what about some whisky?'

'I'm driving,' replied Leo with a smile.

'Stay for lunch,' said Nell quickly.

'All right. Thanks. Whisky, then.' He glanced at his watch. 'Eleven thirty is just about civilised.'

Nell grunted and turned to the cupboard. 'You don't have to worry about that out here. You're not in London now. I drink what I like, when I like. Get out of it, cat!'

Leo watched as she fetched the half-full bottle and two glasses. He loved Nell for the fact that she behaved in such a matter-of-fact manner. No twittering greetings of welcome, no gushing surprise. Just two glasses of whisky and normal conversation.

They sat and talked, mulling over the doings of mutual friends from Cambridge, the whisky warming them gradually, their eyes growing less wary of one another. It must always be at the back of our minds, thought Leo. Even when we're eighty, if we meet, we'll look at one another and think, 'You were my first lover,' and recall how it happened and how it was. Timeless. And yet we shall never mention it to one another now. It's too precious to touch.

'I'll tell you why I came,' said Leo after a while. 'I mean, apart from wanting to see you,' he added, while she gave a grimace of disbelief. 'I wanted to buy one of your pieces. Something as a present for someone.' She looked at him in faint surprise. 'You do still make jewellery?' he asked.

'Oh, yes,' she replied, nodding. She drained the last of her whisky. 'I was in the workshop when you arrived. Come on out and have a look.' She rose and Leo followed her out through the chilly, weedy yard to a low stone shed. They stepped inside, into warm air perfumed with paraffin. Nell went over to the workbench beneath the window. 'Have a look,' she said, then turned and fetched some pieces from a small safe below the table. Leo noticed the fleshy spread of her hips against the cotton folds of her dress as she bent, and thought of Rachel's pale, slender body, its cool skin.

She spread the silver jewellery out on rolls of cotton wool

and he examined each in turn. 'You do beautiful work,' he murmured. 'It's very fine.'

She watched him, saw the way the white winter light glinted on his hair, and wondered, with fleeting pain, why things changed, why time was so cruel, so unfair. She wished Leo had not come. She knew how she would feel when he had gone.

Leo picked up a slender necklace of silver leaves, each different from the other, and held it up to the light. 'I like this,' he said.

Nell gave a lopsided smile. 'You always did like the most expensive things,' she said.

Leo unfastened the tiny catch, put the necklace around Nell's neck and held it there. It lay against the crepy swell of her bosom, the tiny furls of the leaves shining against her reddened skin. Nell felt suddenly horribly self-conscious. I am so big, she thought, I am so changed. And yet, I'm not. I'm still me inside. It was all she could do not to put her arms around him and hold him to her.

Leo eyed the necklace, imagining how it would look around Rachel's neck, lying against her soft, translucent skin.

'I want this,' he said, removing the necklace from around Nell's squat neck. 'And because I'm disgustingly rich, you can add a couple of hundred to the price. To show how much I love and admire you.'

'You're an arrogant bastard,' said Nell mildly, taking the necklace from him to polish it gently before wrapping it up for him.

'Do you sell much?' asked Leo, as they left the workshop and went back across the yard to the house.

'A fair amount,' said Nell. 'I make a good living, anyway. And the tapestries sell, too.'

Nell made them lunch of smoked mackerel and salad, and they talked more generally, argued even. The afternoon crept on.

'I'll have to go,' said Leo at last, 'if I'm to get back to London by this evening.'

Nell picked up their plates and took them to the sink. When she turned round, Leo was writing out a cheque. He tore it

305

from his chequebook and handed it to her.

'That's twice what I would sell it for,' said Nell, looking at the cheque.

'That's what I think it's worth,' replied Leo, smiling and tucking his pen into his pocket.

'What you think *she*'s worth, you mean,' said Nell wryly.

Leo said nothing for a moment, then, his face expressionless, replied, 'No – what *it*'s worth, I'm afraid.'

'At any rate,' she said, following him to the door, 'you're back to girls now, are you? You want to make your mind up, Leo.' She tried to keep her voice mild and chiding, but there was a note of sourness in it.

With a small sigh Leo turned and said, 'Thank you for lunch, my love. And thank you for the pretty necklace.'

She pursed her lips, folded her arms, preparing to watch him leave, and for the afternoon to envelop her in melancholy.

'Come by more often,' she said. She wanted to know about the woman for whom Leo had bought the necklace, just as she wanted to know about all the people, the great chain of them down the years, starting with Christopher, who had taken her first love further and further away from her. But she could not. She watched as his car disappeared over the brow of the hill, thinking, wrongly, that Leo, and that day under the trees near the river, was the reason why she was where she was now, and why things had turned out the way they had.

Chapter twenty-four

Not surprisingly, Mr Lamb did not appear in the office on the day after the Nichols & Co Christmas party. And during the first week of the New Year he was still absent. Word began to get round that he had three broken ribs as well as a broken nose, and wouldn't be back for another week. Good, thought Felicity; he was a pig and he deserved it. But she felt twinges of apprehension. What would happen when he came back? No one had said anything to her about her transfer to the computer department, so she thought it best to sit tight and draw her wages until something happened.

'I thought you was going to another department after Christmas?' Louise remarked one afternoon, as she and Felicity stood by the coffee machine.

'So did I,' replied Felicity vaguely. 'But no one's said anything.'

Rachel, too, was perplexed. She had hoped to have a new and rather more competent secretary in the New Year, but still Felicity sat there opposite her VDU, committing cardinal errors of spelling and grammar, tottering here and there on her spike-heeled shoes, misfiling, mislaying and chattering cheerfully.

'Felicity,' said Rachel at the end of the first week of January, 'what arrangements did Mr Lamb make, exactly, for transferring you?'

Felicity, who was wrestling with a stapler and two thick bundles of documents, glanced up.

'Dunno,' she said. 'He's still off, and no one's said anything, so I'm just carrying on here till he gets back. There. One for you, one for the file,' she added, stacking the bundles together.

'Oh, I see.' Rachel didn't want to approach the other

partners about it, since she had the feeling that this was being done without their knowledge. She could do nothing but put up with Felicity's atrocious typing.

But Rachel had more on her mind than work and the office. That night she was seeing Leo for the first time since he had come back from Wales. After the flat days of the holiday spent with her mother in Bath, life suddenly seemed full of rich and beautiful purpose once more. The thought of him, the fact of him, blotted out everything else. No one, no one, had ever been so much and so gloriously in love as she was. And she could see him that evening, if the slow hours ever passed.

Leo, however, was not in the same mood of happy anticipation. The early part of the year always tended to depress him slightly, and the feeling was exacerbated by the absence of William from chambers. Everyone was affected. Henry, competent and brisk though he was, was struggling beneath the doubled workload of trying to organise the working lives of all the members of chambers, and although they were patient and understanding with him, tempers had begun to fray and there was discord in the normally harmonious atmosphere. Even the typists, without Mr Slee's firm shepherding, were argumentative and bitchy.

Sir Basil, in particular, was morose and gloomy without his head clerk; he had not realised how much he valued the fact of William's contemporaneity, the sense that, throughout the years, he and William were the stout senior bulwarks of chambers. Now the balance had shifted. William's heart attack had been an intimation of mortality. William was growing old. So was Sir Basil. His practice, too, was not what it had been. He was conscious that he lacked the energy, and often the enthusiasm, which some of his weightier cases demanded. Roderick Hayter and Cameron now seemed busier than ever, taking much of the prestigious work which would once have gone to Sir Basil. Financially, Sir Basil knew that it was no longer necessary for him to maintain the high level of his practice. He could retire – but to what? What was there for him besides the law? He had no wife or children, no outside interests. He was the head of chambers, and 5 Caper Court, he told himself, needed him. It would totter without him. Just look at how things fell into disarray without William.

Leo, too, was surprised at how much he missed William and the daily reassurance of his familiar, avuncular presence in the clerks' room. Unlike Sir Basil, however, Leo knew that things would gradually right themselves, that chambers would adjust to the loss of William, temporary or permanent. That was the way things went. Nonetheless, he felt dispirited by the change. It seemed to him further evidence that his world was betraying him. His life seemed to have altered radically, so that he scarcely recognised it. Before last autumn, before he had applied to take silk, he had had no misgivings about his career, had been plagued by no self-doubts. He had performed his work with the utmost energy, aware of his talents, confident of success, and had lived his own private life exactly as he pleased, away from the eyes of others. Now each day brought a new uneasiness; his self-perception was altered. Everything, it seemed to him – his ego, his reputation, his prospects for the next twenty-five years – now depended upon whether or not he took silk. If he failed this year, there would be no point in trying again. There could be only one reason for failure, and that reason would damn his chances for ever. He could no longer view with equanimity the disparate strands of his life, private and personal. All that was gone.

And what private life did he now possess? he asked himself, as he made his way downstairs at the end of the day. Rachel. Nothing but Rachel. Pure charade staged for public benefit, designed to convince the world at large of his orthodoxy, his safety, his harmlessness.

He reached his car and, as he unlocked it, caught sight of Anthony crossing from Inner Temple library to Bouverie Street. His figure seemed more manly, thought Leo, less boyish now. His step was assured, unhurried; he walked as one in complete possession of his world. When I am sixty, thought Leo, Anthony will be at his peak, successful, brilliant. All the things I am supposed to be now. For a moment he thought of locking the car again, catching up with Anthony . . . He suddenly recalled the intensity of feeling they had once shared, and was touched by a sense of loss. Their relationship now was one of only the vaguest politeness.

Leo watched Anthony disappear round the corner, and then got into the car and flung his briefcase on to the passenger seat. He switched on the engine and stared for a moment at the dashboard. I am on my way, he told himself, to spend the evening with someone for whom I feel nothing, when all I would like to do is to spend it with that young man, to sit and watch him, talk to him, enjoy him. No, that was not fair, he thought, as he backed the car out and drove through to Middle Temple Lane. He did feel something for Rachel. How could anyone spend so much time with someone and not feel affection? She was sweet, she was flawless, she was loving, but the habit of her company oppressed him.

In spite of his morose thoughts and misgivings, he was startled, when she opened the door of her flat, by how fresh and lovely she looked. He had quite forgotten. Some trick of his mind managed to make her image insipid when he was away from her, but the reality was quite different. She was wearing jeans, a white woollen sweater with a low neck, and her hair was pinned up loosely.

'You look like Audrey Hepburn,' he remarked, kissing her reflectively, then putting his arms around her.

She breathed a sigh of relief, snuggled against him, and murmured, 'Hello. Oh, hello, hello, hello . . .'

The last two weeks seemed to her the longest she had ever known, but now he was here, and she was safe and happy. So happy that she wanted to tell him how much she loved him. She looked up into his face, marvelling, as she always did, at the perfection of it, its angles, the blueness of his eyes, the distant, musing warmth of his smile. But one did not say those things to someone like Leo. Instead, she simply kissed him again.

Leo allowed himself to be kissed, then disengaged himself from her embrace and took his coat off. She followed him into the sitting room, and he was suddenly conscious of a faint sense of claustrophobia. Such a female domain, he thought. He needed a drink.

'Have you any whisky?' he asked. 'I could do with one. Long January days.'

He sat down on the sofa and watched as she poured him a

careful Scotch from one of the neat array of bottles which stood on the little rosewood cabinet. Her fingers looked thin and white against the glass. So fastidious, he thought. He wished she would just splash it carelessly into the glass instead, wished the room were more disordered and relaxed. Both Rachel and the room gave one the feeling that they had been poised, waiting, beautiful and breathless, for his arrival. He thought of Nell, and smiled suddenly.

She turned with his drink and caught the smile. 'What?' she asked.

He looked up at her. 'Nothing,' he said. 'Just pleased to be here.' He watched as she crossed the room and set his drink down beside him, then said, honestly, 'I had forgotten how beautiful you were.' She smiled her slow, grave smile. 'Are,' he added. She went back to pour herself a drink and he pulled the packet containing Nell's necklace from his pocket and set it down on the table.

'For you,' he said, pointing to it as she sat down. 'A belated Merry Christmas.'

She glanced at him, then picked the packet up tentatively and unwrapped the layers of tissue paper, unrolling the cotton wool. She held the necklace up to the light and gazed at it, entranced.

'Leo, it's beautiful,' she said. 'You shouldn't have,' she added, as she fastened it around her neck, then drew her hand across the tiny leaves glinting at her throat. No, thought Leo, perhaps I shouldn't. Another one of the indissoluble little ties, an added weight in the chain. But in spite of his thoughts he suddenly fished in his jacket pocket for the photographs he had brought from his mother's house.

'I thought these might amuse you,' he said, and tossed the envelope into her lap.

She drew the pictures out and studied them one by one, laughing occasionally.

'Oh, I wish I had known you then,' she murmured, gazing at a young, dark-haired Leo smiling crookedly into the sun. He watched the childlike pleasure on her face, and wondered for the hundredth time how he was to bring this to an end in a few months' time. 'Just think,' she said, looking up at him, 'when

311

you were seventeen, I'd only just been born.'

It would be an utter relief, he told himself. He had never lived so constantly in the company of any woman before, and it astonished him that anyone managed to endure marriage. She is like a long, cool glass of some health-giving drink, he thought. And oh, how he longed for a draught of some swift, brutal and intoxicating passion. The way it had been before. When this was over, it could all go back to the way it had been before. But as she looked up, laughing, holding up a picture of Leo in baggy bermudas and a straw hat, standing next to a punt with Christopher, he realised that the prospect of destroying her trust and affection was appalling. He had not bargained for so much love. Just an affair, an easy affair, something which could be lightly discarded in due course. That was all he had intended. And now he had this.

'Can I keep one?' she asked, pulling out one of the photographs.

'Of course,' he replied. I must do it gradually, he thought. I must devise ways of slipping out of her life, letting the thing go. Perhaps that way she wouldn't be so badly hurt. But it must start soon. Perhaps the affair had already served its purpose, anyway.

Rachel examined the photo she had chosen. 'Who's that next to you?' she asked. 'The blond boy? He's very good-looking.'

'Just a friend from university,' said Leo.

Her eyes met his, and he knew what she was wondering. That must always be at the back of her mind, he thought. Did you sleep with him? Why did you do it? How could you want any man the way you want me? 'He was my lover,' he added suddenly, and plucked the photograph gently from her fingers. 'Choose another one.'

But Rachel merely set the photographs down on the table and slipped her arms around his neck. She didn't care about any of them. That was his past, and it didn't matter to her. What mattered was now, and tomorrow. 'I missed you,' she said, and drew her mouth towards his.

'Aren't you hungry?' he asked between kisses. 'I was going to take you to dinner.' He did not feel like making love. He felt like sex, or food. No emotion, just appetite.

'Later,' she said. 'Come to bed.'

He pulled back gently and studied her face. If he was going to have to go on fucking her for the next few weeks, he might as well make it interesting. 'All right,' he said. 'And this time,' he added thoughtfully, clasping her neck and pressing his thumbs gently against the base of her throat, 'I'll teach you something new.'

'You see, Lord Chancellor, the matter is one of some delicacy – not something which anyone in the Judicial Appointments Group would wish to air openly – but it is clearly one which requires – well, your consideration.'

Colin Crane, a man naturally tentative in manner, spoke with greater emphasis than was customary with him. He had not been looking forward to this confidential interview with the new Lord Chancellor; the subject was a difficult one, and it irked him that he, of all the civil servants within the group, had been elected to broach it with Lord Steele.

'But surely we have seen Mr Davies' personal file?' replied the Lord Chancellor. 'I saw no mention of this there. And his name is already on the final list of suitable appointees.' Lord Steele moved some papers around on his desk in a vexed and aimless manner. He disliked this business of prying into a man's personal life, passing judgments upon his fitness for professional appointments. It was an aspect of his job which he did not relish.

Colin Crane sighed. 'No – well, you see, Lord Chancellor, we have different channels of information. We cannot discount rumours which come to our ears, and I fear that this has a basis in fact. Mr Davies consorted with the young man for several months, apparently. They had, in short, a homosexual relationship. Of course, there is nothing to suggest that the boy's subsequent death and the scandal surrounding it had anything to do with Davies. One can accept that. But the fact does remain that the boy was a male prostitute with dubious, not to say criminal, connections. And there are unsubstantiated rumours that Davies has had other similarly unsuitable . . . liaisons.' Colin Crane paused, folding his long fingers together and gracefully crossing his legs, and waited for Lord Steele's response.

Lord Steele frowned and sat back in his chair. 'I find this hard to believe, you know,' he murmured. 'Very hard. I have met the man. I've met his – well, what would you say? His girlfriend, I suppose. He seemed in every respect a very decent man. I understand his record at the Bar is excellent?' Lord Steele looked up enquiringly at Crane, who frowned and nodded briskly, indicating that this much, at least, was beyond question. 'And, as I say, these rumours do not appear to have merited any mention in his file in the past?' At this Colin Crane could only look grave and doubting, but said nothing. 'Besides which, I have a special detestation of malicious gossip, you know.'

'Oh, Lord Chancellor!' replied Crane swiftly, startled by the evident anger in the other man's tone. 'This information hardly ranks as that. The Judicial Appointments Group thought long and hard, I can assure you, before determining to raise the matter with you. It is supported by evidence. The issue goes well beyond idle speculation. We are all – as I am sure you are – mindful of the importance of ensuring that judicial appointments are conferred upon those whose conduct is beyond reproach – and beyond compromise. I need hardly remind you, Lord Chancellor, of your own recent experiences in Scotland – blackmail, and so forth –'

'Yes, yes, Crane, I do not need reminding of that. The point is taken. I am anxious, however, not to allow any sort of prejudice to enter into the matter of these appointments . . . If Davies is homosexual – and I have to say that I have seen nothing in his conduct or his company to indicate such a thing, I might add – then, what of it?'

'If that were all, Lord Chancellor – if the matter of rent boys did not enter into it, then . . . ' Colin Crane raised his hands slowly and let them drop on to his lap. He did not see the need to elaborate. The information had been imparted, and he had no wish to discuss Leo Davies further. He had been given this unpleasant task, and he had discharged it.

Once again, the Lord Chancellor sighed, raised his bushy eyebrows and nodded at Crane. 'Yes. Very well. You may tell the Judicial Appointments Group that the matter has been brought to my attention and is under consideration.' He paused, drumming his large fingers on the surface of his desk. 'I have yet to have consultations with the judges of the Commercial Court, and, of course, I shall be inviting comment from the Lords of Appeal upon all the applications for silk, including that of Mr Davies. No doubt this matter can be considered further at that stage.' There was a moment's silence. 'Thank you, Mr Crane.'

Colin Crane gave a slight nod in acknowledgment of his dismissal, rose and left.

Leo and his application for silk were slight enough things in the vast empire of the Lord Chancellor's Office, with its many mighty functions, but this little tale of scandal found its whispering way back to the Temple, and to the ears of Sir Frank Chamberlin. What distressed Frank most about this new rumour was its well-roundedness, its factuality. If it were true that Leo had been known to consort with male prostitutes, then his prospects must be seriously compromised. But where had this tale arisen? Who had disseminated this information? No one seemed to know, yet all seemed to share the view that this must damn Leo's chances.

'Not just this year, mind you, but for all time,' pointed out Sir Mungo Stephenson, as he sat with Frank and Sir Mostyn Smith over their whisky in Brooks's. 'I mean,' he added, taking a little puff of his cigar, 'such a thing does not go away. It never leaves a man.'

'I do not like this kind of scandal,' said Sir Mostyn firmly. He had a warm and vivid recollection of Leo's young lady friend, and found it impossible to believe that Leo could ever have been involved with young men, especially prostitutes. It was not within his sphere of moral comprehension. 'And I find it particularly odd that the rumour – for that is all it is, as I see it – should surface now, just when Davies is applying to take silk. There are malicious spirits at the Bar, one must remember that.'

'You are surely not suggesting,' said Sir Mungo, who rather relished all this intrigue, 'that someone would deliberately spread lies about the man? I rather doubt that. Besides, if the Lord Chancellor has been officially informed, then there must be some substance to it.'

'I don't care how much substance there may be to it,' snapped Frank. 'The man's conduct is presently irreproachable, he certainly seems to be a very long way from consorting with rent boys, and he is one of the most able men at the Bar. I don't see why an incident from the past should jeopardise his future. No one is suggesting that he had anything to do with the death of this young man, whoever he might have been, are they?'

'No,' said Sir Mungo, crushing the stub of his cigar into the brass ashtray and picking up his glass, 'but I should have thought that the mere association was taint enough. Still, I concede that it is unfortunate. Very bright man, Davies. Rather lovely girlfriend, too.'

'Mmm. That I *do* find curious. One would certainly never get the impression he was queer,' murmured Sir Mostyn. 'Still,' he added, 'our views will be canvassed in due course. Each of us can take his own line on the matter.'

'I wonder,' mused Sir Mungo, 'whether Redvers will be asked to have his say. Given that he is retiring from the bench this summer, I mean.'

'I imagine he will be,' replied Frank gloomily. 'I don't see why not. One can imagine what his view is likely to be. If Sir Redvers Carlisle had his way, he'd hang every bugger in England.' He sighed and reached for his pen, shaking out his newspaper.

'It will be interesting to see who is appointed in his place. Although I suppose there are a handful of obvious choices,' observed Sir Mostyn, gazing idly at his glass and wondering whether to have another. His doctor had told him to cut down.

'Difficulty Siegfried initially encountered with a horse. Four,' said Sir Frank.

'Snag,' replied Sir Mungo after a moment. 'Well, there's Alexander Porritt. Possibly Carstone.'

'God, I hope not,' murmured Sir Mostyn. 'He has such an ingratiating manner. I always cringe when he is before me.'

'Well, if he's on the bench, you won't *have* him appearing

before you any more. There is that compensation.'

'No, but he'll be around more.' Sir Mostyn made up his mind and rang for the steward. 'Give us another clue, Frank.'

'Retirement from the bank, question mark. Ten. Third letter "T".'

'Withdrawal,' replied Sir Mostyn and Sir Mungo together, then smiled. 'Feeble,' added Sir Mostyn. 'There was a time when that crossword was fairly taxing. Seems to be designed for cretins now.'

'Sir Basil Bunting,' remarked Sir Mungo, lighting another cigar. 'Now, he's a very likely choice.'

'He's head of this man Davies' chambers, isn't he?' said Sir Mostyn. 'Maybe that will help Davies, if Sir Basil is put on the bench. Caper Court may need more silks.'

Frank thought of Stephen Bishop and said nothing. There was no point in mentioning any of this to Leo – why cause the poor fellow more distress? Things looked bad enough for him. He had done all he could to help matters. Now it was in the lap of the gods. He sighed and gazed at his paper. 'Beginners gouge round the shellfish,' he announced. 'Seven.'

Chapter twenty-five

Leo began to take tentative steps towards limiting the amount of time he spent with Rachel. It was not difficult. He could easily plead pressure of work during the weekdays, and February would provide two weekends when he could be away, one watching the Rugby International between Wales and England in Cardiff, and the other at Murrayfield, watching Wales play Scotland. But on the occasions when he did see her, he could not bring himself to change the tenor of their relationship. He was fond of her. He enjoyed looking at her, found her conversation more amusing than that of most women. It was not in him to manufacture arguments, or to behave badly towards her. And, of course, the main impediment to any cooling in their affair was Rachel's great and unshakeable love. Leo had never been the object of such sincere, kind feeling before.

They were lying in bed together one evening when Rachel said it. She had been lying on her stomach while he stroked her back, and simply rolled over, looked up at him and said, 'I love you.'

Leo did not know what to say for a moment. He leaned on one elbow, looking at her, his eyes scanning her face, with its radiantly trustful expression.

'Don't say that,' he said, tracing round her lips with his finger.

'Why not? Don't you want to be loved? Does it worry you?' She was smiling as she spoke.

What was he to say in reply? That he loved her? There was no difficulty in lying, but telling her what she wanted to hear was not the answer. It would only make it more difficult for him to extricate himself.

'I don't think you should love someone like me. I'm too old

for you – '

'Rubbish,' she murmured, and stretched up to kiss him.

' – and, anyway, I'm not worth loving. I don't go the distance. I'm an emotional coward.'

'It seems to me we've come quite a long way already.'

Oh God, this was going to be one of *those* conversations.

'Rachel,' he said, his voice uneasy, 'don't invest too much in me. I'm not worth it. It's not a good idea.'

'Why not?' Her voice seemed to have lessened, shrunk with fear. She had caught the bleak sincerity in his voice. He looked away, but could feel her eyes still fastened on his face.

'You know why.' He paused. 'You know the kind of things I've done, the way I am.'

'But you said all that was over.' She tried to keep her voice easy and cool, but felt the rise of a faint panic.

He said nothing, merely gazed at the ceiling. Then he turned to look at her. 'Just don't expect too much of me.'

'I don't expect anything,' she replied. 'I just want to love you.'

He smiled, deciding that the atmosphere needed lightening. 'You are sweet and adorable and far too good for me,' he replied, and ran one finger down her cheek, then took her in his arms again, which always made everything all right with her.

'Will I see you tonight?' asked Rachel the next morning, as he drove them both into the City.

'I can't, I'm afraid,' said Leo, swinging the car off the Embankment and into Temple Place. 'I have to go and visit our clerk in hospital. I feel rather bad that I haven't been before.' He hesitated as he pulled up opposite Temple tube station, then added with a smile, 'I'll call you.' She returned the smile, nodded, kissed him and got out.

As he went into chambers, Leo met Sir Basil coming out of the clerks' room, pulling on his overcoat with a preoccupied expression. Leo murmured 'Good morning', but Sir Basil appeared not to hear.

'Where's he off to?' Leo asked Henry.

'Lord Chancellor's Office. They called a couple of days ago,' replied Henry, and handed Leo some papers. 'Those instructions from Crump's have come in.'

'Thanks,' said Leo. 'The Lord Chancellor, eh? Well, I think we can guess what all that is about, don't you?'

'Too right,' replied Henry with a grin.

Sir Basil was not accustomed to feeling nervous, but as his taxi made its way to the House of Lords, he was conscious of a distinctly schoolboyish sense of excitement. This summons meant only one thing, and he was still uncertain as to how he intended to respond.

A flinty secretary ushered him into the Lord Chancellor's large, dark-panelled room, where Lord Steele sat behind his desk, flanked by Colin Crane and another distinguished personage from the Judicial Appointments Group, a Grade One civil servant, no less.

Lord Steele rose and shook Sir Basil's hand cordially, and after brief enquiries into mutual health and well-being, invited Sir Basil to take a seat. Then he introduced the two attendant civil servants.

'I imagine, Sir Basil,' said Lord Steele in his light brogue, one blue eye fixed on Sir Basil's serene countenance, the other somewhere to the left of his right ear, 'that you have some inkling of the purpose of the invitation here today?'

Sir Basil coughed, smiled and tried to look deferential and knowing all at once. 'I confess I was not without my suspicions,' replied Sir Basil, at which he and Lord Steele both laughed lightly and the sidesmen smiled and recrossed their legs.

'We wish to know whether, in view of the retirement of Sir Redvers Carlisle from the bench this summer, you would be prepared to consider an appointment by Her Majesty to the position of a judge of the Commercial Court,' continued the Lord Chancellor, his tone slightly more businesslike. 'You are aware, no doubt, that it is my view that we have too few judges on the Commercial bench at present, and that this accounts for our sadly overcrowded lists. I shall be proposing to Her Majesty that two appointments be made at the commencement of the Michaelmas term' – he smiled at Sir Basil, who wondered which eye he should be looking at – 'and we are anxious to know whether you would be prepared to take up one of them.'

Beneath his carefully buttoned waistcoat Sir Basil's heart swelled. Conflicting feelings struggled within him. He had previously determined to reach no decision on the question until receiving this invitation from the lips of the Lord Chancellor himself. Now he paused for a long moment before replying. He thought of 5 Caper Court, of his pre-eminence there, the familiarity of his daily life in chambers. A position on the bench was not financially rewarding, compared with his earnings as a top silk. Then he thought of the prestige of the bench, of the charm of sitting in judgment instead of pleading causes. He was weary of the burdens of commercial litigation, he realised. The offer that the Lord Chancellor held out to him was infinitely tempting.

'I should,' replied Sir Basil at last, 'be honoured to receive such an appointment, Lord Chancellor.' He spoke with decision. Lord Steele beamed with gratification and sat back in his chair, the sidesmen smiled approvingly, and as they fell to the discussion of practicalities, Sir Basil wondered when would be the right moment to bring up the matter of his pension.

He came out into the grey streets of Westminster with elation in his heart. He felt younger than he had done for years. This was a new challenge, and a position that was not without significant honours and advantages. As he hailed a taxi, Sir Basil thought with brief regret that someone else must now become the head of chambers at 5 Caper Court. But he consoled himself with the thought that, in the seven or eight months which must elapse between now and the Michaelmas term, he could indulge in a little political intriguing to ensure that the mantle of authority passed to the successor of his choosing.

'So,' said Colin Crane to his fellow civil servant as they left the Lord Chancellor's room, 'that leaves room for two silks at Bunting's chambers now. And from all I have heard, this chap Bishop is bound to be appointed.'

'I'm afraid,' replied his colleague, 'that that isn't likely to be of much help to Leo Davies, is it? Not as things stand.'

It took Leo the better part of an hour to reach the hospital at High Wycombe to which William had been transferred, and the official visiting hour was drawing to a close.

'I'm afraid you'll only have five minutes,' warned a plump nurse with freckled arms. But after he had exercised a modicum of his charm, she agreed to allow him fifteen extra minutes.

When he went into the private side room, Leo was startled by the change in William's appearance. As he approached the bed, William was lying back on his pillows with his eyes closed; Leo sat down and touched him lightly on the arm.

'Hello, Bill,' he said quietly, as William opened his eyes. William smiled and tried to sit up. Leo helped him, pulling up the pillows. God, the poor fellow looked awful, thought Leo. In just a few short weeks his stout frame seemed to have shrunk. His cheeks had lost their ruddiness and were grey and slack. 'How's it going?' he asked. 'I'm sorry I couldn't come before.'

'That's all right,' said William. 'It's not bad. Better than it was at first. You know. Tell me how things are going in chambers. Sir Basil's been in, but you know how he is. Not always up on the latest news.'

Leo told him all the news he could think of, making it as amusing as possible.

'How's Henry coping?' asked William.

Henry had begun to cope fairly well of late, in fact, although he was clearly in need of an assistant, but Leo merely replied, 'Well, you know Henry. Muddling along. But we're coping. It won't be the same until you're back in chambers.'

'I don't know that I will be back,' replied William, his face despondent, his voice tired. 'They think they can give me some sort of bypass operation, but I don't see me coming back to work. Not any more. Not at my age. I told Sir Basil when he came last week. I'm surprised he hasn't mentioned it to you.'

Leo smiled. 'I haven't seen him for a few days. And at the moment he's probably very preoccupied. I think he's going to be made a High Court judge.'

'Really?' William looked a little more animated at this news. 'Well, well.'

'Nothing official, of course. But I don't think he'll turn it down. His practice isn't what it was. And I think he'd be good.' Leo gazed around at the drips, the jug of water, the flowers, the get-well cards, and felt depressed. 'At least someone seems to be having more luck at moving onwards and upwards than I am,' he added.

'Oh?' said William, his heart sinking as he gazed at Leo.

'I get the feeling that I may not get silk this time around,' went on Leo. 'Possibly never. I've heard from Frank Chamberlin that certain rumours are going around . . . ' Leo paused and rubbed his hands over his face before continuing. He was glad to be able to talk about this to William. There was no one else he could tell. Apart from Anthony and Sir Basil, William was the only person in chambers who knew of his application, and since he was already aware of Leo's hopes, he might as well be told his fears. 'I'm afraid I haven't always led the most blameless of lives, Bill. Committed a few indiscretions here and there, made some unfortunate acquaintances. And somehow word of it has got around.' He sighed. 'I suppose I was a fool to imagine that I could do as I pleased and no one would get to hear of it. But they have. Don't ask me how or why. I've done what I can in the way of damage limitation, but I don't know that it will help. You know what the judiciary are like, and the boys in the Lord Chancellor's Office. Still,' he added, suddenly thinking that he shouldn't be burdening William with his worries at a time like this, 'we shall just have to wait and see which way the wind blows. Nothing I can do now.'

William nodded and looked away from Leo. He felt wretched in his soul. There had been no point in any of this. He had imagined that if both Leo and Stephen took silk, then Sir Basil would be squeezed out, and that people would think he, William Slee, was past it, too, and pension him off. As it was, here he was in a hospital bed, unlikely ever to work at 5 Caper Court again, while Sir Basil was headed for the glories of the High Court. Leo had never been a threat. He would have made no difference to anything. All those rumours, those little asides to fellow clerks . . . Why had he done it? Fear and selfishness. And now Leo was confiding in him, telling him things about himself that William had known for years, unaware that William had already used those things against him. He leaned his head back on his pillow and closed his eyes, weary with self-disgust. It could not be undone now.

'God, I'm sorry, Bill, going on like that,' said Leo, glancing up. 'No doubt the nurse thinks I've overstayed my welcome, anyhow. I'd best be going.' He rose.

William opened his eyes and looked at Leo sadly. 'I'm sorry,' he said.

'What about?'

'Your application. If it doesn't succeed, I mean . . . '

'Good Lord, nothing for you to be sorry about. I'm sure you've given me all the support you could.' He smiled at William. 'You always did.' He patted him on the arm and left.

The time of reckoning had come at Nichols & Co. After taking two weeks' extra leave to repair his injured nose and pride, Mr Lamb was back in the office. Felicity saw him striding down the street towards the office on Thursday morning as she approached from the other direction. She scuttled into a doorway and peeped out at him. His face was grim and his nose, though unbandaged, looked lumpy and odd. She watched until he had gone through the revolving doors and then scurried out, trotting in behind him.

"'E's back!' mouthed Nora to her as she passed the reception desk. The lift doors were just closing on Mr Lamb's stocky figure.

'Yeah, and I've had it,' replied Felicity, gazing after him.

'Why? What's up?' asked Nora, avid for gossip.

Felicity looked at her ruefully and moved her chewing gum from one side of her mouth to the other. She was trying to give up smoking. 'Well,' she said in a low voice, folding her arms on the counter top, 'you remember that bloke who decked Lamb at the Christmas party?'

'Yeah, don't I just. Felt like getting in there and giving him a helping hand.'

'Well, that was my boyfriend.'

'No!' Nora's eyes were wide, her crimson mouth round with astonishment.

Felicity nodded. Apprehensive though she was of the wrath to come, she was quite enjoying this. Nora was always a good audience. 'Yeah, Lamb had been groping me a bit, making remarks and that. So I told Vince. He got really mad, but I never thought he'd do anything like that.' She giggled. 'I wish I'd seen it.'

'Oh, Fliss, it was marvellous!' Nora's eyes rolled heavenwards at the recollection. 'Hold on a tick.' She flipped a switch. 'Hello, Nichols and Co. How can I help? No, he's not in this morning. Yes, I will. Right. Goodbye.' She flipped the switch back and gazed expectantly at Felicity. 'Anyway, what do you think Mr Lamb's going to do? Does he know who it was that thumped him?'

'Well, he should do,' replied Felicity. 'Unless he's had his hand up everyone else's skirt as well, that is.' They both giggled, and the switchboard flashed again. Felicity headed for the lift, fluttering her fingers at Nora, each mouthing 'See you!' conspiratorially to the other.

Nothing happened until after lunch. By that time, Felicity had grown quite used to the idea of being sacked, and when John Parr called her to his office she felt only slight trepidation. She hoped he wouldn't make heavy weather of it. He could be a right pompous arse at times.

John Parr was pacing round his room when Felicity came in, mustering all his authority as second-in-command. He had been highly disturbed by what Mr Lamb had told him, but not entirely surprised. He had never had a high opinion of Felicity. She might be a bright enough girl, but her secretarial skills left much to be desired and he wasn't sure that he found her manner sufficiently deferential to himself and the other partners.

'Please take a seat, Felicity,' he said. Felicity sat down, tugging the hem of her red skirt down on her thighs, taking a deep breath of anticipation and trying not to stick out her chest. She looked up at Mr Parr from beneath her curly fringe, watching him pace around the room.

'Felicity,' John Parr began, 'I had Mr Lamb in my room this morning. It is his first day back in the office since he was attacked before Christmas. You remember that, I suppose?'

Felicity nodded.

'I understand from Mr Lamb that you know something about that attack, and the person who carried it out.' Felicity dropped her eyes and said nothing. John Parr sat down. 'Mr Lamb tells us that you've had some kind of grudge against him since he had occasion to warn you over the standard of your work. Isn't that right?'

'I never had any grudge against him, Mr Parr –'

'But he did warn you that you might have to leave if your work didn't improve, didn't he?'

'Yes, but –'

'And he even went to some lengths to have you transferred, without informing the partnership, so that you would still be able to carry on working here, didn't he?'

'Yes.'

'And yet you still, according to Mr Lamb, held such a grievance against him that you actually got a friend to come to these offices and assault him. Isn't that so?' Mr Parr was, by now, in an exalted state of sorrowful indignation.

'I didn't tell him to do it, Mr Parr! I simply told him about what Mr Lamb had been doing –'

'So you *were* nursing a grudge against him?'

Felicity was close to tears. She might not mind being sacked, but she objected to having the truth distorted in this way. Mr Parr's censorious attitude made her feel bullied. 'I didn't know he would do anything like that! Honestly!'

'Felicity, the facts speak for themselves. Mr Lamb, as office manager, warned you about your lack of efficiency, and that was something which you held against him. So much so that you went to this friend of yours with stories of how unfairly you had been treated by Mr Lamb – who, I might add, was actually prepared to transfer you to another department and give you another chance – with the result that Mr Lamb was seriously assaulted at a party on these very premises. By your friend.'

'But Mr Lamb had been harassing me!' exclaimed Felicity, unable to hold back the tears now.

326

Mr Parr sat back in his chair with a look of cynical disappointment. 'Felicity, I think you have been reading too many tabloid newspapers. I imagine every secretary in Britain who feels victimised through complaints regarding her own inefficiency complains of "harassment". But I'm afraid I, for one, will not wear that kind of nonsense.'

Felicity stared at him helplessly, her eyes blurred with tears. Her nose had begun to run and she didn't have a tissue. She sniffed and wiped at her eyes with the back of her hand. What was the point? How could she possibly begin to catalogue the list of humiliations to which Mr Lamb had subjected her? And what difference would it make, anyway? The blokes in this office would always stick up for each other. The business with Vince was what this was all about. Parr was glad of an excuse as juicy as this to get rid of her.

'No, I'm sorry, Felicity,' went on Mr Parr, clasping his hands before him on the desk, 'this incident is something which I view most seriously. You do realise,' he added, 'that this could result in a police prosecution for your friend?'

Felicity looked at him in horror. 'Oh, no!' she pleaded. 'You don't need to do that, do you?'

Mr Parr relished the pleading tone of her voice as much as he relished the sight of her, her pretty face streaked with mascara, reduced by his authority to a state of wretchedness.

'I can make no promises, Felicity. That is something which we shall leave to Mr Lamb. But you must understand that we cannot allow you to continue working for Nichols and Co after an incident such as this. It is not the kind of behaviour which we expect from our secretaries. The terms of your employment permit you four weeks' notice. I hope you will be able to find employment elsewhere in that time. But I'm afraid I cannot give you any kind of suitable reference. Now, that is all.'

Felicity sniffed back the last of her tears and left Mr Parr's office without another word. There was no point in saying anything else. She'd had enough of them all. She didn't even think she could bear another four weeks in the place, though she'd have to stick it out. She needed the money, and she needed to be able to look for another job.

Felicity made her way to the Ladies and gazed at her

reflection. What a mess. She couldn't go and get her handbag and her make-up without attracting the attention of the Menopausals, and she didn't want to give them the satisfaction of seeing her tear-stained face. She cleaned away the mascara streaks with soap and lavatory paper, then splashed her face with water. Leaning back against the washbasin, she wished she had a fag.

So, what was she to do now? How was she going to get a job without a reference? Oh, well, that would take care of itself. She might as well go and tell Rachel that she *was* being transferred – right out of the building.

When Felicity went into Rachel's room, Rachel was staring at her desk calendar and going over the dates in her head. She was sure she had counted properly. She looked up distractedly at Felicity.

'Can I have a word, Rachel?'

'Of course. What's up?' Either it had been the twelfth or the fourteenth. She was sure it had been an even number. In which case, it might have been the sixteenth. Why hadn't she written it down?

'Well, actually, I've been given the boot. By Mr Parr. This morning. I thought I'd tell you. I'm off in four weeks.'

Rachel sat back, forgetting her own problems for the moment. 'But why? I thought Mr Lamb was arranging for you to go to another department?'

'It's because of Mr Lamb I'm leaving,' replied Felicity, not without bitterness. 'You remember someone had a go at him at the Christmas party?'

'I heard about it. I'd left before it happened.'

'Well, it was Vince. I'd told him that Mr Lamb had been – well, touching me up, making suggestions, and that. And he decided he was going to – sort him out. I didn't have any idea. Anyway, Mr Lamb came back to the office today and he told Mr Parr it was my boyfriend, said I'd had some sort of grudge against him. And that was that. Out on my ear.'

'But you say Mr Lamb had been molesting you?' asked Rachel.

'Yeah. You know the sort of thing. Feeling me up, saying he'd have me sacked if I wasn't – nice to him.'

'But didn't you tell Mr Parr that?'

'I tried, but he wasn't having any of it. Said I'd been reading too many newspapers, that I had a cheek to accuse Mr Lamb of harassing me.'

Rachel was outraged. 'They can't sack you like that, when you've been sexually harassed by a senior member of staff!' she exclaimed, reaching for her phone. 'I'm going to have a word with John Parr.'

Felicity stretched out a hand to stop her. 'No, don't. There's no point. I should have made a fuss a long time ago. It just seemed so stupid. And I really didn't want to lose my job. My getting sacked has nothing to do with that. It's all about this thing between Vince and Mr Lamb. It doesn't matter what you say to Mr Parr, I'll still be given the push. They don't want me here. They've been looking for an excuse for a while. I'm not the world's most brilliant secretary, after all.'

'Look, Felicity, whether you lose your job or not, I can still make things very unpleasant for Mr Lamb. He deserves it!'

'Rachel,' said Felicity wearily, 'I couldn't care bleeding less about him. I'll be glad to get out of here. All I care about is getting another job. Not that I want to go on doing secretarial work. I'm so rotten at it, and I hate big offices. But it's the only thing I've been trained to do. And we need the money.'

Rachel sighed. 'It's your decision, of course. I still think you're wrong not to make an issue out of it. There are too many men getting away with that kind of thing.'

'The way things are in this place, who's going to believe me? They'll think I'm just getting back at Lamb. I know them. MCPs, the lot of them. And that's being kind.'

'Well . . . ' Rachel paused. 'I'll give you a reference, if you need one.'

'Thanks. No one else will. You'll have to bend the truth a bit, mind. I tell you,' she added, tossing back her curly head and grinning, 'I'm going to have a bloody good piss-up when I leave!'

Rachel smiled. 'Why don't you let me buy you a drink after work, and we'll talk about it? I've got a client in ten minutes.'

'Yeah, okay,' said Felicity.

'But don't go slipping me anything this evening, please,' added Rachel.

Rachel was still pondering Felicity's problems when she got back to her flat later that evening, but when she reached the front door they fled in an instant. The door was slightly ajar, its lock smashed, the wood frayed and cracked. Gingerly, Rachel pushed it wide open. The hall was in half-darkness, but the living-room light was on. Why hadn't she noticed that from the street? She hesitated, then stepped into the hallway, feeling for the light switch. The hall sprang into brightness, and she gasped.

A trail of hideous destruction spread throughout the flat. She walked from room to room, numb. Drawers had been thrown around, their contents strewn everywhere. Pictures were smashed, sofas slashed, spilling their stuffing, and the curtains had been wrenched down and ripped, the wooden curtain poles hanging pathetically askew where they had been torn from the plaster. The energy of the violence stunned her. In the kitchen every drawer and cupboard had been flung open and the contents hurled around. Sugar crunched under her feet, mingling with broken glass and the contents of jars and packets. The glass fronts of the cupboards had been systematically smashed. Even the kitchen table had been gouged and smeared with – what? She stepped forward and then drew back in revulsion. The stench of excrement hit her. In the bedroom, the same thing had happened. She could not bring herself to touch the soaking and stinking duvet. All her ornaments and pictures had been broken, the canvases of the watercolours crumpled and slashed. Her computer, television, video, radio – everything was gone. Everything else wrecked. She went back slowly into the miserable carnage of the living room, looking around for the telephone, and realised she was trembling from head to foot.

She began the painful exploration for the phone, lifting up tattered cushions and ripped books, trying to shut out from her sight the deep, disfiguring scratches on the drinks cabinet, on which nothing now stood, pulling back the ruined fabric of her curtains. With each step she could feel the snapping of shards of glass from her precious pictures. When at last she found the phone beneath an overturned chair, its flex had been wrenched from the wall. Rachel straightened up, breathing deeply, and wondered if she was going to faint.

She stood very still for a moment, feeling the horrible thudding of her heart and the uncontrollable shivering of her icy limbs. Then she walked back through the flat and across the landing to the neighbouring flat. There was no answer when she pressed the bell. They were out, as they always seemed to be. Her chest heaved and sobs began to rise. She tried to quell her tears. She had to tell the police. But first she wanted Leo. She wanted someone to take away the horrible sense of violation that she felt. It was as though someone had raped her again, soiling and fouling her, dragging her through some dark swamp. Her private, pretty world, the one where she had sought to make herself secure, had been torn open and desecrated. She would never feel safe there again.

She retrieved her handbag from the hall where she had dropped it and searched with trembling fingers for her car keys, wiping away her tears, pushing her hair back from her face. As she left the flat, she automatically pulled the front door behind her, then stopped. There was no point in that. There was nothing left to steal or destroy.

Chapter twenty-six

It was not until she reached Leo's house that the shock properly hit her. The effort of concentrating on driving there cushioned her against it until then. She dissolved into hysteria as she told him. He soothed her, gave her brandy, rang the police, and then sat, holding her to him.

'Come on, come on,' he said at last, wondering why her tears did not subside. 'Everyone gets burgled once in a while, you know.' He stroked her hair. 'Look,' he said after a pause, 'I'd better go round while the police are still there. I'll ring a locksmith and we'll at least get the place secure for the night.'

'I don't care!' she wailed. 'I'm never going back there again. I couldn't! Not ever! Oh, Leo! When you see what they've done!' A fresh bout of sobbing racked her.

Leo sighed. This was all very tiresome. Wretched for her, of course, but she did seem to be reacting somewhat hysterically. 'All right. All right. Calm down,' he murmured. Then he stood up and fetched his coat. He stood looking down at her. 'Will you be all right here?'

She nodded, but did not look up, hugging herself, torn with misery. He sighed and left.

Two policemen were already at the flat when Leo arrived, one making an inspection of all the rooms, the other standing amid the debris of Rachel's living room, looking around. Leo winced as he surveyed the devastation. He had never seen any place quite so ruthlessly destroyed before.

'Evening, sir,' said the policeman. The radio at his shoulder crackled. 'You the gentleman who rang us earlier?'

'That's right. Mr Davies. This is my – my girlfriend's flat. She's back at my place.'

'I see. Pity she didn't come with you. We'll need details of everything that's been taken.'

'Well,' said Leo evenly, 'it was rather a shock for her, as you can imagine. I don't think she felt like returning straight away. I'm sure she can help you tomorrow.'

'Mmm.' The policeman surveyed the room impassively. 'Yes. It is a bit of a mess.'

Bit of a mess? thought Leo, astonished. Still, they must see this kind of thing every day of the week. The policeman took a few steps towards the door, glass snapping, and Leo followed him along the hallway to where his colleague was inspecting the bedroom. The stench was pungent and Leo grimaced as he looked around. He went through to the shambles of the kitchen and sighed. Oh God, he could not think of a worse thing that could happen to someone like Rachel. The atmosphere of hate and hostile violation was palpable. All Rachel's neat femininity had been despoiled, her sanctuary torn to pieces. No wonder she had reacted as she did. When she said she could not come back here, she probably meant it.

Leo wondered fleetingly whether there might not be something in Rachel which brought this kind of destructive catastrophe upon her. Then he told himself that was absurd. This was just another burglary, with a bit of wanton destruction thrown in.

'She had a television and a video,' he said to the policemen. 'Stereo, computer, all that kind of thing.'

'Yeah, well, it's a pretty thorough job, all right,' replied one of them. 'Doesn't look like kids to me. No sign of damage to the outside door downstairs. Perhaps they got in when someone was making a delivery.'

'Well,' said Leo, 'I wouldn't have thought there's much point in getting a locksmith. I'll get a cleaning firm in tomorrow.'

'Would you mind ringing us first before you do that, sir? Just to make sure our forensic boys have finished here.'

'Yes, of course.'

'Right. We'd better go and have a word with the people downstairs. I assume they must have been at work all day, or they'd have heard something. You ready, Ralph?'

Leo drove back to Mayfair. He found Rachel in the kitchen,

sipping a mug of coffee, her shoulders hunched over as she leaned against the cooker. He went up to her and put his arms around her; she felt tense and rigid. He took the mug from her hands, then pushed her dark hair back from her face, which was pale and drawn. Her body relaxed and she laid her head against his shoulder.

'Poor old you,' he murmured. 'They certainly made one hell of a mess.' She said nothing, merely leaned against him, breathing in the scent of him. 'The police want a list of everything that's been taken. I said you would do that tomorrow.'

She nodded and then drew away from him. 'Thank you for going round. I don't think I can ever bear to go back there again.'

'Of course you will,' said Leo robustly. 'Everything's insured, isn't it? They're only things. Possessions. They can be replaced. God, I need a drink.' He went over to the cupboard and poured himself a whisky.

'It's not that,' replied Rachel. 'It's that sense of intrusion. Like being raped all over again.' She shuddered.

'Come on,' he said, and led her through to the living room, sitting her down on a sofa. She glanced across at the table, where some papers lay, Leo's spectacles and pen on top of them.

'I'm sorry. You were working. I've messed up your evening.'

'Don't be absurd,' he said, and sat down next to her. 'I'm going to put you to bed in a moment with a Valium, and then I'll carry on. I have to finish this before my con tomorrow.'

She leaned back and closed her eyes. Leo sipped his whisky and looked at her meditatively.

'All this has been a bit of an ordeal for you,' he said after a moment's thought. 'I'm going to suggest that you tell your office what's happened, and say that you're taking a few days off. You can go to my place in the country. I'll come down at the weekend.' She opened her eyes and looked at him. 'It's a nice place,' he went on. 'You'll like it. Very peaceful. There's a woman who comes in once a week from the village, waters the plants, moves the rugs around. I'll give you the keys and you can drive down.' He finished his whisky.

She dwelt on this, her gaze tired and far away. Then she nodded. 'Yes. I'd like that. Thank you.' The thought of Leo's country home appealed to her, somewhere safe, away from London.

An hour later she was fast asleep in Leo's bed, while he sat at the table in the living room, Rachel and her burgled flat driven from his mind, his attention and energy entirely fastened on the work in front of him.

When Rachel woke the next morning, she still felt slightly weak from the shock of the previous evening, but in the light of a new day matters began to fall into perspective. She had been burgled, her flat ransacked, most of what she owned destroyed; that was bad luck, but it could be repaired. Even so, she was grateful for the prospect of some time away from the immediate reality of the thing. Thank God for Leo, wonderful, protective, dependable Leo. She felt herself unspeakably lucky to have such a man.

Leo had already left for chambers, but there was a note in the kitchen reminding her to ring the police and to call her office, and saying that he would be back at lunchtime.

When he returned, Leo was weighed down by an array of carrier bags from a variety of expensive shops. He set them down in the middle of the living-room floor.

'I thought you would need a new wardrobe,' he remarked, taking off his coat. He watched with a faint smile as she delved into the bags, pulling out sweaters, trousers, dresses, pairs of shoes, underwear, reams of tissue paper spilling on to the floor.

'Leo! All this must have cost a fortune!' she exclaimed, looking up at him from where she knelt. She drew four cashmere sweaters in muted pastel shades from a Scotch House carrier bag. 'I can't afford these!' She didn't even dare to investigate the contents of the enormous Harvey Nichols bag.

'You don't have to,' said Leo. 'They're a present – not very inspired, I'm afraid, but I did it in a rush. It's to make up for last night.'

'Oh, Leo, you've already made up for last night simply by looking after me. You didn't have to do this.' She couldn't help noticing, looking at the dresses and silk blouses, that he had got her size right. More observant than most men, she guessed.

'Well, what were you going to wear? Most of your things are in rather a mess, from what I could see last night.' Before she could dwell on this, he added, 'Anyway, I enjoyed it. I think my taste is rather good, don't you?'

'It's wonderful,' she replied, and rose to kiss him.

She set off for Leo's house in the early afternoon. The day was raw and blustery; hail spattered the windscreen occasionally from a leaden sky. But the car was warm, the drone of Radio 4 soothing, and with each mile Rachel felt safer, moving away from the horror and destruction she had witnessed the previous evening. She did not dwell on any of her losses, refused to let the image of her ransacked home into her mind. Leo was taking care of everything, and she could look forward to peace and seclusion for a few days in his home, and have him with her for the entire weekend.

In spite of her calm frame of mind, she was surprised by how spent and shaky she felt when she reached the village in which Leo's house stood. Eventually she found the narrow lane that led to the house, and drove up with a sense of excitement and curiosity. Every new revelation concerning Leo, every clue to her enigmatic lover, whom she felt she knew and yet did not know, was fascinating to her.

The house was old and pretty, of reddish brick, set in a large garden bordered by trees, fields on the other side. It was L-shaped, with sloping roofs and gabled upper windows. She parked the car and sat for a moment, fingering the keys which she had taken from her bag. She let herself into the low-beamed hallway and looked around. Then she went through to the large living room, lined with books, furnished in a comfortable, haphazard fashion. It was, she thought, quite unlike his house in London. That had an anonymous, stark quality, whereas this was a friendly room, filled with pieces of old furniture, high-backed sofas and armchairs heaped with cushions, faded rugs scattered about the dark, polished floor, lamps set on tables and bookshelves. She walked over to the windows which looked out across the garden, and sat for a few moments on the bumpy cushioning of the window seat, fingering the soft, rust-coloured plush of the curtains, which were thin and pleasantly old.

This was his. There were more of his secrets here. She looked around, trying to feel his presence in the room, imagining him sitting here alone – or perhaps not alone . . . That didn't matter. She was here now, and in two days' time he would be here with her. The prospect had a settled, domestic quality which their transitory stays at one another's London homes did not. She stood up and walked over to the large fireplace, with its oak mantel. A fire was neatly laid in the grate. Realising that the air in the house was chilly, despite her thick overcoat, she searched around for some matches, found them on the bookcase and knelt down. The scrape and sputter of the match sounded friendly, and there was something cosy and safe about the way the flames licked at the paper spills, then at the wood, which made crackling sounds as it took. She straightened up and put the matchbox on the mantelpiece, and realised she was smiling. Being in this room gave her the same sense of being tucked up and protected when ill as a child. I am being looked after, she thought.

But it was in the nature of an adventure, too. Still with her coat on, she went through to the kitchen. This, like the hallway, was low-ceilinged, but airy and light. She opened cupboards, looked in the near-empty fridge and fiddled with the central heating thermostat on the wall by the door. She would have to ask Leo about the boiler when he rang. Then she glanced at her watch. It was twenty past four. She'd have to unload her things from the car and go out to the shop in the village before it closed, if she was to have any supper. She was looking forward to that little expedition, too, anxious to explore more of Leo's private world.

She took the suitcase which Leo had lent her upstairs and set it down on the landing, then went on a tour of inspection. There were two small bedrooms with single beds on either side of the bathroom, and one larger bedroom with a vast bed. Adjoining this was a dressing-room-cum-study, and next to this a smaller bathroom with a shower. Rachel paced around the little dressing-room, which felt to her very much like a place belonging to Leo, then went back into the bedroom. She stared at the bed, then remembered the girl at Sir Basil's party. Sarah. Just last summer . . . She could not, would not comprehend any of it. She went back out, closed the door, refusing to think about it, and took her case into one of the smaller rooms.

It was a curious feeling, stowing away in drawers and wardrobes these new, unknown garments bought for her by Leo. It heightened her sense of detachment from London and the flat. She smiled at the thought of Leo dashing round Knightsbridge, buying all these things. He'd done very well, really.

At that moment the telephone rang. Slightly startled by the sound in the empty house, she hurried downstairs and located the phone beside one of the sofas.

'Hello?' Her voice was hesitant.

'Rachel?' It was Leo. She smiled, relieved to hear his voice. 'I thought you should have got there by now. Everything okay?'

'Yes. Yes, fine. I got a little lost in the village, but I found it at last. It's a beautiful house.'

'Good, glad you like it.' His voice sounded slightly absent, preoccupied.

'I'm just unpacking, and then I'm going into the village to get some food.'

'Right you are. I forgot to tell you that there's a freezer out in the garage. I don't know what's in it. You might like to have a look. Hold on.' He must have put his hand over the mouth-piece and she could hear a muffled exchange of voices in the background. 'Sorry. What was I saying?' he resumed.

'About the freezer. By the way, how do I do the central heating?'

'Oh, yes. Good point. There's a cupboard in the bathroom, where the hot water tank is, and there's a timer switch in there. It's fairly simple – just set it to whatever you want. You shouldn't have any problems.'

'All right.' She hesitated. 'This is very sweet of you, you know,' she added. 'I'm beginning to feel the therapeutic effects already.'

'Good.' He hesitated, too. He had been about to tell her that some people were cleaning up the flat, but decided against it. She probably wanted to put it right out of her mind at present.

'I wish you were here,' said Rachel, glancing at the fire, which was now burning brightly and steadily.

'Well, I'll be down on Saturday morning,' said Leo in a businesslike tone of voice, the voice of someone who wanted to hang up and get on with whatever he was doing. She felt a little sinking sense of disappointment.

'Yes. Well, I'll let you get on. Bye.'

'Okay. Bye.'

He hung up, then sat staring at the phone. This sudden domestic togetherness seemed to have taken their relationship on to a level even more intimate than before. He sighed. Quite how all this had happened, he didn't know. But he was going to have to be quite ruthless about it. At the end of a week or so, she was going to have to move back into her flat, even if he had to refurnish and decorate the damned place from top to bottom out of his own pocket. This incident had set back his plans to ease himself quietly out of her life. Now she was well and truly settled in his. For the time being. He pictured Rachel in his house, imagining the quiet pleasure she would take in simply being there. Then he wondered which bedroom she had chosen to sleep in. He gave a wry smile at this. He knew her, and her pure, rightminded attitudes. He knew he would find, when he went down at the weekend, that all her clothes and belongings were in one of the smaller bedrooms.

When she had spoken to Leo, Rachel put her coat back on and drove down to the village, slowly navigating the narrow lane bounded by high hedges. There was only one shop, serving as a general store and sub-post office. Inside, she selected a few of the more obvious groceries and wondered what she should make herself for supper. As her mind ranged through the possibilities of omelettes, pasta, chops, she realised that she didn't feel particularly hungry, even though she had only had an apple, with cheese and some of Leo's endless supply of oatcakes, for lunch. She was conscious, too, of the faintly queasy feeling which had persisted throughout the day, but told herself it was simply a reaction to the events of last night.

Suddenly weary, she left and drove back to the house.

The fire had burned down low by the time she returned and she hastily flung a couple of logs on to it from the basket in the fireplace. There were only four logs left after that. Would it be enough for the evening? She didn't know where there might be more, and she couldn't go rooting around in the freezing darkness at the back of the house. She glanced up at the windows as she thought of this, and realised how impenetrable the darkness outside had become. It seemed to stare at her through the cold panes of the window. She got up quickly and went to draw the curtains. Then she switched on two more lamps, so that the room was bathed in a brighter glow. She went from room to room, closing the curtains in each one, until she was reassured that the staring night no longer looked in on her. She switched on the radio in the kitchen for further reassurance as she made supper from the things she had bought, but switched it off after a few moments, aware that she kept hearing sounds in the empty house through the voices on the radio. This way, there was only silence.

She ate in the living room, curled up on the rug in front of the fire, leaning against one of the sofas and watching television, but her mind kept wandering to the night outside, and she began to be unpleasantly conscious of her isolation. She began to wish she was still safe in Leo's mews house in London. This thought brought, unbidden, a sudden memory of her own flat as it had been before the burglary, the destruction, and she found tears welling up.

This wouldn't do. I need a drink, she thought. She searched in the kitchen and at last located Leo's drinks cupboard, below the bookcases in the living room. She pulled out a half-full bottle of vodka and a bottle of tonic. In the other side of the cupboard were glasses. A drink would help her to sleep, she thought, and stiffen her against morbid fancies. But as she was about to unscrew the cap of the bottle, she caught sight of the oily transparency of the vodka and felt a sudden nausea. She put the bottle back, and the glass, and made herself a cup of tea instead.

She locked up carefully, back and front, and checked all the window fastenings before going to bed. She left one lamp burning in the living room; the embers of the fire, settling slightly, glowed cosily in the half-light. Upstairs she sang quite loudly to herself as she got ready for bed, and when she turned over to go to sleep she could not bring herself to turn off the bedside light. She lay for a long time, listening for sounds, before at last drifting off to sleep.

She woke in the early hours of the morning; the light from the bedside lamp was now irritating rather than comforting, and she switched it off. She lay listening to the silence, then gradually fell asleep again. This time her sleep was troubled, and she dreamt of being in her flat, with books, pictures, belongings suddenly flying from walls and shelves, crashing around her head. She woke, trembling, and glanced at her watch. It was six twenty. She lay back on the pillows, trying to calm her thoughts. Then suddenly a wave of nausea overwhelmed her; she sprang out of bed and into the bathroom, where she was sick.

She washed her mouth and stood for a moment on the cold tiles. Her skin felt icy. She went back to bed and pulled the covers close around her. Perhaps it was the cheese omelette she had had for supper. Or perhaps it was still the aftermath of the shock of the burglary. But as she lay, her hands folded across the soft flatness of her stomach, she knew that it was none of those things. Her period was now nearly three weeks late. And she had started being sick.

Oh God, how was she going to tell Leo? The idea, she realised, made her feel afraid, and it threw into clarity the knowledge, hidden even from herself, that she had no idea of the extent of his feelings for her. He had been wonderfully kind about the burglary, and about letting her stay here, but those were acts of friendship, of natural generosity. He made love to her, he spent time with her, but that did not mean he loved her. He had never said so. And some instinct told her that he would not welcome the fact of her pregnancy. There was much she did not know about him, but this much she knew. He would be here tomorrow. She would have to tell him. But first she would have to make absolutely certain. She would drive into Oxford, get a test from a chemist's. She might be wrong. She had missed periods before. But the slight, tender ache in her breasts told her she was not wrong.

That Friday, eighteen miles away in Oxford, Sarah was getting ready to go out when the doorbell rang. There, on the doorstep of the terraced house which she shared with two other girls, stood James. Sarah had last seen him at a club in London during the Christmas holidays, coked up to the eyes, and not pleasant company. She had decided then, in view of the events of last summer, that James was someone who was best avoided. Despite the working arrangement they had had with Leo, he was really no more than an acquaintance. And quite without class. He had shown that. Accordingly, she was not pleased to see him now.

'How did you know where I lived?' she asked coldly, folding her arms.

'I asked around,' replied James, with a nervous shrug. She eyed him; he'd been a careful dresser once, sporting designer labels, vain about his hair, but now he was scruffily dressed and his blond hair had grown long and unkempt. 'Anyway, aren't you going to ask me in, as an old friend?' He grinned, shifting from foot to foot.

'No, James, I'm not,' said Sarah, tossing back her blonde curtain of hair. 'I'm just on my way out, as a matter of fact. Just passing, were you?'

'The thing is,' said James quickly, 'I'm in a bit of a jam.' He seemed to be unable to stop moving, his arms twitching beneath his denim jacket. 'I need to talk to you.'

'You can talk to me out here,' said Sarah, leaning against the doorframe.

He glanced up and down the street. 'Thing is,' he said uncertainly, 'I was wondering if you could lend me a bit of money.'

'No,' said Sarah without hesitation. After a pause she said, 'I know the kind of jam you're in. I can tell just by looking at you. Drugs.'

'Yeah, well.' James grinned uncertainly again, glancing around. 'I've been messing about with smack – a bit too much, I suppose. You know how it is.' Beneath the carefully

342

cultivated, careless Sloane accent there lay a trace of East End. Sarah's ear caught it, and her innate snobbery rose in her. She really should never have had anything to do with this person.

'No, I don't,' she replied. 'Anyway, I can't say you're arousing much of my sympathy by telling me you're into heroin. Do you think I'm going to give you money for that?'

'Come on, Sarah, you used to do a bit of coke yourself,' said James, growing irritable but still smiling and wheedling.

'That was then, James,' she said with sweet politeness. 'This is now. I don't like smackheads.' She glanced at her watch. 'And I'm not giving you any money. Now, I really have to be going – ' She took a few steps backwards and was about to close the door when James thrust out an arm to hold it open.

'Listen, Sarah!' he pleaded. 'I'm really desperate. I wouldn't ask if I wasn't. What about old times? What about last summer?'

'I'd like to try and pretend last summer never happened.' She tried to close the door, but James shoved back, determined to speak to her.

'Yes, but it *did* happen, Sarah, didn't it? And I'll bet you wouldn't want too many people to know about it, would you? A nice girl like you?' He had his foot inside the door now, holding it back with his forearm, his face close to hers. She suddenly let it fall open, and he leaned back against the doorframe. Her face was a mask of cold, concentrated fury.

'Are you threatening me, James? Do you really think you can use last summer against me? Don't you realise that it doesn't matter to anyone? It doesn't matter to me, and it doesn't matter to Leo. Oh, yes, I saw him at Christmas. He couldn't care less about you. No one could! You're a mess, James, and you're pathetic. You don't frighten me. Now piss off!' She pushed at him with both hands, using all her strength. Taken unawares, he stumbled from the doorway and back on to the pavement. The door slammed shut.

James regained his footing. 'Bitch!' he muttered, then lifted his head and stared at the door. 'Bitch!' he yelled, and then shouted it again, louder. 'I hate you both! You and him! You selfish, smug bastards!' His voice cracked with pain and need. He was not feeling good now. His voice died away and he stood hopelessly in the silent street. Then he turned and walked away, wishing he had the courage to put a brick through her window.

In the house Sarah stood, listening to his shouts, and then to the miserable silence that followed. She realised she could not go out straight away. She would have to wait until Alicia came back. There was no way she was leaving the house empty, not with him around.

Chapter twenty-seven

L eo arrived at lunchtime the following day, by which time
Rachel, who had been sick again that morning and was
feeling generally vile, was in a state of nervous tension. The
pregnancy test had been positive. She had stared and stared at
the bright blue tip of the spatula, as if to will it away. She left it
on the ledge in the bathroom, and when she came in a second
time it was still staring at her, blue and accusing.

She had meant to go back into Oxford on Saturday morning
to buy food for the evening, but she could do no more than
wander aimlessly around the house, nursing her secret. She
veered between panicking uncertainty and contained happiness. If only Leo were to take it well, if only he were to smile
when she told him. She had no idea how she was to tell him.

She was standing at the kitchen sink, washing salad for
lunch, when she heard the crunch of car wheels on the gravel;
the bonnet of Leo's dark blue Porsche slid into view. Fear
tightened her stomach. She couldn't tell him straight away. It
would have to wait until the afternoon; but how was she to
find conversation, how was she to take her mind off it until
then?

She went into the living room as he came in through the
hallway. She was wearing one of the dresses he had bought
her, and a big, soft, cream-coloured cardigan which she had
found in the chest of drawers in her room. It smelt of Leo, and
she had had to wear it. It made her feel protected.

'Hello,' he said, kissing her, then chucking his car keys on to
the mantelpiece. 'How is it that you always look better in my
clothes than I do?'

She smiled, they chatted, he followed her into the kitchen
and planted a bottle of wine down on the table next to the half-
prepared salad. Still the knot of fear inside her would not

unravel.

Over lunch he told her that the flat had been cleaned up. 'I went round yesterday afternoon after work. Got a chap to put some new locks on. I think most of the damage can be repaired. There's a place in the Brompton Road that can probably match up the curtain fabric, and I'll get a glazier in to do the kitchen cupboards. The kitchen actually came out of it surprisingly well. You just need a few new cups and saucers. And the sofas can be reupholstered. I can see to all that. Just a matter of a few phone calls.'

'Leo, you can't do all that,' she murmured, watching his face as though she might be able to anticipate, from his expressions and gestures now, the manner in which he would receive her bombshell of news later.

'Yes I can,' he replied. 'Did you get this bread from the village shop? Don't. It's always a day old.'

The truth, as Leo acknowledged to himself, was that he wanted to get Rachel re-established in her flat as quickly as possible, so that they did not become too domestically enmeshed, so that the gentle severing of their relations could recommence. It was easy to be generous, it was easy to let her thank him, but there was more to it than simple altruism. This was for his own self-protection.

They went into Oxford that afternoon and bought more provisions. Driving back, Leo glanced at her face, which looked pale and pinched, and wondered why she was so quiet. Possibly the shock she had received was still having an effect. At last, out of curiosity rather than concern, he asked, 'What's up? You're terribly quiet.'

The car had drawn to a standstill outside the house. She glanced away from him and looked across at the tracery of bare branches against the gathering dusk; a bitter wind swept suddenly, stiffly across the fields and the garden. She turned to look back at him, remembering how, talking to Felicity, she had wondered what it would be like to lose all pride, to love someone so much that you would abase yourself in any way just to keep their affection. She knew now what it was like, she thought. She would do anything, give everything, for this to make no difference to them. But she knew, too, that everything was about to change for ever.

'I'm pregnant,' she said, and dropped her gaze from his face to the steering wheel. Her heart was thudding.

Leo felt as though he had been struck hard in the midriff. 'I see,' he said. There was a silence. 'I see.' He closed his eyes for a moment, aware of impotent anger rising up in him. Then he looked at her. 'Weren't you doing something, taking the Pill?'

She shook her head.

'Why not, for God's sake?' He leaned one elbow on the car windowsill, resting his forehead in his hand, staring at her in wonder. 'Why didn't you tell me?'

'I don't know,' she whispered, wondering if this was a lie. Leo just gazed at her, as if seeing her anew, critically, appraisingly.

'You wanted this, didn't you?' he said at last, unable to keep the edge from his voice.

At the sound of his anger she felt despair, and tears rose to her eyes as she looked helplessly at him. He watched, marvelling at the way the tears trembled, unspilled, above her eyelashes, blurring her blue eyes. 'Jesus Christ,' he muttered slowly, and stared out across the garden. It was as though something was closing in on him, like the night sky gathering across the fields of Oxfordshire. 'How pregnant are you?' he asked, his voice expressionless. She tilted her head back, willing the tears to slide away, determined to control herself, not to slip into pitifulness.

'Five weeks – six weeks. Something like that.'

The tension in his mind eased a little. Still early enough to do something about it. That was something, at least.

'We have to talk about this,' he said after a moment.

'Shall we go inside?' Rachel's voice was tentative, hopeful. Maybe something could be resolved. She was aware, too, of a new feeling which had crept over her since she had told him, since she had seen his face turn to stone and his glance stray away from her into contemplation of the future – guilt.

'No,' he said, with sudden determination in his voice, and turned the key in the ignition. 'I don't want to discuss this in the house.' He could not bear the claustrophobia, the clogging coupledness of himself and Rachel, within the four walls of his

347

own home. 'We're going to the pub. I need a drink.'

They sat opposite one another at a corner table far from the bar and listening ears. It was only six o'clock and the place was almost empty. Rachel sat, eyes fastened on the table, as Leo went to the bar and bought himself a pint and her a tomato juice, and came back with a drink in either hand and a packet of peanuts clenched between his teeth. She glanced up and smiled; the way he was carrying the peanuts cheered her up, for some reason. As though things were nearly normal. But as he put the nuts and the drinks down on the table, she could see that his face was still grim, intense. There was nothing light about the atmosphere. She sipped at her tomato juice, barely tasting it, and struggled to feel brave. She was accustomed to being strong and independent, and she detested the state of abject dependence to which she had been brought.

'So,' said Leo, taking a sip of his pint, then leaning back and looking at her thoughtfully, not unkindly. He had been choosing his words carefully as he ordered the drinks. 'If you want an abortion, we can arrange it. I will pay for it.' The words, which had sounded frank and forthright in his head a few moments ago, now sounded brutal. But they could not be altered or retracted.

Somehow the bluntness of his suggestion gave her strength. She felt instantly detached from him; she and the baby were on one side, he on the other. 'I don't want an abortion, Leo,' she said, her voice quite cool and considered.

Leo ran his tongue along his upper teeth and looked reflectively at the picture which hung on the wall above Rachel's head, a print of a hunting scene.

'Rachel,' he said, looking back at her, 'I don't want a child.'

'It doesn't have to affect you,' she said, thinking that if it had to be so, then – well, it would have to be. The idea of losing Leo tore at her. But at least she would still have something, someone.

He was stung to fury by her mild utterance. She had never seen him angry before, and the effect of it quite shook her.

'Doesn't affect me?' He kept his voice low, but its anger was potent. 'Don't be so bloody irresponsible! Or perhaps it's too

348

late for that. You already have been. You must have known there was a chance you would get pregnant! And yet you said nothing, just carried on as though there was nothing to worry about. Good God! And then you say it needn't affect me.'

She stared at him, stunned. There was a metallic taste in her mouth, one she had come to recognise in the past few days. She stumbled to her feet. 'I'm going to be sick,' she said. 'Excuse me.' And she disappeared into the Ladies.

Leo took several swallows of his drink, and then let out a groaning sigh of exasperation and anger. It occurred to him immediately that he could attempt to sway her, tell her that if she kept the baby she would lose him, but that if she had an abortion, then all could go on as before. But he could not bring himself to tell that last lie. The thing was not going to carry on. He knew how much she loved him, and he could not rob her of her child on the strength of such a falsehood, and then rob her of himself.

She came back, her face white, her expression cold. She did not sit down. 'I think I want to go back, Leo. I don't think there's any point in talking any more.'

He reached up and took her hand. 'Sit down,' he said. 'Come on. I'm sorry. This isn't getting us anywhere. I'm sorry for – for getting angry.' The warmth of his hand and the kinder note in his voice compelled her, and she sat down.

He stared at the table for a moment, collecting his thoughts before speaking.

'Listen,' he said, his tone placatory, 'we have to accept that something has happened to us which wasn't planned.' Not by me, at any rate, he thought. 'It's not in the scheme of things, Rachel. I have my life. I like it the way it is. You are a part of that life – but just you. On your own. No other ties or commitments. If you have this baby, all that alters. I think – I know, that everything would be destroyed. And I don't want that.' Another lie, added to the heap of others. He waited for her reaction, pulling open the packet of peanuts for something to do.

Rachel had been watching his face as he talked. She felt cold inside at the knowledge that he spoke with utter conviction. He was entirely self-centred. Well, he had never made any

349

secret of that. But it was one thing to hear it idly expressed, and another to see it so clearly demonstrated. He didn't want this child. Why should he? She had known all along that this could happen. She had simply willed the possibility away. Or had she? Was this pregnancy the result of some suppressed, subconscious desire? In that case, she was guilty of a double betrayal. Either way, what he had said before was true. She had been irresponsible. Why should she ask Leo to pay the price for that?

But even as she admitted all this to herself, she knew that she could not destroy their child. Amid the confusion of doubts and hopes and recriminations, that was the truth most clearly evident. She could not get rid of this baby. Not even to keep Leo. And here, as she acknowledged this unshakeable fact, crept in the beginnings of hope, little tentacles of illusion spreading out. Maybe when it was born he would change his mind. Maybe before then. He was reacting to news she had given him not twenty minutes ago. How could he have come to a proper decision about this? Surely, given his own feelings for her, their feelings for one another, the issue was more complex than he made it appear? The next words she spoke were prompted by these immediate thoughts.

'Would it be so dreadful, if I were to have our baby?' she asked, her voice filled with genuine, hesitant wonder.

For a second Leo said nothing. He suddenly thought of his mother. Deliberately, he picked up a handful of peanuts and sifted them in the palm of his hand. Then he looked up at her. 'I think,' he replied, 'that it's as much a matter of the timing as anything else.' Immediately he wondered why it was that everything he said sounded cold and calculating. But, of course, he knew why. 'I mean,' he went on, 'you've just joined a new partnership. You've only been there a few months. Another year or so and you'll be an equity partner. Isn't that what you want? Wasn't that the plan?' He felt he had touched a fine nerve here, for her gaze dropped abruptly and she picked up her drink. 'If you stop now,' he went on, pursuing the thread, 'you'll be out of the race. We know what it's like in our profession, Rachel. You can be away for just four months, and bang! Your clients have gone, your practice has shrunk to a fifth of its size . . . That's an awful lot of ground to recover. You should think about it. Think what a baby would do to your career. Not to mention other things.'

She watched him swallow the handful of peanuts. Everything he said was true, but none of it seemed particularly important any more. It was just a job. Didn't he realise that? And then it occurred to her that he had only said all of this as a means to dissuade her from having the baby. He didn't care about her career.

'None of that is important,' she replied. She said nothing more, merely gazing at him, her lovely face calm as the waters of a still pool.

If Leo could have ground his teeth, he would have. He felt like taking her by the shoulders and shaking her. But he merely ate a few more peanuts, one by one, as he considered his position.

'What about us?' he asked at last. 'Don't you care about us?' It was the card he had told himself he would not play, but he played it.

Instantly her expression changed to one of ineffable sadness; he was touched by the sight, and almost ashamed of himself.

'Of course I do,' she replied. 'You are the most important thing in my life. But just because this baby is a mistake, just because it may spoil what we have together – well, I don't see that that's any reason to kill it.'

They talked on and on for another half-hour, until Leo realised he was getting nowhere. Rachel was determined there should be no abortion. Nothing he could say would dissuade her. Leo sighed. Perhaps he should just accept this as a good excuse for their relationship to end. There would be complications, of course. There would be the child, sticky emotional questions, matters of money . . . But if she was so determined to keep it, perhaps this was the best way of utilising the situation, to finish this affair.

Christ, I'm a bastard, he thought, as he weighed the various considerations. He had heard of men who simply cut and ran when this kind of thing happened. He supposed he would be doing that, in a sense. Not physically, but he would use the opportunity to detach himself emotionally from Rachel. In the end, there would only be a distant, practical relationship.

He picked up his drink and swallowed what was left. 'Well, it seems I'm going to have to reserve my position for the moment,' he said grimly. He glanced up at her, wondering what was going through her mind, and said, 'Shall we go? I need some food.' His voice sounded rough and impatient and she suddenly realised that she might be about to lose him for ever. It was as though a small, cold weight had settled on her heart.

Getting into the house hadn't been difficult. Just a matter of busting one of the panes of glass in the window above the sink and groping for the catch. Swinging the window open, James pulled himself up on to the sill and vaulted clumsily over the sink. He crossed the dark kitchen into the hall, then hesitated. Although he knew the house well, he had no idea where Leo might keep any money. When he had lived there last summer, pilfering from Leo had not been part of the game. Leo was too sharp for that. Anyway, he had liked Leo then – it had sometimes felt like more than that. And he had been happy lazing his days away in the house, eating his food, drinking his booze, sharing his bed. Now he couldn't care less about stealing from him, or from anyone, come to that. He'd managed to beg a bit of stuff from friends in Oxford last night, but he needed real money now. Something to keep him going for a couple of weeks.

He bit nervously at the stubs of his fingernails as he considered the options. Then he made his way into the living room, reaching with a familiar hand for the switch of one of the lamps. It was taking a chance, but he couldn't see a bloody thing otherwise. He saw Leo's briefcase lying beside the desk and went over to it. He opened it and rummaged through the contents feverishly. Nothing. Just papers, bloody papers. He thrust the opened briefcase aside, the papers spilling on to the polished floor. He looked around the room at the ornaments and pictures. He had no idea if anything was valuable. Then he saw a small silver box on the mantelpiece. That would do for a kick-off. He pocketed it, and decided to make a swift tour upstairs.

He switched off the lamp and made his way up to Leo's bedroom. That brought back a few memories. Then he realised that he was beginning to sweat uncomfortably, a horrible, flaky feeling coming over his body. This had to be done fast. He went through the pockets of Leo's overcoat, hanging in the wardrobe, then yanked open the drawers of his dressing table, scattering the contents on the floor as he searched. A wallet. He opened it, hands shaking, and pulled out a wad of notes. Brilliant. With a little snickering laugh, James thrust the notes into the back pocket of his jeans and switched off the light. If he hadn't found any money, he'd been ready to trash the place. But he had what he needed. Just as well Leo was down that weekend. Just as well for both of them.

Because Leo's bedroom was at the back of the house neither Leo nor Rachel saw the light go off, and James did not hear the car come to a soft, crunching halt on the gravel outside. He was already downstairs, his hand on the front doorknob, ready to open it and leave, when he heard a footstep and the sound of Leo's voice on the other side of the door. As he opened the front door and switched on the hall light, Leo caught sight of James's figure disappearing into the kitchen. He dropped the bag of groceries he was holding and hurled himself across the hallway after him.

James was already pulling himself up on to the sink when Leo came into the kitchen, without any time to turn on the light. He hauled at James's ankle and James swore at him, kicking backwards with his free foot, which Leo tried to grab as well. He groped upwards for the windowsill, but Leo was dragging him backwards. As his stomach slid downwards over the edge of the sink, James's hands hit the draining board. He felt something beneath his right palm and his hand closed on it instinctively. Leo had pulled him heavily down on to the floor and was bending over him when James lifted the knife to stab at him, raking the blade across the palm of Leo's hand.

It was a sensation, rather than a pain at first. Leo clasped his left wrist with his right hand and felt the wetness, and realised what had happened. He took a step backwards, just as James began to pull himself to his feet, getting ready to lunge at Leo again as soon as he was upright. He didn't care if he killed the bastard. He was getting out of here, that was for sure.

At that moment Rachel, who had heard the voices and the scuffling, hurried across the hallway and switched on the kitchen light. She screamed over and over again, standing slightly bent over, simply staring at them, at the blood running from Leo's hand, and screaming. James was leaning back against the sink, breathing heavily, the knife at the ready, a smear of blood running neatly along its edge. Leo still held his cut hand; the pain was beginning to seep into his consciousness, but he was concentrating entirely on the identity of his attacker and the knife he wielded.

This was James, someone he knew, and that gave him an advantage, an immediate handle. But before he could open his mouth to commence the flow of well-reasoned dissuasion, James went for him again. Rachel screamed even louder. Why didn't the silly bitch go and phone the police? The question flashed through Leo's head as he tried to grab James's wrist with both hands. The pain in the gash on his own hand was mind-numbing as he tried to tighten his grip. He felt feeble against the younger man's strength and fury. He did the only thing he could think of, and brought his right knee up as hard as he could into James's groin. He almost felt for James as he watched him double up, clutching at himself, the knife falling with a clatter to the floor. Leo lunged for the knife with his good hand and picked it up.

'Call the bloody police, can't you?' he called over his shoulder to Rachel, who still stood, stricken, in the doorway. She fled into the living room. Leo stood over James, uncertain as to what he would do if, when he recovered, James got up and went for him again.

But it was not in James's character to continue the fight. He lay curled up on the kitchen floor, the waves of nausea gradually receding, listening to Leo's voice talking to him. By sheer force of personality, Leo reduced James to tears, and by the time Rachel came back into the kitchen he was hunched up against the sink, wiping at his dirt-streaked face with shaking hands.

He was still there when the police car arrived. Rachel was standing in the kitchen doorway apprehensively, her face white, watching James. But Leo stood casually next to him, holding his hand under running water from the cold tap.

As he was lifted from the floor into a standing position, James was looking grey and trembling.

'Do you know if anything's been taken, sir?' asked the policewoman, a businesslike-looking blonde.

Leo glanced over his shoulder, then turned off the tap. 'I don't know,' he replied, pulling open a drawer and taking out a clean tea towel, which he wrapped round his wounded hand. 'I haven't exactly had a chance to look.' The police-woman went quickly through James's pockets and produced the silver box and the rolls of notes, and handed them to her male colleague.

Leo sat down heavily on a chair, suddenly feeling rather weak. 'I presume the money is mine,' he said. 'The box certainly is. Rachel, would you mind checking if there's anything missing from my wallet in the dressing table upstairs? Top left-hand drawer.'

While Rachel was gone, Leo sat watching the policeman and woman. He really felt he'd seen enough of the police recently to last him for the rest of the year. He glanced at James, who seemed to be in something of a bad way, astonished at the change in the boy in just a few months. He'd been a good-looking youth, clean and rather effete. Now he had the look of the streets. Not the faintest notion that he might in some way have contributed to James's altered fortunes flickered across Leo's mind. He believed everyone was responsible for their own destiny. It did not occur to him that he had used or harmed the boy. He did not feel remotely sorry for him.

'Looks like you've got a bit of a problem, son,' remarked the policeman, observing James's eyes and the trembling of his limbs.

James said nothing, but kept his eyes fastened on the wall, his lank blond hair hiding him from Leo's gaze.

Rachel returned with the empty wallet.

'You take the money from this, son?' asked the policeman, holding it up. James said nothing for a moment, then nodded.

355

The money was handed back to Leo. 'Come on,' said the policeman to James, as he and his colleague wheeled him out of the kitchen and towards their waiting car. 'We'll be in touch, sir,' he added to Leo.

As they reached the car, James suddenly wrenched himself round in their grasp and shouted in pent-up, frustrated misery, 'That bastard owed me something, didn't he? I used to live here! I used to live with him! And he just kicked me out, without anywhere to go! He owes me something! You ask him! He paid me to sleep with him! And he owes me!'

Leo stood in the doorway. He had sudden visions of local papers, of this story making its way elsewhere, and he said without hesitation, 'I have never seen this man in my life.'

Still swearing and struggling, James was bundled into the back of the car.

Leo came back inside and closed the door. Rachel was sitting in the kitchen. Maybe I was right, thought Leo, coming into the kitchen and standing over her. Maybe she attracts disaster. It follows her around. She reached up and touched the cloth bound round his hand, blood seeping through it.

'Let's have a look,' she said. He unwound the cloth and disclosed the gash. She winced. 'That needs stitches,' she said. 'Come on. Tell me where the nearest casualty is and I'll drive you there.' She seemed to have recovered her self-possession, taking some strength from the fact of Leo's injury.

They talked little during the wait at the hospital, or on the way back. It was nearly ten o'clock when they got home, but Rachel insisted on cooking two steaks and opening the bottle of wine. 'We both need it,' she said.

As they sat in the kitchen over their late supper, Rachel looked up at Leo and asked, 'Why did you lie to them – to the police? That was the boy who was living here last summer, wasn't it?'

Leo considered this question with weary disbelief. 'Did you expect me to confirm that to them?'

'You could have said nothing at all.'

Leo put down his wine glass. 'Rachel, I have applied to take silk this year. Things aren't looking good for me, apparently. The last thing I need is a story getting about that I had a happy little ménage à trois here last summer and that one of its members is now a junkie who tried to burgle my house and pull a knife on me.' She met his uncompromising gaze. 'I'm prepared to tell any lie necessary to prevent that getting out.'

She said nothing. She was beginning to realise how many sides there were to Leo, how much of him she did not know.

She washed up as Leo went upstairs to get ready for bed. The square of brown paper which she had taped over the window puckered and puffed with the cold night air. When she went upstairs she found Leo sitting on the edge of the bed, his shirt off, staring at the neat, firm bandage encircling his hand. He looked oddly boyish, vulnerable.

'You should take some of the painkillers they gave you,' she said, wanting to sit on the bed next to him, stroke his bare skin, hold him. But something held her back.

'I have,' he replied, then glanced up. 'Are you coming to bed?' he asked. He suddenly badly wanted some animal warmth, the comfort of someone next to him. The shock of the knife attack was only now beginning to hit him.

Rachel hesitated. 'Not in that bed, Leo,' she said, her voice soft and apologetic. She regretted the words as soon as they were spoken.

Leo smiled and nodded. Of course not. She and the baby wanted to be on their self-righteous own. God, he was tired of it all.

'And I've decided,' she went on, 'that I'll go and stay with friends in London next week. Until the flat's in some sort of shape. I should get back to work. I don't need time off – it just gives me too much space to think. And please – I can see to getting the flat straight again. I can afford to. I'll get the insurance money eventually.'

'Yes, I understand,' replied Leo. 'Not pleasant, staying here on one's own, after this evening. We've both had quite a week, haven't we?'

She left him and went into her bedroom, closing the door. In bed, she wept for only a short while, then lay awake in the darkness, remembering the evening when she had first gone to his bed and he had made love to her. The recollection was like a physical pain. Leo, too, lay awake, but the only pain he

357

felt was the insistent throbbing of his hand, and the nagging worry of what James would say, what the repercussions might be.

Chapter twenty-eight

Rachel arranged to go and stay with friends the following day. There was a certain awkwardness between herself and Leo, a sense of unfinished business still in the air.

'I'll call you at the end of the week,' Leo said, as he put her things into the boot of her car. 'We have to sort something out.'

'There's nothing to sort out, Leo,' Rachel replied. 'I'm having the baby.'

'I didn't mean that. I mean between you and me. We need to get a few things clear . . . ' Now was not the time. 'Anyway, I'll call you.'

He kissed her, and for a moment she clung to him, wishing suddenly that this baby did not exist, that everything could go on as before.

Leo spent the rest of the week in court before Sir Frank Chamberlin, in a dreary dispute concerning a joint venture agreement for the operation of a North Sea ferry service. His hand still hurt abominably, and having Frank's lugubrious features before him all day and every day only served to remind him of the oppressive fears regarding his application for silk. The hearing drew to its close on Thursday afternoon, to the relief of all, and as Leo was gathering his papers together and chatting to his instructing solicitor, the usher approached him and handed him a note. 'From Sir Frank, Mr Davies,' he murmured.

Leo opened the note, read it quickly, then crumpled it up. He wasn't sure if he wanted a drink with Frank, but he could hardly decline.

Sir Frank was in his private rooms in the annexe to his old chambers, getting rid of the day's mail, when Leo arrived.

'Ah, Leo! Excellent!' said Frank, and motioned to Leo to take a seat. 'I thought it might be pleasant to have a bit of a drink and a chat after the last four days. What will you have? The usual whisky?'

'Thanks,' murmured Leo, and settled into a chair, glancing round with pleasure at the interesting clutter of Frank's room. He sipped gratefully at the whisky which Frank handed him. Over the past few days he had felt dreadfully tired, as though old age had suddenly overtaken him. He went to bed early every night.

'What happened to your hand?' asked Sir Frank conversationally, glancing at Leo's bandaged hand.

'Oh, just an accident with a knife at the weekend,' replied Leo. 'Rather nasty, actually.'

'Mmm. That's bad luck.' Frank settled back into his chair with his drink. There was a companionable silence for a few moments. Then Frank said, 'I gather there is a rumour that Sir Basil may be joining us on the bench later this year?'

'I think he's been invited, but I don't know whether or not he'll accept. He's very jealous of his position as head of chambers,' replied Leo. He paused. 'It's rather odd, trying to imagine chambers without Basil. He's been the head there ever since I started.'

'Well, I suppose his departure would leave room for a little more weight in chambers, mmm? Improves your prospects.'

Leo sighed. He didn't want to talk about this. He would have preferred general gossip and a few stiff Scotches. 'I don't know if anything is capable of improving those,' he replied.

'Well, you know, I've been canvassing opinion recently,' said Sir Frank with a comfortable air, 'and I'm bound to tell you that, as far as one can tell, not everyone regards this – ah – business of the boy as being in the least bit important.'

'What boy?' asked Leo abruptly. Surely no one had heard of the weekend's events yet, had they?

Frank looked alarmed. 'Oh, you know. Of course you know. About that friend of yours who died some years ago. It has been widely discussed, you know.'

Leo put his glass down on Frank's desk. He shouldn't have come for this drink. It seemed that every time he saw Frank, he told him something which he would rather not have known.

Sir Frank went blithely on. 'Of course, there are, well, a few who will take the hard line on that kind of thing, but you'd be surprised how many take a liberal view.'

Leo shook his head. 'I had no idea that that – incident was known to anyone. What are they saying?'

'Well . . . ' Frank looked less comfortable now. 'That you – um, had a, had a friendship with this young person – I mean, there are those who have it that he was, in some senses, a – I believe the expression is "rent boy".' A pause. 'And that – that, well, a few months after the – the association ended, he was found murdered in his flat – or, perhaps, more accurately, his bedsitting room.' Another pause. 'Not, of course, that there has been the slightest suggestion that your – ah, that your friendship with this young – young person and his subsequent death were in any way related. No, no. No, no. It's just that some see – well, some see the connection as being – shall we say, somewhat unfortunate? More whisky?' He fetched the bottle and poured anxiously.

Leo drank deeply, feeling the tingling warmth spreading from his stomach through his limbs. The gash in his hand began to throb slightly. He said nothing. It didn't matter what Frank said about some taking a liberal view; if this was known in the Lord Chancellor's Office, if Lord Steele had come to hear of it, then the balance was now tipped right out of his favour. The only thing that could be said on his behalf was that it had happened years ago. Nearly ten years. If Rachel, if his conduct over the past few months had had any effect, then perhaps the present could overshadow, if not entirely eradicate, the past. He stared at his drink.

'I have got the – the gist of the thing properly, haven't I?' asked Sir Frank, watching Leo's face. Dear me, he always seemed to be responsible for upsetting Leo these days. But surely he must have heard, must have realised . . . ? Then again, one was often the last to know.

'Yes,' murmured Leo, raising his glass again. 'Yes, that's about right. He wasn't a rent boy, though. Not then.' He took a drink. 'Not,' he added, 'that it makes any difference. It's what people believe that matters, isn't it?' He smiled slightly.

'Yes, yes, I suppose so,' said Frank sadly, thoughtfully. 'But, you know,' he added, 'I think it will make less difference than you imagine. I mean, there is the present to consider. That is what matters.' Thank you, thought Leo. 'It is well known that you have – well, I believe the expression is a – ah – steady girlfriend. That kind of thing matters. They take account of that. And you are so well liked. Very well thought of by everyone on the Commercial bench. I can assure you of that. No, no, despite this most recent rumour – dear me, there do seem to have been so many – very unfortunate, really – I think that, in spite of it, things look less black than they did. I really do think so, you know.'

He sounded so genuinely sympathetic and encouraging that Leo actually felt quite cheered. Frank made it all sound better than he had imagined. Rachel had helped. Image was everything. People's immediate perceptions of one were what counted, not dried-up pieces of scandal from the past. And Rachel had helped, though at a cost that he could never have foreseen.

A few whiskies later, Leo made his rather light-headed way home. He decided to walk all the way, filling his lungs with night air, more sanguine about his own future than he had felt for some time.

He was rooting around in the freezer for something to eat when the phone rang.

'Hello?' Leo's jaw stiffened in a yawn as he answered.

'Mr Davies?'

'Yes.'

'Mr Davies, my name's Alan French, from the *Sun*. Just wondering if you can fill us in on a story we picked up from the *Oxford Gazette*. About this chap who broke into your house last weekend – understand there was something of a bust-up. He says he was staying with you as a summer guest last year, that you had a bit of an interesting household. You and him and a young lady. Would that be right?'

Leo's first instinct was to tell the man where to go and put the phone down, but he hesitated. That would mean they might print the story just as it was. Trying to make his voice as cool as possible, he replied, 'Absolutely ludicrous. I don't even know the person who broke into my house.' But even as he said it, it sounded feeble. He should just hang up.

'But the young lady. There was a young lady?'

'I employed a young woman to look after the house and cook for house parties when I came down at weekends.'

'So you completely deny everything this boy says – including that you slept with him and your – cook?'

'Completely. Now piss off.'

He slammed the phone down and stood, tense and angry. He could see it now. 'Barrister's saucy summer romps. Love triangle that turned sour.' A nice spicy little piece to liven up the February gloom. He rubbed his hands across his face, suddenly feeling very sober and not at all hungry. He must speak to Sarah before anyone else did. Christ, what if they were on to her right now? She could say anything – she had little enough reason to love Leo, after their last meeting. And she had always said, in that flip way of hers, a little toss of the blonde head, that she didn't care what people said or thought about her; she did as she pleased. All very well to say, thought Leo, but she wouldn't come out of this very well if she did tell the papers how things had been last summer. For all that bravado, he suspected she would rather keep it quiet. Still, he couldn't take the chance. He had to get hold of her.

As soon as he reached chambers the next day, he asked Henry to get him the Recorder of the City of London's office. But Sir Vivian Colman was not at his office, and was not expected until the end of the day. Leo rang Lady Margaret Hall and tried to get her address from the college, but they would not give out details of undergraduates' addresses.

It was late in the afternoon when he managed, at last, to speak to Sarah's father.

'Sir Vivian, good afternoon. My name is Leo Davies, from 5 Caper Court, in the Temple.'

'Oh, yes?' The mention of 5 Caper Court lent Leo's enquiry an air of respectability, at any rate. 'What can I do for you, Mr Davies?' Sir Vivian's voice was as fruity and fat as he himself had appeared at Sir Basil's party.

'I met your daughter, Sarah, Sir Vivian, at Sir Basil Bunting's party just before Christmas. Unfortunately, I don't believe that you and I were introduced. But I told Sarah that I would send her some materials on – ah – that is, to help her with her international trade studies.'

'I see.'

'And I find that I have mislaid her address and telephone number. Naturally, her college doesn't hand out that kind of information, and so I hoped that you might be kind enough to help me.'

'Yes, well, I imagine I can, Mr Davies. Just one moment,' replied Sir Vivian plummily. Leo breathed a sigh of relief.

Thirty seconds later he put down the phone, in possession of the information he needed. Leo lit one of his small cigars and dialled Sarah's number. To his relief, she was in.

'Hello, Sarah. This is Leo.'

In her terraced house in Oxford, Sarah smiled and picked up the telephone from the hall table, trailing it through to the sitting room. She settled herself happily in an armchair.

'Leo. How old ghosts are haunting me these days. James called to see me last week.'

This threw Leo for a second. Then he said, 'Oddly enough, he is rather the reason I'm calling.'

'Oh?' Her voice, ever knowing, made him wonder whether she already knew all about the business of last weekend.

'Sarah, have any journalists been calling you?'

'Not that I know of, darling. Why? Have you been doing something indiscreet?' She curled her legs up beneath her and wound the cord of the phone around one finger.

He found it difficult to answer for a second. This had to be handled with care. He could hear from her voice that she was smiling, but Sarah's smile could mean many things, and he did not wish to mishandle this. She could be a sour, spitting little cat.

'I might as well tell you exactly what has happened,' said Leo levelly. 'James broke into the house last Saturday.'

'Goodness.'

'And he and I had a fight. He managed to stab me in the hand.'

'Poor Leo.' Sarah was not smiling now, but listening with interest.

'When the police came and took him away, he started

364

mouthing off about our little domestic arrangement of last summer – '

'Did he indeed?' murmured Sarah, her eyes narrowing.

' – and yesterday I had some chap from the *Sun* ringing up and asking me about it. They picked it up from the local paper.'

'And what did you say?' Sarah tried to keep the anxiety from her voice, but she was touched with fear. Whatever she might airily have said to Leo, she did not wish her family, or her tutor – or anyone else, for that matter – to learn about her working life last summer.

But Leo was too practised at listening to responses, at detecting certain notes in the voices of witnesses under pressure. He heard the ever-so-slight overhastiness of her question, the giveaway.

'I said I had never seen James in my life' – Leo reached for his cigar and stared at its glowing tip – 'that you had worked as my housekeeper and as a cook when I had weekend parties. And that the whole thing was an utter fabrication.'

'Why did you bring me into it?' she snapped, only partly relieved.

'I didn't, my dear. James had already done that. I didn't mention your name, but no doubt James has done that, too. Now, the point is, I think that once Mr French from the *Sun* gets hold of your name, he's going to track you down and ask you about your side of it.'

Sarah smiled and stood up, wandering over to the window with the phone, gazing out at the gathering dusk in the street. She could not resist a little malicious teasing. Why should she give Leo the reassurance he wanted?

'Well, now,' she said in a slow, deliberate manner, 'I wonder what I shall say to him? Mmm? I think you'll just have to start buying the *Sun* each day, Leo.' And she put the phone down.

Leo sat staring at the receiver for a few seconds, until the dialling tone began to purr. Then he replaced it. That bitch. He felt cold inside. She could say anything. And he would be finished. He would just have to hope she was sensible about it – after all, she had something to lose, too.

The odds were stacked heavily against him now, he realised with a sinking heart, first with the story of that boy from years ago doing the rounds, now with this business . . . Even if Sarah backed him up, there would be talk. But he had no more cards to play. He had done everything in his power, and he had this unholy mess with Rachel into the bargain. All because Frank Chamberlin had come up with the ludicrous suggestion that he should get married.

Leo stared for a moment at the plaster covering the wound in his hand. No, that was utterly absurd. The last thing he could do was marry Rachel. That was too big a card to play, even though such a move might redress the balance spectacularly. But it was impossible. It was too much.

He swivelled round in his chair and looked out across the winking darkness of Caper Court. He heard footsteps hurrying over the flagstones, fading into silence. And he suddenly had a vision of himself, old age and obscurity closing around him, his fortunes unchanged, all hopes of further brilliance faded and forgotten, while the gas lamps burned on in the winter's darkness and the footsteps went hurrying by outside, on and on, down the days. If he could do anything to change that picture, he told himself, he would do it.

He opened and closed his left hand slowly, and felt suddenly overwhelmed by an inner weariness. The incident on Saturday night had shaken him horribly. There now crept into his mind a small, questioning doubt – were the events of last summer, the way in which he had simply picked James up and then dropped him, to blame for the way James was now, and for what had happened? He remembered his words to Sir Frank yesterday evening, talking of that poor creature, Ian, whom he had once taken to his bed and then later forgotten, only to hear of his death months later: 'He wasn't a rent boy. Not then.' Not then. Leo remembered making the boy a present of some money – a lot of money, really, for someone of his age. He closed his eyes now at the recollection, and at the memory of last summer. Did he really imagine he could go back to that kind of life now? Even if he was made a QC, the evidence of his senses told him that those things in his life which he had sought to keep private were now rising to the surface like so much scum . . . He had learned, to his cost, that nothing could be kept secret in this life. It had all been mere squalor.

He thought, too, of this child, his and Rachel's, which would eventually be born. It would be a part of him. It already was. He would be someone's father. And he recalled his own father, the longed-for presence so rarely there, and who had ultimately vanished for ever. That was a pain, a crippling loss which he could not inflict upon his own son or daughter. Maybe he could marry Rachel, and lead an ordinary sort of life. Dull, unexciting – but what had been the real excitement of his sordid escapades up until now? It would be possible, he could see that. If he did not love her – he no longer knew what love was like, he thought – then at least he felt affection for her. They had tastes in common. She was beautiful, amusing in a quiet way . . . And above all, this would set a respectable seal on his life at a time when he needed it most. He would have to do it. There was scarcely any alternative.

Twice he hesitated, his hand hovering over the phone. Then he picked it up.

Rachel and Felicity were on their knees in Rachel's office, trying to do a clear-out of old files. Rachel glanced up and noticed that Roger Williams had just passed by for the third time, peering through the glass partition and smiling down at them.

'Felicity,' said Rachel, realising why this was happening, 'I think you're showing rather a lot of knicker, sitting like that.'

Felicity, who was on all fours with her bottom in the air, put a self-conscious hand round to the back of her skirt and sat up. The phone rang and Rachel got to her feet.

'Mr Davies for you, dear,' sang Nora.

'Hello, Leo,' said Rachel flatly. Over the past few days the only tolerable intervals in her life seemed to be those in which she didn't think about him. Morning sickness had become entangled in her mind with despair and rejection.

'I'd like to see you this evening, if you're not busy,' said Leo. 'I want to talk to you about a few things.'

'Yes, I suppose so,' replied Rachel. She remembered vividly the time when he had first called her, asked her to dinner, and how her spirits had soared. Now the prospect of seeing him, although she longed to be with him, was coloured with apprehension. There was nothing light-hearted in their

367

relationship any more, nothing to look forward to.

'I'll pick you up from the office. It's – let's see' – he glanced at his watch; still early, but he hadn't been able to get a damn thing done all day, anyway – 'five forty now. I'll be with you in half an hour.'

'All right.' She put the phone down. Felicity, still sitting on the floor, glanced up at her.

'Cheer up. Can't be that bad.'

'Can't it?' Rachel picked up a heap of the files which Felicity had sorted through and dumped them on her desk.

'At least you've still got a job. What am I going to do in two weeks' time?'

'Haven't you found anything yet?'

Felicity shook her head. 'I'm fed up typing. Fed up doing this sort of stuff.' She chucked a pile of papers down on top of another. 'I want to – God, do you know what I'd really like? I'd like to be one of those PA types – you know, the ones who just go around organising people's lives for them. Tell them where they're going, when they're doing it, fixing up appointments for them, keeping people away from them, letting people in to see them. I'd be good at that.' She sounded morose. 'But I don't know how you get those kind of jobs. Not by being me, I don't suppose.'

'Something will turn up,' said Rachel, unconvincingly. 'Come on, let's get this cleared up. I'm going in half an hour.'

They were putting the last of the files in order when Nora rang to say that Leo was in reception.

'Ask him to come up, Nora. I'm just finishing here,' said Rachel.

'Fourth floor, Mr Davies,' said Nora with her warm, stretching smile, etched in vivid fuchsia today. 'Fifth door on your right.' She watched as Leo got into the lift. Lovely type. Bit old for her taste, though. Looked like a Gemini, anyway.

'Hello,' said Rachel, glancing up as Leo came into her room. In spite of everything, she still felt a glow at the sight of him; his presence seemed to charge the atmosphere.

'Whoops! Mind out!' called Felicity, swooping to pick up a thick file from Leo's path, revealing a hefty amount of cleavage and an expanse of black-stockinged rear thigh as she did so.

'Felicity, this is Mr Davies. Felicity's my secretary,' said Rachel.

'Not for long,' said Felicity airily, flashing Leo a smile. This one was a looker, she thought. She remembered seeing him in reception once. She wouldn't mind a little piece of that action, something on the mature side.

'Oh?' said Leo, stepping aside to let her past with the file, rather taken by her pretty grin.

'Felicity's leaving us soon,' said Rachel, glancing at Felicity with faint apprehension. 'Unfortunately.'

'I'm too much for this place,' said Felicity, this time directing a distinctly flirtatious glance at Leo. 'Don't suppose you'd have a job for me, would you, Mr Davies?'

'Right, thank you, Felicity,' said Rachel quickly. 'I think you can probably go off home now.'

'Okay, night!' She fluttered her fingers at them and left.

Leo found himself smiling, not something he had done much in the past few days. 'She seems rather good fun,' he remarked.

Rachel sighed. 'She is. It's a bit of a rotten story, actually. Office intimidation, I suppose you could call it. Apparently our office manager was coming on to her, and her boyfriend found out and started a punch-up at the office Christmas party.'

'Sounds like standard stuff for an office party,' remarked Leo as he helped her into her coat. He was glad to be talking about something remote from his current preoccupations. They made their way to the lift.

'Anyway,' said Rachel, leaning against the wall of the lift as the doors closed, 'she's been asked to leave because of it. The partners can't exactly give her a glowing reference after that incident – even though it wasn't her fault, so far as I can see – and she's not optimistic about finding another job. I feel rather guilty about it all.'

'Why should you feel guilty?' asked Leo.

'Goodnight, Nora,' called Rachel. They went out into the street; a light rain had begun to fall. 'Oh, I don't know . . . I just wish there was something I could do to help. She needs a job. She lives with her brother, and he's unemployed –

unemployable, by all accounts – and they rely on her earnings.'

'We're always in need of new typists,' said Leo idly, hailing a cab and turning up the collar of his coat against the rain, which was growing heavier now, gusting against them, splashing on to the pavement. 'Especially since we'll be taking on two new tenants shortly.'

They climbed into the cab and it set off down Bishopsgate. 'I mean, if she's badly in need of a job . . . On the other hand, it's a bit of a comedown, being a lowly typist after working as a partner's secretary.'

Rachel turned to him. 'If you seriously think there'd be a job for her, she would jump at it. I mean, she's a bit dizzy, but at least she's used to working for lawyers and wouldn't have to learn the language from scratch.' Rachel regarded Leo, who was staring absently at the rain coursing down the cab window, lost in his own thoughts.

'What?' He turned to her. 'Yes – yes, as I said, we always need new people. If you think she'd be interested, tell her to give Henry a ring. I'll tell him to expect her call.' And he turned his gaze back to the wet, dark streets.

Rachel sat back, reflecting upon this offer. It seemed to be just what Felicity needed. It crossed her mind, fleetingly, that perhaps it wasn't quite fair to inflict Felicity upon the inmates of 5 Caper Court . . . but let them worry about that. How much of a hash could she make of typing up briefs, after all? Thrusting the obvious answer to this to the back of her mind, she said, 'Yes, I'll give her the number. I think she'll be delighted at the chance.'

Leo said nothing and, after a brief silence in which thoughts of Felicity and her problems evaporated entirely, Rachel asked, 'Where are we going?' Her stomach tightened with apprehension as she considered what might be said between them that evening. Until now, she had put the future of their relationship from her mind. Now it could not be put away. The future was upon them with force and immediacy, and she felt afraid.

'Somewhere quiet for a drink and a talk,' replied Leo. 'We can have dinner later, if you like. You say where.' Now that he had settled the matter in his mind, he felt almost celebratory.

He was astonished to find that he was quite relieved at the prospect of a change in his condition. That which he had imagined would be a stricture, an oppression, now struck him as a release. He need not be his old self – the self which now rather disgusted him – any more.

The wine bar in Holborn was tucked away in a back alley, and there were few people in there. It had been converted from an old cellar, and there were a number of small brick alcoves with tables. Leo and Rachel sat in one of these.

Leo bought a bottle of wine and poured her a glass without saying anything. Although alcohol rather nauseated her these days, she took a quick swallow to steady her nerves.

'I've been thinking a good deal over the past few days,' said Leo, unbuttoning his jacket, then leaning forward and turning his glass between the palms of his hands. The light from the candle in the bottle on their table cast saffron shadows on his hands and on the side of his face.

'Oh?' There was a decisive note in his voice which Rachel heard almost with dread. There was a long pause.

'And I think that perhaps it would be best if we were to get married.' He picked up his glass and drank, then set it down again and looked up at her. Her eyes looked large and luminous in the candlelight, her features perfectly still. 'Well?' he said, and smiled faintly. Christ, he thought, what have I done?

'I don't think so, Leo,' said Rachel at last, her voice no more than a murmur.

Leo had hardly expected this. He coughed lightly and looked down at his wine and back at her. 'Why don't you think so? Isn't it the best solution?' he asked quietly.

She shook her head. 'That's all it would be. Just a solution.' She looked up at him. 'You don't love me, Leo.'

At that moment, gazing at her pale, lovely face, the dark, shining hair, listening to the familiar clearness of her voice, he almost felt he did.

'Do you think I make a habit of proposing to people I don't love?' His voice as he spoke was a little grim.

'You said you didn't want a child,' she reminded him, her

gaze shifting to the flickering flame of the candle, the shadows that danced against the walls.

'It's not a matter of choice, though – is it?' he said, then added quickly, 'I don't look at it in that way any more. I was speaking hypothetically. I accept that this is a reality.'

She looked up at him, silent. Then she spoke.

'You once told me not to invest too much in you, Leo. That you didn't go the distance. I didn't want to believe you then.' She hesitated, twisting the stem of her wine glass. 'But I do now. You've given me a lot,' she went on. 'You've freed me from fears I thought were with me for ever, taken away . . . the darkness. Some of it . . . ' There was another silence, one in which Leo, to his surprise, became aware that he felt faintly scared. Of what, he could hardly tell. 'But you know,' she went on, not smiling, merely looking at him with sad earnestness, 'you're not the marrying kind. There's really no room in your world for anyone else besides Leo Davies, is there?' There was not the slightest trace of bitterness or irony in her voice. Merely the frank question.

'I don't know,' he said, and she leaned back. 'I don't know.' God, they were dealing with issues which he hadn't foreseen. He had simply thought that he would put it to her that they should marry, and that she would say yes. 'No, look,' he said, 'I *do* know . . . I do know that I think that we should marry. The baby should have parents . . . '

'The baby will have me, Leo. I'll be more than enough, I promise.'

Leo sat staring at the candle flame, feeling inert and a little old. The faint fear which had crept upon him suddenly resolved itself; it was that familiar fear of late, the fear of rejection, and of loneliness. He looked up at her. 'Do you love me?' he asked softly.

The seconds slid away as they gazed at one another. Rachel knew that she had reached some critical juncture, and felt strangely alienated. What did she know about him after all? He had a past whose sordid details she could only conjecture, and he was offering her a future that must, inevitably, be bound up with that past. But then why should she expect anything but imperfection in her life? Nothing was ever clean and whole.

Everything she touched became disfigured in some fashion. It was her own special curse. Not even Leo could change that. He was merely proof of it. But his question still hung in the air, and she must answer it. They both knew the answer. Dominating every other consideration was the sure and ineluctable knowledge that she loved him deeply, hopelessly. She realised that if she were to refuse him now, there would be nothing worthwhile left in life. Just a dark, gaping void of loneliness that not even Leo's child could fill.

'Yes,' she said slowly. 'Yes, I love you.'

'Then marry me.' He spoke with a determination and finality that surprised even him.

Suddenly she felt weary, all resistance spent. 'Are you sure that this is what you want?'

Leo stared at her, trying to recall all the thoughts that had gone through his mind that afternoon. This was utter madness. Then he thought of the future, of the isolation of failure, of Easter and the difference this might make.

'Yes,' he said. 'It's what I want.' And he waited.

'Very well, then,' replied Rachel at last, with the ghost of a smile. She glanced at him apprehensively.

'Fine,' said Leo, the reality of it sinking in. He picked up his glass, hesitated for a moment, and touched it against hers.

Four days later, his phone rang in chambers.

'You can stop buying the *Sun*, Leo,' said Sarah's lazy voice.

A wave of relief swept him for a moment, then anxiety returned. 'What's been going on?' he asked.

'Well, I simply did what you couldn't possibly do. I paid our mutual friend James a visit. He's in some horrible remand place. I went to see him the day after you rang.'

'And?'

'Well, I have to admit,' she continued with a sigh, 'that I did make a few promises on your behalf. I told him that if he didn't take this business any further – simply kept his mouth shut and didn't talk to anyone – you might be able to pull a few strings when his case comes up. And afterwards . . . well, I'm sure that with your money and connections, Leo, you'll be able to help him a bit. He had come to something of a dead end.'

She paused. 'For which you were somewhat to blame.'

'I know, I know,' sighed Leo.

'And I think if he can stay off drugs and find work of some kind, he'll be okay. If you can set him on his feet, give him a bit of money . . .'

'And I'm meant to be doing all this for him?'

'Oh, yes.' Sarah's voice was cool and bright. 'After all, we're both doing this for you, aren't we? When you think what the alternative might be. Very unpleasant publicity. And don't worry – James hasn't mentioned my name to any journalists, so no one's come near me.'

'You're doing this for yourself as much as for me,' replied Leo curtly.

'Possibly . . .' Her tone was light and reflective. 'But you really should be grateful to me. I'm sure that you'll be able to return the favour when I've finished my Bar course and need a good pupillage.' She laughed. 'Won't you?'

He smiled grimly. 'Sarah, I do not doubt that from this moment on I am eternally in your debt.'

She laughed again. 'Something like that. Now, you will back up these promises I made to James, won't you? Otherwise, well – it's a bit of a let-down for everybody, isn't it?'

'I'll do what I can. Goodbye, Sarah.'

He put the phone down. So that immediate threat was removed – he would worry about the cost of it later. James was easily dealt with from now on. The irony of it was that he had been panicked into committing himself irrevocably to Rachel. He rubbed his hand wearily across his eyes. It seemed that with every step which he took to free himself from his problems, he became further and further enmeshed in new ones of his own making.

Chapter twenty-nine

'I'm afraid I can't – not the fifteenth, Charles,' said Sir Basil, sitting at his desk with the telephone in one hand and his fountain pen in the other. 'No, we are having a small celebration in chambers that evening. Leo Davies is to be married, you know. Perhaps you could have a word with the Lord Chancellor and arrange another evening? Excellent. Goodbye.'

Loyalty to chambers first, thought Sir Basil as he put down the phone. He was hardly likely to lose his appointment to the bench through having to inconvenience the Judicial Appointments Group. He particularly did not wish to miss Leo's drinks party. He felt a vague but unmistakable relief that Leo was at last getting married.

Still with his fountain pen in his hand, Sir Basil stood up, gazing at the little list which he held. He must arrange an afternoon with Henry to go through his cases, working out which he could safely continue with and which would have to be wound down. He would go and arrange that with him now.

Henry was in a little room off the clerks' room initiating Felicity in the mysteries of the photocopier. Felicity, whose first day it was at 5 Caper Court, stood with her hands clasped attentively behind her back, wearing an expression of concerned intelligence. The hem of her skirt was three inches lower than normal, but she had been unable to resist wearing her favourite low-cut blouse. Otherwise what was the point of having a Wonderbra?

' . . . and so you press this button and it collates and stacks everything. Right?'

Felicity nodded and fingered the button thoughtfully. She'd never been very good at getting things into bundles. She remembered that time when the machine at Nichols & Co had started shooting sheaves of paper all over the floor like a demented thing. It hadn't been her fault, but everyone had blamed her. She hoped she was going to be okay with this one.

'May I have a word, Henry?' asked Sir Basil as he put his head round the door. He glanced at Felicity and gave her a faint, courteous smile, trying hard to keep his gaze above her chin. Felicity felt as if she ought to curtsey, and smiled back. Pretty girl, thought Sir Basil, if a little more exotic in her attire than the kind of girl they usually employed.

'Here,' said Henry to Felicity, 'you can photocopy these bundles for Mr Davies for tomorrow's hearing. Four of each, then go through and mark off the pages, just like the original.'

And Henry went off to speak to Sir Basil, leaving Felicity to her task.

At the end of the day, Henry dropped in on Leo.

'How is young Miss Waller settling in?' asked Leo, taking off his spectacles.

'Seems happy enough. Did you get those bundles for tomorrow's hearing?'

Leo glanced up. 'Yes. For some reason all the markers had been moved around. It took me a little time to sort them out, which was annoying.'

Henry raised his eyebrows. 'Felicity photocopied those. It was the first thing I gave her to do.'

'Oh. Ah. I see.' Leo frowned, then glanced away, while Henry tried not to grin. Well, he was responsible for bringing her into chambers. He would just have to hope that it wasn't the shape of things to come. 'It's only her first day,' he reminded Henry. 'She's probably a bit nervous.'

'Yes, probably,' agreed Henry, and left, smiling.

When Henry had gone, Leo, for the hundredth time that day, began to ponder his wedding next week. He had arranged everything with the registry office, they were having a drinks party a couple of days beforehand in chambers, he was taking Rachel to Florence for a week . . . The only thing he had not done was tell his mother. Why? He puzzled at his own reluctance to tell her, to invite her. He wanted no guests at all. Her presence would simply give credence to it all. Family.

With each of these steps – the drinks party, the registry office, the honeymoon – Leo felt as though another hoop of steel grappled him closer to Rachel. And he told himself it was inevitable, part of the metamorphosis. From here on, he was to assume a new persona. It was unthinkable that he should exclude his mother. With this thought, he picked up the telephone and prepared himself to tell her about her future daughter-in-law and grandchild.

On the evening before Leo's drinks party in chambers, five weeks before Easter, Rachel went round to Anthony's flat. She went on impulse, on the off-chance that she might find him in. They had not spoken since Anthony had phoned her and she had told him about Leo, and now she had the feeling that she should say something to him. She felt haunted by guilt about their relationship, and wanted to ease any sense of grievance that he might still feel.

Anthony looked only mildly surprised when he opened the door and saw Rachel standing there. She was wearing an enveloping grey blouson jacket of soft suede, a present from Leo, a white cashmere polo neck, one of Leo's purchases after the burglary, and jeans; she was now, somehow, very much Leo's property, and happy to be so. Anthony was wearing an old rugby shirt and battered cords, and his feet were bare. Rachel was struck by how very young he looked, and beautiful. She had quite forgotten.

'Come in,' said Anthony, and she followed him through to the kitchen, closing the door behind her. The radio was on and the ironing board up. A pile of Anthony's collars lay on a chair and a can of Robin spray starch stood on the table.

'Doing my collars,' he remarked. 'It's a chore I really hate, so I always put it off and finish up having to do about two dozen at once.' He switched off the radio and folded up the ironing board. 'What would you like – a drink? Coffee?'

'I'll have a coffee, thanks,' said Rachel, unfastening her jacket and slipping it over the back of a chair.

'That's a pretty jacket,' said Anthony, glancing at it as he filled the kettle. He knew immediately that Leo had bought it for her; Leo's taste was instinctively familiar to him, he realised with a pang.

'Isn't it?' replied Rachel hesitantly, tucking back shining strands of her dark hair. 'Leo gave it to me – a sort of – '

'Engagement present?' He glanced at her faintly troubled face. 'Don't worry. I do know, you know. We're having a bit of a celebration in chambers tomorrow evening.' He spooned coffee into the coffee machine. She thought she detected a faintly grim note in his voice, and said nothing. She suddenly realised, watching him make the coffee, that she had come round here without any clear purpose. What was she supposed to say to him? Suddenly she remembered Mr Nikolaos.

'We've got some good news on the *Valeo Dawn*,' she said brightly. 'The other side seem prepared to accept the experts' findings about the cause of the fire. We should be able to settle.'

'Mmm,' said Anthony, smiling wryly. 'I was rather hoping that case might become a moneyspinner. Still, I'm glad for Mr Nikolaos.' There was silence again. So even that last little connection between them was severed. Unless she ever instructed him again, which he doubted.

'The coffee will take a moment or two,' he added, fetching a beer for himself from the fridge. He cracked it open and tipped the can briefly in her direction. 'Here's to both of you,' said Anthony, glancing at her and wishing she did not look so heart-stoppingly lovely. It had done him some good not to see her for the past month or two. He had felt only a brief, deep pang when he had heard that Leo was to marry her. The idea of Leo marrying would have astonished him once. Now, nothing surprised him.

'Thank you,' she said faintly. She sat with her hands clasped between her knees, watching him. It was up to her to take the initiative, she realised. She had come here uninvited, after all. There was a pause, during which Anthony got up to pour out her coffee, and she said, 'I felt I wanted to see you, to explain things to you . . . '

'Don't be absurd!' he broke in. She felt grateful for the interruption. 'Why should you explain anything to me?' His voice sounded mild and mocking, but not unkind. He set her coffee in front of her. 'I'm very happy for you. Truly.'

How could he tell her anything of what he really felt? How could he begin to explain to her that the loss he felt most deeply was the loss of Leo, that this news had brought home to him the knowledge that, somehow, he had always felt that he had come first in Leo's heart? That was ridiculous, he knew – he had spurned Leo long ago. Why should he still imagine that he retained the chief part of his affection? But, rightly or wrongly, he had always thought so. Now he knew otherwise. If he had tried to explain any of this to Rachel, she would not have begun to understand. She had come to make an apology where none was needed. He had been in love with her – was still a little in love with her – but that infatuation was eclipsed by his recent awareness of how entire and consuming his affection for Leo had always been. Would always be. And now she had the prize, she had Leo's love and all the rest of him.

Suddenly Rachel looked up and said, 'I'm having a baby.'

Anthony could think of nothing to say. How much he had lost, he realised. Rachel was beyond him – he saw now that she had always been. But to lose her to Leo, to lose Leo to her . . . There was something a little ludicrous about all of it. And then some faint comprehension began to dawn. Of course Leo was bound to marry her – what else would anyone do in such circumstances? He had known there must be some reason, some motive which he could not fathom. He suddenly felt lighter in his heart, as though Leo was not entirely lost to him.

'Oh,' he said at last. 'That's – that's something of a surprise.' Already he was adept at producing the remark designed to elicit the information he wanted, without the need for a question. Part of his acquired skills.

'Yes,' murmured Rachel, ducking her head, unable to prevent her soft smile of pleasure. 'Yes, we were both – well, it was unexpected, I suppose.'

At that moment, the doorbell rang.

'Half a tick,' said Anthony, and got up. When he returned, it was in the company of a stocky blond man, whose voice she had heard booming in the hall, and two girls. The girls were of a type she knew; confident, careless Sloanes with distant, amused eyes, half-smiling mouths, and plenty of easy, bright conversation.

379

' – and so we thought the Bistro Vino, and then a club somewhere,' Edward Choke was saying as he came into the kitchen. 'Oh, I say – hello!' he added, seeing Rachel sitting with her coffee. She smiled back.

'Rachel,' said Anthony, 'meet Edward Choke, who was in pupillage with me. And' – he turned to the girls, who were eyeing Rachel surreptitiously – 'Alexandra and Stephanie. This is Rachel, everyone.'

'Just call me Tiggy,' said the girl whom Anthony had introduced as Stephanie, leaning over and shaking Rachel's hand. 'Anthony, darling, do you have such a thing as an ashtray, or are we in a smoke-free zone?' She curled her arm into Anthony's and gave him a caressing look and a small, swift kiss before detaching herself and going to rummage in the cupboards.

'Look here,' said Edward, who was surprised and enchanted to find this unexpected treasure in Anthony's kitchen, 'why don't you join us, Rachel? We're just off for a spot of supper, then – well, see how the evening goes. What about it?'

Rachel stood up and lifted her jacket from the back of the chair. Alexandra watched as she put it on, wondering how wealthy Rachel might be, and why she'd never seen her around. Rachel smiled at Edward. 'I'd love to, but I'm afraid I can't. Really.'

'Rachel,' said Anthony, laying his arm around Rachel's shoulder, noting that she did not stiffen as he did so, 'is shortly to be married to our own dear Leo.'

'What? Leo Davies? Well, congratulations!' Edward beamed and decided that this was an excuse to give Rachel a kiss. Then he stood back and looked at her, which gave Rachel the curiously unpleasant sensation of being an exhibit whose only interest lay in belonging to Leo. 'Well, well! And I'd always thought he was a raving poofter!' Edward laughed immoderately, while Anthony closed his eyes briefly and smiled. Rachel said nothing, buttoning her jacket up slowly.

Anthony escorted her to the front door. 'Thanks for dropping round,' he said. 'I'm sorry you're going so soon.'

'I've got to go round and sort out a few things at my flat,' she replied. 'I'm putting it on the market next week. I'm staying in

Mayfair at the moment.' Anthony nodded. 'Well,' she said awkwardly, 'I'd better leave you to get on with your evening.'

And my life, thought Anthony, closing the door and leaning against it for a moment, listening to the sound of Tiggy's bright, shrill voice in the kitchen.

In a set of rooms in the House of Lords, dark-panelled, discreetly carpeted, the air laden with a hush befitting the dignity of the assemblies of old men, Sir Basil was mingling at his ease with his future fellows on the Commercial bench. The Lord Chancellor believed in holding regular little gatherings of his judiciary, feeling, as the outsider he perceived himself to be, that it helped to bring an informality and friendliness to his dealings with them.

'And so Leo Davies is to be married?' remarked Sir Bernard Lightfoot to Sir Basil, sipping at his whisky, and thinking that it was really rather superior to the last Lord Chancellor's stuff. Lord Steele clearly knew his malts.

'Yes – yes, we are all very pleased, of course.' Sir Basil smiled serenely round at the little circle, at Sir Bernard's narrow, lofty countenance, at Sir Edward Appleby's gnomelike face, at Sir Frank, thoughtful and jowly, and at the Honourable Sir Roger Ware, who wore his usual imperturbable, knowing half-smile.

'I must say,' said Sir Bernard languorously, 'that some of us were a little surprised. After the rumours which have been circulating, you know.'

Sir Frank sighed; why must Bernard always be so tiresome, making mischief? But Sir Basil must already know.

'I'm sorry?' Sir Basil inclined his white head courteously in Sir Bernard's direction, thinking that he had always disliked appearing in court before this man. He had a mocking, deprecatory manner, as though he found everything, even her Majesty's High Court of Justice, Commercial Division, childishly amusing.

'Well, you know, Sir Basil,' replied Sir Bernard easily, shifting his weight, 'that since Davies applied to take silk his private life has come in for some rather close scrutiny. And not all that we hear has been to the good. Rent boys, unusual proclivities, that kind of thing . . .'

Sir Edward Appleby blinked, making his glasses jump, glancing from face to face as he listened. Oh dear, thought Sir Frank, and took another sip of his drink. Then he rallied, squaring his shoulders slightly, lifting his chin. Taking on Sir Bernard was always something he would do his best to avoid, but on this occasion . . .

'Do you know,' he said suddenly, 'I have been given to understand that all these rumours are purely mischievous, that they have been put about simply to sully Davies's reputation at a critical time. That, in short, they are nonsense. I personally felt that they should be – ah – discounted from the outset. I am surprised, Bernard, that you should still be perpetuating them, given the damage they can do.' Sir Bernard stared at Frank with a face like elegantly carved stone. 'The man has done nothing, to my certain knowledge, that deserves reproach. He is one of our most brilliant up-and-coming men, and I think it ill behoves us to – ah, as it were – to seek to discredit him. He is to be married shortly, he has applied to take silk, and I, for one, wish him well on both counts.'

Sir Edward Appleby nodded vigorously, and Sir Basil, into whose mind a doubt had crept as he listened to Sir Bernard, added, 'Quite. Such rumours are clearly scurrilous nonsense. I very much hope he will be successful.' It gave him some satisfaction to assist in this squelching of Sir Bernard.

Sir Bernard said nothing but, with the faintest of smiles, excused himself from the little group. It broke up shortly thereafter, and Sir Mungo accosted Frank.

'What was all that?' he asked, catching at Frank's sleeve, having heard him speaking in rather sterner and more forthright tones than were customary with him at a social gathering.

Sir Frank drew himself up and smiled. 'We were discussing Leo Davies' marriage. An excellent thing, don't you think? I would say it fairly scotches those rumours we've all been hearing, wouldn't you?'

'Well, I should say it does,' answered Sir Mungo, looking round for one of those chappies to come and refill his glass. A waiter caught his eye and came over. 'Another gin and tonic, please. I knew nothing of this,' he added, turning back to Frank. 'I suppose it's that girl we met at Lincoln's Inn a while ago . . . Oh, you weren't there, were you? Very charming. Very lovely.'

Sir Mungo nodded to himself, waiting for his drink to arrive, thinking of all that had been said about Leo. The last he'd heard was that he was damned in the Lord Chancellor's eyes, and those of his department. Well, now was the time to put all that right. His drink arrived, he excused himself to Sir Frank and ambled off in the direction of Lord Steele. Sir Frank's eyes followed him happily.

'Attaboy, Mungo,' he murmured to himself.

'Well, of course, Mungo,' Lord Steele was saying some ten minutes later, 'I never liked passing judgment on any man on the basis of scandal. I'm very pleased to hear that there is no cause for concern of the kind that the Judicial Appointments Group had feared. You know, of course,' he added, 'that we must be careful in these matters. But clearly we can expect the necessary stability . . . I was always reluctant to pass up a man of Davies' undoubted ability.'

'I think you will find,' said Sir Mungo with determination, 'that when you come to invite comments from the Lords of Appeal, they will be of a favourable nature.'

The Lord Chancellor nodded and smiled; he would enjoy taking a firm line on this with Colin Crane tomorrow morning.

The party at Caper Court the next evening went well; it made up, in some measure, for the abrupt and depressing termination of the Christmas party. Everybody was in high spirits, pleased to have something to lift the gloom of raw early March.

When Leo finally left at nine o'clock, he felt happy, slightly the worse for drink. He would have liked to go on for dinner with the rest of them – had very nearly agreed to do so, as in the old days – but he had realised later that he was no longer part of the younger, raucous element in chambers. There had been a time when he and Michael had been the first to continue festivities of any kind, regardless of whether one was in court the next day or not. But he was conscious that that mantle had now been passed to the likes of William and David. Roderick,

Cameron and Sir Basil had left a little earlier, as befitted their dignity. Now Leo felt that he, too, should bow out and leave the rest to it.

He slipped downstairs and out into the cold air of Caper Court, pushing back the sides of his unbuttoned overcoat and thrusting his hands into his trouser pockets. The Temple was quiet, deserted, as he walked towards the cloisters, his footsteps ringing clear on the cold paving stones.

He heard someone call his name, and stopped to turn as he drew near to the stone pillars; Anthony came towards him through the gloom, his own step unhurried. He stopped as he reached Leo.

'Hello,' said Leo, 'you going this way?' He jerked his head in the direction of King's Bench Walk.

'No,' said Anthony. He paused, and they regarded one another; Leo's face was half in the shadow of the cloisters, his expression neutral, cautious. Anthony had scarcely spoken to him all evening, but had managed to make this meeting look accidental. 'I just wanted to say – well, all the best.'

'Thank you,' replied Leo, a little amused at the sombreness of Anthony's tone. Anyone would think he was leaving on an Antarctic expedition. He suspected that Anthony had drunk a good deal that evening. Suddenly Anthony stepped forward, held Leo by the arms, and kissed him, briefly and firmly, on the mouth. It was all Leo could do not to embrace Anthony and draw him to him. His limbs tingled with emotional electricity, and he remembered, with clarity, how things had been between them two years ago. Anthony had risked much, had confronted himself, in this act. For a wild, fleeting moment, Leo wished that none of the past few months had ever happened, that he could renounce the whole thing, leave the Bar, cease the emotional sham of his life, and . . . and what?

Anthony stepped back, leaning against one of the pillars; now his face was lost in shadow. 'Tell me – ' he said.

'What?' Leo's voice was low, expressionless, lost.

'Do you love her more than you loved me?'

There was a silence of several seconds before Leo answered, pushing his hands back into his pockets so that he might resist the temptation of reaching out for Anthony.

'No,' he answered. 'No.' And he realised in that moment where Anthony's jealousy had always lain, the reason for that scene in Leo's room, the words on the landing just before William's heart attack. He could not trust himself to say more; drawing his overcoat around him, he turned and walked quickly through the cloisters towards King's Bench Walk, away from Anthony.

In the two weeks since they had returned from Florence, Rachel had been aware of a distraction, a restlessness about Leo. The realisation filtered gradually through her own haze of happiness, with days taken up by another of Mr Nikolaos's disasters, visits to her gynaecologist, house details from the estate agents.

'We can't stay here for ever,' Leo had said of the mews house. He no longer wanted to stay there; the place belonged to his past, to a time when he had been another person, his life his own. He did not wish to share it with Rachel. He suggested during their stay in Florence that they should find another place. 'We'll start looking for something bigger as soon as we get back.' But since their return it had been she who had visited the estate agents, going enthusiastically through the bundles of information they sent. Leo had become vague about the whole business.

The vagueness and distractedness, however, she put down to his work and the approach of Easter. It must be stressful, she told herself, waiting to hear whether he would take silk or not, simply having to wait through the days for the letter to arrive.

'If it's big and bulky,' he had told her light-heartedly one evening, 'then it's all right. They have to put in all the bits and pieces about what to wear, where to go, when the ceremony takes place. If it's small and flat – well, that's it, isn't it?'

But Leo had taken soundings, spoken to Frank and others, and he had come to understand that the thing would go smoothly, that he had little to worry about. The rumours had died away, all was as before. James had been given a few hours' community service and told not to do it again, and Leo had paid some money into an account for him and put him in the way of some work in the West End. Since Sir Basil's elevation to the bench, it seemed likely that both he and Stephen would take silk. Had it all been an unnecessary waste of time? he wondered. Need things have been taken to such extremes? He no longer knew. He only knew that the thing was done, that Rachel was his wife, and that his life was now changed completely.

He did not think of Anthony. Since the evening in the cloisters, that was curiously painful. He saw him routinely during the day and all was fine, with no hint of what had passed between them. But when Leo was alone, when his attention strayed momentarily from his work, he had to prevent himself from allowing his thoughts to dwell on the past.

On Wednesday morning in the week before the Easter weekend, Rachel was sitting at the kitchen table in the mews house, going through yet another sheaf of estate agent mail.

'Honestly,' she said, 'they send far too much. If only they'd send the kind of thing we're looking for, instead of all this irrelevant rubbish. Half of it's no good.' She frowned. 'I wish we could sell the flat. That would help. But look,' she added, holding up two sheets of paper stapled together, 'here's the one I was telling you about last night. I've only just found it. Shall we go and look at it this evening?'

Leo helped himself to another cup of coffee and glanced at her eager, lovely face. He felt empty, without any desire to go and look round houses. He wished he could shake off this mood. His life seemed to have lost all its impetus, as though he were falling into a state of fuddled domestic inertia, from which he would never rise. It's just the change in circumstances, the adjustment, he told himself. And this stifling, claustrophobic feeling was probably just the effect of two people living together in a place that was too small for them.

'Not tonight,' he replied, draining his cup and slipping on his waistcoat. He smiled at her, trying to cheer himself, to inject something more positive into his mood. 'I have to go with solicitors to see the director of this pharmaceuticals company this afternoon, the one who's involved in this swap deals case. Apparently he's too important to come all the way down to the Temple. It might go on a bit, and I may be late. Why not fix it up for tomorrow night?'

He heard the apologetic tone of his own words as he made excuses, accounted for his time. He had never expected to have to do that. But he was married now. He was entirely accountable.

He put on his jacket, watching as she rose from her chair, smiling, and put her arms around him. She kissed him happily.

'Aren't you going in to work today?' he asked, running his hand with curiosity over the slight swell of her stomach beneath her robe.

'I'm going in late. I think I've earned a couple of hours at home. Anyway, my new secretary is so tremendously efficient . . . How's Felicity, by the way?'

'Oh, she's doing well. No major disasters so far. Look, I have to run.' And he slipped from her embrace and left, while Rachel went happily back to her house details.

Frederick Seely's offices were housed in the City in a building of sumptuous starkness; one could sense the many hundreds of thousands which had been expended on its apparent minimalism. Leo came in through high glass entrance doors; the reception area, where a uniformed security guard sat, was isolated in a sea of shining marble flooring. Leo signed himself in and took the little plastic visitor's tag which the security guard handed him.

'Twenty-second floor, Mr Davies,' he said, and Leo walked across the gleaming floor to the lift, whose doors slid back noiselessly and swiftly as he approached.

The atmosphere was rather more intimate on the twenty-second floor, but still the whispering voice of vast corporate wealth could be heard everywhere, in the tinkling fountain which played beside the reception desk, in the bank of small video screens on the wall opposite, which gave out soundless images of Seely's scattered empire, and in the lush carpeting and furniture. There was none of the bustle and chatter of a busy office. The heavy carpeting soaked up what sound there was. The polished creature at the reception desk smiled at Leo in an unhurried manner, her movements impressively slow and serene as she informed Frederick Seely's inner sanctum of Leo's arrival.

'I'm afraid,' said Leo, 'that Mr Leslie, who should be with me, has been delayed for half an hour or so. He should be joining us.'

The receptionist smiled and nodded, and asked Leo to take a seat. He sat for ten minutes or so on a glossy, high-backed black leather chair, thumbing through a copy of Seely's latest annual report and reflecting on the habitual unpunctuality of solicitors, until the polished wooden doors which fenced Frederick Seely off from the rest of the world opened and a young man came out. He approached Leo and held out his hand.

'Mr Davies? I am Francis Bryan, Mr Seely's personal assistant. I do apologise for keeping you waiting. Would you come this way?'

The young man was tall and fair-haired, with an oval face and charming features, which bore no trace of a smile. His entire demeanour exuded cold efficiency, and he was impeccably dressed. His movements as he led Leo into Mr Seely's domain were graceful, yet a trifle exaggerated.

'Mr Leslie, the solicitor, should be joining us,' Leo explained as they reached the doorway. 'As I told your receptionist, he has been detained for a short while.'

The young man surveyed Leo's face expressionlessly. He said nothing, then ushered Leo in, leaving him alone with Mr Seely.

The conference was delayed by Mr Leslie's late, puffing, apologetic arrival, and it was well after six thirty by the time their business was finished. Glancing at his watch as he gathered his papers together, Leo was surprised to see that Francis Bryan was still in attendance at that late hour, flitting in and out of the room, bearing Mr Seely the messages which had accumulated throughout the afternoon.

'Look,' said the solicitor, as Mr Seely conferred briefly with his assistant, 'I wish I had time for a drink and a chat, but I have to dash. I'll call you in chambers and we'll go through all this.' And Mr Leslie fled as precipitately as he had come, his briefcase sagging and flapping at its broken clasp, the belt of his raincoat trailing.

It was left to Leo to make the polite murmurs of departure. He shook hands with Frederick Seely and they parted. As he was making his way along the hushed corridor and back to the lifts, Leo was aware that Francis Bryan had caught up with him.

'Allow me to see you downstairs, Mr Davies,' he murmured and, adjusting his graceful, striding gait to Leo's, walked with him past the deserted reception area to the lift.

There was silence as they waited for the lift to come. Leo glanced at the younger man, and their eyes met. Francis Bryan leaned back against the wall next to the lift, his eyes still fastened on Leo's, and looked him up and down slowly. Then he smiled. The gesture was overtly insolent, but Leo felt only a familiar thrill of interest and excitement. He looked away.

The lift doors opened and Leo stepped inside, followed by Francis Bryan.

'There really is no need, you know – ' began Leo.

'I insist,' said the younger man gently, turning his eyes on Leo once again as he pressed the button for the ground floor. As the lift began its slow descent, Leo was aware of the other man's gaze, knew he could not be mistaken. He turned to look at him, and Francis Bryan smiled his charming, affected smile once again. Leo's mouth felt dry as he spoke.

'When will you be finished here?' he asked quietly.

He did not think of Rachel, or of the coming months, or of anything else. He was back in his old world, intoxicated by the pleasurable excitement of this new, wordless encounter, this enchanting young man with the long, graceful legs and insolent smile.

Francis Bryan leaned against the polished steel of the lift wall, his eyes turned to the moving light of the floor indicator, the smile gone from his face. It seemed to Leo that he took a very long time to answer. And in that time, Leo wondered, fleetingly, at his own madness. But he didn't care any more. After the past few months, it no longer seemed to matter.

'In twenty minutes or so,' replied Francis Bryan, still not looking at Leo. Then, as the indicator drew near to the ground floor, he glanced at him. 'There's a wine bar round the corner, in Colvin Street.'

He said nothing more. The lift doors slid open and Leo walked out, across the reception area, into the street and round the corner, to wait in the wine bar.

The next morning, in the mews house in Mayfair, Rachel bent to pick up the sheaf of Leo's mail. A bulky envelope from the Lord Chancellor's Office lay among the others, the little House of Lords crest on the back. She stared at it, turning it over, then carried it back upstairs with the rest.

At the top she paused, aware of the silence in the house, and of the sick uncertainty that lay within her. The wide sleeve of her blue robe slid back from her arm as she reached out to touch the petals of one of the daffodils which stood in a jug on the table. She laid the pile of envelopes next to the flowers. Then she lifted her gaze to the window, to the damp cobbles of the empty mews. Folding her arms, she stood by the window, looking out, waiting.

Chapter One

In the name of love. Leslie Maskelyne had heard the phrase when he was listening to *Start the Week*. Or rather, not listening. Too hard to pay attention to the ramblings of these pseudo-scientists and psychiatrists that Bragg seemed to like so much. They spoke a kind of jargon, delivered in tones and fluctuations of speech which were not comfortable to Maskelyne's seventy-four-year-old ear. People spoke differently nowadays, it seemed to him. From what he saw and read, the world was growing increasingly foreign, full of strangers, the children quite unlike children as he remembered them, young people largely incomprehensible, the middle-aged confused and unsure of their place in the scheme of things. He knew his own place, all right. Either in that bed or in this chair, depending on whether it was a good or a bad day, watching the world turn as he stepped slowly, daily, away from it, taking his medication, pondering everything with the impatience of decline.

In the name of love. It still stuck with him. What one did in the name of love, the man had said. He had not bothered to listen to what the man on the radio thought was or was not done in the name of love, but had wandered off on his own little train of thought. What had he, Leslie Maskelyne, ever done in the name of love? Married Susan, had Stephen and Lydia and Geraldine . . . No, that wasn't quite right. That was not what the words meant. In the name of love. It had a certain grandeur, betokening sacrifice, or nobility of purpose. Marrying Susan had involved neither of those things. While not exactly a marriage of convenience, the attractions had been largely financial. And the children. You could hardly call their upbringing an act of love, more a matter of duty and affection – and hope. Hope that they would turn out decent people,

1

despite the fact that their mother had rutted with half the county, then run off with another man, obliging him to divorce her. Given their handicaps, they were, in their way, not good or bad, merely products of their class and conditioning.

In the name of love.

What about Ruth? It was the closest he had ever come to truly loving someone. But even then he had allowed practicality to get the better of him. A brief affair from long ago, its memory no more fragrant than the scent of withered flowers, was not heroic. The act of lovemaking, no matter from what passion it sprang, did not suffice. Something more, surely, was needed. A demonstration, a proof beyond the merely physical. He had done nothing for Ruth. Everything which had come of that affair, each painful and deadening consequence, was as loveless as anything could be. He was sorry for that. It was not his way to make amends, to feel remorse, but he would have liked something better to have come from his time with Ruth. He looked out at the gardens beyond his window. He liked the plurality – gardens. The rose garden, the kitchen garden, the stone terrace and the lawns which stepped down to the carefully clipped topiary hedge and spread out beyond, the water garden to one side, with its discreet nooks and bowers, more grass and flowers beyond that, the azaleas planted round the winding paths, which drifted eventually into the fringes of the wood, itself a garden when the bluebells came out at this time of year, blurring the shadows with blue. It was all very beautiful, as was the big house in which he now sat, a chairbound invalid, amid all the splendid fruits of his labours. He thought of the lifetime's harvest of stocks and shares in their fat portfolios, the sheaves of gilt-edged bonds. In his mind they almost glistened. Such a satisfying sheen they possessed. The companies, all the controlling interests, rose in his mind like lofty pinnacles, ghostly and glassy. It was a marvel, to have made such wealth. But none of it achieved in the name of love, he reflected. Of power and ambition, yes. But not love.

These thoughts flickered away as Leslie Maskelyne looked down at his hands, lying inert on the tartan rug which covered his withered knees, and saw the faint tremor which galvanised

2

his knotted fingers as the pain began. It always began like a slow, dull glow in the centre of his being, then burning up through him with an unbearable intensity. He knew its pace now, could summon Mrs Cotterell to administer more diamorphine before the monster sank its teeth and talons in to the truest and most terrible depth. It was little enough, but such knowledge made him feel as though he was, if not mastering the beast, at least keeping it at bay. For that was how he now characterised it. In the early days, when the pain had not been intense or spasmodic, he had seen his cancer as some worm crawling through his body, devouring him unseen. But the onset of pain had transformed the laidly worm into a rearing, ferocious, unpredictable foe, something looming so large in his consciousness that he thought of it almost as a being apart from himself. He closed his eyes and reached out a hand to the brass bell which rested amongst his medicines on the table next to him, and rang it sharply, sitting forward anxiously in his chair until he heard with relief the steady tread of Mrs Cotterell's feet approaching the room.

Thereafter, the hours until midday passed in a haze, Maskelyne vaguely conscious of the sounds of the household around him, Mrs Cotterell's presence looming and ebbing, words from the radio, which he insisted should remain on at all times, trickling into and past his mind. In the early afternoon his mind began to clear and his body, miraculously cleansed of pain, reasserted itself. Mrs Cotterell had helped him into bed before administering his diamorphine, and now Leslie Maskelyne leaned over and slid open the drawer of the cabinet next to his bed, fishing around for his cigarettes. He drew one unsteadily from the half-empty packet of Rothmans, placed it between his lips and lit it, drawing gratefully on the smoke as it slid deliciously down into his lungs – what was left of them. He glanced at his watch, whose strap he had had to tighten by a couple of holes in the last few weeks. Nearly one. He smoked for a while, recalling how appalled Mrs Cotterell had been that he should still continue the habit after his lung cancer had been diagnosed. 'You can't mean to go on doing that, knowing that it's killing you!' she had said. That had been after the consultant had told him he only had months to live.

He remembered lighting a cigarette while he told her – as his housekeeper, it had seemed to him more important that she knew before his family. The very fact that she presumed to utter such a thing told him just how horrified she was. Normally Mrs Cotterell was, in a dignified way, the humblest and most unpresumptuous of creatures, to the point of teeth-gritting irritation.

'That is precisely why there is no point in stopping now, Mrs Cotterell,' he had replied. 'I might as well enjoy myself while I can.'

The doctor had agreed with him.

Maskelyne's glance turned to the window, and he noticed with annoyance that Mrs Cotterell had, yet again, drawn the curtain against the late April sunshine. Tapping ash into the heavy glass ashtray on the bedside table, he jangled the little bell and waited until Mrs Cotterell appeared.

'Please don't draw the curtains in the daytime,' he said mildly, gesturing with a thin hand for her to open them. Mrs Cotterell stepped over to the window and pulled the cord, so that the curtains slid slowly back. Gentle sunlight, stippled with the shadows of the creeper round the large window, spilled across the floor.

'Let's clear some of the smoke in here,' she said, and opened one of the windows at the side, settling it on its hasp, so that a breath of spring air flapped the blind for a moment, then subsided. The distant sound of the motor mower drifted up from the gardens. Leslie Maskelyne closed his eyes with pleasure at the sound. It was the herald of spring and summer. He could almost see Reg Fowler astride the thing, battered panama well back on his head, riding the lawns like some proud cowboy, putt-puttering past the yew hedge, while the boy clipped and mulched, performing the more menial tasks.

'Do you feel up to some lunch yet?' Mrs Cotterell asked, moving around the room, plumping the cushions on his empty chair, refolding the tartan rug, rearranging the bottles on the table. All quite unnecessarily. She was one of those bustling women who could not leave anything alone. 'There's some rather nice cold chicken. You could have that with some lettuce and tomato and a spot of mayonnaise. And I could

4

make you a fruit salad.' She touched the petals of the cut flowers in the jug on the dresser, smoothed a hand down the curtain.

The thought of white chicken flesh disturbed Leslie Maskelyne's delicate sense of temporary well-being. His appetite was almost non-existent these days. He would have thought that Mrs Cotterell knew well enough by now that it was all he could do to eat his toast and fruit in the morning, and a chop or piece of fish in the evening. Perhaps it was part of her nurturing nature. Suggesting cold chicken to an invalid must be the next best thing to getting them to eat it, he supposed.

'No, thank you,' he replied. 'I might have something later.' He reached for the cigarette packet and drew out a fresh cigarette. How he liked the look of them in their pristine state, their white, crisp slenderness, the fragrance of the unlit tobacco, the cleanness of the filter before the first drag of smoke sullied it. For years he had taken no notice, just smoked the damn things. Now each one he regarded as a small work of art. His lighter snapped and flared. As he puffed, Maskelyne glanced up slyly at Mrs Cotterell, enjoying her dutifully suppressed disapproval. No doubt she regarded substituting a fag for a nice piece of cold chicken as downright immoral. 'There is something you could get for me, however,' he added. 'Some paper and envelopes from my desk.' He indicated the little writing bureau which stood against the wall beside the window, not far from his chair. It had a lid inlaid with rose-coloured leather, which folded down to form a writing surface at just the correct distance from him when he was sitting in the chair. In it he kept most of his private documents, which he had had moved from the larger desk in his downstairs study when he had become confined to his room. 'And a pen. I had one in the drawer here, but it seems to have been moved,' he added in mild reproof.

Mrs Cotterell fetched him some sheets of paper, a pen, and the bound volume of drawings by Leech on which he liked to rest his work when he was writing in bed. The habit annoyed Mrs Cotterell, for the leather spine was mouldering and rubbed the linen bedsheets with rust-coloured stains, but she never said anything about it. It wasn't her place.

'Thank you,' said Maskelyne, as he settled his glasses on his nose. Mrs Cotterell gave him a hesitant glance, wondering if he was going to ask for anything else. As she looked at him, she reflected for a sad instant on how dramatically his good looks, preserved even into old age, were beginning to shrivel away. Soon he would look like any other bony old bedridden man. Then he glanced up, gave her a small smile, looked back to his paper and began to write. Realising that she had been dismissed, Mrs Cotterell quietly left the room.

By the time half past one came, the motor mower had fallen silent, and only the sleepy chirrup of the birds in the trees broke the silence in Leslie Maskelyne's room. He had laid down his pen, and was lying back against the pillows, eyes closed. Down in the cool peace of the water garden Reg Fowler and his young sidekick, Gary, were lunching off cold pasties and cans of Tango from the village mini-mart. Twenty-five minutes later, the fanfare heralding the end of the lunchtime edition of *The Archers* roused Maskelyne from his doze. He blinked for a few seconds, then glanced down at the letter which he had written. He sighed and read it through again, then folded it, his fingers running a smooth crease along the thick paper as he listened absently to the shipping forecast. The afternoon play would be coming next. He hoped it wasn't going to be one of those socially aware ones, full of gritty reality and people snarling at each other in regional accents. Or a weird one with lots of special sound effects from the Radio 4 stereophonic workshop. He slipped the letter into an envelope, dabbled his fingers lightly in his water glass to wet the gum and seal it – his own mouth too dry from cigarettes and medication to manage this – and picking up his pen again, wrote on it in a slow, sloping hand, 'Ruth Owen'. He jangled the little bell.

When Mrs Cotterell appeared, he handed her the envelope. 'I wonder, Mrs Cotterell, whether you would be kind enough to deliver this for me when you are passing through the village. It's for Mrs Owen.'

Mrs Cotterell turned the long, thick envelope over in her hands, concealing, she hoped, the astonishment she felt. 'I'll take it down with me later, when the night nurse comes,' she replied.

'Thank you,' murmured Leslie Maskelyne, and he slipped off his glasses, pressing thumb and forefinger against the red crease left on the thin flesh, the ever-thinner flesh, of his nose, adding, 'Oh, and could you pick up two hundred Rothmans from the shop for me? I think I'm nearly out.' As Mrs Cotterell left the room, he leaned back against his pillows once more, smiling with satisfaction as the announcer informed him that the play that afternoon was entitled *The Suspect Household*, a drama based on a real-life Edwardian murder trial. Just the thing. But then, try though he might to ignore it, an unmistakable urge gripped his lower innards. With a mild groan, he reached out once more for the bell, this time to summon Mrs Cotterell to help him to the commode.

There were three ways of reaching the village from Hemwood House. One down the driveway at the front of the house to the main road, another at the back down through the woods, and the third by a dusty little track which veered away to the left of the woodland path and ran steeply away from the Hemwood House property into a series of grassy gullies, studded with rocks, clumps of shrubby hawthorns, and tangles of bramble and giant hemlock. In these gullies, known locally as the Dips, the village children played, building dens and forts with pieces of scrap material, hiding behind the rocks to ambush one another, slithering down the slopes on their backsides on flattened sides of cardboard boxes. From the strongest of the hawthorn trees a car tyre hung suspended at the end of a knotted rope, dangling over the deepest of the gullies. This route from the house was too steep and tiring for any adult to bother with, even though it was the shortest, and indeed, since the days when the Maskelyne children had played down there with the other children from the village, it was scarcely used, except by the paper boy. Today Mrs Cotterell took the path through the woods, enjoying the quiet coolness and the lulling coo of the wood pigeons far up in the trees. The path emerged on the far side of the woods, a distance of quarter of a mile or so, then ran down past the scrap-filled back yard of the local garage and became a lane, flanked by the garage on one side and the pub on the other, leading into Church Road, the main street running through the village of Hemwood.

Mrs Cotterell stopped at the off-licence to buy Mr Maskelyne his cigarettes and exchange a few pieces of gossip, then carried on up the street to deliver the letter. Ruth Owen's house was at the end of the street just past the church, narrow and picturesque, its plaster exterior painted pink in typical Suffolk fashion, its door giving straight on to the pavement. Doris Cotterell often stopped off there for a cup of tea after leaving Hemwood House, sometimes picking up groceries that Ruth fetched for her at the supermarket in Sudbury. She and Ruth went back as far as the local mixed infants, had gone to dances together as teenagers up at the American air-force base during the war, taken holidays at Clacton-on-Sea and Walton-on-the-Naze in foursomes with their husbands back in the fifties. Doris thought she knew everything there was to know about Ruth, but that Leslie Maskelyne should write to Ruth was a marvel. She recalled that Ruth's daughter, Abby, used to play in the Dips with Stephen Maskelyne and his sisters when they were little, and in a village this size Ruth and Mr Maskelyne would know one another by sight. But beyond a nod of recognition . . . What would Leslie Maskelyne have to say to Ruth that required to be sealed up in one of those long, ivory-coloured envelopes – especially one that said, not 'Mrs Owen' on the front, but 'Ruth Owen', in that direct fashion?

After ringing the bell, Doris waited for some minutes. Eventually footsteps could be heard in the hallway and Ruth opened the door.

'Sorry, love, I was out the back getting in the washing. Come on through.' Doris followed her up the hallway and into the little kitchen.

Ruth was a tall, big-boned woman, still handsome at seventy. Although her skin was pouched and slack, blooming with fine wrinkles, the high cheek-bones and clear eyes testified to former beauty. Her height lent her poise, and her grey hair was soft and gently folded up behind her head with combs and pins, unlike Doris's, which was crimped and curled in a nondescript, old woman's permanent wave.

'So,' she said, filling the kettle at the sink, 'how's life up at

8

the big house? Oh – before I forget, there's that detergent and biscuits you wanted in the Tesco's bag over there by the door.'

Doris got up and fetched the bag, opening it to inspect the purchases. 'Much the same as usual,' she said in answer to Ruth's question. 'He doesn't get any better. Bad in bed, worse up.'

'Well, he's not going to get better, is he?' said Ruth with only the mildest sarcasm. It had occurred to Doris recently that, however obliquely phrased, Ruth's first questions were always about Leslie Maskelyne. She wondered whether Ruth encouraged her to drop in as frequently as she did just so she could hear about him, about the goings-on at Hemwood House. She thought about the letter, but decided not to produce it just yet.

'He's going to need full-time nursing in a few weeks,' Doris remarked, accepting the cup of tea which Ruth had poured for her, and taking one of the Garibaldi biscuits set out on a plate. She slipped her shoes off and settled back in her chair with relief. This heat played hell with her ankles. They were all puffed up by the end of the day, even though she took her water tablets regularly. 'I can manage his liquid diamorphine, all right – God knows, I was that nervous to start with – but, of course, I can't give injections, and that's what it's going to come to.' She sipped her tea reflectively. 'Mind you, at the rate he's going, they'll be hard pushed to find anywhere to put a needle in. There's that little flesh on him.' Doris gazed at the potted geraniums on Ruth's window-sill and sighed, oblivious of the expression on Ruth's face. Ruth brought her own tea to the table and sat down. 'I'll be glad, mind you, when that day comes,' went on Doris. 'He'll have to have one of those Macmillan nurses. Did you see that programme about them on BBC2 the other week? Marvellous, really. Then at least that'll save my legs. I'm up and down them stairs every fifteen minutes. It's not really what a housekeeper should be doing, nursing an invalid like that. At my age, I should have given up the job by now, but as he's only got a few more months . . .' She shook her head and drank her tea.

'Is he –' Ruth hesitated '– is he all right? I mean, in his mind? In himself?' Her voice sounded awkward as she asked this, and Doris was reminded of the day she had told Ruth about

Leslie Maskelyne's cancer, which she had done in her customary conversational manner. The expression which had clouded Ruth's eyes then had been unfathomable, and though Doris at the time had interpreted the silence with which Ruth received the news as mere neighbourly concern, she now began to think that something more might be read into it. And into this question. Why should Ruth care what Leslie Maskelyne's mental state was? What was he to her? Her mind flew to the letter once again.

'Oh, he's well enough, in that way. He doesn't let it get him down. That's to say, he's got a certain outlook. He just takes it as it comes. I don't know what word you'd use –'

'Stoic,' said Ruth, staring down at her tea.

Doris nodded slowly, watching Ruth and thinking that she couldn't put off mentioning the letter any longer. Making an effort to sound mildly surprised at her own forgetfulness, she said, 'Oh – talking of how his mind is, he asked me to give you something.'

Ruth raised her head quickly and looked at her friend. Beneath hooded and wrinkled lids her deep-set blue eyes suddenly shone with a youthful intensity. 'Something?' Ruth echoed. Then she asked more slowly, 'What thing?'

Doris had got up to fetch her straw shopper. She padded back to the table in her support stockings, fishing past the box of Rothmans and then producing the letter. Ruth stared at it for a few long seconds before reaching out slowly to take it from Doris. She studied her own name written on the envelope, then laid the letter down on the table next to her teacup. She did not look at it again. Her expression was totally inscrutable, and Doris felt a prickle of annoyance. That was the one thing about Ruth which had always irked her, throughout a lifetime of friendship. She wasn't a confiding person. She would be friendly as anything, intimate, capable of having a right good laugh – and they'd had plenty of those – but there were always moments when a sort of shutter came down, when she blanked you out, and you knew that there were private thoughts and feelings she was never going to share with you. Not ever.

'Aren't you going to open it?' Doris could not resist saying.

Ruth picked up her tea and sipped at it, her expression almost absent. 'Later,' she said.

'Oh, well . . .' murmured Doris with mild resentment. She was Ruth's best friend, when all was said and done. You would think, after all this time . . . 'Is there any tea still in that pot?' Doris asked suddenly.

Ruth rose to fetch the teapot. She could feel it in her limbs like a sort of fire, a prickling, intense impatience. It had been all she could do not to open that letter then and there. Or to strangle Doris. Ruth longed for her to be gone, so that she could be alone with her letter. Doris must have divined this, which was why she had asked for another cup of tea. What strange things friends were, thought Ruth, filling Doris's cup again, watching her as she took another biscuit from the plate in an infuriatingly leisurely way. When Doris had arrived, Ruth had been all set to tell her about what the doctor had said about her heart, about the need for tests up at the hospital, had really looked forward to a good half-hour of concern and sympathy. But the letter had changed all that. More conversation with Doris was the last thing she wanted now. She just wanted the minutes to go by until Doris struggled into her shoes, picked up her bag and was gone.

Ruth scarcely listened as Doris passed on the piece of gossip she'd picked up in the newsagent's, merely sipped her tea and waited, reflecting on the ability of time to stretch or shrink according to circumstances. Doris's second cup of tea was interminable. Ruth managed, once, to slide her eyes to the handwriting on the envelope, anticipating and then feeling the painful little lurch of her old heart, which had felt like some tender weight within a shell since her visit to the doctor's that day. Her name, written by him, after all these years.

At last Doris bent to squeeze her feet into her shoes, then rose reluctantly to gather up the Tesco's bag and her shopper. She did not want to leave Ruth alone with that letter, resented the intimacy between it and Ruth which so excluded her. Ruth and her letter. Leslie Maskelyne's letter. The contents could be nothing routine or domestic. Leslie Maskelyne's life contained no activity now which could in any way concern Ruth, consisted of nothing except a swiftly dwindling future. And a long past.

'Right. Well, I'll be off,' said Doris, aware that Ruth had said almost nothing during the last ten minutes, but was merely waiting, burning for her to leave. 'I'll pop in tomorrow,' she added. 'I can pass on your reply to the letter. If there is one.'

Ruth merely smiled as she walked slowly ahead of her friend down the narrow hallway and opened the door on to the street. 'I'll have the kettle on,' she replied. When the door closed, she went back to the kitchen, where the letter lay on the table.

Ruth picked up the letter and opened it, thrusting her forefinger beneath the gummed flap and ripping the envelope quite violently. She drew out the stiffly folded piece of paper and stood for a moment, waiting for this heated feeling to leave her, longing for calm detachment. She thought briefly of the days – early summer days like these – when she had hoped for a letter from him, listening to the flap and rustle of the letter-box with the certain and futile knowledge that he would never write, yet hoping still. He never had written. Until now. What use was now, after so many years? What relevance did now have to the past? She unfolded the letter and stared at the few lines written there.

'Dear Ruth,' it said. *'There is something I wish to speak to you about, which cannot be said in a letter. I wonder if you would come and see me one day, perhaps for lunch? Send me a note via Mrs Cotterell telling me which day would be convenient, and I shall expect you about one. Best regards, Leslie Maskelyne.'*

It was the matter-of-factness which astonished her. The casual tone, as though they were accustomed to communicating, and now something had come up which was more important than usual. They hadn't spoken for over thirty years, not since the afternoon when he had left her standing under the tree down by the river, the midges dancing in clouds over the water, she feeling so utterly bereft it had made her dizzy, fiercely conscious of the last touch of his fingers upon her shoulder . . . God, the memory of that was so alive. Then there had been the weeks of waiting, summer fading into autumn, the passage of months, one after another, turning hope to a kind of dead acceptance. The months had become years. They had spoken once, but it hardly counted. She had been standing outside the produce tent at the agricultural show with some friends – 1975, had it been? A hot summer, anyway – when Leslie had walked by with some other people, and in the murmured exchange of greetings they had said hello to one another with polite formality. That was all. Their eyes had hardly met. Ruth remembered vividly the long time she had spent before the mirror later that day, staring at her forty-eight-year-old reflection, trying desperately to see what he had seen, feverish with hope that she had not so changed that he had been disappointed, hot with anger that she should even care.

As she thought of this, Ruth gave a faint sigh and stroked her withered cheek reflectively, still looking at the letter. She was well past caring about such things now. Old age was something of a relief, in that department. By the time she was going on sixty, she had grown used to seeing him around the village, or at church – perhaps five times in the year – and no longer cared what he saw. By then, everything that had existed between her and Leslie Maskelyne was a precious part of the past. She saw herself as she had been when she was his lover, and it was like looking at a different person, nothing to do with the ageing woman living off her husband's RAF pension and the money she made working part-time at the pub, worrying about her daughter . . . Leslie hadn't changed, though. Not to her eyes. On the occasions when she saw him he looked older, yes, but he remained essentially the same tall, good-looking fellow. Or he had been the last time she had seen him, and that was well over a year now.

She put the letter down and went over to her basket of washing, absently and automatically starting to sort through and fold. How did he look nowadays, though? She didn't think she wanted to see what cancer was doing to him. The things Doris said about needles and so on were bad enough. There was a part of her that wanted to preserve her memory of him intact, to keep the bright, sensuous recollection of that short-lived affair, now that the years had washed it free from pain. Seeing him again, talking to him, might erase all that, the

13

remembered pleasure obliterated by fresh and present ugliness. It might be best, she thought, examining the torn gusset of an old pair of pants, if she didn't see him. Just ignored the letter. They had nothing to say to one another.

She sighed and went to drop the knickers in the pedal bin. They were past it. Things got old and useless, chuck 'em away. Walking back to the basket, she stopped suddenly. Was she thinking the same about Leslie, half-consciously? Perhaps. She picked the letter up once more from the table. *Something which cannot be said in a letter.* For some reason, for whatever reason – age, illness, incipient dementia – he wanted to see her. If she had received such a letter thirty years ago, would she have hesitated? Not for an instant. True, in those days she would still have had hopes and fears, but more curiosity would suffice for the present.

She fetched pen and paper from the dresser and sat down at the table. She hesitated, then pushed the paper aside and picked up Leslie Maskelyne's letter. Turning it over, she scribbled on the back, '*Tuesday the 28th.*' Then she folded it and put it into a fresh, smaller envelope, sealed it shut, and wrote his name on the front. It was as much as needed to be said, for the present. Anything more could wait until Tuesday.

All Orion/Phoenix titles are available at your local bookshop or from the following address:

Littlehampton Book Services
Cash Sales Department L
14 Eldon Way, Lineside Industrial Estate
Littlehampton
West Sussex BN17 7HE

telephone 01903 721596, *facsimile* 01903 730914

Payment can either be made by credit card (Visa and Mastercard accepted) or by sending a cheque or postal order made payable to *Littlehampton Book Services*.
DO NOT SEND CASH OR CURRENCY.

Please add the following to cover postage and packing

UK and BFPO:
£1.50 for the first book, and 50P for each additional book to a maximum of £3.50

Overseas and Eire:
£2.50 for the first book plus £1.00 for the second book and 50p for each additional book ordered

----

BLOCK CAPITALS PLEASE

name of cardholder ....

address of cardholder ....

delivery address
(if different from cardholder)

....
....
....

postcode ....   *postcode* ....

☐ I enclose my remittance for £.............................

☐ please debit my Mastercard/Visa (delete as appropriate)

card number ☐☐☐☐☐☐☐☐☐☐☐☐☐☐☐☐☐

expiry date ☐☐☐☐

signature ....

prices and availability are subject to change without notice